GULF WINDS

SCREAMING EAGLE PRESS

J. M. TAYLOR

This book is a work of fiction. All of the characters are products of the author's imagination. Certain real organizations and locales are used in the settings, however, none of the fictitious events described in the book occurred with these organizations nor at those locales.

Any resemblance to actual events or persons, living or dead, is entirely coincidental.

Printed in the United States of America
First Edition

ISBN: 1-879043-23-8

EAN-13: 978-1-879043-23-7

What Others Thought About
Gulf Winds

The scenes are vivid and the action never drags. I also admire Taylor's ability to milk all the suspense and drama from each action scene.

Ann Turner Cook, Author

I think the characters that are supposed to be good guys are convincingly good, even if flawed, and the bad guys are convincingly bad. The good guys are not perfect and the bad guys are not without their virtues, so I think they're all very believable.

Richard Taylor, Author

Wonderful Book! It didn't end the way I suspected which was fun. **Karen Gibson, Bay Area Greyhounds**

..how impressed I was with Gulf Winds. I thought the story was incredibly descriptive and the characters (Grant, Bennett, Talbot) are ones with a great voice and persona. I could actually picture actors who I would cast for the roles.

**Todd Slater, Founder of
Slater Brothers Entertainment and
former Exec Vice President of
Anschutz Film Group**

A fast-paced story with lots of action and suspense, keeping the reader oblivious to time and anxious to see what's next. There are plenty of complications which are realistic enough to be believable yet with just enough anxiety until the final pages when it all comes to a head and ends very satisfactorily.

Richard Lowery, Author and Critic

Also by J. M. Taylor

Published by Hard Shell Word Factory

Flash of Emerald

Behind the Green Water

Published by Screaming Eagle Press

Missing Sticks

Acknowledgments

My wife Peggy and I met Pete Price with his greyhounds Molly and Lucy at the northern tip of Ozello within sight of the nuclear plant cooling towers across Crystal Bay. Thus began the deep affection I now have for Flash the greyhound, a central character in this book. Pete and his wife Pat have been a great help in understanding the wonderful bonds between adoptive owners and retired racing greyhounds. Maryann Toliver of GPA Tampa Bay and Karen Gibson of Bay Area Greyhound Adoptions added even more insight into the greyhound world.

Once upon a time I recommended against family as readers of draft manuscripts. Perhaps my drafts have improved, but however I got there, I want to thank Peggy, Becky, Richard and Tom for their suggestions, especially Peggy's admonitions about my treatment of Flash.

Ann Turner Cook corrected some of my very first attempts to write, many years ago. Since I seem to continue to make mistakes, she has continued correcting. Many others helped, especially fellow members of the Tampa Writers Alliance, the Florida Writers Association and the Mystery Writers of America. My treasured mentor, Barbara Parker, pushed me in the right direction while she was with us.

Florida locals will see I have taken a few liberties with Homosassa, Florida, moving the Sheriff's substation there from Homosassa Springs. Otherwise, I have tried to keep the locales true and accurate. I also took liberties with the characters in the Florida Departments of Law Enforcement and Environmental Protection. The real people I met in those agencies have no resemblance to the fictitious ones in the book. The same can be said for the Pasco, Hernando and Citrus county sheriff's offices. Although, as an occasional volunteer for the Pasco Sheriff's Office, I have met some characters who do need a book about them, this is not it.

And of course, the remaining mistakes are all mine.

J. M. Taylor

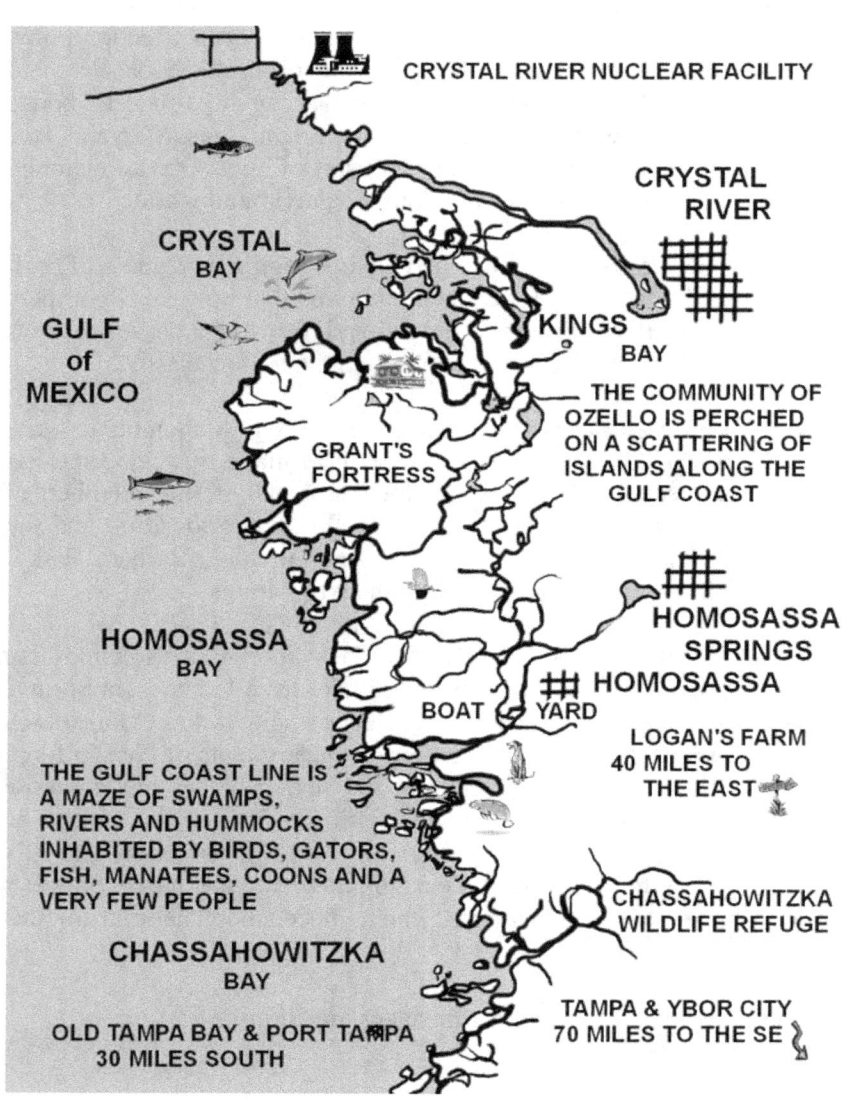

CRYSTAL RIVER NUCLEAR FACILITY

CRYSTAL
RIVER

CRYSTAL
BAY

GULF
of
MEXICO

KINGS
BAY

THE COMMUNITY OF
OZELLO IS PERCHED
ON A SCATTERING OF
ISLANDS ALONG THE
GULF COAST

GRANT'S
FORTRESS

HOMOSASSA
SPRINGS

HOMOSASSA
BAY

HOMOSASSA

BOAT YARD

LOGAN'S FARM
40 MILES TO
THE EAST

THE GULF COAST LINE IS
A MAZE OF SWAMPS,
RIVERS AND HUMMOCKS
INHABITED BY BIRDS, GATORS,
FISH, MANATEES, COONS AND A
VERY FEW PEOPLE

CHASSAHOWITZKA
WILDLIFE REFUGE

CHASSAHOWITZKA
BAY

OLD TAMPA BAY & PORT TAMPA
30 MILES SOUTH

TAMPA & YBOR CITY
70 MILES TO THE SE

PROLOGUE

Today had been a good day—so far. No one Grant knew had died.

Lieutenant Ulysses Grant dropped to a crouch when a bullet splattered against the pockmarked mud wall, followed by the distant crack of a single rifle shot. *Sniper*. He stared across the parched Iraqi landscape. An oven-hot wind churned coarse grit across the sky, peppering his goggles and clogging his nostrils. Across the dun landscape, sand devils swirled toward the Sinjar Mountains. Despite the heat Grant's hands felt clammy. He swiped his palm across his dusty pants, wondering if the sniper had one of his soldiers centered in his telescopic sight.

To his right Sergeant Vicente Madero knelt with his back to the wall separating the schoolyard from the desert, scanning the desolate countryside with a pair of binoculars. "Out about two hundred meters, top of the ridge," Madero called out.

To Grant's left the Humvee cupola swung around as Gunner Snyder trained her machinegun over the shimmering sand and rocks.

Grant flinched at a single ranging shot from Snyder's .50 caliber machinegun, followed by the methodical pounding of automatic fire from the heavy gun, a short, deadly three round burst.

"Got him, L. T." Snyder called down from her cupola.

"Confirmed," Madero answered, and lowered the glasses.

"Good job, Gunner." Grant stood, shaded his eyes. "Vicente. Hang tight. I'm going inside to find the platoon leader." At the entrance to the small courtyard, Grant pulled his goggles up on his helmet.

Spotting Jefferson, the Infantry platoon leader, Grant trotted inside and sprawled beside the dust-covered soldier. Grant jammed his rifle through a gap in a pile of crumbled mud and rock and peered out into the desert. "Gunner Snyder got your sniper. What else is up, Jeff?"

Before Jefferson could answer, sand blasted Grant's cheek. The rock in front of his face shattered, the shot fired from somewhere behind him. Grant twisted around, searching for the shooter.

Automatic fire ripped though the air on the far side of the wall. What the hell was Snyder shooting at now? A shotgun boomed twice behind him, a loud reminder that Madero was close.

"Son of…" Jefferson's words were lost in a second exchange, M4s and AKs roared back and forth, bullets cracking and snapping through the air. Sand erupted in a line of impacts stitched across the sand, heading toward Grant.

Grant rolled to his feet and ran in a crouch to his left, angling out of the line of fire and to get a clear view around the corner.

Two men, one behind the other, the closest in dark shirt and pants, head wrapped in a *gutra*, the traditional head covering favored by the insurgents, sprinted down a gap between the buildings. Grant fired, low, and the man in the *gutra* stumbled against the wall and fell to the ground.

The second turned in a swirl of robes and fired wildly back over his shoulder using his wounded companion for cover. Grant dove to his belly as a hammer blow smacked against his Kevlar helmet. His neck cracked as the impact snapped his head back. He triggered off a wild burst toward the alley. Grant was still trying to get his eyes focused when Madero's shotgun boomed.

The runner slammed to the wall and slowly slid to the ground.

Grant lay on the hard-crusted sand for a moment, breathing the dust and smells of fired rounds and sweat, twisting his head around on stiff neck muscles.

"Uly. You okay?" Madero appeared on one knee beside him, feeding shells into his Remington shotgun. Soldiers from Jefferson's platoon sprinted past them. One crouched and stripped the wounded insurgent of his rifle.

"Good to go, Vince." Grant felt like he had been tumbled in a dryer with a pound of sweaty sand, gear all twisted and jammed with grit.

Madero slapped Grant on the shoulder. "I'll check the rest of the team." Madero trotted though the gap in the wall toward the Humvees.

Grant climbed to his feet, twisted a loose kneepad back to the front and shrugged his shoulders until his tactical vest felt straight again. He took off his helmet and shook the grit out. As he suspected, the camo cover had a tear where one of the zings had turned into a zonk. He worked his tongue around, wincing when he touched where he had bitten his cheek, and spit out a wad of bloody sand.

A medic had Jefferson down on his belly, scissors working on the seat of his pants. "Jesus save me," Jefferson kept repeating.

Grant squatted down beside the prone lieutenant and looked over at the medic with raised eyebrows, questioning. The medic just grinned back at him, shook his head. "Jeff, you hurting, buddy?" Grant asked Jefferson.

"Son of a bitch shot me in the butt."

The medic started laughing.

"Shut up, dammit." Jefferson muttered.

The medic plastered a gauze pad on Jefferson's butt cheek, covered it with an extra strip of adhesive, then used several strips to pull Jefferson's pants closed. "There you go, sir. A nick, but enough for a Purple Heart. Boy, I can't wait to write this one up."

"Yeah, yeah." Jefferson slowly climbed to his feet, the grimace on his face turning to a scowl when he saw Grant's grin. He twisted, peering over his shoulder at his rear end, finally shook his head. "You guys had your fun?"

"You need a med-evac?" Grant asked.

Jefferson spread his legs and looked down at his crotch. "Nope, but inches lower, and my love life would have been a fond memory. Think of all the women who would miss out."

Wilson and one of Jefferson's soldiers lifted the wounded insurgent on to a litter and carried him inside.

"We got a big convoy coming through pretty soon. My guys need to get out of here and clear the route, ASAP. I'll leave that guy to you and your thumbscrews." Jefferson gimped toward the back of the building.

Madero grinned as he watched Jefferson limp away, the tape patch already loose and showing flashes of brown skin and bandage through the slit pants. "*Dios*! That was too damn close." He turned back to Grant. "Snyder got to try out her new gun. Girl just loves that .50 cal. The team's good to go. Everybody's square, L. T."

"Jefferson's boys got everything under control?"

"*Caca pasa*. Rest of the ragheads must have slipped out the back. The two we brought down are the only ones left. Grunts are sweeping the area, but I don't expect them to come up with anything."

"All right, then. Let's go to work. If these guys have an ambush waiting somewhere along the road, we got no time to waste on being sweet. When we start with the wounded one; me good, you bad, O. K.?"

Madero twirled the end of his long-past regulation mustache, put on his *Pancho Villa* scowl and led the way inside.

Grant pushed his M4 around so the rifle hung across his back and helped the medic lift the wounded insurgent, a teenager with a wisp of a mustache, on to a rough wooden table, originally the front door to the room. The kid grimaced when the medic started cutting the bloody pants leg away from a nasty-looking leg wound. Grant eased the folded *gutra* under the kid's head, hand under his neck where Grant could feel the kid's pulse racing in time with the vein pulsing across his temple. "Take it easy," he told the kid. "Doc, here, will take care of your leg. You Saudi? Syrian? Speak English?" Grant asked, brushing a persistent fly away from the kid's face. Fumes stung Grant's eyes as the medic swabbed around the wound with a disinfectant wipe, the ubiquitous odors of a field surgeon at work.

The kid's eyes flicked back and forth across Grant and down at the medic. He shook his head, cheeks sucked in as he tried not to show his pain. "I no Arab. I am *Nokhchi*. My brother live one time in America. He teach me English." The kid winced as the medic tied off the bandage and began pumping up an inflatable splint. He let his head lay back, irises growing large as the muscles in his neck relaxed against Grant's fingers.

Grant watched the kid's eyes, bloodshot brown, blinking away the dusty haze floating through the room. Too much pain to be real tells. "Hey, man, you probably speak English good as I do. I'm just a cracker and my buddy here's a greaser." The kid stared at them, apparently not understanding the slang. His pulse slowed under Grant's touch as Madero handed him a cigarette. "So what's a *Nokhchi?*" Grant asked.

"The Russians call us Chechen." The kid accepted the cigarette from Madero and took a long drag, his eyes now flicking back and forth from Grant to the stocky sergeant.

"So you got tired of fighting the Russians and decided to come down and help the al Queada dogs?" Madero asked, the long tips of his mustache framing a set of crooked teeth. The Chechen's eyes opened wide as Madero took a step forward and racked back the slide on the twelve-gauge shotgun he slid around from behind his back. The medic looked up, alarm clear in his eyes, not sure what Grant's interrogation team had in mind.

Grant shook his head at the boy and pushed Madero back. "Boy, you got sold a bill of goods. You like killing children? Did you plant a bomb here at the school?"

"No, no. I come to fight infidels. *Jihad* for Islam." The vein throbbed across his temple, faster again.

"*Jihad* for Islam, as taught by the word of Allah, written by Mohammad. Very noble of you. Gives you a leg up on going to Heaven over all those who stay home in Chechen, right."

The kid nodded, a tiny look of pride beginning to show. Grant wondered how to work this best. Pride always falls hard.

"What is your name, kid?" Grant asked.

"My father named me Mohammad."

Grant pointed around the blood-splattered room. "And now you're in Iraq, killing innocent Islamic children. Where do you think Allah is going to put you when He decides who stays in Hell and who goes on to Heaven?" He pulled a leather-bound book from the pouch Velcroed to his tactical vest and waved it at the kid. "My Koran says you are going to burn in hell if you kill innocent children. Now, my Koran is in English, so I know some of the Prophet's words might be translated wrong, but aren't you going to be one of those lost souls who end up forever in Hell?"

Mohammad just shook his head, his brown eyes big, glistening.

Why? Grant wondered, probing for a way through the maze of misinformation indoctrinated into this kid by those who claimed to speak for a higher being. Physical pain, moral anguish? *Only Allah knows.* He picked up the flaccid remains of a scuffed and blood stained soccer ball from the floor. "Who killed the child who played with this ball? You? Do you have the child's blood on your hands?"

"No, no. It was a mistake. I did not kill the children. Not I." The cigarette glowed as Mohammad waved it back and forth in front of his chest. "I was only told to watch for Americans coming to the school, not to bomb."

Grant slammed the deflated ball to the ground and held the Koran over Mohammad's face. "Allah's words as given to us by the Prophet said those who kill innocents must pay accordingly. Did you study that *Sura*? The one about women?" He slid the Koran back in the pouch and smoothed the flap shut. "Those who kill believers by mistake must repay the family. Those who kill believers on purpose will burn in Hell." He tapped the pouch. "So it is spoken in the Koran, Allah's words as told to the Prophet." He took a step back and looked across at Madero. "Sergeant. Were these children and their teacher believers?"

Madero nodded. "We found a desecrated Koran in the teacher's clothes. Ripped to pieces by this man's bomb. The teacher was no doubt a true believer, the children innocents." His voice rose from a whisper to a growl. He shifted the shotgun so the muzzle pointed directly toward Mohammad's face.

Grant replaced his smile with a stern look. "Then you, Mohammad, shall burn in Hell, if Allah knows you killed the teacher and the children." He nodded toward Madero and his shotgun. "It may be our duty to send you on the way so you may be judged quickly."

Both hands waved at Grant, the cigarette dropped to smolder on Mohammad's chest. "No, no, please believe what I say. I only to watch for Americans to come. Other make bomb."

"If you want me to believe your word, I will have to find this other man and ask him if he killed the children and their teacher. Where is this man now, the one who left you to die when he and the others ran?"

When Mohammad didn't answer, Madero dragged him from the table and propped him against the blood-splattered school wall, holding him against the wall with one massive fist and slamming the bloody ball against Mohammad's chest with the other.

Time for the ace, Grant thought, *the ultimate humiliation for most Islamic men*. "Snyder," he called out. Gunner Snyder appeared in the doorway, her long hair down, glowing in the backlight of the sun reflected from the hard-packed courtyard. "Miss Snyder. Perhaps it is time to turn this child killer over to you."

The medic started to speak, but stopped when Grant turned his stare on him.

Snyder stepped in front of Mohammad, her long blond hair flowing down over her broad shoulders, arms crossed across her chest. "*Yawm jami*, Mohammad. I believe you might live today, if you have truth in your heart; *Inshallah*." She paused, her face wrinkled in a hard frown. "But, if you lie..." she shook her head, hair swirling, "... then; *Mashallah*." She stepped closer, bent down to look directly in Mohammad's eyes, and pointed toward Grant. "He is not your judge." She shook her head again and pointed at herself. "I am not your judge. Your father taught you properly, so you must know Allah, blessed be his name, is the only one to judge what is true in your heart, what you must do to honor your mother, may Allah bless her for the pain you bring her." Snyder's voice was almost a whisper. "Why have the others left you to suffer for their sins? Who are these sinners who kill the innocents, the believers? Where are they now?"

Mohammad stared at Snyder, then at Grant and Madero, and pointed out the door. "Mustapha, our leader, the Saudi who make explosion, said to meet at a villa two kilometers that way, on the track toward Mosul." His words came out in a rush.

"How many men desecrated this place?" Snyder asked.

"Mustapha and..." He paused, face screwed up, then held up three fingers.

"Three others?"

"Yes, as Allah is my witness."

"Your mother will rest in peace..." She paused, leaned closer, her freckled nose almost touching his. "...if you have told the truth, *Inshallah*." Snyder stepped back and Grant took her place.

Grant tapped his chest, his finger thumping the ceramic plate in the center of his tactical vest. "Allah knows what is in all our hearts, mine and yours, Mohammad. I believe you. If Allah does, perhaps you will get to speak with the virgins in Heaven." He nodded to Snyder. "Thank you, Miss Snyder. Pass the report on to Wilson. Tell him to call it in and ask for instructions."

Snyder nodded, turned and strode out the doorframe, tucking her hair back up under her Kevlar helmet.

Grant, with Madero close on his heels, left the medic helping Moham-mad back on the table and walked outside where Jefferson waited.

"Got what we needed, Jeff. We're going to head home."

Jefferson nodded his agreement. "Take care out there."

"Watch your butt," Grant called out to the departing platoon leader. He pulled a cigar from another of the many pouches attached to his vest. After he lit it, he had to hold his finger over a break in the wrapper leaf to get it to draw, another casualty of the engagement.

"*Inshallah, Mashallah*? What the hell was that all about, Uly?" Made-ro asked as they hurried out to the vehicles.

"*Inshallah*—if God wills; *Mashalla*—whatever God wills; the basis of all Moslem conversation. Even us Baptists can see some truth in that. Plus, Snyder's getting her act down pat. I especially liked the mother touch." Grant grinned.

Specialist Allen Wilson trotted in from his Humvee.

"Uly. The boss says nobody can contact the convoy; for us to leave the Chechen kid with Lieutenant Jefferson. We're to run the road, see what's up."

Grant looked over at Madero, eyebrows raised. "Major Talbot says go; we go." He slid his rifle around to the ready in its sling and patted the M9 Beretta 9mm pistol slung low on his thigh. "Actionable intelligence to exploit. Terrorists to terrorize."

"Uly." Madero shook his head as Wilson just stood there and grinned. "Are you going to get me in a bunch of shit, again? I'm not so anxious for the five of us to get in a tangle out here in the middle of nowhere. Remember, you got to look out for Flash if anything happens to me."

"I've been looking out for you and Allen for years; now just get in the damn Humvee and don't worry about that mangy old greyhound." Grant trotted toward their Humvee and made a circling motion with his hand to the rest of the interrogation team. Wilson joined Snyder and Specialist Franks in the second Humvee. Snyder flashed her smile and a thumbs up to Grant.

He waved back and shouted "Let's go," back to Wilson. Swinging his rifle around to point outboard, Grant climbed in the passenger seat and flipped on the radio and GPS. Madero drove them out of the courtyard, the other Humvee close behind. Grant turned when a shrill whistle pierced the rumble of the Humvee.

Snyder waved from behind her machinegun on top of the trailing Humvee, blowing kisses to the infantry squad pulling security around the school. "Tell your boss he has a cute butt," she yelled. They responded with grins, one finger salutes and friendly cat-calls.

Three miles of a barely discernable trail across open terrain, most of it sand and rock with an occasional wandering goat cropping the sparse grass, and Grant motioned Madero to a halt behind a line of palm trees and low vegetation marking a dry streambed. As Grant slid from his seat, Wilson and Franks spilled from the second Humvee and jogged over for orders, leaving Snyder on top, scanning their surroundings.

Grant pointed toward a mud structure, roof top barely visible over a stone wall. "House overlooks the highway, about twenty meters on the other side of the house. The ragheads will be focused on the road. If they are any good, they saw us coming." He pointed toward a crumbled wall just beyond the trees. "Allen, you and Snyder set up behind the wall so you can cover us."

Grant waited for Allen Wilson to trot back to the Humvee and move it to the edge of the wall where Snyder's machinegun could cover the cluster of buildings.

Satisfied, Grant turned to the third soldier. "Franks, take the left flank and I'll take the right, head straight to the house. Go far enough around that you can see if anyone bolts from the rear. Let's send Mister Madero up the center with his big, bad shotgun. Stay clear of Snyder's line of fire. Don't want to get between her and a target. She looks like she's hot today." Grant watched his team disperse. They had been together in Iraq most of a year, were good people, looked out after each other.

He led the way in a dash across the open ground, scanning the building ahead. Twenty meters to go, Grant held out his hand, palm down. Madero and Franks both dropped behind cover. Grant sprinted across to the house, gear flopping and sweat soaking his clothes. He stopped with his back to the wall, listening. Nothing but flies buzzing around his eyes and the smell of human excrement in his nose.

He signaled with a sweep of his arm, the old Infantry School "Follow Me." Madero and Franks rushed across the open ground, slamming against the wall on the other side of the door.

In front of them Snyder's machinegun thundered a short burst down the far side of the building. Franks sprinted to the corner and dropped flat, edging around the wall on his elbows. Grant felt the first sign of alarm. *Got to keep this under control.*

A voice cried out from inside, followed by the snap and rattle of AK fire through the doorway.

Mouth suddenly dry, Grant ignored the hot sun burning the back of his neck and focused on Madero, poised on the far side of the door frame. Madero, sweat running in filthy rivulets down his temples, held out a frag grenade, eyebrows raised in question. Grant whispered, "Do it."

Madero pulled the safety pin, opened his hand and let the butterfly handle snap open.

Grant's heart raced as Madero paused. One second, two, lips moving with a silent count. With a flick of his wrist, Madero flipped the grenade through the doorway and into the front room. One more count and the wall behind Grant's back rocked with a thunderous explosion. Dust and black smoke billowed out of the doorway as Grant spun around the opening and into the room. His rifle butt high on his shoulder, Grant slid along the inside wall. A tongue of flame stabbed through the thick dust, followed by a shadow charging through the dust. Madero's shotgun boomed, drowning out the snap of Grant's rifle.

A robed man tumbled to the floor. His AK clattered and spun across to Grant's feet.

Grant left the twisted body to Madero and rushed the back room. As he stepped through the doorway, a figure rose from behind an overturned bed. Grant fired, rewarded by a piercing scream.

The insurgent leaped toward an empty window frame.

Grant snapped off a second burst.

Mud clods and dirt spattered from the window sill as the man scrambled through the opening. Rifle fire cracked though the air, Aks and M4s.

Grant ran to the wall, rifle high at the ready, crouched and spun around the window frame.

Outside the insurgent stood on a wall bordering the road, just meters away, and turned to face Grant. He held a black box in his hand, a look of defiance on his face. The red dot in Grant's sight danced across the man's chest. Sand spurted up from impacts in the sand around his feet, Snyder ranging the .50 cal.

A deafening concussion slammed Grant back across the room and ripped the air from his lungs. Clumps of mud rained down on his helmet as he struggled back to his feet, mind racing, wondering what the hell had happened.

He jumped to the side as a whole section of wall collapsed inward. "Christ!" he muttered. Rifle pressed back to his shoulder, he edged around the rubble. He shook his head, trying to clear the ringing from his ears and blurred spots from his eyes.

A bundle of bloody rags lay across a tumble of rocks. A dismembered hand clutched the black box. Wires trailed off toward the nearby roadbed marked by a roiling plume of dust and smoke rising into the sky.

High above, a speck soared over the cloud, either a hawk down from the mountains or a buzzard drawn by another dead body.

Grant huffed dust from his nose and was finally able to spit a gritty mud ball to the floor. "Everybody O.K.?" he yelled, his voice hollow in his ears.

"Clear outside. Gunner just gave me an O. K. wave." Specialist Franks called out. "Highway out there is one big friggin' hole."

Grant looked across the barren landscape, narrowing his eyes to confirm what he saw–a faint line of disturbed dirt leading from the back window toward the road where the bomber had pulled out the detonator wire. He suddenly realized he was dizzy, hyperventilating. He wiped the grimy sweat from his eyes and slowed his breathing.

He yelled back at Madero. "Vince?" Madero didn't answer. Grant ran back into the front room to find Madero on his knees, fingering a hole in the center of his tactical vest.

Madero grimaced and took a deep breath. "Damned bullet caught me smack in the middle of the ceramic plate."

"Sure you're O. K.?" Grant looked around the room where the dust had finally settled.

Two men lay dead on the floor, their blood pooled and black under their bodies. More blood spattered the wall, already attracting flies.

"Vince?"

"Yeah, Uly. Just had the stupid knocked out of me." Madero took a deep breath, hand on his chest, and shook his head. Madero heaved himself up off the floor and walked over to an overturned bookcase. He flipped it upright. "Well, look here. Maybe something worth translating."

"Good. Pack up anything that looks promising. We'll take it back to base where Snyder can go over it." Grant walked through the now silent house. A crude wooden bed frame, the tumbled wall, no cabinets, nowhere to hide anything of interest. A corner of blue paper caught his eye, protruding from a niche uncovered when the wall had collapsed. Grant gently nudged the paper with the rifle barrel.

A thin notebook plopped to the floor.

Grant stood there, frozen, acutely aware that teasers like the notebook could be triggers for a detonator wired to a 155mm artillery round.

He held his breath, blinked away the sweat that ran down his temples and into the corners of his eyes. No explosion. He took a deep breath and grinned, savoring the adrenaline rush. An interrogation mission had turned into an ambush, the ambush into a firefight. Today had been a real combat patrol. This was what he had signed up for, not just interrogating scared kids.

He picked up the notebook and walked back into the front room, thumbing through the pages. "Vicente, I just decided. I'm going to get me a transfer and stay over another tour when the battalion rotates back to Florida next month."

Madero looked at Grant; the corner of his mouth twisted in a wry grin. "You gone nuts, Uly?"

Grant opened the notebook. "Nope. I'm just getting the hang of really living." Arabic script filled the first page, followed by what appeared to be columns of English language abbreviations and numbers. Gibberish. He stuffed the notebook into the pouch with the Koran. "Look at us, man. These ragheads can't kill us."

"Right. Invincible." Madero gathered the scattered documents and stashed them in a canvas satchel.

Grant followed Madero outside and across to the cluster of palm trees screening their Humvee. He scanned the sand and rocks dividing them from Syria. The desert was empty as far as he could see. No more bombers, at least in sight. Franks climbed into the Humvee and called in their situation report over the radio.

Madero took a deep breath, fingering the hole in his vest, and motioned Gunner Snyder and her Humvee forward. "You got a good bunch here, Uly."

Grant nodded. "Don't forget to get a replacement plate when we get back. I can't lose you, buddy." He had known Vicente his entire life. The team had joined the National Guard all about the same time. Franks would make sergeant in a month or two, have his own squad. Gunner, Specialist Snyder, was a deadeye with her machinegun and could read every word of the Koran in Arabic. A well honed team. Now, if he could only get rid of Wilson, life would be perfect.

The second Humvee rolled over from its overwatch position and rocked to a halt, dust billowing around them. Snyder braced herself in the cupola, all business feeding a new belt of ammo in her machinegun. Wilson slouched behind the steering wheel. Grant silently shook his head. His piece of shit cousin had waited out the firefight, like usual, as far away from the shooting as he could get.

Franks waved the radio microphone to get Grant's attention. "Major Talbot says pack it up and come on home," he yelled out.

Grant nodded in acknowledgement, watched the approaching tanker convoy slow and detour around the crater. "Vicente, load up. Time to get out of here before dark catches up with us."

After the convoy had passed and the dust settled enough to see the road, Madero wrestled the Humvee back up on the sand-covered asphalt, detoured around the gaping hole left by the improvised explosive device and turned back toward their forward operating base. Grant lit his last cigar as the adrenaline drained away, and blew the heavy smoke out into the oppressive heat, trying to stay alert as the buzz wore off. He focused on his side of the road, looking for any sign of another bomb buried along the roadside.

Strange. He never imagined he would enjoy going to combat. He had expected to miss the lush Florida swamps and the sparkling waters of the Gulf of Mexico. But those had been picture book, boring days out fishing and fooling around, none of the tension of combat in Iraq. Real butt-puckering thrill. He spat out a bit of tobacco and grit, eyes sweeping over the desolate expanse stretching toward the distant mountains to the north.

A long day. Even the circling bird had flown away. Grant forced his eyes and mind back on the harsh Iraqi desert, the dark sliver of roadway.

Ahead a Bedouin prodded a small herd of goats toward a patch of sparse grass lining the roadside ditch.

"Uly!" Madero suddenly roared.

Grant snapped his head to the front.

An old Renault slide sideways toward them, the wide-eyed driver hunched over the wheel. The car snapped around, straightened, careened across the crown of the road, back end swinging around, out of control.

"Son of a…" Grant lurched in the seat.

Madero swerved toward the ditch. Tracers from Snyder's machine-gun snapped through the air, chewed through the Renault's windshield and obliterated the driver's face.

Grant kicked at his door and tried to get his rifle untangled from all the other gear bouncing around his legs. The Renault lifted up on two wheels and rolled across the road, filling their windshield. He grabbed the radio mount and braced. They skidded at an angle toward the side of the road and the scampering goats. The Humvee finally jolted to a rest half perched over the edge of the ditch.

With a screech and grinding of metal and glass on asphalt, the old Renault rocked to a stop on its side, inches from the Humvee's hood.

Grant pounded the door with his shoulder. He kicked the door again. The instant his heel connected with the side panel, the Renault vanished. All around, the air roiled into a terrible mix of brilliant colors, followed immediately by a horrific explosion, battering him from all directions. A deep blackness replaced the colors.

He gasped. His face was smashed down in the damned dirt. Grant spat and pushed his helmet up off his eyes. How the hell did he get here, sprawled face down in a ditch, a swath of Kevlar from the Humvee roof spread over his back along with bits of debris and chunks of windshield? The radio and the GPS lay on the ground beside him, torn from their mounts.

He rolled clear of the wreckage and clawed his way up the side of the Humvee with his arms, no feeling in his legs. Madero lay sprawled across the driver's seat, covered with a mangled mess of blood and blackened vehicle parts and charred documents. He stared up at Grant, blinked, silently screaming for help. Grant yelled back, but nothing came out, nothing he could hear. Flames flickered up from the floorboards around Madero, singeing the hair from Grant's arms as he tugged at Madero. He yanked again, but tangled cables and bent metal clung to Madero, refusing to let go. Grant's sleeves burst into flame.

On the far side of the roadway, Snyder swayed behind her machine-gun, teeth bared, helmet askew, soundless gunfire pouring out in short spurts as she continued to fire into the mangled wreckage that had once been the Renault. Wilson flopped out of Snyder's Humvee. Blood streamed down his face He waved at Grant with one hand as he slowly raised his rifle with the other. Wilson's mouth moved, but Grant couldn't hear a word, couldn't hear the gunfire, couldn't hear himself think. He tried to stand, assess what had happened, take charge, get them out of this mess, take care of Vicente like he had since they were kids, clear the bees buzzing between his ears. The Humvee windshield shattered as he tried to focus. Something slammed into his helmet. Grant forced his head around to see Wilson crouched behind the second Humvee, rifle pointed directly at Grant, a big grin on his face.

Why didn't Wilson come over to help?

A bullet pounded against the ceramic plate in the back pouch of Grant's tactical vest, slamming his gut against the Humvee. Before he could gather his breath, a searing pain sliced under his vest and across his kidney. Grant pulled his Beretta and forced himself to turn around despite the pain. Now he saw what Wilson was trying to tell him. The goat herder was running toward him, an AK at his shoulder.

Grant fired his Beretta. Once. Twice. The goat herder stumbled, went down. Heat from the flames swept around Grant's face. The acrid smell of burning rubber and plastic stung his eyes. Fighting against the pain pulsing from his back, Grant tried to keep the pistol pointed at the herder, but the next 9mm round only kicked up more dust as the man struggled to his knees, yanking on the AK's charging handle. The AK came up and a red rose, edged with sparkles of flame, spouted from the muzzle.

A line of tracers arced over Grant's shoulder and the *gutra* flew into the air, followed by a white skull cap. Another burst of tracers flung the man across a boulder, AK smashed into splinters. Grant twisted back to see Snyder still in the Humvee, firing into the desert. Wilson stood in the middle of the road, a wild grin on his face.

A faint sound reached his ears, screaming. His head filled with the sour smell of burning diesel fuel and rubber. And flesh. He looked down at his arms. The world suddenly turned black.

He woke to a soothing vibration and disturbing smells. Disinfectant, hydraulic fluid, alcohol, other odors he didn't want to identify. He forced his eyes open to see the bottom of a bunk overhead. Back on his old boat, he thought for a moment, until the woman in an olive drab flight suit leaned over, so close he had to blink to focus on her tired eyes. She held something in his view for a moment, then laid it on his chest and smiled down through the mist floating over his eyes. He recognized the leather binding of his Koran. *Dear Lord, she thought he was Muslim.* What would momma think? He patted the right side of his chest where he kept his battered Army-issue New Testament. Not there, of course. He looked around for Vicente. He wasn't there, either. He had lost everyone.

The nurse's lips moved, but he couldn't hear her words. He closed his eyes and let it all drift away. Out of control.

CHAPTER 1

The day was getting late. Fishing was slow. But it was a good day. No one Uly Grant knew had died today.

Bennett, the woman fidgeting in the front of his flats boat, had insisted on spoiling his Sunday afternoon by pretending to fish. She also pretended to be a government clerk of some sort. She needed to take acting lessons for both. Clerks don't hire fishing guides. But then, most fishing guides don't make their money scamming funds from hidden al Qaeda accounts. Grant figured they were even. Nothing left to do but relax, like Flash.

Flash had it right, sprawled along the deck, long head resting on a boat cushion, back paws twitching. The lanky greyhound was probably dreaming about the day he won the Million Dollar stakes down at Derby Downs and the stud offers that followed. Grant wished his own dreams were so good.

Bennett stood, feet in a wide stance to steady against the gentle rocking, and stared over the low islands toward the Gulf of Mexico. Beyond her the sun, orange turning red, dipped toward the Gulf and the line of grey storm clouds boiling along the horizon. Bennett looked at her watch and then at Grant. "What time do you have?"

Grant shrugged. "I don't wear a watch anymore. Time doesn't matter a lot to me, just day and night; and I can tell them apart without a watch." He kicked off his boat shoes and ran his toes over Flash's smooth back. *Be nice*, he reminded himself. Whatever Bennett wanted, she was a paying customer. He leaned back against the poling platform, sliced the tip off a cigar with a bait knife. He lit the cigar with his battered Zippo, blowing the acrid smoke toward the mosquito buzzing around his head. "Be dark soon," he offered. "Time to get back."

"Well, I think it's time to get to why we're out here in the middle of this godforsaken place." She turned to him and dropped her fishing rod to the deck. A cruising snook, spooked by the racket, swirled and fled into deeper water.

Grant stabbed the knife into a cutting board. "You think?" He'd been waiting all afternoon to figure out what they were really doing out here. He spat a tobacco flake into the snook's wake. "Go ahead. It's just me and you and Flash out here and it's getting late. Say whatever you've got to say. Flash won't talk."

Flash lifted his head, stared at Grant for a moment, stood, stretched and shook his back, skin rippling over his lanky frame.

Bennett tucked her faded red Florida State ball cap between her knees while she combed a tangled thatch of sun-streaked hair back with her fingers. She smiled when she saw him watching. "Are you really a fishing guide?" she asked. She pulled the cap down over her eyes and fed the pony tail through the cap.

If he wasn't a fishing guide, what the hell was he doing out here? Grant struggled to think of an appropriate answer that didn't include tossing her off the boat. Lord, this woman was trying his patience. He was supposed to be recuperating, not dealing with this crap.

Bennett stared up at the stars starting to show through the deep indigo sky. "Listen," she finally said. "I know how to make this trip more than worth your while."

"Like how?" Grant wondered what she could offer him. Even as he stared at Bennett's figure in faded jeans and sweat-soaked shirt, he doubted she had anything of interest to him. Pretty face, narrow shoulders, light tan on what he could see in the late afternoon glow; the rest of her figure hidden under the loose blouse and jeans. He guessed somewhere around twenty-five, a couple of years younger than he, about the same age he was before he had aged a lifetime in Iraq. She smiled when she saw him watching. Crazy look. One corner of her mouth up, the other down, as if she couldn't make up her mind.

The boat rocked as Flash moved to the side and stared across the water. Grant dug the push pole into the mud, stopping his shiny new Ranger flats boat snug up against a low screen of mangroves. Flash's ears twisted toward the horizon.

A line of high clouds climbed up toward the wispy plumes left by the airliners heading south toward Tampa; growing, twisting, golden giants that towered over the squat cabbage palm marking the next island across the water.

Flash leaned his head out over the gunwale, as close to looking excited as Flash got. One ear perked straight up like a deer, the tip of the other flopped over, his thin tail curled under his body. He could hear something Grant couldn't.

Grant finally spotted the plane. Coming fast and low out from under the clouds, heading directly toward them out of the sun. He worked his finger in his ear. The drone of the plane's engine drowned out the faint insect chirping. He craned his head back and followed the dark silhouette as it flew directly over them, blacker than usual without the required running lights.

The plane's engine throttled back. One, then a flurry of bundles tumbled out, almost like a stick of bombs from a big B-52 paving the way toward Baghdad. An irregular trail of phosphorescent blooms marked the impacts in the shallow water, pale mimics of the Buff's deadly incendiaries. The plane turned and climbed, heading south down the Gulf coast to join the stream of commercial aircraft inbound to Tampa.

In its wake a string of phosphorescent lights bobbed in the water, markers for whatever had been dropped, each connected by a flickering orange trail of rope. His brain finally locked into gear. *Square flounder, the Mexican kind.* Definitely not the kind of fishing he had signed up for.

CHAPTER 2

Grant spat his cigar into the water. "Sit down, lady. Now!" He shoved the boat away from the mangrove roots and stowed the push pole along the side of the boat. *Wrong place, wrong time.* He dropped into his seat behind the console and reached over the ignition key, paused in mid reach when the bellow of an unmuffled airboat engine replaced the buzz of the airplane.

Spray flying, the airboat shot through a gap between two islands, heading toward the glowing markers. Airboats were restricted from this part of the Chassahowitzka Wildlife Refuge. But Grant doubted this driver was lost, not as the boat bounced over the water toward the phosphorescent markers dropped by the low flying plane.

Before he could start the Yamaha outboard, a high intensity search-light from the airboat sliced over the water, brilliant against the twilight sky. The light swept across the bundles and back, sweeping along the islands. The blinding glare pinioned them against the low bank.

The airboat skittered in a long turn. Away from the markers. Toward them.

Grant had been here before. A careening car. Stark fear. The need to scream. He should bail. Abandon his passenger. Run. Instead, he froze in place. Not in fear. He was the guide. Bennett was his responsibility. *Damn her*!

Spray glistened in the light beam as the airboat skimmed the shallow water, coming directly toward them. Grant tried to slow his heart rate. Docs said he should relax, hasten the healing process. *Right*.

The driver perched high on the airboat, silhouetted against the last vestige of the sunset's glow. A second figure stood alongside the driver's platform, hanging on to the seat supports. The driver cut the engine. The boat kept coming, fast. Faster than Grant could get his mind to work.

The airboat's wide aluminum bow slammed into the Ranger, flinging Grant to the deck. Screeching metal slid inches over his face, pinning him against the console. Grant bounced against Flash's bony ribs as the boat rocked with the impact. Over his head the poling platform crumpled and folded with a shriek of twisted metal. The broad nose of the airboat stopped, jammed against the big Yamaha. With a final squeal of metal on metal, the airboat rocked back enough for Grant to scramble through the bent tubing, grab the steering wheel and pull himself to his feet, groaning with the effort. Add a few more bruises to his litany of pain. He squinted and held his hand up to block the glare as the light swept over his boat. With relief he spotted Bennett huddled in the bottom of the boat. Then the rage began to rise, blood pound in his head. Grant took a deep breath. *Relax?*

"Ain't ya'll out a little late for tourists?" A laugh followed the question out of the darkness. "What you think? You going to get some for your own self?"

Grant recognized the voice from the Homosassa marina dock. Billy—a tattooed ex-con who knew who and what Grant was. Or at least the broke-soldier-fishing guide part. Grant silently cursed. Complacent, drifting around the scattered islands during the day and puttering with his computers at night since his release from Walter Reed, he had let his mind erase, forgot about the fiends, thinking they all wore red-checked *gutras* on their heads and vented their evil a world away. He suddenly wished he had his M9 Beretta where its weight, sand and desert heat once rubbed him raw. Even his cigar knife was gone, flung somewhere out into the mud by the impact.

He cleared his throat. "What the hell you guys want?" Besides the bales. Uly glanced at Bennett, suspecting she already knew the answer. Billy confirmed it.

"You ain't got nothin' I want, Uly. Just you look there at your piss-ant boat. All messed up. You need a real boat like this one, something with a Chevy V-8, not some crappy Jap motor." Billy laughed, a deep chuckle, hawked and spit into the mud. "But the woman might be worth a little time. She one of your Mex whores?"

Billy stepped from the airboat and across to the bank, a hulking silhouette behind the light. Big, over six feet tall. Only an inch or two taller than Grant, but with a big belly and broader across the shoulders. And no discernable limp. "You at the wrong place, boy. Sit down!" Billy bellowed. "You screwing in our business."

Grant took a deep breath and sat back down as the blood pounded behind his eyes. *Damn!* His only weapon was the H&R Tamer, a single-shot .410 snake gun stashed somewhere in the mangled mess that had been the console. Grant suspected these guys had something bigger. And probably didn't give a damn if they used it. He felt for the Tamer in the wreckage. Flash looked back, a strange look in his eyes, and edged toward the gunwale. He whined, low; a sound Grant had never heard from the greyhound before.

"Holy shit!" Billy yelped as Flash sprang across the gunwale. A shotgun boomed from the airboat, red fire spitting out toward the leaping hound. Grant's boat shuddered as shot tore through fiberglass and spattered into the mud. The muscles across Grant's back grabbed, puckering around his old gunshot scars. The shooter racked a fresh shell into the pump shotgun. Grant forced himself to relax, back down to a tremble, resist the urge to leap after Flash. Two men, with guns. Flash was on his own. He prayed the dog was still alive.

Grant groped along the shattered fiberglass. His fingertips brushed smooth polymer, then the Tamer's cold nickel barrel.

"Get out, bitch," Billy ordered, pinning Bennett with the light beam.

The light reflected from the flats boat enough for Grant to recognize the pistol, a shiny, chrome, long-barreled .357 magnum revolver, tiny in Billy's tattooed fingers.

Grant slid his fingers around the snake gun's grip and eased it free of the wreckage.

Billy waggled his pistol toward the higher ground behind them where the twilight was fading into darkness. "Both of you. Git!" he yelled, shining the light on Grant and Bennett.

When the light paused on Bennett, Grant stood and slid the short barrel of the snake gun down his back and under his cargo shorts until the tip of the nickel barrel stabbed his calf, the polymer stock cold and wet against the small of his back. The light flashed back around to him. He stepped onto the bank, palms extended. He backed away from Billy toward the center of the tiny island. "No problem, man." He tried to make it sound like a whine. He didn't have to try too hard.

Bennett's head snapped toward him. He was glad he couldn't see her eyes. She'd led them to this hell, but that didn't mean he liked what was about to happen.

"Look, we ain't got any reason to mess around in your business," Grant continued. His mind churned for some story to distract the men, something to slow them down.

"You're right, boy. You ain't." Billy stopped and hollered back to the man on the airboat. "Hoop. I'm gone need the light to do a little chicken parts inspection."

"Get on up to the hummock, Billy, and do it if you can get it up. Get rid of these assholes and get your butt back here. Damned airboat sprung a seam. Moon's coming up, so I can see to patch. When I fix it, we gotta find the weed before it floats to Clearwater."

Grant had lost too much weight. His waistband was loose and the gun kept working its way down, threatening to drop out of his shorts. Eat better, the doctors had said. He should have listened. He heard the rip of duct tape torn from a roll. He wondered if it was for the boat or for them. Hoop and Billy had used each other's names. Get rid of them, Hoop had said. A bad sign. Grant looked toward the mainland where a line of low clouds glowed with the hint of the rising moon. No help coming out of that swamp.

Billy kept the light on Bennett as he herded them to the higher ground. "Honey, you look like a coon up in a tree, big old eyes. Shoot fire, you fixing to have lot's more fun than any coon. Now move, the two of you."

The ground rose slightly as they walked away from the water. Bits of shell and twigs sliced at Grant's bare feet. Faint in the stray beams of light, palmetto fronds poked up over the low mangroves. Hundreds of nesting ibis, ghostly white bodies scattered across the low trees and bushes, muttered at the trespassers. Sawgrass blades clawed at his ankles. The Tamer dropped, caught in his inseam as it threatened to slide to the ground.

"Stop. This here's fine, honey." Billy brushed the light across Grant. "You just stand there, Uly, and watch. You might learn something." He turned the light back on Bennett. "Drop your drawers, gal. Let's see if you're as sweet for me as you are for your hotshot Mex loving guide."

Grant focused on the gun in Billy's hand, ignoring the mosquitoes walking across his arms and the stings where the sawgrass had sliced his ankles. He blinked, trying to regain his night vision, and listened for the second man, Hoop. He heard ripping tape. Or was the sound in his mind?

Bennett had a distant look on her face. She had gotten them in this damn mess, and now she stood there, looking at him, eyes big, waiting for him to do something. What did she expect?

"Come on, baby. Don't fuck around. Drop your pants."

The light flashed back over Grant. He held both hands out in front as the light swept over him, head down, trying to give Billy no cause for alarm. *Stay in control*, he reminded himself. Not the time for battle rage.

Billy dropped the light in the grass and moved closer to Bennett, the chrome pistol glittering. "That's right, boy," Billy called out to Grant. Every word sounded more contemptuous to Grant. "You just stay there shivering, you scarred up crip."

Grant's head jerked back up. He worked his jaw, fighting the building rage. *Crip? Fucking crip!* The son of a bitch had shot at his dog. And whatever her intent, Bennett had hired him. He was supposed to keep her safe. Even she didn't deserve Billy.

The throb in his leg worked up to a pounding in his head. He slid his hand behind his back, over the Tamer's pistol grip. He was tired of waiting, being patient, in control. Heart pounding, he tugged at the gun.

The hammer, something, snagged on his waist band. One of the .410 shells popped out of the Tamer's stock, bounced off his foot into the mud.

Bennett yelped when Billy slapped her across the face. Billy reached down and tugged at her jeans. She jerked back. Her jeans popped open, slid down her hips. She stumbled to her knees as she struggled to pull her jeans back up.

Billy laughed; unbuttoned his fly.

Grant gave the gun nestled against his butt a savage jerk. This time it tore free with a loud rip.

Billy stayed focused on Bennett. He stepped closer to her, moving between Grant and Bennett.

Grant worked it through his mind. This close, buckshot might go through Billy, maybe hit Bennett. He carried both birdshot and buckshot shells in the gun. Which was loaded tonight?

Grant thumbed back the hammer, a click that Billy ignored. Grant leveled the nickel barrel at Billy's back. Paused. The gun trembled in his one-handed grip, barrel lustrous in the growing darkness as he waited. *Come on Billy. One step to the side.*

"I said drop them britches. You best pay me some mind," Billy repeated. "Less you want to stay down there on your knees." He laughed. "But that'll do for a start."

Bennett pushed herself to her feet. Billy reached out and jerked Bennett's jeans down as she stood up, her face as pale as her white panties gleaming in the moonlight.

Grant's finger tightened on the trigger, praying Bennett would fall on her ass in the mud, anything to get her out of the line of fire.

She staggered back, jeans tangled around her knees, pushed Billy away and twisted to one side. "Bastard," she screamed. Her fists were a blur across the light beam when she swung at Billy.

Almost clear.

Billy swept her arm away with the pistol and jammed his fingers into the waistband of her panties, jerking her toward him until the fabric ripped free. He slapped the pistol across her chin, snapping her head around. He laughed, flinging the remains of Bennett's panties in the air.

Still too close together.

Billy took a step back and picked up the light.

Almost.

He played the beam over Bennett, now naked from the waist down to her jeans tangled around her feet. "Now ain't you a pretty." He turned to Grant. "See what you're missing, boy?" Billy stepped to the side so Grant could see.

Grant saw. Slim legs. Smooth belly, indistinct in the background as he focused on Billy and steadied the Tamer.

The light swung toward Grant, blinding.

The .410 Tamer bucked in his hand, a puny 'boom' compared to Hoop's twelve gauge pump.

The light beam sliced across the sky.

The air around Grant filled with the frantic flutter of wings as white ibis swirled in confusion around them.

"You chicken shit!" Billy yelled, arms flailing at the birds swirling around them.

Birdshot.

"Billy. What the hell?" Hoop yelled from the direction of the airboat.

Grant blinked sweat from his eyes and fumbled with the shotgun. Billy screamed and staggered toward him. A shell slipped from Grant's fingers and plopped into the mud. Grant clutched at the remaining shell as Billy finally figured out how to work his legs. Grant slammed the slender shell into the chamber and snapped the breech shut.

Billy snarled, lips bared in a primal growl. He changed directions, reached out, faster than Grant expected, and grabbed Bennett. He yanked her close, chrome barrel wavering between Bennett and Grant.

Bennett screamed something, unintelligible.

The concussion from the shotgun blast still rang in Grant's ears. Blue jeans whirled though the air as Bennett kicked them free, struggling in Billy's grip, his gun under her chin.

Grant cocked the Tamer's hammer back. "You're the loser, you shit. You let an old crip bloody you," he screamed.

Billy slowly turned toward Grant, fury on his face. He shoved Bennett away and raised the pistol in both hands, lifting as if he were moving a mighty weight.

Grant fired. He could tell the difference this time. The Tamer slammed back, the recoil felt all the way up to his shoulder. Buckshot, five double-oughts that ripped a ragged circle in Billy's overall bib.

Billy tottered, then collapsed on his back in the grass, gurgling as air leaked out of his lungs.

"Billy," Hoop yelled, this time closer.

Grant dropped the Tamer and grabbed Bennett, half crouched in the mud, by her shirt collar. He dragged her, feet kicking, naked butt and all, though the mangroves to the opposite side of the island. Splashing out until they were waist deep in the cool water, he crouched and pulled the struggling Bennett down to her chin. "Be still."

Her breath came quick, short, scared, too loud.

Hoop's head momentarily appeared through the mangrove screen, then disappeared out of Grant's view. "Damn, you, Uly and your whore!" Hoop yelled into the night. Hoop's shotgun boomed, spitting flames across the island.

Grant flinched and ducked close to the water. Pellets tore through the mangroves, splashed and ricocheted into the glow of the rising moon. Another boom, and pellets splatted to the side, skipping away until Grant heard the crackling of branches and muted squawks from a nearby island. He pulled a shivering Bennett lower as the light swept up and down the island, pausing on Bennett's panties dangling from a palmetto. He could hear the distinctive clacks as Hoop reloaded his shotgun.

The light swept across the small island, moving their way. Hoop must be tracking their footsteps in the mud. Grant pulled Bennett further back into the water and toward the tip of the island.

"Wade away from the island. Stay low. I'll be back," Grant whispered. He eased into deeper water and swam away from Bennett, circling back around the island. When he rounded the tip of the island he gathered his feet under him and crouched in the shallow water.

Hoop bellowed something across the island and fired again, the shot falling harmlessly in the water.

Grant leaned around the mangrove roots, face just above the water, air rich with the smell of island mud and bird shit. Ten, twenty yards away, a dark mass rose out of the water. Silhouetted against the bright stars and the light of a half crescent moon still low on the horizon, the mass resolved into the rudder and high platform of the airboat. Slowly the propeller cage took shape in the evening glow.

He looked back toward where he had left Bennett. Nothing but water and star reflections rippling across the surface. Back on the middle of the island a light beam whirled across the sky like a searchlight, coming his way.

As the light flickered across the mangroves, stars twinkled in the branches. Grant blinked. A dark shape, thick as his arm, fell so close water splashed his face. The flickers weren't stars. They were snake eyes.

CHAPTER 3

A heavy salt marsh snake broke across the reflection of the moon and swam lazily beside Grant, within arm's reach, as if he knew this was his kingdom and Grant was only a temporary intruder.

Grant tried to ignore the wavering shape as the snake kept pace with his breast strokes. Grant slowed to a stop at the edge of the airboat and let his knees sink into the muck as the snake disappeared into the mangroves. Grant reached into the bottom of the boat, groping for anything he could use as a weapon. His fingers brushed across a rubber gas line, dry and scaly. He sensed, felt more than heard, a low hiss as he squeezed the line in his fist, forcing gas up into the engine. The acrid smell of gasoline and motor oil floated through the heavy air.

He slid his hand around the hull until he found a stubby bait knife in the litter of beer cans and chewing tobacco bags. He looked back toward the island. The light was gone. No sound from either Bennett or Hoop disturbed the lapping of the water against the side of the boat. Or more likely he was stone deaf from the gunshots. Grant sawed at the gas line with the bait knife until he felt the cold ooze of gas from the ragged cut. He twisted and sawed until gasoline squirted out of the hose in a tiny stream, still under pressure from the tank after baking in the afternoon sun.

A movement caught his eye, a small slither over the bow, silhouetted against the silver glow of the rising moon. Grant eased his way around the boat to the bank. Crouched low, he squinted into the darkness. If only the moon could give him a little more light, he might figure out if there was a real weapon on board, something better than the bait knife.

The high intensity beam pinned Grant against the boat.

"Hey, asshole. What the hell ya'll think you're doing? Drop that goddamned knife. And don't go nowhere. This fuckin' twelve gauge will get you quicker'n you can say snot. Bigger damn holes than you put in Billy."

A shotgun barrel glinted in the sharp light beam.

"Git on the boat, face down on the deck. Business first, and then I'll figure out what the hell I'm gone do with you. And it ain't gonna be nice, you shit."

The boat lurched as Hoop shoved them free of the mud bank and stepped on board. The insects returned to full volume, a yowl in Grant's head. He tensed as a damp shape slid across his bare skin. Moonlight flickered on the undulating lateral stripes that marked the snake's contractions as it crawled across Grant's foot and on to the stanchion. The snake wound its way up on the casting platform and vanished into the open bait well.

Hoop played the light over Grant. "Old Billy's dead, shit head. How'd you do that? You still got a gun? Stand up so's I can see."

Grant stood, willing away his pain. He glanced past Hoop. Bennett was nowhere to be seen. The snake had disappeared into the blackness.

Billy looked Grant over, then climbed up on the driver's platform and flashed the light around the boat, stopping on the fluorescent floats bobbing in the water. He cranked the engine and leaned down to shout at Grant, brandishing the shotgun for effect. "First you're gonna help me pick up the weed. Then we're gonna find that woman. I'll really take care of the bitch this time. Both of you." Hoop poked Grant with the shotgun barrel. "Now git outa my way." He slid the shotgun into a scabbard lashed to the frame and shined the light down on a pistol stuck in his belt. "Don't fuck with me. Billy's magnum will turn you into fish chum."

Grant grabbed the platform support when Hoop shoved the throttle stick forward and gunned the big V-8. In response, the open exhaust roared into the night, spewing orange flames into the sky. Grant froze as the snake slithered out of the bait well and coiled around the platform leg, tongue flickering, and head moving in time with the boat's slow rocking. It constricted and stretched in the peculiar way snakes climb, twining around the platform post, slid across Grant's hand and climbed on up to the boat seat.

Hoop pushed the steering stick forward and swung the boat toward open water. The crickets were drowned out by a sudden burst of raw noise from the engine.

The light swept across Grant with the motion of the boat. He reached behind him, found the fuel hose and twisted, back and forth in time with the swaying of the boat.

Hoop leaned back, intent on the glowing bits of blue and orange dancing across the water. The snake's head appeared, swaying as the snake wound along the platform by Hoop's head. The airboat tilted to one side, bounced over the water in a wide sweeping curve. Hoop twitched and pranced as he tried to follow the snake's progress with the light as the snake slid down to his leg. The snake clung to Hoop, tail waving around as Hoop gyrated, trying to dislodge it. The boat surged and slowed as Hoop danced on the platform, trying to smash the snake's head under his heel.

Cool liquid washed down Grant's arm, cooler than the Gulf waters. The heady odor of gasoline floated around his head. The engine skipped, backfired. He dug his Zippo from his pocket. Hoop's wild maneuvers slung him to one side of the boat, then back against the propeller cage. Grant shook the water from the brass lighter and thumbed the wheel. A tiny spark, but no flame. He blew into the lighter, thumbed the wheel again. The boat rocked over the crisscrossing wakes.

Hoop stomped on the platform with both feet, screaming at the snake, then at Grant.

The motor sputtered, and the boat spun to a stop, flinging Grant against the platform. One of Hoop's boots kicked Grant's hand, jarring the lighter in Grant's wet fingers. He snatched at the lighter with both hands, balancing against the dancing boat, and flicked the wheel again. A small flame fluttered from the wick, died, grew.

Hoop yanked out the shotgun, long barrel glistening in the moonlight, and swung it toward Grant.

Grant tossed the lighter toward the bottom of the boat and rolled, half-dove, half-fell over the side. He hit the water an infinitesimal tick before the shotgun roared. Grant clawed toward the bottom as pellets slapped his butt. The roar of exploding gasoline drove him even deeper.

Grant's chest slammed into the bottom muck, pushed down by the pressure from the blast, smashing the air from his lungs. He jammed his fingers into the muck and held himself on the bottom. Waiting. Seemed what he did best, anymore. Finally, out of air, he ignored the yellow and red flames dancing overhead, wiggled his fingers free of the bottom mud and pushed his way to the surface. He gathered his legs under him and crouched low in the water. He turned back toward the airboat drifting toward the open Gulf. The engine gave one last cough and spout of flame. Small fires raced up the framework, consuming bits of flammable materiel left after the explosion. A charred mass sat upright in the driver's seat.

Grant straightened in the waist deep water and splashed away the lingering flames. Still sucking for air, he gasped in a deep breath and shivered, the taste and smell of gas overpowering. He stuck his head back under the surface and rinsed out his mouth. He stood and scrubbed the mud away from his eyes, spitting out gas-tainted salt water.

Everything tasted and stunk of gas. And something else. That particular combination of odors made chills run down Grant's back, a putrid brew he had smelled on the road to Baghdad. Grant gagged, staggered through the shallows to the island.

Grant's stomach churned until he remembered the threats and forced himself to stare for a moment at what remained of Hoop. He wondered if the snake had made it out of the inferno. Hoop? Hoop got what he deserved.

The crickets returned to full volume all around him, gradually drowning out the drip of the water from his cargo shorts into the shallows. Overhead the moon glow barely bested the twinkle of stars overhead.

Someone had finally died. At least not a friend. *This time.*

He looked back toward the palmetto. Bennett's panties fluttered in the moonlight as the onshore breeze picked up, a white flag of surrender. Grant waded over to the flats boat jammed against the bank. With a splash Bennett emerged from the water on the far side of the island.

Now where was that damned Flash hiding?

CHAPTER 4

Ivan Karkoff eased back the throttles and let the Bertram roll across the long cross swells generated by the massive ships churning up Old Tampa Bay. For a moment the distant tanker laden with refined gasoline disappeared from sight as its low profile slid behind a container ship stacked high with orange and white boxes.

Satisfied he had correctly identified the tanker as his prime target, Karkoff spun the chrome wheel and steered them on a curving course west across the bay. On his right a constant stream of vehicle lights flashed over Gandy Bridge connecting Tampa and St. Petersburg. Below the lines of vehicles, bobbing white lights marked the night fishermen anchored around the bridge pilings.

Karkoff picked up the binoculars and scanned the waters. Aft of the Bertram, the low riding tanker receded into the distance as a pair of ninety foot tugs nudged the vessel into a Port Tampa berth by the petroleum tanks, presenting an even better target. Flood lights lit up the tank farm, reflections dancing in the lenses as the Bertram rolled over the wake spreading from the container ship.

Karkoff turned back to the controls and tapped the throttles forward. The twin Detroit diesels built to a roar and ten tons of fiberglass, mahogany and chrome surged through the water, close enough to the small boats floating around the Gandy Bridge to irritate the fishermen. This was one operation in which Karkoff wanted to be seen, the boat identified. He roared down the slow speed zone along the causeway, passed the Bartow Power Plant with its array of exhaust chimneys, on toward the narrow entrance leading behind Weedon Island.

"*Prepárese para la acción.*" Karkoff yelled. The old military command, prepare for action, still sent a thrill through his soul. He had been out of action far too long.

Chrome stanchions holding up a canvas awning, and then the awning itself splashed into the water behind the motor yacht as his team cleared the flying bridge overhead. The big Bertram cabin cruiser had been an excellent choice with the broad flying bridge, a perfect platform for the improvised rocket launcher.

Zakariya al Bandri looked over at Karkoff. "What are you doing now?" The Arab grabbed at a corner of the console, his face noticeably pale even in the waning light.

Karkoff smiled at al Bandri's discomfort. The Arab might be a brave fighter, but he was a terrible sailor. He clapped the slim man on the shoulder. "My team is preparing the launcher. Soon you can demonstrate your expertise, my friend."

Petite clambered down the ladder from the flying bridge, followed by Agustín, who began unlashing the inflatable boat secured to the transom. Petite stepped up behind Karkoff and slid her fingers over his neck.

"All is ready, Ivan," she whispered in his ear. "Your father will be proud of you."

"*Sí*. Very soon." He slid an arm around her waist. "With a little help from our friend." Karkoff turned and motioned the Arab toward the hatch above. "It is time for you to ready the missiles."

Al Bandri nodded and scrambled up the swaying ladder to where the *Katyusha* rockets awaited.

Karkoff glanced down at the glowing instruments and confirmed the rapidly shoaling water. Fifteen feet, then eight feet under the keel. He steered in a giant sweeping S-curve through the cut until the bow lined up with the lights marking the dock at the end of the small cove. Karkoff gripped the wheel tightly. Deviate a few feet to either side of the channel and the boat would run aground. The chart showed a shallow bar ahead with a depth of only two feet at high tide. At low tide, as it was now, the bar would be exposed, shiny mud. A fast approaching dark line confirmed the imminent collision. He smiled at Petite, her short black hair glistening in the glow of the instrument lights, her arm tight around his waist, warm body pressed against his.

Karkoff leaned closer to the windshield, staring hard into the growing darkness. Dead ahead the tips of the tall reed tops at the far end of the channel waved in the slight breeze. He glanced back at the stern where Agustín clung to the transom rail, staring back toward the Port Tampa lights, now almost five kilometers across the bay. Karkoff eased the throttles back and let the boat drop down from a plane. Pushed ahead by the following wake, the boat skated toward the exposed bar. Almost at a stop, the boat lifted, groaning as the bow slid up on the mud. With a nudge of the throttle, Karkoff jammed the hull onto the mud. The boat shuddered to a stop just shy of the reeds. Using the power plant chimneys as giant aiming stakes, he rocked the big boat with the twin throttles until the stern pointed precisely across the bay at the docked tanker and surrounding fuel depot tanks. He left the engines in idle as he checked the GPS for range and azimuth to the target. Satisfied, he gave the throttles one final nudge, settling the boat into the mud.

"Petite." He shoved the woman toward the stern. "Help Agustín with the inflatable. I will check on al Bandri." Engines secured, Karkoff scrambled up the ladder to where the Saudi squatted, a small flashlight clamped between his teeth. Karkoff took a deep breath of the bay air, almost the air of his beloved Havana. "This is much different from the sands of Afghanistan, yes, Zakariya?"

Zakariya al Bandri nodded, not looking up from his final adjustments to the rockets, and attached the electrical firing leads to the *Katyushas*. Karkoff slowly walked around the four missiles perched on the metal rack, bending close to inspect al Bandri's application of lessons taught in the hidden valleys of Afghanistan before the Americans had disrupted the Taliban's rule, their excellent pay for Cuban instructors and Karkoff's introduction to the international drug trade.

Al Bandri removed the flashlight from his teeth and wiped at the sweat dripping from his forehead. "Yes, much different. Desert heat is good, frees the soul. This is like African heat, like the hell all Americans shall find on their final journey. But I will not complain as long as I can bring death to the Americans, Allah willing."

You may see your Allah sooner than you expect, thought Karkoff. Aloud, he asked, "Do you have your Koran?"

"Of course." Al Bandri patted his breast pocket. "I am never without the words of Allah as written by his faithful servant, Mohammed."

"*Bueno.*" Karkoff bent down to sight across the rockets, aligned directly over the power plant stacks and in line with the glow from the docks. He shared at least a part of Zakariya al Bandri's goal. He hoped many *Norte Americanos* died tonight. Karkoff would be glad to share the credit with the Saudi.

CHAPTER 5

"Grant! Where are you?" Bennett called out, her voice shrill, on the edge of hysteria. Silhouetted by Billy's flashlight shining into the sky, she hopped around on one foot trying to pull on her jeans and avoid stepping on Billy's sprawled body at the same time.

Grant stared at her dance, wondering what to do now. He was tempted, for just a moment, to leave her out here with Billy and the crabs. Damn her for getting him in this pile of shit, all for a bunch of drugs. Holy mercies, he had his own drugs. VA issued prescriptions, but they got the job done. He tried to remember if he had stashed any on the boat. He really needed a handful, right now. Bennett's sharp curses brought his attention back to the island. "Put your britches on and get over here, Bennett," he called out.

At the sound of Grant's voice Bennett stepped back, stumbled over Billy's body and fell backwards with a scream, jeans flung into the air.

Grant climbed over his flats boat and slogged through the muck and mangrove roots to the light. He switched it off, ignoring Bennett thrashing around in the sawgrass. Across the low mangroves a sudden tongue of flame flicked up from the channel, followed by a final muted "crack" from the dying airboat. As his night vision returned, the moon climbed through the low lying mists hovering over the islands to join a scattering of stars in the night sky and the lights of a jet rising up from Tampa to the south.

The soft pad of steps came toward him from the end of the island.

Grant dropped to his knees and felt through the grass and mud for the Tamer. Hoop, Billy, accounted for. Had someone else been out there with them? The pounding behind his eyes returned with a vengeance.

Grant's fingers slid over the Tamer's metal barrel and on down to the pistol grip molded into the polymer stock. He picked it up. It felt too light. All the shells were gone from their compartment on the side of the stock, fired or scattered in the melee. Behind Grant a light footstep crunched in the mud. He froze. Another crunch, closer, and he spun to his feet, Tamer barrel gripped like a club. He stifled a groan as a sharp pain fired down his bum leg and his knee collapsed, dumping him face down in the churned up mud.

Grant jerked his head back to focus on a pair of eyes staring into his. And a long grey muzzle. With bad dog breath. "You damn dog." Grant reached a muddy hand out and stroked Flash's sleek head. Grant eased up on his elbows and knees, ignoring the sting of the sawgrass cuts and the dull pain from his leg.

Flash pawed at the mud. Brass glimmered in the moonlight. Two shotgun shells.

Grant wiped them clean, loaded the gun with one and snapped the other one back into the stock.

"Bennett," he called out as he climbed to his feet.

"Over here," she answered, a tremble in her voice. She stood by the battered flats boat, jeans in hand. Bare skin glistened, disappeared as a cloud drifted over the moon, then reappeared, pale in the moonlight. Bennett shook out her jeans and stepped into them.

Grant joined her. The shotgun blast had done a job on the boat. The steering console was a pockmarked mangle of shattered fiberglass. His brand new Ranger was now well on its way to being fiberglass toothpicks. Grant wondered how he would have written up the insurance claim. If he had gotten insurance.

Flash hopped into the boat, ready to go. Much slower, Grant followed him. No gurgling sounds, no water in the bilge, but the battered Yamaha hung off the stern at a strange angle.

Bennett stood on the bank, looking out over the water toward the florescent markers. "This thing still float?" She stepped onto the battered boat.

He shook his head at the tangled mess. "The motor kept the airboat from cutting me in two, but I doubt it'll run." He slipped the Tamer into the side compartment with the extra rods, moved up beside Bennett and dropped the electric trolling motor from the bow. To Grant's relief it hummed when he stepped on the foot control. The boat shook, bad wounded, but eased away from the island and Billy. "How about you. You all right?" She smelled of marsh mud and bird shit.

The boat lurched as Bennett crouched by the gunwale and turned her head toward him, eyes shimmering in the moonlight. "Sure. Just fine." She trailed the ragged remains of her panties into the shallow water and used them to swab off some of the muck smeared over her arms. She dipped them again, wrung them out and stuck them in her back pocket. "Guess this a regular day for you. Shooting, killing, all that soldier stuff?" She fished her crumpled cap from underfoot, stared at it.

"Not so much." Grant had lay in bed many sleepless nights, his mind focused on a melody, George Shearing's piano riffs in *Lullaby of Birdland* or the opening drum set in Brubeck's *Take Five* to keep his mind off days like today. He looked back across the island to where Billy sprawled somewhere in the sawgrass, if nothing had dragged him away yet. *Foolish thought.* Crabs would get Billy, bite by bite, battling the buzzards and gulls. He steered toward the channel that would take them through the islands and back to the dock in Homosassa. "We got to get back. Call this mess into the sheriff."

"Wait a minute, Uly." She leaned toward him, her cap askew on her head and wild strands of hair over her face. For a moment her eyes reflected the sliver of moonlight. "You've seen my bare ass. I can call you Uly, can't I?"

Grant resisted the urge to push her hair back. Even in the darkness he really wanted to see her eyes. "Who are you," he asked. "For real? Where do you really work? Are you part of some sting set up by the FDLE?"

She cocked her head to one side. "Florida Department of Law Enforcement? Not hardly. I'm who I said I was, kinda. And stop calling me Bennett like I was one of your soldiers. My name's Katrina. Kat, with a 'K.'" She took off her cap, ran her fingers through her hair and pulled the cap back down square on her head, as if her mind was made up.

She pointed toward the bobbing lights, pulled by the outgoing tide toward the Gulf. "Come on," her voice suddenly frantic, almost as desperate as when Billy had grabbed her. "That's our paycheck getting away." She pulled a boat hook out of a side bracket. "Those assholes are dead, their own doing. The bundles are floating away. When you talk to the deputies, what are you going to tell them? You shot these two because they spoiled your fishing? I got enough problems. I don't need to be tangled in a murder investigation. Damn it, Uly. At least help me get the stuff before it floats back to Mexico!"

Grant glanced south, toward the glow along the horizon marking the string of condos, clubs, tourist traps and restaurants along the beaches. As he watched, a fiery plume arced up from the skyline, moving westerly, fast, toward Tampa, followed by three more just like it. A year ago he would have said it marked the trajectory of a *Katyusha*, the old Soviet 122mm rocket. Tonight, somebody was just having a good time with an early Fourth. But his leg hurt, and he didn't really care what it was. Just home and a couple of pills, forget tonight and this insane woman.

The boat rocked as Bennett reached out with the boat hook and snagged a dark bundle. Finally, she was fishing.

CHAPTER 6

At Karkoff's command, al Bandri had launched the rockets in a shower of flame, one after another, leaving the smell of smoldering paint and charred fiberglass and a pall of grey smoke floating around the boat. On the far side of the bay, four distinct impacts marked the skyline with pillars of flame.

Spectacular! Karkoff fished a wooden match from his pocket. Petite took it from him, struck it with her fingernail and lit one of his dwindling supply of Vegueros, a celebratory cigar to commemorate their first strike against the *Norte Americanos*.

Karkoff savored a deep, intoxicating draw from the cigar, and slowly exhaled the smoke that floated upward and mingled with the aftereffects of the rockets. Enough celebration. His sister, Delina, had insisted that time was important.

Al Bandri stood in the back of the boat, staring at the flames across the bay, oblivious to the three Cubans in the front of the cockpit.

"Agustín," Karkoff whispered. He nodded toward al Bandri's back. "It is time to terminate our friend's contract."

Agustín hefted the remaining stanchion, sliding it around in his grip.

Al Bandri turned, mouth open to speak as Agustín reared back in his best home plate stance and started a home run swing toward al Bandri's head. Al Bandri, eyes wide, started to twist away. Too late. The stanchion slammed against al Bandri's wind pipe. He clutched at his throat and fell back against the rail, gasping.

Agustín swung the chrome pipe again, smashing the pipe into the Saudi's temple.

"Careful!" Karkoff caught Agustín's arm on his back swing. "Do not damage his face, especially his teeth. He must be identifiable. Remember, his friends, and enemies, must understand he fell, a terrible accident, while executing this attack against his great Satan."

Al Bandri lay crumpled in a dark pile by the transom. Agustín tossed the stanchion overboard and dragged al Bandri's body into the galley. He returned with two AK-47s draped over his shoulders and a pouch of grenades dangling from his hand.

Karkoff ran the engines full up, worked the throttles and rocked the boat back and forth. With a sudden release, the twin screws clawed into the water and dragged the Bertram out of the mud bank, twin diesels roaring. He cut the throttles and let the boat drift. "Petite. Open the sea cock, enough to start the boat settling."

Karkoff hated to abandon the Bertram. Stephan had painted his favorite boat name across the transom, *Anita*, in honor of Ernesto, the one *Norte Americano* he admired. He could see himself on the *Anita*, basking in the Havana harbor with his lovely Petite and a pitcher of tangy lime *mojitos*, heavy on the rum, and an endless supply of Vegueros cigars, a hero of the new revolution. And of course, wealthy from his newly mastered trade.

However, as he had expected, the damage left by the rocket exhaust would require too much new chrome hardware, fiberglass patches, new paint. He had also expected a more extraordinary result from the *Katyushas*. He stared across the bay, tracing the smoky path left by the rockets.

The rockets had launched as commanded, trajectory right in line with the big tanker tied up to the dock and in the process of unloading thousands of tons of gasoline. Across the bay flames shot up into the air, followed by muffled explosions that rumbled; one, two, three, perhaps fuel tanks exploding. Low flames reflected from the water appeared to be dying, not growing. Not the massive disaster for which he had hoped.

Al Bandri had accomplished the first part of his assignment. Ivan's sister, Delina, had emphasized that it was most important to make sure the dead Arab completed his remaining mission. Their father had agreed, so Ivan made sure. Karkoff dropped down into the elegant galley where an unlit candle waited in the sink. He patted his pockets, cursing under his breath. No more matches. At his feet al Bandri's arm waved, already awash in the water. Remembering the Saudi's distaste for Karkoff's dark Veguero cigars and proclivity for American cigarettes, he quickly rifled through Saudi's pockets, ignored the small Koran and pulled out a heavy lighter. Karkoff lit the candle's wick and carefully placed the flickering candle on the lowest part of the decking. He watched the flame steady and grow until he was satisfied it would stay lit.

Back up on deck, Karkoff paused, long bush knife poised, until he heard the low rumble of the small outboard. Satisfied, he took one last draw on the cigar, threw it overboard and stabbed the plastic container. He stepped back as gas dribbled from the puncture and splattered across the deck.

"*Ivan. Venido rápidamente, por favor.*" Agustín pleaded, eyes focused on the gasoline flowing toward the open cabin.

"Go. Into the boat." Karkoff glanced back, the smell of gasoline heavy in the night air, and followed Agustín into the inflatable. He grabbed a rope and hung on when Petite gunned the small outboard and steered them away from the Bertram.

The sudden boom and flash from the Bertram caught him by surprise.

Karkoff gave the sinking Bertram and his Arab comrade a salute, "*Adios, Anita, mi amor. Y tu*, Zakariya." He crouched low as Petite drove the inflatable toward a light signaling from the shadowy end of a nearby dock.

Once on the dock Karkoff flipped open his cell phone and placed the call. "General," he said when the old man answered. "We have completed the mission as planned, and on target. Unfortunately, the results were not as impressive as I hoped."

"Of no matter," was the curt reply. "Full destruction would be best, but the psychological impact will serve our interests. Did our Arab friend do his part?"

"Completely," replied Karkoff. "He did his part most well."

"Excellent. Delina has another matter for you to attend. Intercept a transaction intended for that Silva. Your sister will provide the details."

"Of course, father." This Silva's competition had siphoned far too much money from Karkoff's personal enterprise, in addition to thwarting Delina's goals. He held al Bandri's lighter up to the dim glimmer of a distant street light, admiring the Arabic engraving in the heavy silver. "I will call Delina as soon as we are finished here." He slipped the phone back in his pocket. "Stephan," he called out. The fourth member of his team trotted up, a flashlight in his hand. "Have you found us a vehicle?" Karkoff fished a slightly crooked cigar from his shirt pocket, licked it to seal the cracked wrapper and lit it with the silver lighter. He snapped the lighter shut with a satisfying clack, the sound reminding Karkoff of a rifle bolt chambering a round.

"Over there," Stephan replied. He flashed the light on a rusty red Jeep Wagoneer with a boat trailer hitched behind it. "Old, but easy to hot wire, not like the new cars with the coded electronic keys."

Karkoff listened for a moment. Across the bay, blue flashing lights turned their way, bouncing across the water. On the land side a siren warbled in the distance, also coming in their direction. Flames from the burning boat flickered from beyond the marsh grass. The blues lights were closing on the drifting *Anita*. "Move quickly now." He shoved Petite toward the Jeep. "Agustín. Pull the inflatable onto the trailer. We can dispose of it later." He followed Petite and sat in the darkness, waiting for Agustín to drag the boat onto the trailer while Stephan fiddled with the ignition wires under the dash. He took a deep breath as the siren came closer, joined by another in a weird warble of noise.

Karkoff's cell phone rang.

"*Hermano*, are you well?" his sister asked. "I am watching the news, and see there has been a problem in Port Tampa."

"We are fine, Delina." Karkoff frowned as he watched Stephan strip the ignition wires. "Father instructed me to go to a fishing village to the north. Is this at your instigation?" As he spoke the blue flashing lights slowed by the burning hulk. The sirens sounded close, too close. "Stephan. We must go. No lights." The Jeep rumbled to life and Karkoff returned his attention to the phone. "Quickly, sister."

"*Sí.* My friend in the FDLE warned of a man and a woman, working with this Silva," she replied. "Stop them, and Silva must find other ways to finance his operation. It will be of benefit to you and father."

And you, Karkoff thought, *especially you.*

The Jeep lurched as Stephan snatched it into gear, and they pulled away from the boat ramp. "Do you have any specifics for the mission?" Karkoff listened to the woman's name and description of her car. He interrupted his sister. "Enough over the phone. I will find them." He glanced over at Stephan. "Your special friend here sends his fondest regards. Do you want to speak to him?" Karkoff laughed at his sister's response and ended the connection. "My sister wishes you well, Stephan."

Stephan nodded. "Please Ivan. Do not joke. I admire your sister greatly."

"Careful, comrade," said Petite from the back seat. "Delina has her own plans. She will turn the General against you if she believes she will benefit."

Karkoff shook his head, inhaled a deep draw from the cigar and watched the smoke whisk out of the open window. "No fear. We are family. Perhaps, Stephan, one day we will all be family. After we kill more *Americanos* and make our fortune from their addictions."

CHAPTER 7

"I hope to God this is the last bundle." Grant trudged up the sandy path from the dock and tossed the plastic wrapped bale into the pickup bed. It had taken them a couple of hours to capture the bundles and motor their way back to the dock, electric trolling motor whining all the way. He was far past whipped. The dried salt eating through the sawgrass scratches and oyster shell cuts stung like hell. His leg just plain hurt. God Almighty, his leg hurt. He stopped and leaned against the side of his truck. Sweat streamed down his face, clammy in the sultry night air. And he still hadn't figured out why he had let Bennett talk him into this madness.

Bennett stumbled out of the darkness, a glistening black plastic bag hanging from each hand. "The last ones." She leaned against the truck and grunted as she tossed a bag into the truck bed. Bennett straightened, clutched the last bag to her chest and pointed over his shoulder. "Uly! Someone's coming."

He pulled Bennett down behind the truck. Lights moved toward them, flashing up and down as the vehicle slowly navigated the potholed road from the public boat ramp. It rolled by so slowly the crunch of the tires on the oyster shells made distinct crackles, even to Grant's damaged ears, as its headlights washed over Bennett's Mustang. Too dark to see inside. Grant could just make out the shape of an old Jeep Wagoneer, made back when his mom called them station wagons. Yellow headlights, followed by faint taillights. He had gotten pretty good at picking up vehicle nuances at Iraqi checkpoints. This one had a right headlight askew, pointing more up than out over the road, and the muffler rumbled with a leak appropriate to its age. A dog barked from across the road. The Jeep sped up, stirring up a cloud of dust. The light from the single bulb that glowed from Overmier's Bait and Tackle across the shell road shimmered in the dust.

Grant stood, the dull pain burning inside his hip slowly crawling out to his leg like a damned worm. Jesus. Kill two men, and suddenly he was paranoid. Killing wasn't so new. Just the locale. For killing. He watched the Jeep bounce and rumble along until it disappeared from sight and sound behind a stand of oaks, thick with Spanish moss. He rubbed the ache in his leg and watched the dust settle in the light from Overmier's. No one else stirred. Distant heat lightning flickered over the Gulf. The loud croaks of the tree frogs announced the impending arrival of a thunderstorm. A little early for the season, but not unusual. Down the road and just beyond the oaks a cluster of frame houses sat quiet and dark behind a row of tall cedars.

No new lights, no one about, just the solitary dog barking. Old Betsy, the Overmier's watch beagle, Flash's buddy. She'd bark at a cricket. A light mist was beginning to roll in from the Gulf, mixing with the dust. As his breathing slowed, Grant thought he could hear the lap of water against the river bank and the groan of a boat rubbing against a piling. Could he actually hear, or was it just the need for medication washing around between his ears?

Flash slid up beside him. A low woof floated through the mist, Flash's answer to Betsy.

"Shut up," Grant muttered. "Greyhounds aren't supposed to bark." The crickets, joined by a frog chorus, opened up in full volume, so loud even Grant could hear them. Grant smiled into the darkness. Fumes from the bags either had opened up his ears or his imagination.

Four muted dings echoed across the small boat yard. Bennett, still squatting in the shadow of the truck, looked up at him. "What's that?" she whispered.

"The dinging? Just the clock. Up there." He motioned with his head toward a cabin cruiser by the edge of the canal, perched up on a heavy wooden carriage braced by angled four by four timbers. "Four bells. It's two in the morning." He took a deep breath. "That's why I'm so tired."

A rain drop plopped down on one of the plastic bags. Grant pulled a tarp out from behind the pickup seat and threw it across the truck bed, hiding the glitter of the damp garbage bags. He hadn't even peeked into one. Didn't want to. Didn't care if it was Mexican cow manure.

Flash slowly walked up the inclined walkway and looked back down at them from the top platform. Grant had built the incline so he and the retired greyhound could reach the boat's deck. Like Grant, Flash's legs were beginning to go. The steep steps propped against the stern had been more than either Flash or Grant could handle.

Bennett leaned against the rusty truck. She had pulled her hair back, but mud still smudged her face, like horror movie makeup in the dim light. She looked up at the scarred hull towering over her. "That where you live? On that thing?" She wiped at a rain drop that spattered on her face.

"She's not a thing. She's got a name. *Rum Runner*." Grant smiled into the darkness. "She's my office, too." A plywood sheet with *Gulf Winds*

Guiding Service in crude hand-painted letters was a key structural component to the incline.

"Office and home, all on the boat?" She walked up to join Flash. "The *Rum Runner*? I thought this was a junk yard when you met me here."

Grant was careful about the truth. "Office, home, boat yard, junk yard." He motioned toward the dim outlines of the derelict boats that had come with the old boatyard. "It all works for me," he replied. "Now we got things to do. Ready to go?"

"Can I wash off some of the mud and change? If you don't mind, I'd like to put on some panties. My mom wouldn't approve, my running around bare butt. What if we have a wreck on the way?"

Was it her style of humor, or was Bennett just evasive? It was after midnight, and they were both covered with mud and dried salt. Grant pointed at a hose hanging over the rail. "Shower below deck, or hose up there. Both cold water, your choice." She made a face, but Grant could care less. "Light switch on the right bulkhead, inside the hatch."

Bennett pulled a small bag from the trunk of the Mustang and started up the ramp. "You win the hose. I'll try out the accommodations. Then we'll talk about what to do next."

Talk? This had been a strange day ever since she showed up. He had just killed two men and brought home a load of what was most likely Mexican marijuana, and she wanted to talk. He lashed down the corners of the tarp, jerking the ties snug. Damn this Katrina Bennett and her talk. She can shower and do herself up all nice, but the dead guys and the bundles weren't going away. Best face Deputy Rankin sooner rather than later.

Grant climbed into the cab of the pickup, fished the key from under the seat and tried the starter. The tired Chevy straight six turned over twice, three times. One more time, the charm. He turned the key again, but charm didn't start the truck. Grant rolled his forehead over the top of the steering wheel. Maybe Bennett was right. Daylight wasn't far off. He was exhausted from chasing the floating bundles with the electric motor. Clean up, get a little rest and their stories together, and then find Eustis Rankin. He knew in his heart that he didn't want to talk to Deputy Rankin, either. The difference was, he knew his own motives. He had no concept what Bennett's were.

"Kat." The tree frogs hushed when he said her name out loud. He wasn't sure he liked it. Or the person. Any more than the frogs did.

He dragged a battery charger from under the truck seat. The hood creaked like it felt as bad as he did. He propped it open, connected the battery terminals and plugged the charger into the orange extension cord he used to power his tools. He closed the charger under the hood, out of the rain that had turned into a steady drizzle, and walked up the slick incline, grimacing in the dark at every step. He stepped over the polished mahogany rail, down onto the box he and Flash used for a step and into the cockpit of the *Rum Runner*, thankful for the long roof that protected him from the rain pattering down though the oaks. He shivered as he held the hose over his head and sluiced the mud, sweat and dried salt from his body and out the scuppers. Sawgrass and shell scrapes scarred his legs, ankles and feet, but no deep cuts. He slipped off his cargo shorts, twisted his body so the light from the hatch painted his pale skin, trying to see if Hoop's final shot had broken his skin where a splatter of dark splotches marked the cheeks of his ass.

No sign of blood, just the sting of a bunch of blood blisters. He toweled dry, chilled by the damp rain, and pulled on a pair of quasi-clean flannel athletic shorts from the clothes line strung across the cabin. Beginning to warm, he stared out across dark waters of the Homosassa River. No sign of any lights out toward the islands, just occasional heat lightning. Didn't look like anyone had missed the airboat or the two men.

He leaned against the boat transom and squinted into the dark. No one was moving around the boatyard, just the frogs hollering along the canal bank welcoming the rain. Something big, a coon or a red tailed hawk, rattled around high in the big oak trying to find a dry place. Old parts left over from installing the new boat engine littered the deck; paint cans, scraps of hose, odd pieces of mahogany planking. The original Chevy 283 marine conversion block dangled from a hoist just aft of the boat, awaiting a trip to a real junk yard. When he got rid of Bennett and her dope he could get back to the boat and his life. Like him, the old boat just needed a few repairs.

Flash walked over, toenails clicking on the teak deck, and sniffed Grant's hand. Ignoring the pain, Grant squatted down and ran his fingers over Flash's damp hide, down to his paws.

"You sorry rascal. I don't know if you saved my butt or were just having fun out there." Grant poked and prodded the hound. No blood on Flash's coat. Caked mud, but no obvious wounds marred the dog's thin skin. Flash didn't flinch when Grant squeezed his paws, just pulled his lips back in his stupid looking grin. Grant dipped a big handful of the high priced dog food from the raccoon-safe can and filled Flash's bowl.

Flash gingerly ate a couple of bites. Satisfied he wasn't being poisoned, he devoured the rest of the food.

Grant rubbed the top of the hound's head when he finished. "I'll give you a better look over in the morning, clean up your coat. You go rest, old man."

Flash ambled back to a pile of towels in a corner of the cockpit up next to the bulkhead, out of the rain splatter. Two times around the bed and Flash sprawled out, head resting on his outstretched legs.

"Come on down, Uly. I'm out of the shower." Bennett's voice floated up from below.

Grant pulled the screened hatch shut behind him and stepped down into the cabin where Bennett sat on the edge of the padded booth. She scrubbed at her hair with a towel, shivering. Clean, her shoulder-length hair was a sun-streaked brunette, almost blond. She had his old terry robe wrapped around her, the shadow from the single bulb hiding her expression. Grant pulled a stool from under the galley counter and sat in the middle of the small cabin, grimacing as he eased his bruised butt onto the seat. "You doing all right?"

Bennett looked at him with her strange grin. "Never seen anybody killed before. Never been that close to being raped." She glanced through a port hole. "Never been around that much weed, either. So yeah, I'm okay. Just different." She pulled the robe over her legs, covering the skinned places left from tumbling around in sawgrass and oyster shells. She looked like a prize fighter the day after, bruised, a cut on her chin.

"Look, Bennett. Killing those two out there in the islands was bad enough, but stopping here with that weed was dumb. Get your clothes on. We're going on down to the sheriff's office."

Rather than getting up, she just sat there, scrubbing at her hair. "We really need to talk about that, not rush into things."

"Why are you so all fired hot to sit here and talk? Way you say 'talk,' it sounds like an euphuism for 'do something else.' Like take the dope and run." Grant shook his head, "That what you want to do? If so, you better leave now, because I'm not going to be a part of that. We're going down to report the dope, the whole mess, to the sheriff's office." He motioned toward an old Bakelite rotary phone sitting on the galley counter. "I'd call now, but I doubt I could tell a convincing story over the phone."

She squinted up at him through the glare from the light bulb. After a moment she said, "I'll swear; I never know when that Allen Wilson is making a fool of me." She smiled again, as fake a smile as he had ever encountered in any interrogation. "He said you would be the right man in a fight."

"Allen said that?" Grant should have known better when his cousin had phoned and set up the trip. "When he called he said he knew you from work. I should have figured he was in on some crackpot drug deal."

Bennett's smile faded to a worried frown. "Allen said you all were old friends. He went on and on about how he knew about computers and such, but you would be the right person to help if something went bad. Especially if it might not be quite legal."

Quite legal! Damn Wilson. "How do you know a Florida Department of Law Enforcement computer guy?" Grant wondered if Wilson had figured out more than he should.

Bennett's frown turned to a scowl. "I thought I could trust Allen." She shook her head, her damp hair flicking around her eyes. "We met at lunch. I went out with him a couple of times last year. He said you were very good. And discreet. And that you knew the waters around Chassahowitzka; you could help with the weed. Then he would help me with some computer hacking."

Grant took a deep breath, shook his head. "Allen's full of shit. He's setting us both up, the jerk." He squeezed his eyes shut, forced his mind to slow down. Cousin Allen was at his best again. "Look. What's your computer problem? You need something hacked, removed, altered? Personal or government files? Sensitive, proprietary, classified? I just spanned the range from misdemeanor to felony to treason, so you've got to be a little more specific."

"Allen warned me you might be a little hard to get along with. But he said I could trust you." She studied him as if she were making a major decision.

"Allen Wilson? Trust? Change of heart for Allen."

"He said you would do a lot of things for money." Bennett pushed stray strands of hair back behind her ears.

A different smile, even faker than before, crossed her face. She was going to try a new tact, a defiant look on her face.

"Look, Uly. I found out about the drop and thought I could hijack it, with a little help. Allen said you wouldn't mind breaking a few laws if need be. I thought I set those guys up so they would be at least an hour late, get to the drop long after we were gone." She shrugged. "From the way Allen described you, I thought the weed would be enough of a payoff." She stared at him, slowly shaking her head. "Killing anybody was never supposed to be a part of it. And I guess I got your breaking the law part wrong." Her eyes narrowed. "Or did I? You just waiting to get rid of me and take the whole load for yourself?"

"Jesus Christ, woman. No! I'm not going to hijack you. Like it was ever yours—or mine." The pain from his leg shot all the way up until he thought his head would explode. Grant pulled a bottle of Ybor Gold from the small refrigerator and rummaged around in a chart drawer until he came up with a bottle of pills. "I don't know what got into Allen's head, sending you down here, even implying I'd help steal a load of weed, for

Christ's sake. Maybe what I do isn't always by the book. And I've been in some firefights. But until tonight, not here, not in my backyard."

He slammed the drawer shut and chased down a pill with a long swig of beer. He traded Bennett the bottle for the towel and scrubbed his hair so hard his scalp hurt. "What you got going so important you need a gajillion dollar load of weed to pay for it? Woman, you must be in a shit pile of trouble."

She motioned with her hand, palm down, several inches over her head. "About up to here."

He sensed it. Here came a better version. Maybe not the full story, but at least a different one.

"I work for DEP, the State's Environmental Protection Agency."

"O. K." Grant did a little work for the FDLE, Allen's office, but not the kind of jobs he would or could tell her or anyone else about. He didn't know anything about the DEP. Grant's hand twitched, rattling the blue OxyContin pills around in their container. He shook a second pill out into his palm. He took the beer back and finished it, washing down the second Oxy.

Bennett looked up at him so the light fell directly on her eyes. "The dope belongs—belonged—in a way—to my boss, Bobby Silva. I made a mistake. Now I can't get him to let me alone." She blinked her eyes, looked down at her hands, avoiding his stare.

Grant had to bite his tongue to keep from telling her to get out. Right now. She was lying, or at least hiding something. He didn't need to see her eyes. He could hear it in her voice.

"Bobby's tied in with some drug transporters. He's the wholesaler, some kind of middleman for the dope. He knows I found out about his drug deals. He forged some computer files, implicating me, holding them over my head. I thought I could get him off my back if he lost the shipment, cause him trouble with the dopers." She was back to her original smile, the crooked one. "I wanted Allen to hack my records out of Bobby's computer. I was going to use the dope money to pay him."

So now we're getting to the meat. She was a drug dealer and was using him to get her out of a jam. And damn near got them both killed. Grant wondered just how much she knew about him and his other businesses. A nuisance or a real problem? Before they trooped off to see the sheriff he needed to know more—a lot more.

Grant threw the pill bottle back in the drawer and tried to will the twitching to stop. He sat for a moment, trying hard to follow Bennett' chatter, but the Oxy was beginning to shut down his mind. "What are you going to tell the deputies when we go in? I can't sit on what happened. This boss of yours who's causing the problem. I don't think he'll believe you just happened on the drop by chance. Like you always go fishing where a drug drop is planned?"

Bennett pushed her hair back. Her fake smile flickered across her face for a moment. She bit her lip, her face serious. "Uly. I need this. I don't have a lot of money. I was desperate. Allen said you would help, that's all. I didn't know I was fixing to get either of us in this kind of a mess."

Grant blinked his eyes. The blue bombs had his head whirling as he tried to focus on her eyes. So sincere. Hell, he might even trust her. He squeezed his eyes shut. *What the devil was he thinking*?

Grant tossed the towel into the miniature galley sink. "Let's get rid of this weed loading down my truck. Then you and Allen can deal with Silva and his files." He blinked at Bennett, trying to keep her face in focus. "We'll figure out payment later."

Bennett cocked her head to the side, shrugged. "Allen told me you had a hard go in Iraq. That he saved your life." She flicked her gaze to Grant's scarred hands for a moment. "That he thought you would do this as a favor to him."

"Allen ought to keep his mouth shut. And to tell you the truth, I don't exactly remember him saving my life." He looked down at the puckered burn scars on the back of his hands. "But I did come home." The scars brought back memories he tried hard to forget, emotions he fought to hold in check. He blinked back a tear. "Alive, despite Allen."

He took a deep breath. *Damn*. He was losing it in front of this infuriating woman. Maybe she was right about one thing; going down to the sheriff's office could wait. He glanced over at the phone, thought again about calling. Who? If he called 911, the dispatcher would have some yo-yo screaming out to the boatyard, lights flashing, sirens yowling, and they'd both go immediately to jail.

Her voice was beginning to get all blurry. Do sounds get blurry? Bennett looked up enough that he could see her eyes. They weren't exactly blue. But they were blurry, too. Why was she trying to distract him? Bennett's face swam in front of his eyes. He focused on her mouth. The lips sometimes told as much as the eyes. Bennett grinned at him. A lying grin or a real grin? Old blue was flowing full tilt through his system now. He recognized the OxyContin lethargy settling in.

He focused real hard on her face.

"I'm running down. Got to go to bed."

"Great. Means I won't have to worry about you climbing into the sack with me." She arched one eyebrow. "Right?"

Grant grunted. "Right. Especially since I've see your skinny butt." He pretended not to notice her blush. Actually, he couldn't remember if her butt was skinny or not. Things like that hadn't seemed very important to him since he woke up on the medevac flight.

He grabbed at the hammock hanging from the bulkhead, missed it the first time, snagged it on his second try. He pointed toward the bow. "You use the forward bunks. Booby hatch is cracked. It's cooling off and should be enough breeze. I'll be in the cockpit with Flash."

She leaned over to look out the porthole at the dim shape of the truck. "Trust me not to bolt with the bundles?"

"Lady, I'd just as soon you and them be gone when I wake up." Grant looked at the brass clock swimming around on the bulkhead. Three o'clock. "Dawn pretty soon. In just a few minutes." He hoped his speech wasn't blurring like the rest of the world. His tongue felt like a thick wad of old rope in his mouth.

He staggered up to the cockpit and strung his hammock over a snoring Flash. Luck and a toy shotgun had kept him alive tonight. He might need more before this was over. He knelt by the engine compartment and hoped the spiders were all asleep. He fished around in the dark until his fingers found the cold metal of his Kimber, a modern version of the venerable Army .45 caliber automatic, stashed in a waterproof bag. Heavy but small, it was a copy of the Colt officer's model .45 issued to general officers, with a three inch barrel small enough to carry in a cargo pocket. Grant slipped under the mosquito net and rolled up in a tattered poncho liner, the aluminum and steel Kimber a cold weight on his chest. The OxyContins would work their magic, and the pistol would keep him safe. In the morning he would wake up and laugh. Tonight had all been a dream. Or a nightmare, like most of his nights. The rain stopped, and the frogs joined the crickets in an all-night gospel sing, so loud even Grant could hear them until the OxyContin took control. Lately they had been his best buddies, next to Flash.

Best buddies?

The OxyContin or the crickets?

He wasn't sure which.

CHAPTER 8

The steam from the coffee cup Grant held under his nose pushed away the musty smells of the nearby marsh. He tried to keep his mind loose, let it appreciate the red glow of the sun rising behind the cedars. A jay squawked from the top of an abandoned sailboat, answered by another across in the oaks. Before Bennett and her mess, he had planned to work on the old boat. Let time slide by and forget Iraq and his many mistakes. Let it all go, wash down the canal with the falling tide.

But Billy and Hoop hadn't been a dream that would fade in the sunlight like his other nightmares.

He stared at the extension cord draped from the *Rum Runner* to the low hanging oak tree limb. He had forgotten to turn the power on last night. He flipped the switch with a loud clack, sending power down to the charger and prompting a trio of cardinals balanced on the phone line to shuffle across toward the utility pole.

The killings he could get over. Hoop and Billy deserved to be crab food. But he wasn't sure if he could deal with Katrina Bennett, alive somewhere up in his boat. She had slept through his rattling around the galley making coffee. Even when he slipped a faded blue shirt from the locker from under her berth. she slept on, an innocent tangled in the sheets.

The sun found the gaps among the tall cedars and washed across the boatyard. Good and hot, but not blistering. Too early for the march of tropical storms from Africa. Grant folded the Kimber into the shirt and followed Flash down the incline. He brushed away a green anole and opened a driftwood board cabinet bridging two sawhorses. The lizard, still lethargic from the night air, climbed on a fern leaf to soak up the sun and show off its chin flag. Grant laid the shirt and gun in a dry corner, picked up a sanding block and began long, slow strokes across a ply-wood patch, blending the edges into the original curve of the boat's hull. The soft scrub of the sandpaper on the damp wood kept his mind from focusing too sharply on the present, on the woman on his boat, on the dead men stinking up the islands.

The old boat had been bad broke when he found her laid up in this very yard, holed and rotting. He had patched and painted; replaced parts, installed a new engine, dug out far too much wood rot, rewired and rebuilt the boat as he recovered from his own wounds and mourned dead friends. Not much more to do. Some more sanding, a little mechanical work and the final coats of paint, and the *Rum Runner* would be magnificent, a pocket yacht, restored to resemble the pictures he had found stuffed in a drawer from when some movie star owned her. Her scars told a story, too, most of which he hoped he would never know. He had enough of his own to forget.

Two soft chimes followed by a single ding had the cardinals dancing. Six-thirty.

"Morning, Uly." Bennett's face appeared over the boat rail above. She waved a cup of coffee at him.

Grant nodded. "Miss Bennett." He kept on sanding as Flash strolled by, heading toward the Logan's and a share of Betsy's breakfast.

She smiled her crooked grin down at him. "Forgot already? My name is Katrina. Thought we got that straight last night."

"Nice name." He scratched the back of his head with the sanding block. He had wondered in that brief moment before sleep came if Katrina Bennett really was her name.

She started down, her gait a bit crooked and a grimace on her face. She looked up to see him watching her sidle down the incline "Don't laugh. I've got scratches from my toes to my elbows. But the ones on my knees and behind are the ones that the jeans snag on. Make it hard to walk when the weather is tacky like this. My goodness gracious. I should have brought some shorts. I didn't plan on staying overnight."

Where did "Miss Grits" come from? Another act. Grant put down the sanding block, worked the stubby pistol out of the shirt folds and dropped it into his cargo shorts pocket. He shook an errant gray spider off the shirt, checked for more multi-legged cousins and slipped the shirt on, covering up the web of scars across his back. Overhead a nesting dove cooed down at him from the thick leaves of the chinaberry tree that shaded his impromptu work bench, undeterred by the intrusion. One calm soul in this entire calamity. He hid a grimace as he tucked the clean shirt over his own fresh set of scratches and bruises. He turned to Bennett. "Ready to face up?"

He looked up to see her staring at him, so he stared back. Clean jeans with a little embroidery down the legs, snugger than her fishing outfit, and a bright blue blouse with little red flowers. Hips a little broader than he had thought, but a skinny waist. No makeup, but clean face, the tangles gone from her hair. The cut on her chin had scabbed over. Her canvas shoes gave her away with dark smudges of mud from last night's tromp across the mangrove island. The early morning sun glistened in her eyes, but all the juice and excitement from last night had died out. She looked as tired as he felt as she walked up to him.

She touched his arm with her fingers. "How about if you go by yourself and just leave me here. Really. I'll find some way to pay you back."

Grant jerked his arm back. "You got some other reason you can't go to the law? If this guy Silva is blackmailing you, tell them. Let them sort it out. Or does he have something really, really crappy on you? Something you haven't told me about?"

She shook her head, streaked hair flying until she caught the loose strands in her fingers and smoothed them back over her shoulders, painting a look of calm over her face like a mask. "I just know Bobby will figure out a way to screw me if he finds out that I had anything to do with his losing the marijuana."

Up close, Grant got an even clearer look into her eyes. Pleading, but still lying. He hadn't been an interrogator for almost a year now, but all his skills hadn't evaporated. "Come on."

She followed, her reluctance showing in her eyes and gait.

Grant headed toward her Mustang, its dull maroon finish and a Florida State Seminole decal barely visible under a thick coating of rain splattered dust. He wondered what she was lying about now. "Got your car keys? The truck battery's still charging, and I'd just as soon leave all that weed here until we sort out things with Rankin."

She was persistent, like she had an edge. *Had Allen told her so much she could screw him up with the law?* The thought kept nagging at him. He opened the door and slid into the passenger seat. Faded upholstery, a beat up Mustang. Not a classic collector item. More a junker four-cylinder model. Guess she really did need the weed. She didn't look especially rich, not with this ragtag car of hers. Grant wondered how Bennett had fronted the hundred and fifty dollars to book her fishing trip.

Forget that. Other things to worry about. Even if Allen had blabbed to Bennett, which Grant doubted, his cousin didn't know any real specifics about Grant's financial manipulations. Allen wouldn't say anything out of school, Grant hoped, but with a seed of doubt. Allen had never been his best friend.

The growl and whine of the underpowered four cylinders forced him to focus on survival as Bennett ground her way through the gears and fishtailed the Mustang down the dirt road, leaving behind a cloud of oyster shell and sand dust. Too damn fast. Everything happened too fast around her. He rolled down the window. Air conditioning apparently wasn't included.

GULF WINDS

Bennett slammed on the brakes and skidded up to a black asphalt road, dust drifting in the open windows. "I came in from the left, through a teeny little community. That where we're going?"

"Yep," Grant answered. "Don't be snooty. That's historic Homosassa."

"Right." She roared by a scattering of a low concrete block houses and the old sugar mill and park. Without slowing she bounced by a couple of old cracker shacks with rusty tin roofs, all waiting for the real estate developers to raze them and build modern cracker houses with fake rusty roofs.

Grant pointed at the upcoming stop sign, post wound with morning glory vines and purple blooms drooped over the red marker. "Turn right at the next corner." As they came up to the intersection an old Jeep caught his eye, half hidden back in the tangled scrub along the canal.

He craned his head back, but before he could see more, Bennett accelerated around the corner. She slowed when the pavement widened to include overgrown sidewalks on each side of the road with a short row of faded one story brick buildings on the right. On the left, a parking lot fronted a small chain grocery, not one of the big shiny jobs, but a dingy local version anchoring a row of shops and the ever-present convenience store. Bennett pointed at one of the brick storefronts with the green star painted on the glass on the right. "That where we're going?"

"Yep." Grant glanced over at Bennett. Her hair hid her eyes, but her knuckles were white with the strangle hold she had on the steering wheel, a tell in itself.

Bennett slowed as she drove by the sheriff's substation, a deeper shade of old red brick and plate glass sandwiched between the peeling green-painted brick front of a café on one side and a hardware trying to retain an old rustic look on the other. Only a few people were out, mostly parked in the diagonal parking spaces in front of the café or gassing up at the convenience store pumps. It was still too early for the tourist trade or shoppers. Most of the traffic was construction, fishermen and farm pickups, men and a few women grabbing breakfast at the café before the Florida heat bore down.

Grant motioned toward the strip mall. "Turn into the parking lot. We'll walk across."

The morning sun had begun to beat on their shoulders by the time Bennett parked across the street from the substation. The sidewalk fronting the row of stores trying to be authentically antique or cutsie boutique sandwiched between the grocery and the convenience store still offered enough shade that a trio of dusty cats sat in a row, preening.

Grant climbed out of the Mustang.

Bennett still sat behind the wheel. "Isn't there some other way we can do this?"

"No. There's not. Come on. Last night isn't going to evaporate."

Bennett stood and slammed her door; apparently still not happy with the way Grant was handling the situation.

Grant felt the sweat on his palms. Not just the heat. He didn't want to face Deputy Rankin any more than Bennett did.

Bennett nodded toward the café, a red sombrero painted on the window. "Can't we at least get a bite to eat first? I'm starved. All you had on that damned boat was dog food and canned junk."

The Mustang's shocks creaked when Grant leaned on the rear corner. No sign of life in the substation. He wasn't hungry, but his stomach growled, part of the weirdness in his life. And still tired and half dopy. He needed to eat something, even at *El Sombrero Rojo*.

"Uly!" a squat man in a straw hat coming out of the café saluted Grant and climbed into a faded lime green Dodge pickup parked on the street.

"*Buenos dios*, Juan," Grant yelled back

Bennett looked at Grant eyebrows raised. "Friend? Our buddies last night said something about Mexicans." Her statement had a question in it.

"Yeah." Grant nodded. "I know most of the locals. Their families came to work seasonal crops, migrants living in crappy temporary quarters. Juan's older than me, but I went to school with his brother and sister. Some settled around here. Worked hard, raised families. Real people."

Suddenly Bennett's eyes got big, reflecting a flash of movement. The lines in her face reminded him too much of the way she had looked at him when Billy had them at gunpoint. She ducked down behind the Mustang as an old muffler blatted and tires squealed behind him.

Grant spun to see a red Jeep skid to a stop in the parking lot. Three people sprang from the passenger doors, one small, maybe a woman; one dark guy, big and bald, came out of the back seat. The third popped out of the other side, out of Grant's view except for feet under the Jeep door. The bald man, slick head gleaming in the sun, pointed toward him and yelled at the others.

Grant's knees popped as he instinctively crouched.

The woman sidestepped away from the Jeep door and snapped off a ragged volley of shots from a rifle, a damned AK from the sound.

Grant dropped flat on the hot concrete. Bullets slapped into the side of Bennett's Mustang. Grant covered his head when a bullet twanged off the body work and thumped into the tire next to his head with a whomp, followed by a hiss and the smell of stale tire air. Grant scuttled backwards, trying to put as much of the Mustang between him and the shooter as he could.

Wen the firing paused, Grant clawed his Kimber from a cargo pocket. He brought the automatic up, elbow on the concrete. Sweat and dust stung his eyes.

The woman with the AK knelt beside the Jeep door, bracing the rifle against the door.

Grant snapped off a quick shot. Glass shattered from the open door, splattering over the pavement. The woman tumbled back to the concrete, then scrambled behind the Jeep's door. The third man wound up like a major league closer, leg high in the air, and started his throwing motion.

Grant popped a quick shot at the would-be closer. Too quick. Wide. A dark lump arced high up in the air, bounced in the parking lot and spun like a toy top.

The woman moved clear of the door on the other side, feet wide apart, rifle at her hip. Grant shifted, got a two-handed grip and fired again as a bust of automatic fire rattled from the AK. The woman spun, fell to the pavement.

Recoil drove Grant's elbows into the concrete as he fired blindly at the jeep, now a blur in the sweat stinging his eyes. The firing from the jeep stopped. Grant blinked his eyes clear.

The thrower dove back inside as the bald man dragged the woman into the Jeep. Smoke poured from the Jeep's rear tires as the driver punched it and accelerated backwards. The engine roared as the Jeep backed, weaving across the parking lot. The open door caught on a van parked at the end of the lot and ripped free with a screech. The Jeep swerved and dropped over the curb, almost tipping over. The roar of its open exhaust muted the reports from the AK bucking in the bald man's hands. The Jeep slid sideways and roared down the side street spewing steam and dripping oil. In its wake a muffler spun across the road.

Fast. It always happened too fast. No time to think, just react. Every firefight, he had tried to focus, but sometimes it seemed he focused on the wrong things. Like the jeep instead of the lump still spinning on the empty concrete.

Grant had one last clear shot at the bald man hanging out of the door frame. Before he could pull the trigger an explosion lifted Grant up, slammed the top of his head against the Mustang's undercarriage and dropped him back to the hot pavement. Stunned, he squinted through the shower of dust, oil and oyster shell fragments that rained down from the chassis. The hair on the back of his neck stood on end as the pungent smell of gasoline washed over him. Eyes watering he scrambled from underneath the car.

CHAPTER 9

Clear, Grant rolled away from the Mustang and the dripping gas. Shivering, he climbed to his feet, suddenly cold in the Florida heat, and sucked in a ragged breath. The odors clogged his nostrils, exploded in his sinuses.

Blood on hot concrete, fired gunpowder. Acrid bite of gasoline and urine, all dulled by a stirring of dust. It smelled just like the road to Baghdad.

Bennett stood on the other side of the Mustang, a terrified look on her face. Real, this time. He walked past her toward the convenience store gas pumps. Her lips moved, words lost in the ringing in his ears. He turned on a water hose and carefully rinsed off the thin stream of blood running down his arms from his skinned elbows. When he held the end of the hose over his head, blood and water mingled with gas coursed down his shirt and cargo shorts, turning the concrete at his feet a pale pink. He held the nozzle of the hose to his pants, rinsing away either piss or gas, and shook the water from his eyes. Around him faces began to show, peeking from around corners and over cars. Through the water running over his ears he could hear emergency vehicle horns bellowing, a hint of the high pitched wail of sirens.

"Uly?" Bennett took the hose from his hand. Her voice echoed in his ears, a dull noise lacking all the high tones. She took the hose and played it across his back and shoulders. "Who were they?"

Grant turned his head to look into her eyes. No lies, now. Just fear. "Somebody who knew you and your Mustang, I'd guess. Maybe your Bobby Silva's friends." He looked at the blood seeping from a cut on his hand. The water danced across his chest as Bennett squeezed the hose in trembling hands. "You hurt?" he asked.

She brushed at the dirt smudges on the front of her blue blouse and picked a glob of grease from a red flower, then twisted to look at her elbows. "Scraped a little, but not shot, thank goodness." Her voice shook. She looked more vulnerable shivering in the sunlight than she had the night before with her jeans at her feet.

A broad-beamed white man and a lanky black, both deputies by their shirts and gun belts, spilled across the street from the café. They converged toward Grant, guns in hands.

A fire truck blared its horn, urging on gawking motorists who clogged the street, and eased its way through the stopped traffic. Firemen bailed out from the still moving truck and pushed through the gathering gaggle. A sheriff's cruiser squalled to a stop, blocking the street on one side of the fire truck. A second cruiser roared into the parking lot, red and blue lights reflecting off the store front windows. Firemen started hosing down the Mustang with thick white foam, giving it a Christmas look.

Grant shook his head, trying to clear the ringing and stupidity away. *What the hell had just happened?* He looked around, dreading what he might see; knowing what to expect. In Iraq, attacks always hurt more innocents than targets. The shops along the parking lot stared back, gap toothed. The explosion had shattered a florist's front window, leaving a hanging pot dangling by a single wire. The windshield was missing from the white van, one tire flat. A young man in cutoffs and ragged tee shirt stood staring at the van, hands on hips. The man hopped back, stumbled to the curb as smoke boiled up from the van's engine compartment, followed by flames. A pair of firemen nimble in their heavy boots and protective clothing ran over with portable extinguishers and smothered the fire, followed by an EMT who trotted over and knelt by the man, medical kit by his side.

Grant drew another great, deep breath. No maimed kids, no charred remains. No best buddy bleeding all over the roadway. Another good day.

The hulking deputy slowed to a walk. He holstered his pistol and hitched his belt up when he got to Grant. "You still trying to be a fucking hero, Uly?" Deputy Rankin shook his head at Grant. Rankin turned to the deputy close on his heels. "Ben. Tell the fire guys we need some EMT support over here. No hurry. After they finish foaming down the gas and take care of that other guy."

The second deputy started toward the firemen, trotting backwards as Rankin continued, "You're in charge of this mess out here until the crime scene techs get here," Rankin added, upping tone and volume a notch to the old drill sergeant voice Grant was so familiar with. Rankin pointed toward the van. "See that kid standing there like a fool?" Rankin bellowed. "Get him, everybody out of the parking lot. Don't touch nothing. Tape the whole area off, and then make sure the scene is secured."

The deputy nodded and detoured toward the van, tools of the trade flapping against his hips.

Rankin turned back to Grant, shaking his head, sweat dripping off his nose. "Ben and I finally got a chance to eat a decent breakfast, and here you come to town with your frigging circus act. Jesus, Uly. Wish you would just stay out on the water in your fancy new boat, not spoil my Monday morning like this." He hitched up his belt, watching the deputy hustle the kid away from the van. "Good man, that Wellington. You never know, I might be in for a promotion. Bosses keep sending me new minorities to train. Probably since I did such a good job training Iraqis. " He turned back to Grant. "You still got some of them ragheads chasing you?" He turned to stare at Bennett. "You with my buddy, here, miss?" He pulled a big handkerchief from his pocket and swiped at the beads of sweat.

Bennett nodded in mute agreement.

"Well, come on with me and tell me what in hell's going on." Rankin led the way toward the substation. "Spit it out. What hornet's nest you stir up now, Uly?"

"Damned if I know, Eustis. The shooters are a mystery to me." Grant followed Rankin across the street.

Rankin stopped and looked back at Bennett. She had remained in the shade of the gas island shelter with the water hose in her hand, trying to blend into the gas pumps. Rankin turned to Grant. "She's too pretty to be with you." His raised eyebrows made it a question.

Grant's mind churned, mulling over how to explain Bennett. His story was awfully thin with her. Without, it was a fairy tale. He motioned for Bennett, to join them. She didn't move at first. Finally she dropped the water hose and walked over.

"Miss Bennett. This is Deputy Eustis Rankin, a friend. We've known each other far longer than I ever wished. Eustis, this is Miss Bennett, a fishing customer of mine from Tampa."

Bennett opened her mouth, but nothing came out.

"Don't worry, honey. The Lieutenant here is just envious he ain't somebody of stature in the community, like me." Rankin patted Grant's wet shoulder. "I don't think he's even a Lieutenant now. An old back woods fisherman, like his daddy was before he took off. What's your daddy doing now, Uly?"

Grant stopped walking, fist balled. He swallowed his anger, slowed his breathing. Rankin always could pull his chain, ever since high school when Rankin was the hero jock, and Grant was the fishing camp bastard.

Rankin looked back with a bigger grin on his face. "Don't get all riled up. You're the one always told me them stories you made up about your old man being a great fisherman. What kind of fool story you got today?" Rankin opened the door to the substation, plate glass frosted with condensation, and nodded for Grant and Bennett to go inside.

Grant shivered, part the chill air, part being inside the station. He hadn't been a favorite with local law enforcement when he lived in Homosassa as a kid. Despite their wild days, he and Eustis and the Madero kids had managed to stay out of the jail growing up, mostly because old Deputy Tillman would simply put them in the back of his black Plymouth patrol car, threaten to put them in jail for life, and then take them home.

Rankin's presence as the new generation Tillman had dissuaded Grant from hob-knobbing with local law enforcement, not to mention his desire to stay far under their radar. So the Homosassa substation was new to Grant; one large room with a couple of battered desks and two doorways leading to smaller rooms in the back, the AC cranked down to freezing. He cringed as another reason he avoided Rankin, probably the principal one, flew through the door, breathless, long black hair flying, flower print and pastel nurse's uniform smudged with blood.

She looked around and homed in on Grant. "Eustis. Why didn't you call me? I heard shots, a terrible explosion. I was across the street, helping the EMTs, when Maria from the café said Uly'd been shot." She started pulling at Grant's shirt, still dripping from his hosing. "Let me look at you." She pulled his face close to hers and squinted, looking deep in his eyes. "Pupils are fine. No knock on the head from the explosion? The parking lot looks like—" Her face puckered up for a moment. "—like you said it was, over there. *Dé gracias a Dios*, it was a miracle no one was killed." She smiled at Bennett. "Hello. I'm Chantico Madero. If you are Uly's girl friend, watch out. He's nothing but trouble."

Grant blinked, trying to focus on Chantico's face, but the gasoline fumes rising from his skin still had his eyes watering. He scrubbed at his eyes with a sleeve. "Jeeze." The stinging intensified.

"No cussing, now. You aren't with a bunch of soldiers." Chantico wiped at his face with a tissue, hands warm and soft, her touch as gentle as he remembered.

"Now, Chantico, this here's just Uly," Rankin said. "Let him be until the EMTs come over. He ain't dying or nothing. Besides, I got to interview him before the Watch Chief gets here."

She ignored Rankin, gently unbuttoned Grant's wet shirt and peeled it away from the tacky scabs, making tutting sounds with each scratch uncovered. Grant looked from Rankin's glare to Bennett's quizzical stare.

Humiliation at the hands of an ex-girlfriend, he didn't need. Much as he didn't like Rankin, it was time to get to police business. And a tiny matter of ten bales of marijuana in the back of his truck and two dead ex-cons, and Lord knows what happened in the parking lot. He pushed

Chantico's hands away and took back his damp shirt. "Eustis is right, Chantico. I'm fine."

"What? You shy, now. I've seen you with your shorts off before, remember? What the devil's wrong with you, Uly?" Chantico stood, hands on hips, dark bangs framing her face. "Just because you got a new girlfriend don't mean I can't take care of you. Like always." She looked at Bennett and smiled.

Rankin grunted. "Like Uly took care of Vicente?"

Chantico whipped around and punched Rankin in the chest. "Shut up, Eustis. You turd. I know where you were when Vicente died. You were on R and R. Screwing all those nurses. No wonder your wife left you. Trash." She looked back at Grant. "Both of you." She spun on her heel and stomped out.

"Now that last was uncalled for, Eustis." Grant shook out his shirt. He grimaced as he wiggled his arms into the sleeves, the damp cloth still stinking of gas fumes. At least the cut on his hand had stopped bleeding, just a sting now. The skint place where he had tried to move the Mustang with the top of his head stung like ninety.

"You were there. I weren't. He died. You didn't. I don't call that looking after the troops, L. T." Rankin walked over to the window. "Chantico's just mad. She gets that way when you remind her of her brother." He shook his head. "Does look kinda like Fallujah or one of those fart hole places out there, doesn't it?"

Firemen and deputies swarmed outside, appearing cool through the green tinted plate glass window half obscured by the five pointed star painted over the glass. With the uniformed deputies cordoning off the area and sweating firemen rolling up their hoses, the parking lot resembled all too closely the photos of Iraq he had emailed home. Wicked looking scraps of metal lay scattered over the concrete, each being carefully photographed and tagged by a crime scene tech and then studied by a pair of detectives slowly walking over the pavement. Except for the mortally wounded van, the other vehicles in the lot only suffered a scatter of puncture wounds. Bennett's Mustang? Who knew, under all the foam? Grant finally realized that chunk of hell spinning around on the concrete must have been a grenade.

Rankin yelled out the open door, pointing at the cluster of deputies, "Ben. Tell Sam and Mike we don't need them killing time here anymore. The detectives and techs will take care of the scene. Get your ass in here. Toot sweet. Come on. Don't let all the damn cold air out." Rankin hurried the deputy along with a wave of his hand.

Wellington came across the street at a trot.

"Everything secure out there?" Rankin asked, barely giving Wellington's heels time to clear the sill before he slammed the door shut.

Wellington nodded, sweat running down his face. He held up an ornate silver cigarette lighter by its corners and dropped it into an evidence bag. "I found this by the van, saved it for the crime scene techs before somebody else policed it up. Might belong to the shooters. The detectives said to tell you they would wait and review your report before they conduct follow-up interviews. Too much going on today to spend time out here until we figure out what's going on."

"Damn right. Those old boys know who runs this corner of the county. Right, Uly?" Rankin looked at Grant for a long minute. He turned to Bennett. "You in Tampa last night? Down around Port Tampa, MacDill Air Base?"

Grant shook his head. "Nope. Out fishing with Miss Bennett." This wasn't getting off to a good start. Mislead Rankin, and there would be hell to pay in the end. "But there's more to it, Eustis."

"Damn right. With you, there's always more." Rankin said, shaking his head.

CHAPTER 10

Karkoff clenched his teeth, suppressing a howl of rage. Petite lay in his arms, gasping for breath. He pressed his hand over her chest, blood oozing around his fingers. She coughed, spewing a bloody froth across his arm.

"Ivan. We should go," said Stephan. "Find a doctor."

Karkoff stared at Stephan, blinking the splattered blood from his eyes. "My Petite; she's dying. Too late for a doctor."

Petite shuddered, than fell still. Her face relaxed. All of her pain was gone, with all of their dreams.

He picked up Petite's slim body, carried her back under the tangled vines and laid her on the soft leaves. He had left too many friends in the jungles and deserts. Most because of some damned American. This one, the one who shot Petite, he would track down and kill, with his own hands if necessary. Damn his sister and her missions.

Stephan pointed at the blood seeping from Karkoff's arm. "And you?"

"I need no doctor." How many comrades had he left on the battlefield? Too many, from Angola to Afghanistan to this miserable swamp. But Petite was special, so much more than a comrade. He felt the old rage building, the battle haze he first felt in Angola, cherished in Afghanistan. He strode back to the Jeep, pulled out an AK and checked to make sure the magazine was loaded. "Come." He shoved Agustín toward the Jeep. "Agustín. You drive. Stephan. You find us a new vehicle and meet us back here." He chambered a round, ignoring the throbbing in his arm. "I have someone special to kill."

CHAPTER 11

Grant took a deep breath of the substation's chill air. The pounding gradually left his head leaving a constant ache. He held his hands out. Fingers were still. No sign of tremor. Maybe he was dead.

Rankin turned to Wellington, dispelling Grant's wishful thought.

"I got a bit of conflict of interest here. I know this fine gentleman. Known him too damn long. He even thought he was my boss when we deployed to Iraq. So you take him into the other room and get his statement while I speak to the young lady."

Wellington frowned, wiping his face with a soaked handkerchief. "What are we looking for, Corporal? Anybody read him his rights? Has he been searched for weapons?"

Rankin scowled at Wellington and turned to Grant. "You carrying?"

Grant looked down at his hands, remembered firing at the men, then the explosion. "Had a pistol when this started, but it's gone. Black, short barrel .45 automatic, a Kimber 1911. Got away from me when the grenade or whatever it was went off. Your people out there probably will find it under the Mustang. And I got a damn carry permit, so don't get in an uproar about technicalities."

"Jesus, boy, calm down. You are a case. Least you learned your lesson about ballistics and stopping power in Iraq. No more 9mm popguns that just irritate people." Rankin turned to Wellington. "Please make sure you inform Mister Grant of his rights, in case he's killed somebody." He stared, pointedly, at Grant. "Again." He turned back to Bennett. "Now, miss." He herded her toward a desk. "You come with me, and we'll chat about things."

Bennett glanced over her shoulder at Grant, a question in her eyes.

Grant wished she had told him the truth, the whole story. Now he had his story; she had hers. Which one would Rankin believe? Grant began to shiver as the cold air chilled his wet clothes and his anger. He focused on the faded photos on the walls. Men held up long stringers of fish in the yellowed prints. Familiar odors gradually replaced the stench from the parking lot. Grant lifted his chin, lightly inhaled through his nose. Hair tonic. He focused on the room and remembered. This was Ralph's Barbershop, back when farmers and fishermen were the big spenders in town, before the county became a tourist haven and bedroom community for Tampa. This was where his mama forced him to get his head sheared once a week, before he gathered up enough courage to rebel and grow the pony tail that lasted until he joined the Guard.

The three chrome and plastic chairs, the full length mirror along the wall, the tall chair in the corner where George, the wise old black man had shined shoes back when old black men did things like that, all were gone. Two government issue battered desks, two wood chairs and a table remained, along with the lingering smell left by years of Vaseline Hair Tonic splashed onto the floor.

Wellington got Grant's attention with a little wave. "Sir. Come with me, please." Grant followed the deputy to a back room where Wellington motioned for Grant to sit at a small desk. A computer and printer sat on one end of the table. Behind a pair of two-drawer file cabinets on the other side of the room a faint outline, not fully covered by a low bid paint job, marked where a huge piece of furniture once had covered the exterior wall. Old memories seeped back. This was Ralph's office where the barber stashed the good magazines, the ones the older men didn't let the kids see, in a giant rolltop desk. The other room had been a bathroom, probably still was. The door on the back wall led to an overgrown alley that meandered behind all the stores and down toward the river. He had been here before. That was the door Grant had snuck through to study the forbidden magazines.

Wellington sat down at the computer and looked at him expectantly. "Full name, please."

"Ulysses NMI Grant." Grant pulled out a chair and sat down at the end of the table, tucking the damp shirt into his dripping shorts. He stifled a groan. Explaining blood blisters from a shotgun would have to come later.

"Enema?" Wellington grinned. "That's a different middle name."

Grant shook his head, wincing at the twinge of pain that shot down to his feet. "November, Mike, India. Army abbreviation for no middle initial. My mama figured Ulysses Grant would get me as far as I needed to go, so that's all she gave me."

"You served?"

"Actually, I'm still in, on convalescent leave from the Guard. Your Corporal and I served together in Iraq."

Wellington said, "I ate my share of sand back in 2003. I was an MP with the 101st in Mosul when we took down Saddam's sons." Wellington stopped, that thousand mile stare in his eyes Grant recognized from his time in the desert, blinked and shrugged. "Back to business. We need to start with last night. And actually I know what NMI means."

A sense of humor?

Grant's mind raced as he got past a few more stumbles like the ambiguous address of the boat yard as his home and office. He knew how to ask the questions from his time in Iraq running an interrogation team. He should know how to answer. Rule one: Only answer the direct question. Rule two: Don't lie. Neither would work, not today. So he started with Bennett hiring him. As a fishing guide. They were fishing the flats, and, to their amazement, an airplane flew right over them and dropped a bunch of bundles, right in front of them. Then the airboat showed up. Grant skimmed though the details so he could get to the meat, that is Hoop and Billy, without too much fanfare.

Then Wellington asked Grant to recount the shooting in the parking lot. The deputy was a good listener. He seemed to believe Grant's story better than Grant did. Grant wished Wellington had worked for him back in the sandbox. The deputy's soft way often paid dividends with some types, especially younger Middle Eastern men. Except that many of the Arabs looked down on blacks.

Wellington paid attention, even to the parts that Grant had trouble believing, and typed on the computer with nimble fingers, interrupting Grant's narration of events, going back and asking him to repeat details as any good interrogator would, stopping to confirm the last known locations of Hoop and Billy's remains. Wellington did look up with slightly raised eyebrows when Grant told him they were saving bales of what was probably marijuana in the bed of his Chevy pickup.

"Ten bales?" Wellington's eyebrows went up another notch with the count. "Leave it out in the open? If anybody gets a whiff when the sun gets to it, it'll be gone before we get there. You really should have brought it with you."

"You're right, Deputy." Grant agreed wholeheartedly. "Truck wouldn't start, so we left the bundles. You know, kind of like compacted hay bales, maybe twenty pounds each, but in garbage bags. Left them in the back of the truck, in the shade and covered with a tarp." Grant left out the part about how he would have come in last night, except he had washed down two big old blue opiates with a mighty refreshing Ybor Gold brew and zonked out on the deck of his boat. *What does Wellington know that I don't*? Grant wondered. Why doesn't he ask why we didn't come in immediately? Why didn't he ask about the Jeep? Grant decided Wellington's interrogation technique was either excellent or stupid. And stupid didn't seem to be the correct answer.

"What's it worth?"

Grant shrugged. "No idea." He looked up at Wellington's grin. The deputy was good.

Wellington laughed. "Probably over a thousand bucks a pound, whole-sale, if it's good stuff. More on the street. You left a small fortune in your pickup. Course you probably know that, too."

Grant shook his head. "Not my thing."

The deputy leaned back from the keyboard. "The two men on the island. They sound like a couple of Aryan Brotherhood members we're watching. You got any connections with the Brotherhood or their allies, the Mexican Mafia?"

Grant shook his head. "I remember hearing about the Brotherhood at a counter-terrorist briefing, long time ago, before we deployed to Iraq." He shrugged his shoulders. "Don't know anything about any Mexican Mafia."

Wellington canted his head when Grant mentioned the Mexicans. "Mexican Mafia, EME. They're out of California, another one of the gangs that spread through the prisons. Somehow made an alliance with the Brotherhood, mostly to sell drugs. And you don't know about them, with all your Mexican connections?"

Grant just shook his head, wondering exactly what the deputy knew about his Mexican connections. "I've kinda kept to myself since I got back. I'm still on some pain meds, so I don't spend any time in the bars. Booze really winds up my meds." *And my head*, he thought.

Wellington added a paragraph to the report and hit the print key. The deputy nodded toward the pages spitting out of the printer. "Read over your statement and mark up any corrections while I check with Corporal Rankin."

Grant looked up from the first sheet when a flash of reflected sunlight glimmered into the back room. Through the tinted plate glass out front, the world outside had returned to Florida normal. The firemen, crime scene tech and detectives were gone, leaving a foam covered Mustang, barricades and yellow tape to decorate the parking lot. Rankin stared through the door at Grant and picked up the phone, shaking his head.

A vehicle skidded to a stop outside the glass, indistinct through the condensation. Rankin looked up from the phone and stared back at Grant, an angry look on his face. A shadow fell across the plate glass window and a face peered inside. The bald man, from the parking lot, big gun in hand, maybe an AK. His eyes focused on Grant.

"You git inside, with Uly. Now!" Rankin shouted. He threw down the phone, grabbed Bennett's arm and shoved her toward the door and Grant. With his other hand he reached for his pistol. "Just what kind of fool do you think you're playing me for, L. T.?" Rankin yelled. Wellington and Bennett looked at each other, apparently as bewildered as Grant by Rankin's actions.

GULF WINDS

A row of glittering holes shattered the plate glass. Bennett dove toward Grant and the open door. Rankin pulled his pistol, the tip of the barrel barely clearing his holster when another long burst ripped through the star, sending fracture lines across the window. Chunks of heavy glass fell to the floor with a crash, background to the staccato roar of gunfire echoing through the office. Bullets slapped and chewed into the brick wall behind Grant. A hurricane of hot, humid Florida air gushed into the room, sucking out all of Rankin's precious cold air.

Rankin backed away from the window. He jerked his pistol clear and fired toward the falling glass, yelling, "Get down, get down." A spray of bullets splintered the desk top in front of Rankin. He spun as if hit by a passing car.

Grant reached out for Bennett as she scrambled on all fours toward the doorway, got a hand on her collar.

Shards slowly fell away from the window frame like icicles melting from a roof. Except the temperature was closer to ninety and the icicles were hand-sized chunks of glass. Grant's face stung as a sliver sliced his cheek.

Rankin slammed against the wall. A streak of red stained his green shirt. On one knee, Wellington had his pistol clear of his holster. Another burst of gunfire rattled through the empty window frame and Wellington fell, face down. Splatters of crimson blood spread to the stained floor, glittering on the glass.

Grant jerked Bennett through the doorway and into the back room. The bald man stepped in front of the empty window. One arm hung to his side, sleeve dark stained. The other held the AK.

"*Puta*," he screamed. "I kill you and your *asesino amigo*. The one who killed Petite. Where are you?" He sprayed another burst of automatic fire around the room.

Bullets buzzed over Grant's head and thudded into the old brick walls. He slammed the door shut and shoved the table over to block the door. When the next barrage of bullets hammered the door, Grant pressed flat against the old oak floor. The shooting stopped. Quiet enough to hear his heart pound. Then the shooting started again, a fresh magazine. Bullets ripped into the door with a drawn out rumble, adding new dimples to the metal sheet.

Bennett grabbed his arm and frantically jerked at him. "Is there a way out?" She shook him. "I told you this wasn't a good idea. Now your friend's dead, shot by those bastards from the parking lot. Come on; come on. Let's go." She tugged him toward the back door.

On the other side of the door to the front a voice boomed out, "*Perra*. Come out, *pronto*. Maybe you live." More bullets thudded into the door.

"Maybe nobody get hurt, 'cept maybe that stupid bastard who shoot Petite. No Yankee kill her and live. Him I kill myself."

Grant jerked his arm back from Bennett's grip. Something big rammed against the door, hard, loud, then harder, louder.

Grant backed away from the door. Eustis Rankin was in the next room, down, wounded if not dead. And Wellington, with his soft brown eyes, on the floor. And a big guy cussing in Spanish who had stopped shooting to pound away at the door, slow reverberating blows at first, the cadence and volume building like a concert timpani coming to a grand finale, segueing into the drum solo in the middle of *Take Five*.

When they were kids, Rankin had always ragged him about not figuring the odds, always taking on someone too big, too fast, too mean. In Iraq, Grant had learned to funnel his anger to a controlled battle rage. Now he felt helpless, unable to think, much less act.

Brightness flooded the room. Bennett had opened the back door. The door frame darkened for a moment as she hopped through the opening, Alice into the rabbit hole. She stopped, turned, looked back at him. "Uly?"

He looked back at the door. He had never, ever run from a fight, left men behind. Another smash and the door frame around the metal door cracked, jagged splinters thrust out around the hinges. "Forgive me, Eustis," he whispered and hobbled after Bennett into the morning sun. He broke into a run as the door crashed open behind him.

CHAPTER 12

G rant turned toward the river, ignoring the new sharp pains and the old aches. His loose boat shoes flapped as he ran down the ruts that marked the old alley, across the abandoned railroad tracks, pounding footprints into the patches of blooming railroad weed.

"Uly!"

He looked back. Bennett had turned to the opposite direction. "This way," he yelled. Sirens wailed in the distance. A gunshot echoed between the buildings.

Bennett spun and ran by him, quashing the tiny snapdragon blooms poking up from the abandoned rail bed.

No more gunfire. Behind them the sirens and emergency vehicle horns yowled, a hope for Rankin and Wellington.

Ahead of him, Bennett edged away. Bits of railroad gravel flew back from her feet.

A familiar trail ahead. "Bennett! In here." He turned into the swamp bordering the canal. Grant crouched and entered a long, low cavern formed by a mix of wild muscadine grape vines and sawgrass briars, all tangled with dead branches and leaves. He led Bennett from bright sunlight into a dank, shadowy tunnel of vegetation, following tiny tracks down the game trail. He could hear Bennett's light stride, tight on his heels. Deer, raccoons, red foxes, all the wild life that lived on the edge of urban Florida had kept the way clear, if you had sharp eyes.

Grant had followed this trail as a kid. It would lead them back to the boat yard and his truck. At least that's what he thought.

But he hadn't been a kid for a long time.

Grant squinted at the bright light ahead where the trail angled closer to the canal. This wasn't right. The trail should twist by the tall pines and skirt the gator slough before it broke out into the clear by the oaks. Grant suddenly slowed. Bennett slammed into his back at full tilt, stomping his heel and tripping him up. He grunted when he hit the ground. Every inch of his body hurt, compounded by Bennett's elbow in his back as she sprawled across him.

Bennett glared at him, her face inches from his, splotched with damp decayed leaves and sand from the trail floor.

"Damn it, pay attention," he whispered.

Bennett shook her head and leaves flew from her hair. She spit sand from her mouth. "Somebody's shooting at us, Uly. I'm not inclined to stop unless some fool falls in front of me." She pushed up to her knees. "Why'd you stop here?"

"The trail was supposed to lead all the way back to the boat yard. Developers bought up all the old canal frontage, cleared it, filled the swamp. Now they're putting in new houses."

"So?" Bennett started to her feet.

"Wait!" Grant pulled her back down and pointed. A faded Jeep sat empty at the far end of a row of parked construction pickups. Grant stared through the underbrush. It was the same one from the parking lot, same skewed headlight, with new bullet holes in the side by the missing door, back glass starred. A figure appeared from the shadows heading for the Jeep.

Grant dropped flat, face down in the muck when a report echoed from the unfinished houses, followed by the sound of slamming vehicle doors. He glanced over at Bennett. She was slowly worming her way off the trail toward the canal, out of sight of the road. Grant poked his head through a tangle of undergrowth. A swarm of roofers climbed over the peak of the far house and began their drill on the near side, slapping down rows of shingles. A shirtless man fired nails into each shingle with a steady rap-tap-tap of his nail gun.

Grant froze as a foot long water turtle, a cooter with a dandelion stem in its heavy mouth, lumbered across the path, yellow-streaked neck outstretched in its search for water.

"Uly. Come on."

Grant wiggled his way across to Bennett. "We'll backtrack and cross over the tracks, find some other way out."

"No. Come on this way." Bennett grabbed his arm and tugged Grant after the water turtle, toward the canal, dark in the shade of the tall pines draped with wild grape vines.

He pulled back "We don't want to do that. I've killed gators in this canal. I don't want to give them a chance to get even."

Bennett nodded toward two big lumps slowly floating down the canal. "We've got an escort." She slid down a muddy gap in the bank and into the water. She looked back at Grant expectantly as one of the lumps rose to the surface and blew.

Grant eased into the placid water and let his head slide under the surface. Even without a mask he could make out the friendly nose of a big manatee inches from his own face, drifting along, enjoying the cool water flowing down from Homosassa Springs. A flipper slowly waved, turning the ten foot long sea cow enough to snatch a clump of floating vegetation. As the cow turned, Grant spotted a calf tucked under her, long as Grant was tall, but tiny in comparison to its mother. Grant let the manatees drift by, aware of Bennett's fingers gripping his shirt tail and her quiet breaths by his ear. With a quick glance at the roofers, he slowly kicked, towing Bennett toward the far bank, putting the manatees between them and the Jeep.

Grant exhaled and sank to the sand bottom, pushed off and let his head pop high enough to see over the plastic barrier intended to keep the construction wash out of the canal. No one but roofers in sight. The gentle current pushed them past the construction and behind a stand of live oaks whose low limbs, draped with Spanish moss, hid them from the road. The water was cool, soothing to his cuts and bruises. Bennett jerked on his shirt, followed by a second frantic tug reminding him they were not yet safe. Grant blinked the water from his eyes and spotted the silhouette of a big man standing on the bank, staring back toward town, AK in one hand. Grant quietly exhaled and sank behind the cow. A dark shadow drifted across the surface as Grant slid his hand along the manatee, gently grasping a flipper and letting her tow them downstream, his shirt pulled tight in Bennett's clenched fist. After a long forever, Grant quietly broke the surface, and Bennett's face rose close beside. The man was gone.

Not a word said, the four of them floated toward the Gulf, surfacing only to breathe and take a quick scan of the bank. A sudden bump in the small of Grant's back shoved his face into the water. He opened his eyes to a face only a mother could love staring back at him. The baby manatee had slid up close, checking him out. Grant gave the calf a gentle scratch along its algae coated back, and together they drifted down toward the boat yard.

The next time he surfaced, a dog yapped, close by, insistent.

Betsy. Flash's buddy.

They were home. He left the manatees behind and silently breast stroked toward the bank. Bennett passed him, her strokes powerful and smooth. He grabbed her ankle and pulled her down when she started to climb up the bank. Grant shook his head and pointed back toward the bank. He eased his head through a cluster of water lilies, wound his fingers into a clump of weed and dragged his body out of the water. He tilted his head, draining the water from his ears. Voices murmured in front of them. He inched through the weeds until he could see the *Rum Runner* up on its braces. "Damn," he muttered.

Bennett slid up alongside him, body pressed close. "What?" she asked, then fell silent as she parted a clump of grass and stared across at the boatyard.

A gaggle of uniforms surrounded the boat. Green shirted deputies stirred around the cockpit as a handful of people in dark windbreakers, useless in the late spring weather except for big FDLE printed across the back of the jackets, milled across the boatyard. Grant's Chevy pickup was gone. FDLE? Must be DEA guys, ATF, too. Guns and drugs.

A clap of thunder boomed through the clear sky, for a moment drowning out the sounds of multiple sirens coming their way.

Grant shook his head. Maybe the guys in jackets were smarter than he had thought. The sky darkened. A cloud scuttled overhead and rain started pattering down as he slid back into the water. He pulled Bennett down with him. She seemed to be a good swimmer, and he had been swimming out into Crystal Bay for weeks now, trying to loosen up and get some muscle tone back. They could swim out of here. But where to?

He pulled her head close, whispered in her ear. "Place is full of law enforcement."

Bennett pushed her straggly hair away from her eyes, sparkling with the reflected lightning bolts that marched across the Gulf toward them. "Why don't we just walk over and say hello? Christ, Uly. We aren't the ones who shot the deputies."

He towed her back into deeper water so he could stand, his chin touching the water, holding Bennett by her arms, her face close to his. He could feel her legs slowly moving, treading water. "Dead cops, dead drug guys on the islands, a pickup full of Mexican dope. Oh, yeah. And a shootout in a parking lot, probably with more drug guys. If Eustis and his deputy are dead, I bet we get the pointy end of a bunch of bullets before these guys ask any more questions. Nope. I don't think walking up to them is really smart."

Although, Grant thought, *maybe I'm the dumb one, not thinking things through.* He hadn't had an Oxy since last night, just a handful of Tylenol with his morning coffee. But to his surprise, Bennett seemed to agree, nodding her head.

She said something, but the rain and thunder drowned her out. Large drops splattered down around them.

He shook his head.

She put her arms around his neck and pulled close with her head touching his. "Where to?" she whispered.

He rested his forehead against hers for the moment, thinking. "The flats boat. We can hide in the Wildlife Refuge, get away from Homosassa. I've got some friends who will help."

GULF WINDS

Side by side they swam through the rain toward the dock and the battered flats boat, now a ghostly white fiberglass blob in the downpour gusting in from the Gulf. When they reached the dock Grant motioned Bennett into the boat.

With a grunt she slithered over the side. "Yikes!" she yelped.

Grant pulled up and peered into the boat. Bennett lay sprawled in the bottom, nose to nose with Flash. The greyhound licked the water from her face, tail thumping the side rod compartment. Another friend had deserted him. "Untie the bow line."

Grant stretched across the boat to jerk the power cord charging the trolling motor battery clear from the dock receptacle. He eased back down into the water, warm compared to the chill rain drops, and untied the stern line. He centered himself behind the boat and pushed it away from the dock. Slow, even kicks and soon he had them out to where the boat twisted in the tidal flow.

Grant dragged his body over the scarred gunwale, every muscle and joint complaining. Cold rain drops smacked against him, sucking away his body heat, leaving nothing but his aches. He looked back at the dock, as they drifted away. A solitary figure walked out to the end, one shoulder all wrapped in white. The man leaned forward, staring through the rain, directly at them.

CHAPTER 13

Grant blinked the water out of his eyes. Could the man see him in the rain? Stupid. Grant could see him; the man had to see them. The man on the dock pulled a windbreaker over the white bandage, stared at Grant for a moment, then reached up and tipped his cap. He turned and slowly walked back toward the line of law enforcement vehicles lining the road back to the *Rum Runner*. Deputy Wellington was alive. And had let them get away.

Grant let the tide float them out away from the bank until the dock disappeared into the driving rain. He eased the fiberglass push pole from its clamps and shoved the boat toward the dark trees marking the edge of the Chassahowitzka Wildlife Refuge. He glanced back. Still no alarm. A few easy shoves and they were in the Homosassa River channel, too deep to pole. Grant stowed the push pole and made his way to the bow.

Flash and Bennett grinned back at him, huddled in the bottom of the boat.

Grant dropped the electric motor over the bow and steered them deeper into the Wildlife Refuge, meandering in what he hoped would look to an outsider like a random pattern through the twisting channels of slow moving water. The boat glided among the tiny islands studded with cabbage palms and an occasional cedar tree, red mangroves along the edges.

Peaceful if you liked thunderstorms, Grant thought, glad he was in a low flats boat with no antennas and the poling platform a tangle of twisted tubes and fiberglass crushed down over the Yamaha. He instinctively ducked as lightning flashed down into the swamp, instantly followed by thunder snapping across the water. Not the good old rolling rumble of distant storms, this one had the snazzle and crack of a .50 caliber bullet fired about a foot from his head. His skin tingled with the built-up static electricity. A swirl of wind twisted the boat in the channel and drowned out the whine of the electric motor. The motor was barely making headway against the howling gusts. He didn't want to lose power here. The tide would push them back toward the dock and the emblazoned jackets who would take great pleasure in a little interrogation that would make Grant's Iraq experiences look tame.

He glanced back and confirmed the big outboard needed more work than he had tools or time to give before he could use it again. In the bottom of the boat Bennett had pulled her cap down tight, curled up with Flash, the two of them burrowed into a pile of boat cushions and life vests. Harder gusts swirled around the boat, whipped the tops of the tall pines back on the higher hummocks and churned the water. Water drops stung Grant's face as he steered them up close to the underbrush lining the twisting channel, wondering if he could find his way without the GPS, another victim of the collision.

"Uly!" Bennett called out, her voice shrill over the howl of the wind. "Are we going to sink?"

"No," he yelled back, more of a hope than an answer.

"Anyone following us?"

He looked back and shook his head. "Storm will slow anybody trying to find us." He started to shiver as the wind whipped his soaked clothes around him. The wind abated, the storm blowing over as quickly as it had swept over them. In the distance he could hear the whap of helicopter blades turning into the wind and the closer squeal of the helicopter's turbine. He headed deeper into the Refuge, scanning each big cypress and tangled hummock for a familiar sign.

The helicopter flashed overhead and a rip of machinegun fire tore through the trees, accented by Bennett's yelp. "Son of a bitch!" Bennett climbed to her knees. "Stay down," Grant yelled at her.

What the hell has everyone so trigger happy?

Grant nudged them deeper into the thick mangroves through the maze of channels, winding through the tall cypress and tangled underbrush until he finally spotted the gap tooth row of rotting pilings that were once a dock. He steered the boat past the pilings until the electric motor prop surged as it caught a blade in the bottom. Mangrove roots bumped along both sides until the boat jerked to a stop.

The helicopter whap was almost directly overhead, son of a bitches reconning by fire. Homeland Security must be involved. Locals would never be so damn ready to shoot. Grant grabbed a branch and pulled them deeper under the trees

A section of the rubber bumper on the boat's gunnels, torn loose by Hoop's airboat, snagged on a protruding limb. Bright sunlight speckled down through the trees, leaves still twisting in the fitful gusts that refused to give up. The whap of the blades almost directly overhead, Grant pulled the bumper free, ignoring the urge to scan the limb for resident snakes.

"Whap, whap." The helicopter had slowed, moving almost at a hover, very close.

Grant pushed aside a palmetto frond. A rusty marker nailed to a tree ahead beckoned. He gunned the electric motor, ducked as the flats boat scooted under an old tin shack perched over the water, scraped against weathered stilts and drifted into a silvery tangle of spider webs. Grant killed the motor and grabbed the rotting stub of a post, stopping the boat. He took a deep breath and winked at Flash, staring up at him from the bottom of the boat. Flash stood and did his familiar shiver, like he was going to shed his skin. "Hold on to Flash's collar. He probably wants to get out and take a leak," Grant cautioned.

"He's not the only one," came back a muffled reply. "Was that somebody shooting?" Bennett emerged from the pile, head turning as she stared into the dim light. "Where are we? What the heck is this place?" She held her arms clasped tight over her chest, still shivering from the chill rain.

"Fishing shack. Pretty deep in the Wildlife Refuge." He ignored her question about shooting. That one he didn't know the answer for. He pointed at the thick tangle of vines twined around the stilts and the cypress trees surrounding the shack. "Spring and summer when the cypress trees are greened out like this, you can't see in here from ten feet away. I've never flown over, but I doubt you could see the shack from the air. And if you did, all you would see is a rusty tin roof. It's not very big, longest side maybe twenty feet, just big enough to hide the boat."

The insistent whine of a helicopter moved closer.

He pointed at the plank roof floor over their heads. "Most important, the tin roof on top should block their FLIR if we stay down here." He pulled the boat to a middle stilt and stood, hanging on to a crude ladder. He shoved on the floor over his head with the upturned palms of his hands. Dust and bits of dried vine floated down as a trap door flopped open, adding a bit more light to the shadows. "We'll go up after things calm down. But stay in the boat until the helicopter goes away."

Bennett sat up. "Ugh. Too many spiders." She cleared away a thick network of webs drooping around her head. "FLIR. Is that like the night vision things on the police helicopters?"

Grant nodded, suddenly too tired to answer.

Flash sat up on his rear haunches and rested his chin on her leg.

Bennett ran her hand over his head. "Where did you get this old hound? The two of you kind of go together."

Grant stared into Flash's eyes. The hound grinned back at him and twisted his pointed nose so Bennett could rub his ear. "The woman back at the station, Chantico, the nurse."

"Oh, yeah. The one that jumped on you and the deputy." Her grin died. "The deputy. You said you had known him a long time. A friend? Law enforcement guys I know don't talk to civilians the way he talked to you, unless they are friends."

"Flash belonged to Chantico's brother, Vicente. Vicente was killed in Iraq, and I inherited Flash when I got back. Vicente, Eustis, Allen and I ran around together, joined the Guard the same day when we were still in high school." He slowly shook his head. "God, I hurt." With the memory as much as the pain. He clambered past Bennett, Flash and the remains of the console, and opened up the storage compartment under the crumpled remains of the poling platform. He dug back in the corner of the compartment and came up with two bottles of water and a prescription pill container half full of blue capsules. He held the container up so the light shined through the brown plastic; shook it to confirm there was some relief to be had. It wasn't noon yet, but the day already had been too long.

"You and she have a thing?" Bennett held out her hand.

For a moment Grant thought she wanted his pills, then realized she was looking at the water. He handed Bennett a bottle of water. "Not anymore. Not in years. She'd set her sights on Eustis, I think. That's the way Chantico is, seems. The more she likes you, the meaner she gets. She hit me over the head with a stick hard enough to give me a knot when we were dating, years ago."

He had all the questions, but seemed Bennett was the one asking. The capsules began to jiggle in his hand. Time. His leg told him so. He washed down a capsule, stared at the container and popped a second down his throat. Bennett took a long drink of water, pretending not to watch his self medication.

"I hope Eustis is all right. At least Wellington got out alive. Maybe that big guy focused on us long enough that...." He stopped and looked at Bennett. "*Puta. Perra.*"

"What are you talking about?" She sat the water bottle down. "*Perra?*"

"Whore, bitch, in Spanish, I think. That's what the guy with the gun yelled. He came back for you. Not me, not the deputies." Grant and Flash both watched her eyes. Either Bennett was totally confused or back to her acting job, and doing a better job this time.

"You know that big guy, the shooter? He know you?" Suddenly spooked, Grant searched the swamp around them, wondering if they had somehow been followed. "I'm pretty sure he didn't think the green star on the door meant a five star restaurant. Surely he knew where he was going and what he was doing."

"He might know me, but I don't know him," she insisted. "For crying out loud, they were shooting at both of us. Look. I don't understand what this is about. And Wellington. Wasn't he the deputy? How do you know he's all right? I hope he is, but what makes you think that man didn't kill everybody in the office?"

"I saw Wellington. Back there, on the dock. He tipped his hat at us, turned and walked away."

Bennett stared at him, her mouth twisted in disbelief. "You fool. If Wellington's alive, we can just go back. He'd vouch for us." She started to climb up the ladder. "I'll go up and wave down the damn helicopter; get out of this jungle and get me something to eat."

Grant grabbed her dripping pants leg and hauled her back to the boat. "Wait a minute. Think about what's going on. Let the helicopter guys get tired of looking first." *And shooting.* He turned her loose, and she sat back down, a frown on her face. He looped a line through the post and sat back on the remains of the cushioned seat behind the console, feeling the contents of the two OxyContin capsules bubble and cook through his system. Slowly he relaxed, steam rising off his wet clothes as the blue bombs dissolved, pulsed through his body and into his brain.

Overhead, the whap of the helicopter blades came closer. Grant leaned back against the broken motor and closed his eyes. Wave at the bird. It would fly away. He no longer cared. This was his safe place. His daddy could never find him here. No one could.

CHAPTER 14

"Uly," she whispered. Grant didn't move. Bennett lifted the dog's muzzle from her knee, listening to the tin shed creak and insect whine that had replaced the helicopter noises. A light breeze whispered through the trees. Birds twittered and flitted through the twisted vines. Grant seemed to be dead asleep, oblivious to it all.

Bennett leaned back against a life vest and stared at her watch as the second hand marked off another minute. What had she done? She thought the drug money would be the solution. Instead, she was in more trouble than she had ever been in her entire life. The sawgrass scratches across her behind itched. A swarm of mosquitoes seemed to be homing in on her ears. She batted at the mosquitoes and squeezed out the remaining drops of water clinging to her hair, leaving it sticky and stiff with dried salt, mud and damned bits of spider webs. She smelled like wet dog. She looked down at Flash. Both of them did.

Grant's head had fallen back, mouth open. Flash deserted her and ambled back to lay his muzzle on Grant's foot. The two of them began an unsynchronized snoring duet. Like a hillbilly cartoon, if everything wasn't so damn serious. Salt and grit in her hair and up her behind, she was stuck in the swamp with Ulysses Grant and his wonder dog Flash. She needed to get out of here.

Bennett eased her way to the ladder, paused and glanced back at Grant. Flash raised his muzzle and lazily opened one eye for a moment. He laid his head back down with a soft grunt. Grant's eyes remained closed.

Her handbag lay in the bottom of the boat where she had left it last night, all excited about having convinced Grant to retrieve the bales. She bent down, cursing the pull of the salt stiffened jeans on her raw skin, and maneuvered her cell phone out of a side pocket. Bennett looked at the phone and then at Grant. He had taken two of those blue pills, but she didn't know what they really did to him. Sleep looked like a good bet, but how long and how hard? She shrugged her shoulders. Who cared? All she wanted now was to get out of this alive—and figure out how to deal with Bobby Silva.

She slipped the phone in her pocket, grabbed the half-rotten ladder and waited for the boat to stop rocking. Grant didn't move. She eased one foot on to the bottom rung of the ladder. The wood felt as if it would crumble and drop her back in the boat. She put more weight on the rung and pulled up with her hands, trying to distribute her weight. Three, four rungs and she had clambered up and through the hole in the floor. She stepped through an open door looking out into the swamp, all green matted vines and palmetto fronds over dark swirling water, steam rising up toward the sun. Nothing between her and nowhere but a tiny porch under a tin roof that wrapped around the shack. Sweat dripped from her chin as she walked out onto the porch.

Not a human sound, no planes, boats. Nothing but the murmur of the slow moving water and the clatter of a big pileated woodpecker pounding away on a tall pine rising over the palmettos. Bennett pulled out the phone and clicked it on, quickly pressed it against her stiff shirt with both hands when the damn thing chimed. The way the day had gone, she had expected the phone to be dead. She looked down at the display.

Miracle! The little icons indicated a signal. She stared at the display for a moment. What would she say? All she had to do was stay calm, and she'd handle Bobby. Like she'd handled Grant? She'd let Uly Grant lead her into the middle of nowhere. That had to change.

She punched in Silva's number.

"Silva," was the scratchy answer from the other end.

"Bobby," Bennett cooed into the phone. "I had a little—" She paused for a moment, visualizing her foam covered Mustang in the parking lot. "No, make that a major problem with my car this morning. Must have been a short of some kind, darn thing caught on fire."

"Kat. Are you hurt?" he interrupted.

Son of a bitch almost sounded sympathetic. She could play that, too. Bennett looked down at her skinned elbows. "I'm fine. Just a little scrape when I fell down getting away from it. I'm all right. But I'll take the rest of the day off if that's O.K." She took a small breath. "Everything go all right with you?"

"Sure," he answered, all nonchalant. "Look. I got to go. I've got to get over to Port Tampa and you need to get back to the office as soon as possible. Things have turned to shit." A pause. Papers shuffled in the background.

"Right," she answered. "Tell Marcy to hold everything for me, please. I'll be back soon as I can get a ride. Anything you can tell me?" She tried to sound a bit distraught but business-like. The distraught came easy.

"Not over the phone, honey. Got to go now. Call me later. Bye."

"Bye, Bobby." She clicked the phone shut. Business-like was not too hard either, as she thought through what Silva said. Not a word about the drug deal gone wrong, nothing about her being in a shoot-out. Then, with the two crackers dead in the swamp, who would tell him. Not her, for goodness sakes.

She pushed her phone back into a hip pocket. What could be so important that Silva had to go to Port Tampa? Maybe he had a meeting with that crooked senator, the intended recipient of the proceeds of the drug sale. After Bobby's slice off the top, of course. Fool that she had been, for a while she had included herself in the scheme.

After all, dope was just dope, Silva had said. Everyone uses, so why not make a whole lot of money. You need the cash, he had insisted, more money than either of us will make in this dump, waving his hand around the Department of Environmental Protection Oil and Gas Section office. That Clyde Butcher print on the wall probably cost more than her analyst's job brought her for a full month, he had argued. He had been right about that part, so she had agreed.

She may have been fooled then, but she had sensed a change in Silva's voice, even over the phone. Had the bastard sent those men to kill her? Had he discovered she had changed the drop times in the message? What a fool she had been for letting Silva sweet talk her. Everybody didn't do dope, and the ones who did usually eased into coke, meth, crack. She had seen it back home. She knew better. She flipped open the phone and dialed again. The phone picked up after the first ring. "Liz. Hi. It's Kat. How's Chris doing?" She tried to make her voice cheery. No reason to get Liz in an uproar. God knows, she was doing her best to cope.

"I'm not sure we can delay any more," the answer came back. "Chris needs—no, not needs—must be in the center and treatment started by next week to keep him in remission."

Bennett felt her stomach lurch at Liz's answer. "Look. I know I promised you and Logan I would figure out how to help. But there have been some complications." *God, the complications.* "What's the hold up this time?"

As always, Liz's answer had to do with the damn medical system and money. More than Bennett ever had squirreled away, more than Logan, her ex, would ever make. "Soon," Bennett promised. "I'll find a way. You tell Chris I love him." She paused, took a deep breath. "We'll make it work, Liz. I promise." Bennett snapped the phone shut and closed her eyes. *Money.* She had already sold her soul, for naught. Now she was making bad promises.

Water under the bridge. She looked around. Water. Trees, vines. Everywhere. Out in the swamp a gator roared. Great. Stuck in a swamp with a druggy and his dog.

She shook her head. Too cruel. Except for his gimp, Grant had seemed like a typical guy when she first met him, brusque, but all right. Today, his face was drawn, eyes a bit whacky. But he had saved her from those two yahoos. And then in the parking lot and in the substation. But none of that was her doing. Now she had to focus even harder on Chris.

She took a deep breath, ignored her growling stomach, waited until her breathing was steady, and made one more call.

CHAPTER 15

Grant blinked the fuzz out of his eyes, still groggy from the meds. His shirt and shorts clung to him, salt sticky in the heat, a haven for the flight of mosquitoes that had discovered his bare arms and legs. Dust motes drifted down from the boards overhead, a hint that Bennett had made her way up the ladder. Flash whined and stretched his head around, looking for a bit of land. Grant rubbed the greyhound's muzzle. "We're starting to get old, ain't we, buddy?" Flash groaned and looked aggravated, in a lethargic way. Grant untied the boat and shoved them toward the hummock.

Grant glanced at the sky. Late afternoon by the sun. No more water. No more helicopters spraying the swamp with random machinegun fire. He still wondered what had caused such a violent reaction. Fire from a helicopter meant Federal intervention. They were in deeper than he had thought. He let Flash hop out and take care of business after a quick sniff of the pine tree. It had been a long day. It would be a longer night in the swamp without food or water. He needed to figure out how to get home. The boat battery was about half gone. First, though, he'd see what Bennett was up to. At any rate, he wasn't moving until night. He called Flash back and pulled the boat under the shack until the trap door was directly overhead. He gathered Flash in his arms and lifted him through the opening until old quick thinking Flash used Grant's head as a step and scrambled up, claws scratching across Grant's scalp, then clattered up on the old floor boards.

Grant blinked through the dust. Flash's nose appeared, then those eyes, staring down, followed by his stupid grin. "All right, all right," Grant muttered. "Coming up."

When he pulled himself though the opening in the floor, muscles screaming, Bennett walked in from the porch that ran around the outside of the fishing shack.

"Ready to go?" she asked.

He leaned against the old wood timber until the woozies flowed out of his head. "Where?"

"Out of this damn swamp. Uly, I'm sorry I brought you into this, but I got to get back to civilization. I don't think anyone, sheriff, DEA,

FDLE, has anything to charge either one of us with. Surely that Deputy has told them we weren't the one's shooting. We should be safe. I'm getting out of here, with or without you."

Grant walked onto the porch and looked out over the swamp, dizzy with the effort. He reached back and steadied himself with a hand on the door frame. He let the pain killers drain out of his system, leaving behind a dull ache in his leg and a buzzing inside his head. A real mosquito buzzed around his eyes. A pileated woodpecker pounded at a big pine and a second settled on a limb, squawking at its mate below, all conspiring to make his head hurt more than Bennett's remarks. "And how do you plan on getting out of here, pray tell? You walk on water?"

Flash walked over and stuck his head around Grant's legs. The two of them stared at Bennett. Grant saw the outline of the cell phone in her pocket. "Crap. You called somebody? You know the damn cell can be traced, tracked." Grant thought of the solid tips signal intelligence had passed down from NSA to his unit on the ground in Iraq. He peered out through the trees and heavy foliage. "Probably on the way, right now."

Bennett shook her head. "What did you think I would do? Sit around and starve out here in the swamp with you two? Yes, of course, somebody's coming to get me. He said he knew about the shack. All we have to do is wait just a little longer." Her voice climbed in pitch, a bit of desperation creeping into her tone.

"Wait for somebody you trust, more than me? You sure you got any friends left?"

"Uly, I don't think trust is the issue. We live in two different worlds. Goodness, I'm not sure I even know where yours is. You want to get out with me, fine. But I'm not waiting around for another killer to show up."

He thought for a moment, watching her eyes. She seemed to believe her own words. "If anyone comes, he'll be after you."

She stared at him, mouth twisted in anger, or resignation. He couldn't tell which.

"God, why did I ever listen to Allen?" She looked down at her watch. "When does it get dark? My ride should be here pretty soon."

Grant shrugged his shoulders. "You can deal with the law on your own, fine," he said. "You all self sufficient now?" As he spoke, Grant wondered why he even cared. She didn't owe him any loyalty. And he sure as hell didn't owe her any.

"I don't need, want, any drugs. I'm not like you, Uly, I'm clean. What I really need is about hundred thousand dollars. Got that stashed away in your boat?" She crossed her arms and stared at Grant, her face hard. "All I wanted was a little help. Damn Allen! Damn you and this whole mess!"

GULF WINDS

For a moment Grant thought the rumbling noise was blood boiling through his ears until Flash poked him with his nose. "Shut up!" Grant hissed to Bennett. He slid down to the floor, pulling her down with him. She jerked away from his grip. "Get down!" He tried to whisper, but it came out a horse rasp. He grabbed her blouse and tugged her to the floor, gathered Flash in his arms and gently stroked the dog's smooth head. The dog he could control. Bennett, nope. "Don't be a fool," he hissed at Bennett.

Eyes narrowed, Bennett stared at him for a moment, an obvious look of disgust on her face, and jerked away.

"There's a boat nosing around. Who're you expecting?" Grant asked. Before she could answer a boat burbled past, half hidden behind a screen of air potato vines and palmetto fronds.

Bennett stood and let out a piercing whistle. She leaned over the rail and waved, a big grin on her face, this one real. The boat slowed and backed against the current. The single occupant, a tall man, biceps straining the sleeves of a tan shirt, stood behind the console, weapon holstered at his side.

"That's Matt." Bennett sounded like she had just received a pardon from the Governor. "He's with Fish and Wildlife, an old friend."

"If you had such a good buddy already in the Refuge, why the devil did you get me involved?"

She looked down at her feet for a moment, then looked Grant in the eye. "Matt Olsen is straight as an arrow. Not a crooked bone in that pretty body. I couldn't bring him into this. Remember, Allen said you were the guy if I needed to break the law."

Bennett left him standing there with Flash and clambered down into the tattered flats boat.

When they were out here building this shack, old Morris, wiser in the way of women, had warned him there would be days like this. Grant walked over to a corner of the shack and slid a floorboard aside, another under it like a Chinese puzzle box, until he uncovered a plastic bag that he slipped into his pocket. Morris also had told him you would never know when you might need to be someone else. How right the old man had been, about everything.

"Come on, boy." Grant slowly worked his way down the ladder with Flash sprawled across his shoulders, fireman carry style, to find Bennett standing in the back of the boat waiting for her friend.

Bennett hopped into the Fish and Wildlife boat as it glided between the stilts and under the shack, her grin, if anything, broader.

Hatless, the Wildlife officer smiled back from under a blond crew cut. "Hey, Kat," he greeted her with a hug. He leaned over and stuck his hand out toward Grant and Flash. "Ranger Matt Olsen, Mister Grant. I've seen you around, but don't think we've ever spoken. Sure have heard a lot about you today. Must say, bit of a surprise when Kat called and said she was with you." He took a long look at the listing flats boat. "Appears you been in a mess somewhere along the way. Maybe popped a seam somewhere under the decking. You two, and your dog, O.K.?"

Grant slipped Flash off his shoulders, stretched across and shook Olsen's hand, wondering exactly what Olsen had heard, and from whom. "Considering, I think we're doing all right. Good of you to come when Miss Bennett called. She's anxious to get out of the swamp; be back with friends."

Olsen sat down and looked from Grant to Bennett, and back. "Before we go, you two got a problem we got to talk about. At least one I know about, maybe more. Mister Grant—"

"Uly. When I get bad news, I like to be called Uly."

Olsen nodded in agreement. "Uly. I'm Matt." He brushed back a crew cut that didn't need brushing and swatted at a buzz of mosquitoes. "Be dark soon, and we need to get out of the swamp, but first I want you to understand. There's a warrant out for your arrest." He glanced back at Bennett. "Both of you. Drug trafficking, plus they want to talk about an assault on the sheriff's substation. I saw the report on the incident at the substation. Speculation is that you were part of some drug deal gone bad. I don't think they really have any convictable evidence, but the warrant is to get you in for questioning, and the fact that the Sheriff's office was assaulted didn't go down well. Lots of cops are ready to shoot first, plus Homeland Security has FBI ninja guys running around armed to the teeth. I got the impression that I was the only one who thought you didn't do the shooting." He grinned at Bennett. "And that was only because I believed it was too weird for you to be involved in anything like that, Kat. With everything else that happened yesterday, every law enforcement agency around is spooked; FBI, ATF every alphabet around poking their nose into every incident report. Now, just so everything gets off on the right foot here, officially; I have placed you both under arrest."

He held up his hand when Bennett started to speak. "Kat, hon. Just let it be. Anything you tell me will be admissible, so just don't tell me anything. Then I won't have to report anything. You get back and explain to whoever the bosses decide has jurisdiction. I'm sure it'll sort out." He hesitated for a moment, staring back at Grant. "Uly. You coming in without a problem?"

It really wasn't a question. Grant had seen law enforcement stares before. And Olsen had the gun. "Sure, Matt. It'll all sort out." Grant figured a little lie at this point was the diplomatic way to get the hell out of the swamp without getting his ass shot off.

Olsen picked up a line. "Good. I'll rig a bridal line and we'll tow your boat out of here." A couple of quick knots and he snugged the harness connecting the two boats. "By the way, Kat. After you called, I rang up your office and let them know I would get you back safe. I was concerned someone would do something drastic, so I called your friend in FDLE to see if I could get them to back off."

"Allen Wilson?" Bennett asked.

"Yeah. But he wasn't in the office. I left a message with the FDLE secretary that I planned to bring you back to the Refuge dock. So don't be pissed at me if a gaggle's waiting for us when we get back."

Grant sat in silence as Olsen started his engine and slowly towed Grant's listing boat under the overhanging limbs out to the river channel and back toward the Wildlife Refuge dock, pondering why Allen had ever sent Bennett to him. The only thing he knew for certain was that he didn't have the vaguest idea what was going on. Was the OxyContin still buzzing around in his head, or had he just gone stupid?

Olsen eased his boat up to an empty dock, the battered flats boat trailing behind with Grant and Flash. "Nobody home," he announced. "Gal at FDLE must of thought I was full of crap. Or maybe they're all tied up with the Tampa incident."

Grant wondered what had happened in Tampa that was more important than a law enforcement shooting, surprised at the lack of reception. No lynch party. The dock was deserted. The Wildlife Refuge was closed to the public after dark, but he figured that gaggle of logo'ed jackets he had seen milling around the *Rum Runner* that morning would be assembled, handcuffs gleaming. He looked up to see if the helicopter was about to unload on them. Nothing but a flock of buzzards wheeling around the tree tops.

Olsen climbed out of his boat and helped Bennett up the ladder and onto the dock. "Uly?"

Grant turned and rummaged through the bait well, searching for his pills. "Got to get something."

Olsen's hand moved a fraction closer to his holstered weapon.

"I'm coming, Matt. Just hold your horses. I need to find some drugs."

Olsen stared down at him, a frown creasing his forehead.

Grant laughed at Olsen's look. He held up the brown container. "Prescription. Traceable directly to the docs at James Haley VA hospital in Tampa."

Just as Olsen took a step toward him, hand out to help him up, a shot rang out. Olsen lurched, pulled out his pistol. Blood spurted out over his uniform shirt. He looked down at Grant, betrayal in his eyes.

"Matt." Bennett screamed.

Olsen began to crumple to the dock. Bennett caught him under his arms, staggered under his weight. Olsen's pistol tumbled into the battered boat, thumping down on top of a startled Flash.

Grant struggled to his feet. "What the hell's going on?" Bennett stumbled to the edge of the dock, Olsen in her arms. A second, louder report echoed over the water, a different weapon. Bennett screamed and followed Olsen head over ass into the water, showering Grant with a huge splash.

Grant dropped the pill container and stood, hand on the piling to still the rocking boat. He peered over the edge of the dock.

The baseball closer from the parking lot was coming fast in a low crouch, pistols in both hands like a wild west cowboy. A second man followed the shooter, an AK at his side flopping around like he had no clue. Back at a white pickup a man waited, a big bald black guy. The crew from the parking lot, minus the woman.

"Uly, help." Bennett grabbed the side of the boat and struggled to hold Olsen's head above water. Red stains swirled in the tidal flow. Olsen's feet floated up to the surface, long pants ballooned full of air.

Grant grabbed Olsen's collar with one hand and yanked Bennett half over the gunwale with the other. "Get in the boat. Shooters coming." Footsteps pounded across the gravel. Bennett slid into the boat and grabbed Olsen's shirt. Grant splashed his fingers through the warm water filling the rod compartment, found the plastic grip and pulled out the dripping snake gun. He cocked the hammer back just as the footsteps slowed. A last crunch of gravel, then a thud as footsteps moved onto the creaking boards of the dock.

A face leaned over the edge of the dock followed by the muzzle of a pistol.

Grant fired the Tamer as a ball of flame licked down at him, slamming the Tamer back into his chest. The face flew backwards and a mist of blood floated down into Grant's face. A gun roared in his ear. As Grant fell back he saw Bennett with Olsen's pistol, firing up at the dock.

Olsen was gone.

Then, suddenly, so was everything else.

CHAPTER 16

Another damn Renault. Must have been. Grant had that light feeling, floating, spinning. Maybe they would put him on the medevac flight soon, get him out of this God forsaken land.

"*Como estas*, Uly?"

Grant shook his head in disbelief and struggled to get up at the sound of a familiar voice. Thank the Lord. Vicente had survived the car bomb. Grant tried to shrug the sandbags from his chest. His left arm felt strange. His left arm had never hurt before, just his leg.

"Uly. Open your eyes and talk to me."

Grant forced his eyes open, blinked. Juan's wrinkled face and silver hair hovered over his. Grant sank back. Vicente wasn't alive. Instead, Vicente's older brother, Juan, hovered over him. Grant squeezed his eyes back tight, wishing the dream were true.

Grant's stomach churned. Antibiotics, pain pills, all the stuff that made him nauseous roared like a cyclone around his gut. He tried to breathe slowly and calm his stomach. He opened his eyes again to see Chantico elbow Juan from his view. Grant blinked once more, this time trying to keep the tears from washing down the sides of his face. He had so wanted the voice to be Vicente's. Grant closed his eyes and felt the tears flood his cheeks.

Chantico smiled down at him as she wound a bandage around his arm. He blinked the tears out of his eyes. He was in a bed, half naked. Chantico's face hovered on one side, Bennett's on the other. Had him trapped.

"Matt's gone, Uly. Those men from the parking lot shot him. I tried, but he got away from me. He's gone," Bennett's voice whispered in Grant's ear.

A tear ran down Bennett's nose and dripped onto Grant's bare chest. She scrubbed at her eyes with the back of her hands and took a deep breath. Her hair hung all glossy around her face, the mud and twigs gone. A fresh washed face had returned her to being an attractive woman, except for her red eyes. The flowered blouse had been traded for a loose white tee shirt with a *Cinco de Mayo* logo embroidered across the front, one he remembered seeing on Chantico, once upon a long time ago.

Chantico slowly shook her head. She wore that same sad smile Grant remembered from the ceremony at the Florida National Cemetery when they put Vicente to rest.

Grant tried to speak. His throat felt raw, sandpapered. He swallowed and worked his tongue around until he could get the words to come out. "Where are we?"

"Chassahowitzka. My house, silly." Chantico wiped his face with a damp cloth. "Flash brought you home. With a little bit of help from Juan and your new girl friend."

Grant sat up. The room whirled around him and his stomach lurched. "I didn't shoot quick enough, did I?" he managed to croak.

Chantico put her hand behind his neck and held him steady. "Hush, Uly. You said something just about as dumb about Vicente. You couldn't stop the car bomb, just like you couldn't stop whoever shot you, so don't be an ass."

Grant looked over at Bennett. "You all right?"

She shrugged her shoulders. "Not shot." She looked at him and brushed her hair back. Her cheeks were red where she had scrubbed away the tears, but her eyes were cold. "The bastards killed Matt. I grabbed Matt's gun, fired up at the men. When I got untangled, one was dragging the other one back to a truck. I emptied the pistol at them and the bastards drove away."

"They're still after you, aren't they?"

Bennett didn't speak for a moment. "After me?" she finally asked, lips pursed and a puzzled look on her face. After a moment Bennett nodded her head as if a great truth had finally dawned on her. "Is it Bobby, you think? Would he have me killed so I won't mess up his plans anymore?

Chantico shook the cloth in Grant's face. "Uly. Did you get her into trouble with this Bobby?"

"No, Chantico. For crying out loud. I didn't know anything about him. Or her." He tried to sit up straight, blinking into the glare of the sun reflecting from the polished linoleum floor. The sun spread across the floor, a morning sun unless Chantico's house had turned around since Vicente's wake, Grant's last painful visit here. Grant's mind whirled, trying to put a logical progression on what had happened. "How did we get here? Flash's smart, but I don't think he can drive."

Bennett swiped at her nose with a tissue. "I used the electric motor and went back up the canal to behind the café."

"Old Flash came and got me." Juan's broad face beamed down at Grant. "I stopped by *El Sombrero Rojo* for a beer after work, and to find out what had happened at the sheriff's office yesterday. Man, everybody talking. Rockets, shooting, bombs. Like a war, man; like you say about Iraq. Then old Flash came wandering around the corner. I knew you would be close. I followed him to the canal and there you were. Sleeping like a baby in the boat with *Señorita* Bennett holding your face out of the water. Then I bring you here." Juan, broken teeth and all, grinned at Bennett. "Uly, he's a good friend. Sheriff deputies, I don't let them see you, bring you to Chantico. She always take good care of all of us, like Uly do."

Bennett raised her eyebrows. "What's he talking about, taking care?" she asked Grant.

"Chantico's looked after all of us since we were kids."

"If I hadn't been around, this *stupido* would still be a virgin." Chantico winked at Bennett.

"And you," Bennett asked Grant. "What do you take care of?"

Juan rubbed his fingers together and answered for Grant. "*El dinero.*"

Grant shrugged. "That money you are always talking about. Sometimes I take it from people who shouldn't have it and give it to people who should." He took Juan's arm and stood up. A surge of nausea and a swirl of bright spots made him squeeze his eyes shut. He was talking too damn much.

"Uly, you hurting?" asked Chantico.

He shook his head, slowly so the swirling spots wouldn't return. "Noooo. Feel good. Better than in a long time." He grinned at Chantico. "What you give me, baby?"

She slapped the cloth against his butt. "Just two of your OxyContins. Not so you feel good, just to keep your damn mouth shut. It worked. You slept all night. And you not a hero this time, either. Katrina says the man shot holes in the boat." Chantico pointed at Grant's arm. "Only a tiny little cut. Juan said the bullet smashed up that little shotgun you keep in the boat. You got one big bruise on your forehead and a little gash where the bullet went across your arm. The wound is clean and you didn't lose much blood, thanks to Katrina. Keep it clean, no infection, and your arm should be all right."

Bennett stared at Grant, frown lines furrowing her brow. "What about the money? Is that why the gunmen are after you?"

Always about the money with this woman.

"Son of a bitch. You've been blaming this shit on me and Bobby Silva. How do you know it's not somebody out to get you for stealing their money, for crying out loud?"

"You're the one he called the *perra*." As soon as the words left his mouth, even in his drug reinforced stupidity, Grant wished he hadn't.

"Who's the *perra!*" Chantico's volcanic temper erupted. She stood and punched him in the chest so hard the room swam around in front of his eyes.

Grant knew better. Mamma Madero had told him when they were kids that Chantico had been named for an Aztec goddess of fire. "Not you, Chantico, not you. That's just what the man said, the one who shot Eustis."

"Just who is the bitch, then?" Chantico asked. She waved the cloth in his face. "And watch your tongue."

"What are you two talking about?" Bennett asked.

Grant sat back down before Chantico could deck him. "We're talking about the man who shot up the substation. He said he was after the *perra*, bitch. I thought he was talking about you." He looked around the room. "Eustis. Is he all right, Chantico? I saw the other deputy, Wellington, but haven't seen Eustis since we ran out of the substation."

"Papa's gone to Heaven to be with my other papa," a tiny voice piped up from the corner.

"Come here, Angelica." Chantico sat and lifted a small girl into her lap. "This is Uncle Uly. He's Katrina's friend, and both your papas' friend."

The two women and one girl all stared at him. Juan shrugged his broad shoulders and walked out of the room, followed by Flash, who at least was thoughtful enough to grin at Grant as he left.

Chantico hugged the little girl to her chest. "Angelica came to her papa's funeral, and now her mommy let her stay with us."

Grant smiled at the cherubic face, and looked at Chantico for an explanation. He still didn't have the foggiest what she was talking about. Chantico had always been able to read him, and her disapproving frown showed she obviously did now.

She slid Angelica to the floor. "You go find Juan and he'll help you get some of Flash's special treats, sweetie."

The girl skipped across the floor into the next room.

"Apparently Angelica's mother, some tramp from Ocala, had Vicente's child, but never told him about it. She played DCF as an unwed mother for all the support she could get. When she heard about Vicente's funeral, she dumped Angelica on us when the Army balked at giving her Vicente's insurance money. Eustis and I planned to adopt Angelica." Unexpectedly, a tear rolled down Chantico's cheek. "After we were married."

She scrubbed at her face with the wash cloth. "You still don't understand, do you? That man you were arguing about. He killed Eustis." She shook her head. "I don't get to marry Eustis; Angelica doesn't get to have him for her new papa. We don't even get to bury him." The tears began to stream down her face. "Eustis' ex is still on his will as executor of his estate. She says she will take him to Illinois or someplace to bury him, probably just so she can get his Social Security money. Bitch probably put him in a cardboard box and bury him in a field. And nobody but me and Eustis wanted that poor child."

She patted her face with the cloth and pulled her shoulders back. "Now. What to do about you."

Grant put his aching head in his hands. "Dear God." Vicente, now Eustis. Dead. And his head whirling around so he couldn't think straight.

Bennett broke the silence. "Uly. I have a couple of friends who might help." She stood. "Where's your phone, Chantico?"

"Wait." Grant grabbed a handful of the her tee shirt and tugged her back down. "We can't call from here. I've brought too much shit down around Chantico and Juan. And the kid. Too many people are dead, and we're right in the middle. There'll be so many court ordered phone traps in Homosassa the techs will be going nuts listening to them all. You call and they'll find you."

"Then let's go some place we can call from. Tampa? Somewhere we'll be lost." The determined look faded from her face. "How can we get there? My car's a smoldering wreck." She jerked loose from his grip. "I'm not getting in that damn boat again and let you lose me in the swamp."

Her determination seemed to come and go as fast as the truth.

Chantico stood. "First, I fix everybody breakfast. Then you can take your truck. Do what you need to do."

Grant didn't know if the confusing facts or the OxyContin were making his head swirl. "My truck? I thought the cops had it."

"Eustis called me. He said you were in trouble," Juan explained. "He told me to get your Chevy from the boat yard, and hide it down by the river until Ben Wellington can come get it." Juan spread his hands in apology. "This just before the shooting at the station, I think. The truck is still by the river. I hid it pretty good."

"Still loaded with dope?" Grant asked.

Juan grinned and sniffed at the humid fresh air coming in the open window. "Can almost smell it from here. Maybe you better take my Dodge, leave the weed. When I get a chance I'll dump the stuff in the swamp."

Grant slipped on his shirt and sat down at the old wood plank table. Bennett met his look across the table, the expression on her face implying she had decided what she was going to do. He was just too addled to figure out what.

Spicy aromas floating through the house took his mind away from the puzzle and the lingering smell of gasoline that had not been completely washed out of his shirt. Grant bowed his head with the others as Juan prayed the breakfast of *Huevos Rancheros* be blessed and their family and friends be kept safe.

Family. Friends. Of which he had precious little, outside of this house.

Flash curled, nose to tail, in his old bed in the corner that had been his home when Vicente went to war, only to come home in a coffin. Grant's fault, according to Eustis. Only now Grant couldn't even argue about it with Eustis any more. If he had wanted to. But Angelica's chatter about the pictures she had painted with her fingers at the church day care center made the morning almost seem right. Vicente had left something good back home.

As Grant finished his last bite, Chantico appeared in her nurse's uniform.

"The van from the clinic will pick me up for work soon and to take Angelica to the day care center. You call, tell me you are all right, both of you, when you can." She motioned toward the door. "*Vamos*. Leave, so I can clean up this mess, in case someone comes by looking for you, *comprende*? I'll be home early, so call if I can help. And take care of that arm."

Grant stood. His stomach stayed in the right place, but his head throbbed, and in the OxyContin buzz he wasn't sure he could even feel his hip. There was no way he could drive. "Thank you, Chantico. And Juan."

Grant put his good right arm over Juan's broad shoulders and let him maneuver him down the steps and into the Dodge pickup.

"Here." Juan slid a pistol from his pocket and into Grant's hand. "One of my *amigos* picked this up from the street. I save it for you."

Grant looked down. Juan's gnarled hand held the black Kimber Grant had lost in the parking lot. Grant tucked the gun in his pocket as Bennett climbed up into the cab and behind the wheel. "I'll be in touch as soon as I can," Grant called out as Bennett ground her way through the gears and bounced across the ruts.

Grant slumped in the corner of the old green Dodge cab and watched as Bennett leaned forward, the tip of her tongue sticking out of the corner of her mouth. She held the steering wheel in a death grip, weaving a bit at first until she got the hang of the Dodge. She followed the dirt track out onto the highway leading toward Tampa. The littered floor rattled with tools, and an errant seat spring threatened to fling Grant out the window. A sun beam shining through the green, white and red Mexican flag decal on the back window played across Bennett's hair, whipped by the humid wind blowing in the open window. She leaned back and grinned at Grant as she sped down the highway, quickly at home driving the old rattle-trap truck. Grant closed his eyes as the trees flew by. Too damn fast.

Grant wondered why Rankin had told Juan to hide his truck and the weed. What had Bennett told Rankin in the substation? She had been so sincere back at Chantico's. He stared at her profile, jaw working, intent on maneuvering toward Tampa and plotting her next lie. No doubt, she was the best liar he had ever met.

Grant waited in the truck while Bennett registered them at a fancy motel around the corner from Busch Gardens. She smiled at him when she climbed back in the truck and handed him a newspaper. "Hi, Mister Bennett." She drove around to the back and parked. "Such an early check in. Desk clerk thinks I'm screwing my lawn guy." She slid out and slammed the door. "Come on. Nothing new. You've already slept with me."

Grant followed her into the air conditioned hallway. She unlocked the room door and stood back as he headed toward the bed. He kicked off Juan's Keds, flopped back on the bed and closed his eyes. The OxyContin was beginning to wear off. The new pain in his head vied with the old pain in his leg, all clamoring for his headache to let them be. He reached down and pulled the spread over his bare legs. Her comment finally worked its way into his brain. "What are you talking about, we already slept together?"

"Chantico put us in the same bed last night. She thinks you and I are together. Heck of a joke, huh? I just let it ride. You were zonked on your pills, and I just wanted—" She stopped and sat down next to him on the flowered spread. "Uly. I'm scared. Why are people shooting at us? Who's their target? Me? You? Why? I don't think Bobby even knows I tried to take his weed. Matt's dead. Your deputy friend's dead. None of this makes any sense." She picked up the bedside phone. "I'll make some calls. See what my office thinks is going on. Bobby will be royally pissed if he found out what I did. But surely he wouldn't have me killed; I just can't believe he would go that far." She looked at Grant for a moment. "That bald man; he was screaming at the substation about you killing somebody. Maybe that's what this is all about. Allen said you were in a lot of stuff, not all of it legal."

"Dammit!" Grant finally lost his temper. "Allen doesn't have the vaguest what the fuck he's talking about." He closed his eyes and took a deep breath, reminding himself—rage might win in combat, but not in peace. *Was this peace?* He opened his eyes. Bennett had replaced the phone and stood in front of him, waiting.

"Whatever you want to do. Make your calls." He scanned the newspaper headlines as she dialed. They hadn't even made the top section. Some

Islamic terrorist had fired rockets at the fuel tanks farm at Port Tampa. Now everybody was on screaming terrorist alert. That's what all the fuss was about. The stories had little substance, mostly old quotes from Homeland Security officials. The shooting at Homosassa barely warranted a blip on the bottom of the front page with a follow on page eight. Grant flipped through the paper until he found the story buried below a big car advertisement. Sheriff's spokesperson confirmed that one unnamed law enforcement officer, a hero from the Gulf war, was killed as a result of an apparent drug turf war, no details until the investigation made further progress. Suspects, but no names. Grant laid the paper down and listened to Bennett's side of her first call.

Three calls later she slowly replaced the phone and lay back on the bed beside him.

"Nobody wants to talk, huh?" The room was cold. He put his right arm around Bennett's shoulders and pulled her closer.

"You making a move on me now?" Her breath was warm in Grant's ear.

He grunted. "Haven't made a move in a long time. Doubt if I ever will again. So just be quiet for a bit. Let me rest, and then we'll figure out what to do next." Grant took a deep breath and closed his eyes, her warm body soothing against his aching leg, wondering if she would be there when he woke.

CHAPTER 17

Exhausted, Bobby Silva rushed down the hall. He had been at Port Tampa all night. God damn terrorists had screwed up his schedule. He needed to check on the delivery, find out if the money drop was still on, track down Bennett, make sure she hadn't screwed anything up. His phone rang as he stepped in his office.

He jerked at his tie and picked up the phone. "Silva."

"Hey, Boo, your boys ain't coming wid the stuff. They dead, man. I done saw one of your Aryan Brothers body bagged on TV, other one a crispy critter. Somebody else got your weed, or it floating back to Mexico. Now, you let me know next time you want to deal. But get real. Don't you go hook me up with no shootin' ain't my business. If my EME boys want somebody dead, I'll do it in a heartbeat. But that ain't the deal 'tween you and me. We just got a little business thing going, *no mas.*"

"Beetle, what the hell are you talking about? You didn't get anything? Nothing? Dammit, you better not be pulling no scam on me. I'll be on you in a New York minute. Don't you forget how we made our connections. The Aryans I know ain't going to let you off the hook for a deal."

"Don't you get Yankee fancy with me, Boo. Ain't no deal. Ain't nothing showed up, 'cept what's on the news. You need to lay back in your crib, *amigo*, stop trying to lay your shit off on me. You call your Wilson boy when you get straight. Till then, forget about me, my crew. I don't need that shooting shit."

The phone went silent.

Silva slammed down the receiver. "Son of a bitch," he muttered. "That damned Bennett. She said she wanted out, that the drop would go bad. Bitch and her stupid pot head buddy Wilson, setting me up. Who the shit they think they're screwing with?" He looked around the office, suddenly aware of the bustle of people outside his door, scurrying around too busy dealing with the rocket attack on Port Tampa to listen to his rants. Good. Let them deal with some jerk-off pretending to be a terrorist. In the short run the explosions were good news. Oil prices would skyrocket. Long run, probably more of the same. He had never seen the energy sector fail to take advantage of any reason to increase profits.

He kicked his office door shut, picked up the phone and dialed the Russell Petroleum Resources main office in Houston. "Mister Russell, please. Tell him this is Robert Silva."

Two clicks and a voice boomed over the line. "Howdy, Bobby. You get everything I sent? Some especially good inventory, I was told."

"Darrell—" Silva paused, then decided telling all now was a lot better than waiting. "We got a bit of a problem. Your email, the one with the delivery schedule?"

"We ain't got no problems, son." Russell's voice lost all its joviality. "My problem is getting more refined product into Florida and scoring me some of these fine profits that we deserve. Don't you worry about that leak crap off New Orleans. Americans need their oil. They'll suck it up. Now. You got a problem?"

"Yes, sir. Apparently a woman in my office intercepted your email and changed the delivery times. Then all hell broke loose. My contractors in Homosassa are dead and the shipment's lost." He waited for the explosion.

Instead, Russell's response was calm. "Way I understand the Florida legislative process, we got to have Senator Fuller and all his influence in our camp when that vote on Gulf exploration goes to the floor. Soon! You listen close to me. I got my eye on Desoto Canyon, the rest of that Gulf deep water on the Florida side. Boy, I've already signed leases for three more drillships, got them ready to move over from Green Canyon. My ass is extended way out yonder, betting I can pump a million barrels crude a day, just me and my little piss-ant company. No need for them big dog consortiums, the Russians and them Arabs to get all that money, now is there? Me and you, we need to get our share. Listen close, boy." He paused, hacked into the phone. "Now, have I got that right?"

Silva could imagine the cloud of cigar smoke surrounding the oil man. "Yes, sir."

"Bobby, boy; I don't give a shit about your people or what happens at your end. I sent the right stuff to you, plenty enough for you to get the job done with Fuller. So far as I'm concerned, you got it." Another coughing fit. "Now. You going to make Senator Fuller and his votes happen, or have I got to take action from here?"

"No—I mean, I didn't get the shipment, but I will get the job done." Silva kept his voice steady. But he could see his plans all falling apart. "Don't worry; I'll get it all together. I only wanted you to know I had a problem. Nobody likes surprises. One thing I do need. I got to shut this woman up. Can you send someone over to take care of her?"

"I told you before, Bobby. I got my problems. You got yours. I take care of mine, and I damn sure expect you to take care of yours. You came down with a good rep from New York, a reputation for taking care of

GULF WINDS

business, good connections. That's why I brought you into the deal, you being right there in the Department of Environmental Protection and all. Now you take care of this woman before she really screws up our arrangement." A short cough and his voice got softer. "And if my name's dragged into your problems, I'll send someone over, but not just for her. Texans can take care of business same as you New York boys, *capishe?*"

Silva rubbed his forehead. He got it. "Sure. Don't worry. It's done, Darrell. Senator Fuller, the votes, everything will be taken care of. I'll make sure everything gets back on track."

"Good boy. Votes coming up soon. You damn well better have the vote cinched before then. Do it. And don't forget. I got a long reach. You don't think that screw-up out in the Gulf was an accident, do you?"

A click and the connection went silent. Silva hung up the phone. The Florida portion of the deep water Gulf of Mexico oil drilling legislation was scheduled for a State Senate floor vote before the end of the month. Feds and big oil were already pushing the benefits; but the opposition, prompted by the big spill, was still fighting the legislation. Senator Fuller had made it clear his support was contingent on at least a hundred thousand dollar down payment. With the Senator and his good old boy network onboard, the vote would be a shoo-in. Next was rights bidding, and Fuller had already promised he had that all tied up.

Silva needed the profits from this last drug shipment to fill the coffer, plus pay some overdue debts up north. He didn't want to face the alternative. He slammed his palm down on the desk, teeth grinding in frustration. He had maneuvered for months to assure Russell a lock on the prime drilling sectors. With the crude oil prices bouncing up and down and the economy going to shit, Russell had promised they would all be wealthy beyond expectations. The hundred grand would just be a drop in the bucket. Now the deal was all falling apart because of that bitch.

This deal had to work. The guys up north were pressuring him to make good, sooner rather than later. He knew how they collected debts, and wanted no part of it. He had to find the weed before Russell sent his Mexican friends; or it would get two way ugly. Plus, he had picked up rumors that a major local grow house operation was beginning to cut into the market. Shit! He had to get the senate deal back on tract. Right now. Then get rid of Bennett, and everything would fall back in line.

He snatched up the phone and dialed.

"Florida Department of Law Enforcement, Wilson speaking"

"Allen, you son of a bitch. You know anything about what happened?"

A pause. "Christ, what are you thinking? What are you doing calling me here?"

"Got your cell?"

"Yeah."

"Go outside, take a smoke break. Take your phone. Now!"

"I don't smoke."

"Don't play stupid with me. Get your ass to where we can talk. Go."

Silva slid his issue Glock 27 from his desk drawer and clipped it on his belt, carefully smoothed his blazer over the pistol, and signed out on the board by the door. He tried to calm himself, pulling on his driving gloves as he walked out to the parking lot, stretching the deerskin until the leather was smooth on his hands. He slid into the bright red Corvette and punched in Allen's cell number. It rang as he drove out of the parking lot and headed across Tampa, northwest, toward Homosassa. The phone rang, and rang. Silva had to grip it and his temper tight to keep from throwing the phone out the window. Allen finally answered.

"Bobby. What the hell is going on? Why you calling me at work?"

"Those two jail house crackers botched up the drop. Got their asses killed. You got any idea how? You better not have set me up."

"Christ, Bobby. I just put you in touch with them through my dealer. I don't have any direct connections with these guys."

"You know them enough to do business with them, asshole. If you screwed me, I'll have your balls, jerk-off." Silva blew through a red light and turned onto the highway. "You been talking to Kat?"

A pause. Long enough to confirm in Silva's mind that Wilson was screwing with him.

"I talked to her, maybe a week ago. But not about this," Wilson finally added. "I'm smart enough not to mess in your deals."

"Well, I think she's in the middle, and you damn well better not be. So if you know where she is, you better shut her up, or you'll wish you still lived on the reservation." Silva snapped his cell phone shut without waiting for a reply. When he pulled into the lot across the street from the Homosassa Sheriff's substation he grunted with satisfaction. Bennett's old mustang sat there festooned with yellow tape, barely recognizable under the dried foam. Whoever shot it up should have finished the job, her in it. But then he wouldn't have the pleasure. Silva dug the little Kel-Tec .380 pistol, his personal throw-down, from its hiding place under the dash and dropped it in his back hip pocket. He pulled off his driving gloves as he got out of the Corvette and stuffed them in the same pocket, covering the pistol. The humid subtopic air slapped him in the face as he smoothed his tie and scanned the street. No one about in the afternoon heat who looked like trouble.

The substation looked like it had been smashed in by a hurricane with sheets of plywood nailed across the window. Slivers of glass on the sidewalk sparkled in the afternoon sun. Silva walked down the sidewalk past the boutiques, taking his time, scanning the sidewalks, and crossed over to the café. No one he recognized, just a bunch of Mexicans laughing as they filed through the door. His stomach growled. The day was so screwed up he had missed lunch. He paused and listened to the muted Latino music from the café. No one out on this side of the street. Across at the convenience store, a woman screamed at a kid in a car seat while she gassed up a minivan.

Silva pushed the substation door open and walked in, a concerned look plastered on his face. The office looked as if vandals had gone amuck with smashed furniture stacked in a corner and holes punched in the walls, but at least the air conditioning had chilled down the place. In the center of the debris a deputy pecked away at a laptop with one hand, a half eaten sandwich on the table. He looked up from the computer and the papers scattered across a folding table.

Silva stifled his surprise. He hadn't expected to see a lean, chocolate skinned deputy in this backwater cracker town. "Excuse me. I'm Robert Silva." He flipped his Department of Environmental Protection Enforcement Division identification at the deputy. "I'm looking into the disappearance of one of my employees, a Katrina Bennett."

The deputy leaned back and took a long look at Silva. "Didn't expect you to come up here. I figured all the DEP folks would be in the Hillsborough Emergency Management Center working on last night's incident at the port." The deputy leaned closer, stared at Silva's badge and scribbled a note on a yellow note pad by the computer. "Have they figured out what caused the explosions down at Port Tampa yet? You guys think terrorists are involved, or just some longshoreman not paying attention?"

Silva shook his head. "Nobody knows for sure. Homeland Security has taken the lead. You know them. They'll figure it out." Silva felt beads of sweat starting to gather on his upper lip under the deputy's steady stare. He reminded himself he had a reason and a right to be here. After all, it was one of his employees missing. And he had law enforcement credentials for emergencies like the rocket attack. He was just doing his job, so play the part. He looked around the office. "Looks like you had a bit of a mess here, too. I don't mean to bother you. I thought I would stop by and see what you could tell me about Miss Bennett."

Wellington stood and offered his left hand. A green sling cradled his right arm. "Sorry, Mister Silva. I'm a little bushed. I'm Deputy Wellington. I interviewed Bennett yesterday, here in the office."

Silva held his breath for a moment, wondering if the drug drop and his involvement had surfaced in the interview.

"I don't know where she's at now." Wellington continued.

"Don't—" Silva cut his outburst short. "Sorry." He scrubbed at his two-day stubble. "It was a long night for all of us. I still haven't made it to bed. I want to make sure she's safe. I also want to make sure her special knowledge of the State's energy resources is protected. Especially in light of last night's crisis."

Wellington sat on the edge of the table. "You know Miss Bennett a long time?" The deputy stared at him like he knew something Silva didn't. "Friends?"

Silva glanced down at the deputy's holstered pistol, calculating. With his own Glock under his jacket, he couldn't out draw Wellington. Foolish. Surely Bennett wasn't stupid enough to implicate him in a drug buy. No reason to cowboy, here, now. Best talk his way through this. "Actually, not really close, just an employee. I was really hoping I could find her and make sure she was alright. I haven't had a chance to read any of your reports, with all the emphasis the office has on the Tampa crisis, but I'm pretty sure she's not involved in any illegal activity."

Wellington drummed his good hand on the desk. He finally smiled and said, "I expect you're right. She didn't seem like the type who would be involved in drugs. But you never know, do you?" Wellington picked up a set of keys. "I was getting ready to close the office for the day, do a little patrolling. I can take you a couple of miles out in the sticks to some folks who can likely help. Just down the road in Chassahowitzka. Let me lock this stuff up."

When Wellington disappeared into a back room with a folder stuffed with papers, Silva took a deep breath of relief and glanced at the note pad. Wellington had scrawled "Silva - FDLE" across the pad, followed by a row of question marks. Silva ripped off the note, stuck it in his pocket. The bitch had jacked his weed, and damn near got her ass caught. Now just play this deputy; the drugs and Bennett would be his.

Outside, Wellington looked at Silva's low slung Corvette parked across the street. "Why don't you ride with me? I wouldn't want you to take that beauty out through the brush. Won't take long."

Silva climbed into the deputy's cruiser and watched Wellington reach across the steering column to shift gears with his left hand. This was going too easy. If he had to take down this county cop to get Bennett, so be it.

Wellington drove them through a winding labyrinth of country blacktops that finally ended in an overgrown dirt road. Deep ruts led them to an old frame house set back against a line of tall cypress trees.

As Wellington maneuvered through the puddles from yesterday's storm, Silva spotted an old man in a battered straw hat leaning against a rusty red pickup. Silva pressed his elbow against his Glock, confirming it was still in place and ready. The little Kel-Tec poked him in his butt, a reminder he had backup if needed.

Wellington let the cruiser roll to a stop in a patch of bare sand that passed for a front yard. "Come on. I'll introduce you."

When they got out of the cruiser the man in the straw hat nodded at Wellington and stared at Silva.

"*Buenos Dios*, Juan. Chantico here?" Wellington called out.

Juan took off his hat, ran his fingers through a thick shock of silver hair and motioned inside. "*Buenos Dios*, Benjamin. Chantico, she's feeding Angelica supper, I think." He nodded toward the pickup. "You come for the truck?"

"Nope. Not yet. Hold on to it until we can catch up. Too much going on. I just brought someone out to talk."

Silva glanced back at the cruiser's communications set up. Laptop, radios. Nothing that looked like a GPS that would automatically report the car's location. Good. He slammed the cruiser door and followed Wellington on to the porch. When he walked by the pickup the distinct aroma of marijuana floated from under a tarp draped over the bed.

Beautiful. This was all a set up. These bastards stole his weed and thought they could lose him, the dumb city boy, in the swamp. He let his arm swing against his jacket, the hump of his holstered Glock reassuring. He'd show them dumb. He reached back, eased the driving gloves out of his pocket and slid them over his fingers. Silva forced himself to keep a steady pace and smile at the Mexican. Heavy muscles, calloused hands of a construction worker, but no sign of a weapon. Didn't look like much brain. Not a problem. He had dealt with his kind in the Bronx where a dead Latino was just another pile of garbage. He put the Mex out of his mind and focused on business. For the immediate moment, Bennett and the dope were his business. A little of her south Georgia pillow talk, and he had gotten too loose with his bragging. Then she got greedy. He hoped she was inside the house. He'd finish this right here and now.

He followed the deputy up the block steps where a skinny hound stared at him. Silva glanced around. The Mex had come up behind them onto the porch. He wandered over and squatted down by the dog, scratching the dog's ugly snout. The squeak of a screen door drew Silva's attention away from the homey scene on the porch. A dark haired beauty pushed the door open.

"Hey, Ben. Who's this?"

The hound bolted past his legs, through the screen door and into the house. Startled, Silva took a step back, hand half way under his jacket.

The woman smiled at him. "Don't mind old Flash. He's just a little skittish around strangers in suits."

She reached out and gave Wellington a peck. "Come in, Ben. How your shoulder doing?"

"I'm fine, Chantico. It's late, so we won't stay long. This is Mister Silva. He works with Katrina Bennett and wondered if she was safe. I thought maybe you might know where she was; if everything was all right."

Chantico's smile went from real to a mask, frown lines on her forehead. With her look, Wellington turned back to Silva, his eyes suddenly intense.

Silva felt the whole deal slipping out of control. He raised his hands, palms forward in a conciliatory gesture. "It's all right. I'm not here to arrest anyone. Kat and I work together."

The look Chantico gave Wellington further convinced Silva something odd was going down. Procedure, and Wellington would have called in his location to Dispatch. This wasn't right, cop wise. Silva's pulse beat in his temple. He bet Wellington, this whole *Latino* crew was in on the hijacking.

Chantico eased the screen door shut and leaned back against it. She had a look somewhere between terror and anger as her eyes flicked back between him and Wellington. She swallowed, cleared her throat and spoke. "You're Robert Silva?" she asked. She stared down at his gloved hands.

Silva didn't respond, didn't need to. The bitch knew who he was. Bennett had talked to her.

"Ben. Would you come in for a minute? I need to talk to you, private. Something personal." She opened the screen door behind her.

Before Wellington could move, Silva grabbed Chantico by the arm. He drew his Glock from under his coat, jerked her out of the doorway and kicked the door shut behind her. He wound his hand in her heavy black hair and spun her around, twisting her between him and the deputy.

"Don't you fucking move, deputy." Silva had to laugh at the deputy's hound dog look. He had made his moves so smooth the deputy hadn't taken a step.

CHAPTER 18

Wellington stood hopeless on the porch, almost in tears, his arm dangling out of the sling, fingers twitching by his side.

"Touch that gun; she dies first and I pop you," Silva snarled. He felt the floorboards shift under his feet. He rolled his back against the rough cedar clapboard wall. To Silva's left the Mex froze, crouched on the porch. A knife blade gleamed in his hand.

"Stupid move, taco. We'll see who the gators get for supper."

The Mex charged.

Silva flicked the Glock's muzzle toward the Mex and fired across Chantico's gut. She jerked, screamed some Spanish shit, elbows pummeling back into his gut. The first .40 caliber MagSafe round took off the stupid hat. The next shot slammed into the Mex. Eyes big, he tumbled off the porch and to the sand. Silva pounded Chantico's head against the boards. "Shut the hell up," he roared as he caught a movement out of the corner of his eye.

Silva spun to his right. He snapped a shot at Wellington as the deputy dove off the porch. Silva turned back, distracted by that damned Mex. On all fours, the old man clawed up the steps, teeth bared. Silva couldn't believe the silver-headed fool was still alive. He fired twice more, all the time the bitch screaming in his ear, fingers digging into his arm. This time the Mex collapsed to the porch floor, still.

Silva threw the shrill woman beside the Mex and dashed down the steps. Where was Wellington? Silva knelt in the sand and peered into the shadows under the porch. A dark form moved in the shadows. Silva fired once, again, two rounds on each side of the concrete steps. A grunt answered his last shot. Silva squinted though the late afternoon glare reflecting off the sun-bleached boards. *Nothing moved now, by damn.*

He looked up when he heard the screen door slap shut. Silva sprang up the steps, across to the door and jerked it open. Against the far wall Chantico looked back at him with a terrified expression on her face and a phone in her hand.

Silva raised the pistol. Before he could fire, a shadowy shape slammed into his chest with a guttural growl. Silva fell back across the threshold. The back of his head bounced on the hard pine porch floorboards; stars swirled around inside his head. He blinked away the stars and dug his heels into the planks to get away from an onslaught of snapping teeth and sharp claws that tore at his chest. Foul smelling slobber sprayed across his face as yellow fangs slashed at his chin.

Silva shoved the dog's muzzle back with his forearm. He levered the pistol muzzle upward and fired.

The dog howled and sunk his teeth into Silva's wrist.

Silva punched the gun toward the dog's boney ribs and fired again.

As suddenly as the dog had attacked, it collapsed, releasing a flood of urine on his leg. Silva pushed the limp dog off and stumbled back into the house. The woman was gone, phone abandoned on the floor. Silva picked it up and listened to the dial tone humming through the set. She hadn't had time to call. In the next room someone cried out, shrill.

He threw the handset to the floor and stomped, crushing it under his shoe. He jerked the nearest door open. Chantico stood with her back to a window, arms spread wide. Behind her something flashed across the trees. Stupid bitch was protecting the fucking dog. Silva raised the Glock. The slide was locked back, magazine empty.

With his left hand he pulled the Kel-Tec from his hip pocket, popped off two quick shots to shut up the screaming woman. She fell to her knees, shook her head, hair flying around like a horse's mane. She struggled to her feet, leaped toward him, still screaming. Another jerk of the trigger and finally she shut up, her face suddenly sad. She staggered back and fell across a bed. Ears ringing, Silva jammed the pistol back in his pocket and glanced around the room. No one else.

Silva popped the Glock's magazine. Hands trembling, he dug around in his blazer pocket until he came up with his spare magazine, slapped it in his Glock, let the slide go forward and holstered the pistol. He took several deep, slow breaths and wiped the dog slobber from his face. Once his hands stopped shaking he searched the house, room by room. A crucifix hung from one wall over a table with a vigil candle, incense and a box of matches. He lit a candle and fed a handful of newspapers into the fire until the flames licked up the side wall toward the crucifix. The paper and cardboard backing of a cheap religious print curled and burst into flames. Smoke swirled up around the old icon. Wood floors, cheap plaster board walls on wood frame, the place was a tinder box. No worry about prints, traces.

Silva ran out to the front room. His eyes began to water as dirty flames flickered through a heavy pall of smoke building in the room. He pushed the screen open and picked up the scattered brass from the porch and sandy ground, making sure he had all the fired cases. No sign he had ever been there except for the Mex bleeding out on the porch and some smudged footprints. The .380 brass from the Kel-Tec he didn't care about. He'd just lose the throwdown. Dog was gone and the cop stuffed dead somewhere under the porch. Both buzzard food. He jumped off the porch and sprinted to the cruiser.

Locked. No keys.

"Fool," he spat out, angry at the dead deputy for not leaving the keys in the cruiser. He furiously sorted out alibis in his head until the loaded pickup caught his eye. "Forget alibis; get the weed," he muttered. "Go with the money." He bet the cops down here were as dumb as the cops in New York. He felt under the cruiser's bumper until he found a magnetic box and a spare key. He ran over to the pickup and yanked the tarp clear. A pile of garbage bags lined the truck bed. He ripped the top bag with his gloved fingers and a handful of dried marijuana seed pods popped out. He crunched the pods in his fingers, sniffed them. *Good as gold*. He quickly transferred the bundles from the pickup bed to the cruiser trunk.

With all the bags stuffed in the Crown Vic trunk, he looked back at the house where smoke tendrils bled through the screen door and curled under the porch roof. He jumped back when the interior ceiling collapsed, flinging burned boards through the doorway. In seconds, flames flickered from the porch floor and around the Mexican's body, racing across to the straw hat. Silva snatched up a burning timber and smashed it through the pickup's driver's window. Flames filled the cab. "Teach you to screw with me, fucking hicks."

He jumped into the cruiser and fishtailed across the ruts. Back out on the highway Silva punched the accelerator, passing several cars, each pulling over to let the sheriff's cruiser pass. This late in the afternoon, no one wanted to get in the way of a deputy. Everyone was too busy going home, avoiding speeding tickets.

When he had caught his breath Silva made a quick call on his cell. "Hey, Allen. That shipment the crackers lost before they could deliver. I got it. You call the EME boys to come to pick it up, right now. Just bring money, like we set up." He whipped off the road and into the alley behind the substation along the railroad tracks. "The stuff's in the trunk of a sheriff's cruiser parked behind the Homosassa substation. Key's on the driver side floor." Silva laughed. "Yeah, in the cruiser. Nobody's the wiser; the deputy won't bother nobody, so don't you worry about him. You tell them to come get the stuff, right now, hear me! And quit whining. All you got to do is find out where the bitch and her new boy friend are hiding. Yeah, Kat. Who the hell you think I'm talking about? When you find them, call me. I'll take care of Bennett as soon as I get my hands on her. You just make the damn call."

He stopped the cruiser in the alley, pulled out his shirt tail and rubbed the key fob, steering wheel and door clean, any place he might have touched, not trusting his gloves completely. He scrubbed his pant leg stained with dog urine across the seat. Dog piss, weed traces in the trunk. Let their forensic techs sort that shit out.

Sirens wailed in the distance rolling toward a thin wisp of smoke that rose up from the swamp. Even if they identify Wellington's body, once they find traces of weed in the cruiser the cops would link Wellington to the pickup and Bennett. Just walk away and he was clear—after he found that conniving bitch and shut her up. Silva slid out of the cruiser and slammed the door shut with his elbow. He tucked his shirt in and strode down the alley. He stopped at the street, empty in the lazy afternoon sun. He strolled across the street to his Corvette, buttoning the middle button of his jacket over the rumpled tie and ripped shirt. His wrist throbbed where the dog's teeth had broken the skin. He hoped the damned dog had lived through the shooting and burned to a crisp.

Silva window shopped, admiring a large assortment of ceramic alligator ash trays until a black Expedition slowly cruised by, passengers unseen behind their dark tinted windows. The tag had a soccer ball with the letters 'EME' and the number 13, the Mexican Mafia gang bangers. The Expedition eased around the corner toward the railroad tracks behind the stores. Silva strolled past a temporary plywood sheet nailed over a store front and stood facing a cracked window, watching the street behind him in the reflection. A growing column of smoke rose in the distance and a fire truck roared past, siren wailing

Minutes later the Expedition nosed back out and down the street. It pulled over close to the curb to let a fire rescue ambulance race toward the smoke, horn blaring and lights flashing. Silva took the opportunity to walk out to the curb. The passenger window slid down and a dude wearing a Duke University cap dangled a stuffed beach bag that Silva grabbed. Silva walked over to the Corvette and looked around. Satisfied no one had noticed the exchange, he unzipped the bag. "Hot shit," he muttered. The bag was stuffed with bundles of old bills. He tossed the bag behind the Corvette's seats as the Expedition accelerated out of town. Skim some from the top, he'd still have enough left to pay his debts and get Darrell Russell off his back.

Silva slid across the Corvette's soft leather, wondering how the next part of his task would work out, when his cell rang. The number was from the Tampa area, no one he recognized. "Hello?" He smiled at the answer. The bitch, herself. "Honey. I was worried about you. Where in the world are you?" He patted the Kel-Tec in his hip pocket. He would have the .380 all ready for her.

CHAPTER 19

Something stunk. Grant opened his eyes, blinked away the crust. He sniffed, then realized the smell of marsh mud and gasoline oozed out from the spread he had wrapped around himself. He was the one who smelled so bad. Thank God, his nausea had cleared, along with the dizziness. Old blue was long gone, replaced by the familiar ache in his leg and a new throb in his arm. And a general weariness. But he was alert. Too alert. He could clearly hear every word Bennett whispered into her cell phone, even with her back turned.

"Bobby. Look. This has been a crazy couple of days. Believe me, I don't know what happened to the shipment. I didn't want to bother you, but I had to check out a new clinic for Chris. I know I needed to call you. But my old Mustang still doesn't run." She put an extra little plea in her voice. "Honey, can you come down and get me after work? I'll be at the clinic. About five? I'll be ever so grateful."

Grant closed his eyes. Another lie. All right. Let the jerk come get her, if she thinks she will be safe that way. Sounded like a frying pan, fire thing to him. He relaxed on the bed until he heard the toilet flush in the bathroom. He sat up on the side of the bed and let the dizzies rush through his head until all that was left was a blinding headache.

"What now?" he asked when Bennett appeared, tucking the tee shirt into the waistband of her jeans. "What lie now," he didn't ask.

Bennett walked over to the window and stared out. Grant followed her stare. In the distance a tall, twisting roller coaster car eked its way to the top and spiraled down with breathtaking acceleration. The window glass shimmered with a view of the African plains, or at least the lush Busch Gardens Africa version.

"Bobby's coming to pick me up." Her voice was quiet. Her tone had reverted to her soft Georgia twang. "The men. The ones shooting at us. That was the bald man's doing, not Bobby's. That's just not him." She looked at Grant. "I'll figure it out somehow. Anyway, I can't afford to walk away from my job. Bobby's tough, from New York, the Bronx," she said. "He'll protect me, not kill me."

What in the hell had Grant been doing for the last couple of days, playing ping pong? "And who will protect you from Silva?" He shook his head before she could reply. "None of my business. You do what you want. Money. Drugs. You guys have at it." Grant looked beyond Bennett, staring out at the south Florida Serengeti where long giraffe necks floated among the trees and flocks of sea gulls soared in great wheeling circles watching for tourist handouts. Shadows were getting long and his stomach felt empty. "What time is it?" Grant pushed off the bed and gimped his way toward the bathroom. He flexed his arm, lifted his elbow up to shoulder level, as far as the bandage and his pain tolerance would let it go.

"Damn it to hell!" He stopped in the middle of the room. "I need your help." He nodded toward his arm. "Pull this damn shirt off, would you?" Nurses, therapists, doctors; seems he was still too dependent on other people; more than he ever wanted. Now he needed a drug trafficker to help take off his shirt.

Bennett helped him out of the shirt, staring at his bruised, scarred and undernourished body. "You need to eat better." She lifted his bandaged arm and unwrapped the bandage, carefully peeling it away from the wound.

Grant nodded toward the bandage. "You've done this before?"

"I got a kid. Kids always need bandages, nose wiped, told to take a bath, go to bed. Like you. You stink. Get in the shower. I'll go downstairs and get you some new underwear, shorts and a button shirt, something to put on your boo-boo." She motioned toward the shower. "Now go."

"Juan's shoes are too tight. Get me some cheap boat shoes. Tens, if they have something like that."

"Just get in the damn shower. I know how to buy clothes, too."

Not until the hot water had swirled away the dried mud, salt and stink did the soreness ease up. He gingerly scrubbed at the fresh arm wound with a soapy rag, relieved that Chantico was right. The wound wasn't very deep, more of a scrape. Looking at the bruise on his forehead, Grant wondered if the Tamer had survived at all. He finally stepped out and wiped the towel across the mirror. Bloodshot eyes stared back out from over sunken cheeks, along with a—he had to stop and count—three day beard. Suddenly he was hungry, ravenous, despite Chantico's breakfast.

The door opened a crack. "Decent?" Bennett asked through the steam.

"Nope." He watched her in the cleared streak in the mirror as she placed underwear, a pair of plaid shorts and a new shirt on the toilet top. "Shoes?" he called out to her.

"Out here, waiting on you," she answered. "All the motel shop had were old man Bermuda shorts, tourist stuff. Lots of pockets, though, like you like. I wasn't sure of the waist, so I bought the ones with elastic. You can play shuffle board in them." A pause. "Come on, Uly. You slept through lunch, almost all afternoon. I've got to go pretty soon." Her impatience brought her tone up close to shrill.

A pack of sterile pads and antibiotic ointment lay on top of the clothes. A dab of ointment and Grant slapped the pad, already affixed with an adhesive backing, on his arm. He threaded his arms though the shirt sleeves, easing the cloth over the bandage. The floral and parrot motif was not what he would have selected. He had become accustomed to subtle tones, desert camouflage and dark tans mostly, or a faded blue, even pink, if it was a genuine fishing guide shirt. But around Busch Gardens, a Canadian in Florida disguise seemed appropriate, he supposed. He closed his eyes for a moment. So much thinking hurt his head.

Grant pulled the plastic wrapped packet of credit and identification cards he had retrieved at the fishing shack from his dirty shorts and stuffed it into a pocket of the new Bermudas. He stared at the mirror. The shirt was too big, drooped over his skinny frame, but the too-long sleeves covered the bandage, so he wasn't going to complain. Nobody around who would listen, anyway.

The old shorts slid to the floor with a clunk as he collected his dirty clothes. Grant retrieved the Kimber from the cargo shorts. The pistol had chunks of floatation foam and bits of indistinguishable crap all over it. Grant popped out the magazine and racked the receiver back, grimacing at the sandy grit that fell out onto the bath mat, along with one .45 caliber metal jacketed round. He could see one more copper jacketed bullet remaining in the magazine.

"Uly?"

"Couple more minutes." Sitting on the closed commode lid, Grant quickly field stripped the pistol and wiped it and the two rounds clean with a dry facecloth. Using the corner of the cloth he cleaned the sand from the groves and crevices, reassembled the pistol and worked the action a couple of times. He reloaded the rounds into the magazine, slammed it back in the pistol. Dry, no oil. Two rounds. About all that will cycle through before it seizes up. *Need to take care next ambush*, he thought, and slipped the pistol back into a back pocket with the packet. Hanging around with Bennett, another ambush seemed inevitable.

When Grant stepped out of the bathroom he found Bennett sitting on the edge of the bed with her back to him, shoulders hunched. He knew he didn't owe her anything, but felt like something needed to be said. "Kat. Before we go."

She scrubbed at her face, but didn't turn.

"I'm sorry Allen told you I could help. Maybe I could have with the computer part, the files, but not with this other drug business. Seems we got into this all wrong."

She nodded and pointed toward the television. Grant picked up the remote and turned up the volume. The announcer gave a dramatized version of the violent incidents at the substation and hazarded a theory that a missing wildlife ranger was somehow connected to the two suspects, according to unnamed sources. Then the mug shots. One of Grant in Army uniform right out of college with his shavetail crew cut; a separate photo of Bennett, looked like maybe a college photo with her hair all in some weird bouffant. No one would recognize them from those, especially with his scrubby beard and shaggy hair. And the stupid shirt. The image shifted to a swarm of investigators at the wildlife refuge dock. The view panned to a pair of divers rigging the remains of the Wildlife boat to a wrecker boom, water streaming out of holes in the bottom.

He sat down on the bed. "What?" Grant asked. He wondered if finally she was going to tell him the real truth. When she did turn to face him her eyes were puffy. So she did have regrets. Bit late for the ranger.

The television shifted to a gas station pump where a customer agonized over the horrendous rise in pump prices. The picture faded to a bar chart showing how gas prices had skyrocketed, the reporter's words, since the incident at Port Tampa, with the announcer in the background saying she had no expectation prices would decrease significantly in the near future.

Grant turned off the television. "When I get a chance, I'll call Allen, ask him to pass along what happened to Olsen, and that I'm going to get lost. Lots of boaters in the area. Olsen's body will show up sooner or later, unless a gator drags it home."

She looked at him with a mixture of horror and disgust.

"That's the way it is, Kat." He had seen worse, but she probably hadn't. Whatever, she had talked on the phone too long. They needed to get out of here. "Maybe this rocket attack thing will draw some of the heat away from us."

Bennett finally turned to him, lower lip clenched between her teeth in a full face grimace, but no tears. She walked over to the big mirror by the door and patted powder on her face from a compact.

"Come on, Kat, didn't you see them? The driver at the dock was the same guy who killed Eustis at the substation. Sooner or later either the shooters or whichever law enforcement agency takes charge of the investigation will run us down unless we hide, deep. You heard what Olsen said. Both of us are considered fugitives. Not a problem for me. I can disappear if I have to. You need to think about what you are going to do. You really think you're safe with this Silva guy? Especially with our names all across the news."

Bennett didn't answer. She continued in front of the mirror, now working a tube of lipstick.

He slipped his feet into the new boat shoes. "O. K. You do whatever the hell you want to." He stuffed his dirty clothes in the hotel laundry bag and looked around the room. Time to start covering his tracks. He walked around the room, detoured through the bathroom and cleaned off the obvious fingerprint surfaces. No need to make it easy. He would be long gone before anyone could get DNA samples analyzed, if the cops even considered them worth the expense.

"So. How about I drop you somewhere and we go our separate ways?"

When she finally looked away from the mirror, her eyes were clear, but flat, blank, as if she had made up her mind to do something very distasteful. "Drop me at the children's cancer clinic on the University of South Florida campus. Know where that is?"

Grant paused. This wasn't the right thing, cutting her loose. But he was tired of arguing. "Your call. Let's go." Using the dirty shirt as a glove he pulled the door shut and led the way out a back entrance to the Dodge pickup parked in the midst of a pack of shiny rental cars.

Bennett didn't speak on the short drive over to the university campus. When he stopped at the clinic entrance, she looked at him, her eyes clear, blue. "This didn't go right, did it? But I still don't think those men were after me. No one knew what I was doing, not Bobby, nobody else. I hadn't told anyone, except Allen. I'm sorry about Chantico's deputy, and Matt. But I don't know why anyone would want to kill me." She got out and leaned back in the open window. "You take care, now. Tell Chantico thanks for me. But you need to think. About who might be after you."

Grant glanced at the rear view mirror as he pulled away. Bennett stood at the curb beside a flower bed full of multicolored impatiens, hands in her pockets and shoulders slumped. *Enemies after him*? Bennett had sounded so sincere since they drove down from Chantico's house. Good liars always sound sincere. But he had looked straight into her eyes and, if he hadn't totally lost it, Bennett thought she was telling the truth. Grant's mind raced as he drove off. Was somebody from al Qaeda tracking him? Possible. If terrorists had attacked Port Tampa, who knew what else they had going on in South Florida. He had never detected even a hint they had detected his financial manipulations. Other enemies? None that he knew of.

A thought distracted him for a moment. His most recent domestic financial target was a dirty casino controller. He wondered if some alert casino manager had detected his skim of their skim of the casino take and tracked him down. Those guys would send big bald shooters, for damn sure.

In some twisted way, could some law enforcement agency be after him? Maybe, but they didn't send big bald shooters—did they?

Out of the corner of his eye he caught a glimpse of two men in a flashy Lexus sedan parked on the opposite side of the street. The passenger, a long haired blond, had some kind of black portable radio to his face. The driver stayed hidden behind a cap. Two men, swish new car with chrome spinner hub caps. Drug dealers? Or cops in a drug forfeit vehicle? Grant turned the corner and accelerated around the block as fast as he could maneuver the old Dodge.

He slowed when he spotted Bennett.

She had her big artificial smile plastered on for the driver of a red Corvette stopped at the side of the road. Bennett stepped to the curb and bent down to the low window. She reached out, took something from the man. Her smile disappeared and she jerked back, flung the object back into the Corvette, pivoted and started running, cutting the curve back toward Grant. Not to him. Eyes wide, she was just running. Long strides, the loose tail of the tee shirt flew behind her like a whitetail deer flushed from the swamp. The Corvette's tires smoked as the driver punched the gas, reversing after Bennett. Gunfire, a single shot from inside the Corvette, punctuated the tire squall. Bennett stumbled and ducked her face behind her arm as glass shards sprayed from the side window.

Grant slammed his foot down on the accelerator and swept around the curve, back end hopping. Dead in front of him the Corvette's brake lights flashed. Grant crunched low behind the steering wheel when the Corvette's driver twisted around and pointed a pistol at him. Grant kept his foot and the accelerator flat to the floor. Grant's head snapped forward when the Dodge's bumper slammed into the Corvette's rear deck.

The tail lights exploded as the Corvette flew ass-crooked up and over the curb. The Dodge's front bumper tore chunks of fiberglass from the Corvette's butt end.

Foot still to the floor, metal groaned and screeched as Grant rammed the Corvette across the impatiens and into a concrete planter. Grant slammed on the brake and jammed the pickup into reverse, transmission grinding, his gear shift quicker than his clutch foot. The passenger door flew open. Bennett dove across the seat until her head was in his lap.

"Get us the fuck out of here," she screamed.

Back in first gear Grant punched the accelerator and twisted the steering wheel. The Dodge crushed the left rear corner of the Corvette, spun it sideways and into a cabbage palm by the clinic's portico.

Across the street, the Lexus doors opened. The driver brought up a pistol, black finish dull in the sun.

Rear tires squalling, Grant swerved toward the Lexus and prayed the car's passengers weren't too quick on the trigger. Grant clipped the half open door as the driver dove back inside. Sheet metal clashed as the pickup fender slammed the car door shut. The blond popped up on the far side of the car, big eyes followed by a gun's muzzle. The truck fishtailed, hooking the rear bumper into the Lexus. Grant sawed at the wheel trying to regain control. In the mirror Grant saw a spinner roll lazily down the street in their wake. The mirror exploded as gunfire sounded from behind them.

Bennett pulled herself up and stared back at the wreckage. "Son of a bitch! Bobby set me up. Did you see what he did?" She grabbed Grant's shoulder as he slammed the Dodge over a curb and cut across a parking lot, between buildings and down an alley, ricocheting off a wall on one side and a fence on the other. "Where're we going?"

"Close by. Suitcase City. I know the layout there." Grant focused on the streets ahead, winding his way quickly off campus and into his old haunt. "What'd he do? Bobby, that Silva guy? Was that him in the Corvette?"

"Yeah. He handed me a little pistol, said I might need it. Like a fool, I didn't realize what he was doing, took the damn thing. Then he pointed his pistol at me with this look—I don't know—like he was going to kill me. I tossed the gun and ran. Bastard tried to shoot me. He set me up. Bastard set me up!" she repeated, clutching Grant's shirt with both hands as Grant whipped into an even narrower alley.

The Dodge fishtailed and slapped a garbage can with a rear fender. Grant fought to keep the truck under control as they slid out into the street. The steering had an odd feel to it, likely a tire going flat. Grant cruised past rows of low duplexes where chain link fences enclosed unkempt yards and staring faces, trying to remember the street names. Finally recognizing the Chinese restaurant on the corner, he turned into a seedy strip mall and let the truck roll to a stop. The engine coughed, then shut down. Steam hissed from the radiator, the smell of antifreeze heavy in the air. For the moment they were hidden from the street. A plumber's van shielded them from view on one side, a load of lawn turf on the other. He turned and leaned toward Bennett, good arm extended. "Pull off my shirt." He wiggled his shoulder and Bennett tugged at the sleeve. Grant grunted as Bennett pulled the flowered shirt over his head, blood seeping through the gauze pad on his arm. "Put this one on, over the white tee shirt. Hurry. We got to get away from Juan's Dodge without being recognized."

Bennett slipped the flowered shirt on over the white tee and buttoned up the front, her face devoid of emotion, in shock. Grant reached over the seat and pulled his old blue fishing shirt from the laundry bag. It still stunk of gasoline, algae laden swamp water and sweat, but was better than running around with his ribs showing.

Grant climbed out and took the laundry bag with him, but left the keys in the ignition as he slammed the door.

"Someone will steal Juan's truck," Bennett said, tucking the flowered shirt into her jeans over the tee shirt.

"Let them take it, if it'll run. Let's hope they do, get it away from here." Fumes floated up from the shirt as he struggled to slip it on. "Get your mind back into what's happening." Grant scanned the parking lot as he struggled with the shirt. "Anybody who takes the truck better be bullet proof. If the law spots it; Silva, cops, somebody will be all over this parking lot in an instant. Anybody in the truck, or even around, will be in trouble, but they might buy us some time."

Bennett reached back in the open window, grabbed a grimy ball cap off the dash and jammed it down on her head. The logo said she did landscaping work. She shivered, arms clasped across her chest, a lost look in her eyes.

Grant took her by the shoulders. "Come on, Kat. We don't want to be here when they find the truck. Follow behind me until we get away from the main streets, far enough back so it won't look like we're together." He tugged here toward the street.

She pulled back. Emotions finally washed over her face, first fear wrinkles followed by the clenched jaw muscles of anger.

Grant lightly shook her. "Think. This Silva, he's probably got the cops looking for us, along with homicide charges and an armed and dangerous tag. Take a deep breath, listen to me and we'll get out of this."

She put a hand over his as if to push it away. "You were hot to dump me when we left the hotel."

"Damn right. I still am. But I'm not leaving you here for your buddy Bobby to shoot down in the street. Now shut up and follow me, just not too damn close." Grant turned and started down the street. If she followed, he'd take care of her. If she didn't? So far as he was concerned, she was on her on.

He sure as hell wasn't going to let her lead anymore.

CHAPTER 20

Moving as fast as his leg and hip would let him, Grant cut through an alley and came out in the middle of the next block. He chanced a quick glance back. Bennett, a block behind, walked right by a parked police cruiser with her head down, arms clasped across her body. Apparently she had missed his detour through the alley, mind on something else. Separate was okay, keep the cop from connecting them. Grant picked up the pace, focusing on eliminating the limp his leg insisted on. He ignored the cruiser, took easy strides, let his joints and muscles and tendons loosen up and steered around the pot holes, all the while wishing he had a handful of pills in his pocket. Without breaking stride he dropped the laundry bag into a garbage bin by the curb. Next corner he looked back long enough to confirm Bennett still trailed him, the woman in the stupid flower shirt and filthy cap.

Grant slowed when he came to the next house and turned to walk along a side hedge of leafy bougainvillea. The bougainvillea tumbled over the side fence, creating a spiky barrier between the yards, mostly bare sand and weeds except where scattered pin oak leaves fell. No fancy lawns here in Suitcase City, named for the preponderance of transients, college kids and a swarm of immigrant workers who lived in the low duplexes and dingy apartment buildings. Grant stepped into a gap in the hedge and waited.

Behind Bennett, the police cruiser turned the corner, slowly rolling toward her. She strolled nonchalantly along the cracked sidewalk. Grant silently urged her to move faster, then stopped his attempts at telepathy. Her unobtrusive amble was the right thing, as long as the cop didn't stop her. She finally tugged her cap down tighter and glanced toward him.

Grant stepped deeper into the gap. The cruiser pulled up even with Bennett. She glanced over toward the cop and gave a little smile and turned toward Grant as if she had been going that way all along. When Bennett reached the break in the hedge, Grant pulled her into the opening.

"Damn, Uly. That hurts," she complained, as the bougainvillea spikes poked at her bare skin and snagged in the flowered shirt.

Grant squeezed through behind her as he glimpsed the white nose of the cruiser, stopped at the far corner. He squatted and pulled Bennett down beside him in the tangle of leaves and thorns.

"Are they coming after us?" she asked, a resigned look on her face, her makeup streaked by tear tracks.

"Don't think so. Cops patrol this area pretty heavy, anyway." He grinned at her flowered shirt over the tee. "Shame you had to cover the *Cinco de Mayo* bit. Fits in around here. Cop probably figured you for a hooker." She grinned her crooked grin back at him. Weak, but this time a real grin. Grant wiped the sweat away from his eyes and scanned the weed-filled yard and house.

"What are we doing here?"

"I lived here once. With your old buddy, Allen. We both went to South Florida, him on a Seminole Tribal grant. Momma and I didn't have squat for money, so I joined the National Guard when I was in high school. Florida Guard has a tuition free program. Only catch is you have to go through ROTC and accept a commission. But that's what I wanted, anyway, to get away, do something different."

"And all this time, I thought you were just a crooked fishing guide." Bennett pulled the cap down over her eyes and peeked back at the cruiser. "So you and Allen really are old friends."

"Friends? Not so much. Come on. If that cop spots us hiding here he'll be all over us."

He poked his head through the hedge. A glistening wrecker sat in the driveway. Polished chrome glittered in the midday sun. Volunteer red impatiens struggled to cover an old tire leaning against the wall. A jungle of flower pots hung around the small slab porch, spreading a profusion of color across the shaded entrance. Then Grant realized most of what he thought were yard weeds really were flowers, just planted in haphazard patterns.

Grant stood and trotted around the wrecker, pausing in the shadows for Bennett to catch up. He laced his fingers through Bennett's and pulled her behind him into the entranceway hidden behind a tangle of Hoya tentacles drooping down from hanging pots, dripping clusters of tiny pink blossoms. The cruiser U-turned at the corner. Between the two doors to the duplex units, exotic looking red, yellow and orange orchid blooms, some small, some gigantic, stared out from pots arranged along shelves between the corner posts and the wall. Grant grabbed onto the nearest post as a dizzy wave washed over him.

"Hey, you!"

Grant dropped Bennett's hand and slid his fingers deep into his cargo pocket and around his pistol. He slowly turned toward the open door, blinking the dizziness away. A heavyset black man filled the door, inches from Grant's face.

"What the hell you doing sneaking around in my yard?"

Grant tried to smile, gave it up and just shrugged. "Used to live here. I was taking my girl friend over to see the Picataras next door."

The police cruiser had completed the U-turn and started back toward them.

"Hey, buddy. Can we come in, look around a minute?" Grant asked.

The man glanced down at Grant's hand, still in his pocket, and took a step back. Grant shoved Bennett into the room and closed the door behind them.

"Cops after you, huh? Reckon they'll come in here shooting?"

Grant just shrugged his shoulders and glanced around. The front of the house was one big room, kitchen on one end, couch and TV on the other. An old Formica chrome dinette table and two chairs divided the kitchen from the living side. Surprisingly clean, considering the neighborhood. The old linoleum squares gleamed with fresh wax. No stack of dirty dishes, half empty peanut butter jars or empty take out boxes like when he had lived here as a student majoring in beer. No TV blaring. Maybe this guy didn't know they were killers on the run. He unwrapped his fingers from around the pistol and stuck his hand out. "My name's Uly Grant." He nodded toward Bennett. "She's Katrina Bennett."

The man took Grant's hand. "Ha. We ought to get together. I'm Randy Sherman. Sherman and Grant. If you play guitar we could go on the road." He laughed, a deep rumble and enveloped Grant's hand with a powerful, callused grip. "You live around here now?"

Grant shook his head as he retrieved his fingers, hoping they were all intact. "I shared this house with a buddy when I was in school, bunch of years ago. Bennett and I were just going through the yard to see Mama Picatara. Does she still live next door?"

"The Mexican family, nope. They moved out last year." Sherman stared at them, his gaze shifting from Grant to Bennett and back. "You really kill the deputy and the park ranger?"

So Sherman did watch TV.

"We were there, but sure as hell weren't the shooters." Grant leaned back against the counter, both hands in the open, trying to remember how to look friendly, not certain what showed on his face at the moment. He glanced at Bennett, willing her to help with the conversation. Instead, she walked over to the window. "Kat. Stay back from the window," he warned her.

"You're carrying, so am I in trouble here?" Sherman asked, glancing down at the lump in Grant's pocket.

So Sherman had eyes, too.

"No way, man," Grant reassured him. "A bunch of people are after us. Some of them have been shooting first, haven't even got around to asking questions. We're just trying to get out of town before someone kills us."

Bennett stepped back for the window. "Uly. Quit screwing around and figure out something in a hurry. The cruiser stopped outside and the cop is heading this way."

Sherman stared at them for a moment, smiled a toothy grin and said, "Come on, you guys." He motioned for them to follow him into the next room. He shoved a dresser to one side and pulled the metal grill from an oversized air vent opening. "Through here. Quick."

Bennett dropped down and squirmed through the opening. Grant knelt, grimacing at all the strains and pulls. He watched Bennett's hips wiggle over the metal frame. As her feet disappeared he dropped to the floor, slid flat and started through the opening.

"Get with it, man. He'll be at the door any minute," Sherman urged Grant with a shove against the soles of Grant's feet.

Grant squirmed and pulled himself through with his good arm, letting the left drag behind.

Behind him someone pounded on Sherman's front door. Bennett grabbed Grant's hand and pulled, jamming his shoulder against the side of the frame. A shove from behind and the old shirt ripped. Another shove and he was through and in the empty half of the duplex. By the time Bennett had helped Grant to his knees, the vent register was in place behind him. Muted sounds of the dresser scraping across the floor floated through the opening until the dresser covered the opening.

Bennett took off the cap and shook her hair free. She slowly combed her hair with her fingers. Tiny shards of glass tinkled to the worn linoleum floor. She grimaced. "Must be from Bobby's Corvette."

Grant, still on his hands and knees, let his head hang for a moment. He could feel the blood pounding through his temples.

"What now?" Bennett whispered as muted voices on the other side of the wall were followed by a slamming door. She slipped out of the parrot shirt and handed it to him to replace the shredded rag that had been Grant's favorite fishing shirt.

Grant pulled Bennett behind the kitchen island cabinet and slipped on the shirt. They both crouched as someone rattled the front door knob. "We wait," he whispered back, sliding down to a sitting position in the dark room. Grant sniffed. His imagination, or could he still smell Mamma Picataras's cooking, lots of chili peppers and onions, more Tabasco than his stomach really liked?

Bennett pressed against him, shivering. "Wait for what? The cops to break down the door? Sherman to decide to turn us in?" She eased up and peeked over the counter, then dropped back down.

"Oh my God. I saw Bobby looking in the window," she whispered. A flashlight beam washed over the wall behind them as Bennett buried her face in Grant's shirt. "Dear Lord. He's going to kill me."

Grant took her face in his hands and stared into her eyes. "He's not going to kill you. Take a deep breath." He could smell her sweat, her fear. "Is the cop with him?"

She nodded, her face bobbing in his hands. "I think I saw another man."

Grant pushed her down, eased the Kimber out of his pants pocket and slipped off the safety. "I can sure as hell shoot Silva. But I don't know who the other one is. Probably a friend of Silva's. Maybe one of the guys in the car we sideswiped back at the clinic. Shit! I can't just start a shootout with a bunch of cops." Grant sat on the cool floor, back against the counter. He flexed all the parts that hurt. *Damn near everything.* Bennett pressed close to him, still shivering like she was freezing. Strange. She felt so warm to him. Grant tried to think, to plan, but came up blank. "You got any ideas, where to go, what to do?" he whispered.

"Not back home. Bobby knows where I live. He even has a key." Her voice was muffled as she whispered into his shirt.

Grant had no answer that made any sense.

Why are you flat on your butt, Grant thought. What's next? Get away? Make a plan. Find a ride, get back home and move on to parts unknown. How? The back door stood directly in front of them. Grant wondered who was on the other side.

Window glass crashed. A thunk vibrated against the other side of the island cabinet.

His ear drums must be healing. He actually heard the butterfly handle click open, the clatter of the grenade rolling across the linoleum, the thump as it bounced off the front side of the cabinet.

Grant screwed his eyes shut and pulled Bennett across his chest, contorting until one hand covered his eyes. With his free hand he covered his left ear as a flash seared its way through his eyelids. He blinked away the dancing globes of light, let the thunderous boom wash through his head. He scrambled to his knees and grabbed Bennett, all rolled up into a ball behind the cabinet. He dragged her toward the wall somewhere behind them. One second, two seconds passed. These jerks weren't regular SWAT. Amateurs, no sense how to clear a room. The stun grenade had slowed them as much as it had him. Still half blind, he slid his hand over the wall until he was sure he was at the back door.

He flopped on his back and kicked the door hard with both feet. A sharp pain shot up his leg as the frame splintered and the door flew open. He shoved Bennett out and crawled after her. He rolled across a concrete stoop and into sand, spinning back to face the door as he pulled his pistol, blinking in the bright sun until he could distinguish the outline of the doorway. He fired, high, through the door and into the ceiling to slow whoever was in there, hoping some uniform didn't come bursting out, gun blazing.

Grant scrambled to his feet and grabbed Bennett's arm. She stumbled, mouth working, probably saying something very important to him, cap askew. Grant looked around as he pushed her toward the hedge. No one hot on their heels with MP-5 submachine guns. Even Eustis would have someone covering the back. The thought made him stop, turn.

The blond from the Lexus stood by the corner of the house, working a finger in one ear. A pistol dangled from his other hand. The blond looked up, stared at Grant, mouth open as he yelled back over his shoulder and raised his pistol.

Grant fired first, intentionally high. He couldn't take a chance that maybe these were good cops, sucked into this by Silva. *Shit.* For all he really knew, Silva was the good guy, and Bennett was the dealer. Grant's .45 caliber full metal jacket slug splattered the yellow stucco, ricocheting into the neighborhood. The blond dove out of sight behind the corner of the house. Grant glanced at his Kimber. The slide was locked back, empty. Bennett jerked at his sleeve, insistent. It suddenly occurred to Grant that running was a damn sight smarter than just standing stupid with an empty pistol. He spun, shoved her through the hedge and followed, ignoring the thorns tearing at his arms.

As he burst through the hedge the chromed wrecker slid to a stop, blocking their way. The door flew open and Randy Sherman grinned out at them. The wrecker was already moving by the time Grant scrambled in behind Bennett, speeding away from the duplex. Sirens sounded, close. Grant ducked when a pair of cruisers and an unmarked Crown Vic roared down the street. He slid down to huddle in the floor with Bennett, the two of them curled up together in a tangle of arms and legs; Bennett talking, mouth going ninety miles an hour. Grant still couldn't hear her. A painful buzz of white noise bounced between Grant's ears. For once he was glad he couldn't hear. He was too tired to argue. As he watched her lips moving he saw a trace of blood seeping from her nose. *Wounded in action.* He pulled her face to his and kissed her nose. Her arms slowly slid around his neck and her lips finally stopped moving, pressed against his.

CHAPTER 21

"Where you folks want to go?"

Grant was surprised. What he thought was white noise left by the grenade blast was rather the rumble of the big wrecker. He could actually hear Sherman's question. When he answered his own voice seemed louder in his head than in his ears. He looked down, surprised to see the Kimber still in his hand. He reached around Bennett, her head resting on his shoulder, popped the magazine and let the receiver go forward. "Anybody following?"

Sherman glanced at the two big side mirrors before he answered. "Not that I can tell. When I went to the door, two dudes pulled up behind the cruiser in a battered 'vet. Looked like what was left of a Corvette that had been in a hell of an wreck. They had guns out, Glocks. I figured them for undercover cops, especially when one of them, coat and tie type, started giving orders to the uniform that pulled up behind them."

"The Corvette was no accident, and the shooters weren't either." Grant climbed up onto the bench seat. He slapped the magazine against his leg, reseating it back in the pistol, and tucked the gun into a pocket. Bennett stayed on the floor, leaning against his legs, working her jaw like she was trying to clear air pressure from her ears. "First off, get us away from Suitcase City."

"Right." Sherman gunned the wrecker through an intersection. "We're almost out of Tampa, but I probably shouldn't drive too far. I'm way, way behind on my fines, and if a road patrol spots me they'll probably pull me over." He paused for a moment to scan the cross street before he busted through another red light. "I'm heading toward my yard, just a couple of more miles."

Grant cringed as Sherman cruised through a stop sign, his armor of invincibility the rotating yellow lights that reflected back from the shop windows along the streets.

Bennett ran her hand over a long scar running along the top of Grant's leg. "Randy."

Sherman reached down, flipped off the yellow lights and kept driving.

"Louder," Grant said to Bennett. "We're all half deaf."

Louder this time, she said, "Randy. Won't the cops connect you to what happened back there?"

Sherman glanced down and shrugged. "I was real polite, and they told me to leave the house. This one slick-looking shit seemed real agitated, said there were some dangerous suspects in the area. The uniform even helped me back my truck out. I went around the corner and waited, just to see what would happen. Then this son of a bitching explosion blew glass and crap all over the place. I got to tell you, I damn near messed my pants. Probably blew all my orchids to high heaven. Couple of rounds popped, then you came flying out." Sherman slowed as they came up to a red light, flipped his yellow lights back on and gunned the wrecker through the intersection. "Are you folks like real secret agents or something?" He glanced down at Bennett, then over to Grant. "You two are the good guys, right? Hope you didn't shoot any of those cops. They ain't all bad, you know."

"Not today," Grant assured him. "Whoever the hell was chasing us threw a stun grenade, a flash bang. Unless they set the place on fire, everything should be okay. I'm pretty sure I didn't shoot anybody."

Sherman looked down at Bennett leaning against Grant's knees, and flipped off the yellow lights again, his big grin back on his face.

"What?" Bennett asked.

"Who dresses you? I thought secret agents were suave. Grant's shorts look like my grandpa's."

Grant laughed. That would have to change. He pointed toward a convenience store with a neon ATM sign in the window. "Pull over into that empty parking lot, away from any cameras. I'll get us a little bankroll." He opened up a pack of gum from the console.

"Uly, no." Bennett grabbed his arm. "Don't do anything stupid."

He shook his head. "Legally, Kat. I'll get it legally, at least as legal as anything I do." He grabbed a pair of sunglasses from the dash and slipped the landscaper's cap from Bennett's head to his own. Grant stuffed several sticks of gum into his mouth, chewed them into a wad and worked pieces between his cheeks and his teeth. He grinned down at Bennett. The sunglasses sat cockeyed on his nose, the frame all twisted and a serious scratch on one of the lenses.

Bennett shook her head. "Ugh. Anybody who knows you wouldn't admit it now."

Grant nodded, afraid the gum would spurt out if he tried to talk. He slipped out of the truck. On his way across the parking lot he unwrapped the packet retrieved from the fishing shack. *Who would Morris want me to be tonight,* he wondered? Somebody smarter than the jerk that let a panicked woman get him into all this shit. He selected a debit card and fed it to the ATM. Two hundred dollars, the cards limit, whirred out of the slot, and he bought a box of donuts, sunglasses and a Tampa Lightning cap from the clerk, chewing on the gum and just nodding in response to the clerk's wary greeting. The clerk seemed edgy. Grant glanced at his reflection in the window. Who wouldn't? Stupid shirt, dumb shorts, broken sunglasses on a cloudy afternoon; poster child for a meth head. He glanced back at the ATM and considered using one of the other cards. Suddenly he felt the weight of the empty pistol pulling at his shorts, and hoped the clerk didn't come around the counter with a shotgun. He smiled at the clerk through the chewing gum. Sweat began to run down his sides. Grant wondered if he smelled as bad as he looked.

Pushing my luck here, he thought, and strolled out of the store. He crossed the street and walked down the street to a credit union ATM. On the way he spit out the gum and flipped the landscaping cap and sunglasses into a trash can. He pulled the new Lightning cap down over his forehead. Donut in mouth and new glasses perched on his nose, he selected another ATM card from the thin stack. Smiling behind the donut for the camera, his old friend Louis Anderson enticed five hundred from the credit union's machine. Or at least Anderson was the name embossed on the ATM card.

Five minutes later Sherman turned the wrecker into the entrance to a parking lot half full of cars and trucks scattered behind a chain link fence. He set the emergency brake and pointed at the sign by the curb, *Randy's Reckers*. "How you like it? My own shop. Trouble is, I got a couple traffic tickets too many, and the durn Sheriff's office stopped calling me for pickups."

Grant opened the wrecker door and slid down to the pavement in front of an old concrete block building that maybe had once been an early Forties filling station, with the remains of the two pump island and portico still recognizable. While Sherman unlocked the gate to the lot and then the office door, Grant helped Bennett unwind from the floorboard, and they both followed Sherman into the office, Bennett balancing the donut box on one hand, waitress style. The interior matched the outside architecturally, but everything was freshly painted. Even the linoleum squares shined with a wax polish. No surprise, a row of potted African violets lined a broad window sill, prolific purple blooms bursting from the lush green leaves.

Sherman, vehicle retriever and horticulturalist, draped his cap over the top of a skinny lattice that still waited for an indistinguishable bit of greenery in a pot to climb up.

Nice, but not what Grant was looking for. "Got a computer with Internet access?" he asked Sherman. Traffic rumbled by outside, rattling the glass in the old windows. He shivered as an air conditioner rumbled in the background and a draft of cool air brushed across the back of his neck.

"Sure." Sherman unlocked a desk drawer, pulled out a laptop and plugged it into a power strip. "Anything you leave out in the open, somebody relieves you. I keep all the good stuff stashed." He admired another donut from the box and took a huge bite.

"Clothes?" Bennett reminded them. "I saw a Wal-Mart down the street."

Grant peeled away several twenties and gave them to her, along with the new cap. "Go down and buy us another change of clothes and pick up some burgers or something. Cargo pants for me this time, lots of pockets." He took Bennett's hand, gently twisted her arm and checked out the scrapes and scabs on her elbow and forearm. "Don't forget a first aid kit." He tugged the cap down over her eyes. "And stay out of trouble."

"Maybe if you stay here. With you along, I never know what's next." Bennett pushed the cap up. No grin in return this time. She didn't seem to find any humor in their situation.

What happened to the kiss, the arms around my neck? Grant wondered. But business first. "I'm going to fix up Randy. After that we'll let him get back home before the cops think he's part of the gang."

Sherman leaned on the desk as Bennett took the money and walked out. "What you going to do for me?" he asked, sugar dribbling from his chin.

"First, clear your driving record. Which jurisdiction is the problem?"

"Most of my tickets are up here in Pasco County. Got a deputy buddy that keeps writing me up."

"Randy, you shouldn't break the law. Driving like a bat—" Grant stopped. Who the hell was he giving advice to?

"Yeah, right," Sherman said. "I take advantage of the flashers sometimes. You gotta remember, I haven't shot or blown anything up, lately."

"Me, neither." Grant replied. "Nothing that counts." He let the computer boot and logged through a series of servers. To anyone less skilled than FBI techs or cousin Allen at the FDLE Computer Crime Center, his next login would appear to be from a Pasco deputy's patrol car. He sat back a minute, sorting through the access codes in his mind. He tried one. He grimaced at the flashing red screen that resulted. He logged off and routed back through a different set of servers and tried again, this time with what he hoped was the correct password. A black screen filled with colored lines popped up. He nodded with satisfaction and clicked though a series of screens. A short sequence of key entries, and Grant accessed the Sixth Judicial Circuit of Florida Clerk of Court's database as the IT administrator, and from there the traffic violations outstanding lists. Grant paused, resting his tender left arm for a moment.

"Cool," muttered Sherman. He tapped a second donut, letting the powdered sugar float down to coat a violet on the desk.

"What's your driver's license number?"

Sherman fished out a billfold attached to a chain, and spieled off a series of numbers.

Grant entered the data and a file flashed on the screen.

"Holy shit." Sherman sat down on a rolling stool and stared over Grant's shoulder.

Grant scrolled the mouse, highlighting a list of violations. "Randy. What the hell is this all about? Equipment citations, parking tickets. Only one really good speeding ticket in the bunch." He hit another key. "Oh, I see." He looked at Sherman. "Those were last year's. Here's this year's." Grant shook his head as he ran down the list and cleared each offense, waiting until a "paid in full" response notation appeared opposite each charge. "I wouldn't bug the county about towing contracts for a while. Let this clear the next audit cycle, end of the month, I think. But all your tickets have been paid." He stopped a moment and leaned closer to the screen, reading down the entries. "What's up? Every one of the moving violation tickets was written by the same officer, half of the cheap ones."

Sherman grinned. "Officer Mallory. Tom and I dated the same lady friend for a while." The grin turned into a laugh. "He lost. They got married. He gets even by writing me up whenever he sees my truck."

They both looked up as Bennett came through the door. She dropped a McDonald's bag on the counter and disappeared into the restroom with a couple of Wal-Mart bags.

Sherman picked up a violet from the desk and turned the pot under the incandescent light. Apparently not satisfied, he twisted it another ninety degrees, apparently not satisfied. "Neat girlfriend you got, Uly."

Grant shook his head, grinned back at Sherman, feeling his grin was as fake as Bennett's as he tried to sort their relationship in his mind. "Not my girlfriend, least not the regular sort. We just kind of got thrown together."

Sherman turned to look at him, started to say something, then stopped.

"The kiss?" Grant asked.

Sherman nodded.

Grant shrugged. "Just happened. Didn't mean anything."

Did it?

"Oh. Right." Sherman carefully sighted down the line of pots and tapped one back in alignment. "Yep. I figured that. Secret agent stuff. You two just passing messages in your chewing gum."

Grant laughed, shaking his head. Sherman was good company. The first laughs he'd had since he met Bennett.

Grant backed out of the citation files and closed the computer. "Now I need another favor. One of the cars outside. Any out there you think are pretty much abandoned? And runs?" He handed Sherman half of what was left of the crisp new ATM money. "Gas money. For a vehicle no one will be looking for the next few days."

Sherman counted the cash. "I don't think anything on the lot is worth this much." He tucked the money in a pocket and thought a moment. "Most's been so long abandoned I need to drag them down to the salvage yard." He walked over to a board of cup hooks, stared at the dangling keys for a moment and took one down. He handed the key to Grant and pointed out the window. "How about that? Runs good. I got no title or registration for it, but if you get stopped, paper would probably be the least of your worries. Tag is still valid, so it shouldn't draw attention on its own." Sherman pulled a burger and drink from the bag. "That work for you?"

Grant nodded. "That will do just fine." He rolled the desk chair back and looked up at Sherman. "What's up, Randy. Is there a reward notice out? You got this Mallory waiting around the corner for us? I was in the Army too long to believe in the tooth fairy."

Sherman took a monster bite from the burger. Finally swallowing, he said, "Me, too." He wiped his fingers, pulled open a drawer and shuffled though some papers, finally digging out a couple of snapshots and handed them to Grant. "The Army part, not the tooth fairy. I still believe in the tooth fairy." The first photo showed a slimmer Sherman in the old forest pattern camouflage fatigues perched on top of a huge armored vehicle. From the background, Grant guessed the shot probably was snapped in the Grafenwöhr Training Area outside of Nuremburg.

"Looks like an M88, a tank retriever." Grant shuffled to the next photo, Sherman behind a .50 caliber machinegun, this time in full tactical gear.

"Nope, the new model, the M2 Hercules. I had one of the first ones in Iraq, took it over from Germany." He pointed at the second photo. "Ended up with the 3rd Infantry, assigned to the Band of Brothers, the 101st Airborne Division task force. When I saw on TV that you had a run-in with a car bomb over there, somehow I couldn't figure you for a bad guy."

The next photo showed a convoy running down a highway in the middle of a desert. "I kind of got used to driving fast. Hard habit to break. I keep waiting for somebody to light me up, IED or sniper. Today was the closest I've come since I got back." He shook his head and put the pictures back in the drawer with a wry grin. "When that grenade went off, *hooah*, got to tell you, sounded all too damn much like an RPG."

"*Hooah*!" Grant echoed the old Army version of "damn right."

They both looked up when Bennett came out of the restroom. She pirouetted, showing off a knee length skirt, loafers and a pale rose blouse to an appreciative whistle from Sherman. But what got Grant's attention was her sheared hair, now black, dark as Chantico's. Grant inhaled as she walked by, the smile on her face accented with a touch of lipstick. The scents; deodorant, powder, all those exotic smells that always left Grant wondering, filled the room. He touched the tip of his tongue to his lips, remembering her soft kiss, and quickly looked down at the blank computer screen. He shook the thought out of his mind. Focus. He needed to focus on getting them away from Silva, somewhere safe. He looked back up to see Bennett watching him. "Where're my new clothes? And your old clothes?" he asked.

"I left your clothes in the restroom. I stuffed my old clothes in the trash, with all the bottles from the dye kit. Sorry about the mess, Randy. I tried to clean up, but I couldn't find anything to bleach away all the stains."

Randy grinned at her. "I'll have the cleaning lady take care of it tomorrow. Mrs. Cortez will think I have a new girlfriend." He winked at Grant. "Maybe a little jealousy will help her clean better."

Grant got up. "I'll be back in a minute." Inside the restroom he swabbed at the grime and sweat with a damp paper towel and smeared the deodorant Bennett had left sitting on top of the clothes under his arms. He grimaced at himself in the mirror at the effort; the bullet wound to his arm more of an itch, his leg the same big ache. The bruise on his forehead was beginning to yellow. Grant stopped for a moment, staring in the mirror. *His leg*. He chuckled silently to himself. He hadn't even thought about his leg since the flash bang. The bandage on his arm seemed reasonably clean, no blood showing, even after the tumble from the duplex. The cut on his hand looked inflamed, but that he'd have to live with. Grant glanced in the remaining bag and confirmed it was men's clothes. He traded the Bermudas for khaki cargo pants. A fishing shirt replaced the parrot shirt; more his style, cream white, outfitted with all the little Velcro tabs and pockets for fishing gear. One last look in the mirror. He still needed a shave. Behind the heavy stubble, his cheek bones showed more than he ever remembered, now almost POW gaunt.

He stopped, hand on the old style brass knob. Voices in the office. He put his ear to the thin door panel. He couldn't make out any of the words. When he tried to squat, the old pain slammed into him. That leg he had forgotten about. He grabbed the sink to keep from falling, went to his knees and looked through the old style keyhole.

In the office Bennett was smiling, talking to someone else out of sight. She sat in Sherman's lap, her arm around the big man's neck. The source of the other voice came into view. Polished high boots, riding pants. Grant suddenly realized he was looking at the bottom half of a mounted patrolman, either a horse or motorcycle. His guess was motorcycle. Then the rest came into view, a squat, tough looking cop, helmet under his arm.

Bennett kissed Sherman on the cheek. Grant squinted. Was that a blush on the back of Sherman's black neck? The cop said something and then turned toward the door. Bennett stayed on Sherman's lap for a long couple of minutes, her head slowly turning as she apparently watched the cop leave. She kissed Sherman again on the cheek and turned to the restroom. "Come on out, peeping tom."

Grant pulled himself up, trying to ignore the reminder that he wasn't a man who really kissed, or did much of anything romantically anymore. He opened the door just enough to get a good look around the office. "Mallory?" Grant asked.

"The one and only. I think finding Bennett in my lap kinda disappointed Tom. I suppose that son of a bitch still wants me to take his wife off his hands." Sherman put a big arm around Bennett's shoulders and hugged her. "This must have been a bummer for him when he saw a beautiful gal like you smooching on me."

Bennett grinned at Grant from Sherman's lap, running her hand over Sherman's burr haircut.

"Kat, you want to stay here with Randy, or go figure out what's going on?" Grant's harsh tone startled his own ears.

Bennett frowned at him, shook her head, stood and straightened her skirt. "Let's go. Randy's been too good of a friend. He doesn't need us around to bring him trouble."

Sherman looked at Grant, his eyebrows raised in a hint of a question, then gave a tiny shrug to his shoulders as if he didn't want to get in the middle of a lovers' quarrel, especially when one of the lovers was carrying.

Grant held out his hand to Sherman. "Thanks, Randy. If we get stopped I'll tell them I'm just test driving the flatbed; considering it for my boat business."

"You got a boat business?"

"Sure." Grant shrugged. "I'll take you fishing one day. Thanks, buddy."

Sherman stabbed the last donut with a thick finger and waved it at Grant. "You guys watch your back."

Outside, Bennett stopped and turned back to Grant as the last bit of sun slanted across the sky. "O. K. Where are we going now?" Her jaw was set, not even a crooked grin.

No more kisses for him. He limped over to a rusty and scarred flatbed farm truck, rubbing his stiff leg. "Someplace Silva won't find you. Someplace I can find some answers. Get in and drive."

CHAPTER 22

A broken seat bracket poked her in the behind, irritating the scabs on her butt. The pedals were too far away and the cuts and scrapes from the last couple of days itched. But none of her aches and pains bothered her as much as the man slouched against the far door. She thought Allen Wilson would connect her with some small time criminal who could help her siphon away some ill gotten gains. Now she was supposed to drive a derelict flatbed truck loaded with a stack of empty fruit boxes, sitting beside an enigma, running for her life from Bobby Silva and God knows who else. She pushed her doubts aside and tried to focus her energies on what was real; who was important.

Chris. All the trouble was for him, so she would work it all out, somehow.

She tossed the bag of clothes behind the seat. "Was this the best you and Randy could come up with?" She turned the ignition key. A cough and the big truck engine grumbled to life, exhaust rumbling like a hot rod. "I can't drive this monster." She stared at the unfamiliar dash.

Grant waved his bandaged arm at her. "I could if I have to, but I sure as the devil don't want to." He pointed at the steering column. "Automatic transmission, power everything. It's just a little longer than you're used to, that's all."

"About ten feet longer." She sniffed, wrinkled her nose. Randy's wrecker had smelled like a precision machine. Juan's pickup had smelled of jalapeños. The flatbed just stunk like a worn out old truck. She expected a mouse to pop out of the cracked seat cover any minute. She wished she were back in her old Mustang, that she had never gotten involved with Bobby Silva and his schemes or Uly Grant and his deceptions. But it was too late to whine now. Bennett yanked the bench seat forward, adjusted the rear view mirror.

"Just drive it, Kat. Couple of blocks, you'll feel like you belong in it."

"Right." Bennett twisted the big side mirror and stared back at the long flatbed behind her. "All we need is a load of produce in those boxes." The wind teased her damp hair; cool blowing through the open windows as she came up to speed.

Grant shrugged. "This was the best Sherman had on the lot, at least that ran." He pointed at the intersection ahead. "Take a left up here at the light. Keep it slow and easy. I need to take a little side trip before we go home."

Bennett almost felt comfortable driving the big truck when Grant pointed again after only a few miles.

"See the big building ahead on the right. Turn into the parking lot and park in the back. I've got some business to take care of."

She hunched closer to the windshield; stared at the confusion of lights. "Where?"

"The driveway just ahead. Turn into the parking lot where that pickup is parked." Grant pointed out a big black truck that glistened with raindrops, dark tinted windows hiding the interior and sporting a University of South Florida Bull decal on the back window. Wrong school, but Bennett suddenly wondered how much her makeover had changed her. Would an old Florida State acquaintance recognize her? She shivered at the memory of Silva's face, his pistol pointed at her. She glanced over at Grant. Was she better off with or without this guy? Was he saving her ass or getting her in deeper?

She swung the flatbed in a big circle and eased into a slot close to the building, positioned so she could pull straight out. "What now?" She rolled up her window as Grant opened his door.

He looked back. "You sit tight till I get back."

"No way. You're not leaving me, not again, not until this is sorted out." She shook her head, wondered what in the world she was doing. She pushed the door handle down. Stuck. She pounded her shoulder against the door frame until it popped free.

He limped around to the front of the truck. "Each our separate ways. That was the way we both wanted it. Least that's what I thought," he said.

She hopped out on the running board, rubbing her shoulder, and on to the ground. This would be her opportunity to leave his ass right here, but the words spilled out anyway "Well, we're not thinking that way now. You go in; I go in." She stared at the neon sign as it flickered to life, spelling out *Best Rest Retirement Center* in buzzing green and red neon tubes. "What's here anyway?"

"Ease up, Kat. I need to do this." Grant turned toward the entrance, massaging his thigh as he walked. "But keep your mouth shut; I don't want us to be recognized."

She glanced at her reflection in the oversized door mirror. "New clothes, new hair. You think I enjoyed chopping off my hair, dying it with drugstore crap out of a box? Lord, it'll all fall out in a few days.

Look at us. You look like a meth junkie with that scrubby beard. We're different people from the photos in the paper."

If she was going to turn what had happened into any gain for Chris, she still had to get this skinny man to follow up on the computer files. Sherman had told her about Grant clearing his tickets while she was at the store, enough to convince her Grant could do what Wilson had promised with the files. She still had to get him to help. How? He had saved her skin, and seen her naked, but didn't seem to care one way or the other. Other than the kiss. She still wondered how that had happened. She slammed the truck door and caught up as he pushed the entrance door open and limped over to the receptionist's desk.

Bennett followed him in, fighting to suppress the shudder that tried to work its way down her spine. The long hallways, the subdued fluorescent lighting and, most of all, the odors. Too much hospital, but with that bit of dead and dying nursing home ambiance that she never tried to analyze too carefully, not really wanting to know the answers. She had seen and smelled the inside of too many medical facilities in recent years. And this one was sort of the end of the road. Not what she wanted to think about. She glanced over at Grant. A jaw muscle worked under the beard stubble. As she watched out of the corner of her eye, he took a deep breath and let it out slowly. Apparently he wasn't too fond of hospitals either.

The receptionist at the desk smiled up at Grant after a quick appraising glance Bennett's way. "Good evening, sir. How may I help you?"

"My name is Howell. I'm here to see my aunt, Mrs. Grant." He looked over at Bennett, obviously trying to send her a message with the expression on his face. "This is Mrs. Howell."

Oh. That message. Bennett returned the receptionist's smile, but gave Grant a different kind of look as she clasped her hands behind her back. Grant should have warned her. She could have bought a band at Wal-Mart. What wife walked around without a ring? Stupid men.

The receptionist opened a notebook and ran her pudgy finger down a list, paused, and smiled up at Grant. "May I see some identification, please."

Bennett watched the receptionist's eyes as Grant pulled a card from his hip pocket and signed the register. A slight turn of her head and Bennett realized the receptionist was looking at his left hand. The one without a wedding band.

"You and Mrs. Howell go right on down. I'm sure Mrs. Grant will be pleased to see you." The lady's double chins waddled as she talked. "She always seems a bit better after visitors. She was delighted to see that young man just a while ago. Don't forget, now. It's getting on a little late, so please don't stay too long. Your auntie needs to be asleep by eight."

Grant stared at the register for a moment, scanning the names. "Thank you," he finally replied. He took her hand in his and led her down the hall.

"Mister and Mrs. Howell?" Bennett gripped his fingers as hard as she could, trying to put as much pain in the squeeze as she could muster.

Grant didn't respond as he led her past an orderly pushing a sleeping man in a wheel chair to a room midway down the long hallway. He stepped inside the room, pulled his fingers free from her grip. He closed the door behind them and turned toward a woman propped up in a lounge chair by a collection of bright flower-print pillows.

The woman's wrinkled face lit with a thin smile when she saw Grant. "Oh, Charlie, I'm so glad you came." The old lady took Grant's hand. "And who is this nice young lady with you? Couldn't Chantico come over for supper? My, she's always so busy, taking care of that little girl of hers. Did I tell you I met her child? I'm sorry; I can't seem to remember the little one's name."

Grant kissed her on the cheek. "Are you feeling good today? Who came to see you this afternoon?"

"Lordy, Charlie. You know, I just don't know who that was. But he was awfully nice, one of Uly's cousins, I think, asking if I knew where Uly was. Sweet boy brought me some flowers. See them over in that pretty little vase."

Who is Charlie? Bennett wondered. She stood back as the woman chattered on, Grant's hand clasped in her thin fingers. The old lady appeared frail but healthy in her flower print bathrobe and pink slippers. Bennett had to close her eyes for a moment as the reek of disinfectants and dying people washed over her; made her pray she could keep Chris out of a place like this, reminded her why she had gotten in so much trouble.

"Would you look at that!"

The woman's loud exclamation brought Bennett's attention back to the room.

"Why that's you, Charlie," the old lady exclaimed, pointing over Grant's shoulder. "What in the world are you doing on the television, and in a bathrobe, for goodness sake?"

A new picture of Grant filled the screen of the muted TV on the wall behind them. This one captured him, even more haggard than he was now, in a bathrobe and on crutches. The caption below mentioned Walter Reed Medical Center. Grant picked up the remote and turned up the sound when the picture shifted to a reporter standing in front of a tangle of police tape and barricades. The reporter's coiffured blond head craned up to interview a tall man with his arm in a sling standing in front of a massive stone building, a helicopter circling in the distance.

Grant leaned toward the screen and muttered, "Oh, crap," then fell silent as the reporter continued.

"I understand you were here at Port Tampa City Library when the attack occurred night before last. Tell us, what exactly did you see, and were you seriously injured?" The camera angle shifted to an overhead helicopter shot of the Port Tampa tank farm. Twisted wreckage smoldered as firemen poked through the debris. Boats with flashing lights cruised around the water side. The land side looked cordoned off by a mix of police and military.

"National Guard troops," whispered Grant.

"I spotted the rockets trails inbound, coming across Old Tampa Bay, right at dusk. Thank goodness, the missiles missed the tanker. It did hit the tank farm, and they lost some fuel. Fortunately, the tanks are isolated and bermed up so the fire didn't spread to other tanks or the community." The witness lifted his arm in the sling and shook his head. "Dumb fracture. I broke it myself, diving under a table."

"And you believe the damage was caused by terrorist weapons, not just some kind of out of control fireworks?"

"I witnessed several rocket attacks around Baghdad. Same kind of smoke trail, speed, same kind of explosion. I'm sure the ATF investigators will have a more technical finding, but my experience tells me I saw *Katyushas* or a similar variant rocket. Not very accurate, not a very big warhead. If I am right, and one had hit the tanker or one of the larger storage tanks, it would have been a different story. No one was hurt, a miracle in itself."

The screen divided into a live shot of the interview and a different photo of Grant, the old Grant, a burr cut soldier in the his desert camouflage uniform, sleeves rolled up over muscled arms. The reporter smiled into the camera. "One account links the attack with the murders in Homosassa involving an Army National Guard soldier on convalescent leave, a Lieutenant Grant. I understand you know the Lieutenant. What do you think happened?"

Bennett watched the Grant standing in front of her, not the one on the TV. His fishing guide tan seemed to drain from his face, replaced by a pallor made even greener by the room's fluorescent lights.

The man on TV shook his head. "I seriously doubt Lieutenant Grant had anything to do with the Port Tampa incident. In fact, the short time I knew him in Iraq, he was a dedicated soldier like most of our service men and women; saw a lot of combat. He's from right around here somewhere. That's how I got to know him. We talked about fishing, getting back home."

"Come on, Lester, don't blow it for me," Grant muttered.

"Thank you, Mister Scanlon." The reporter turned back to the camera. "That was Master Chief Petty Officer Lester Scanlon, retired Coastguardsman, now a civilian employee at Central Command on MacDill Air Force Base just a few miles from where we are now in the Port Tampa community on old Tampa Bay. Yesterday in Homosassa, Ulysses Grant, a missing fishing guide who was severely wounded in Iraq, allegedly was involved in a drug related series of murders about the same time unknown attackers fired what Master Chief Scanlon believes were terrorist rockets. The apparent target was a fully loaded fuel tanker docked at Port Tampa close to MacDill. These incidents happened barely fifty miles apart on the same night. One deputy involved in the drug investigation is dead and another missing, both suspected to be linked to this man—" The photo of Grant popped back up on the split screen. "—after a series of attacks at a Citrus County sheriff substation, all in broad daylight. Were these events really coincidence? At least one authority doesn't think so, but we'll have to see what the federal authorities conclude. This is Francine Garcia, reporting from Port Tampa, the scene where experts are attempting to determine if a series of explosions were an accident or, as suggested by our witness, a deliberate terrorist rocket attack. Now, back to our weather center and the latest on the tropical storm moving into the Gulf of Mexico." The scene cut back to a TV weather map.

Grant clicked off the TV. "Mom, I got to go, take my friend home before it gets too late, okay?" He smoothed out the old lady's sleeve. "Don't let any of that TV upset you. Remember how stupid those soaps are."

Bennett pushed her hair back from her face, brushing back the still damp strands that barely reached her ears. Had she heard correctly? Grant's aunt is really his mother, and he's really Charlie Howell. Had she put her life, her Chris's life, in this charlatan's hands?

Uly's or Charlie's aunt or mother, whoever she was, spoke after a moment. "That reporter and that other man, the tall, thin one, talked about a Ulysses Grant. They don't mean my Uly, do they? He's a good boy, hardly ever gets in trouble. And for goodness sake, he's way too young to be in the Army."

"Don't you worry. I—Uly's doing just fine. Now we've got to go. Do you need anything?"

"I'm fine, Charlie. You take this girl home safe and get back to your fishing. Why, goodness, I think I'll just rest awhile." She closed her eyes, and instantly it seemed the old lady was asleep.

This was too much. Bennett didn't wait for Grant. A catalog of questions swirled through her mind as she strode past the receptionist and out the door, away from the hospital smells and into the steamy afternoon air.

She opened the truck door and climbed up on the running board as Grant limped across the parking lot, a distant look on his face. *What kind of fool has he taken me for?* Behind the neon sign, crimson streaks radiated toward them from the setting sun. She thought she had figured out the mishmash of gunmen and threats. Simple—she had believed—Silva was trying to kill her, and had enlisted some goons to help. But all the rockets and terrorist threats were way beyond anything she knew about. Did Grant? From the look on Grant's face, he and the Coastguardsman knew each other. How, she wondered.

Fleeting pink clouds raced in from the west, covering the remains of the sun. The sky turned dark as she waited for her enigma. The lacy clouds turned gray, then heavy black, threatening a new storm. A wind gust rocked the truck and a single heavy raindrop battered the windshield. Grant broke into a gimpy run as the rain pelted down harder. He pulled himself up into the cab, slammed the door and wiped the rain from his eyebrows.

She rotated the key one click in the ignition, enough to start the wipers. She turned toward Grant. It was already too dark to make out his expression. "You got some explaining to do, Uly. Which is it? Aunt? Mother? What was that TV reporter talking about? What friends got murdered? Were they talking about friends I don't know, or that deputy, or Matt, or someone else, for God's sake?"

Grant stared past the stuttering wipers into the darkness. "First, drive. Back to Homosassa."

She shook her head. "Answers, *Charlie*, or whoever the hell you are. No more lies. I want some answers." *What was she thinking, driving around a mystery man who killed as easy as he did, without a tremor?*

"Allen Wilson. That was the name in the receptionist book. The one who came to see my mother this afternoon, the same Allen who sent you to see me. Now you tell me that was a coincidence. You give *me* some answers."

Bennett glanced over at Grant. He was staring at her.

"Another of one of your damn phone calls?" he asked before she could answer.

Bennett shook her head. *Why was she on the defensive?* "Not me, Uly. I swear."

Grant cleared his throat. "My name is Uly Grant, like I told you the first time. Charlie Howell was my father. The woman back there is my mother; she just gets a little mixed up sometimes. Now start the truck. I want to know why people are trying to kill us, even more than you do. I want to find out why Allen came to see my mother, for the first time ever, so far as I know. I got things to tell you, and you damn well better have things to tell me. First you drive. Let me think a minute."

Bennett pumped the gas and turned the key until the truck started with a roar. She wheeled out onto a river of black asphalt that glistened in the dim headlight beams. "Where to?" She steered between the white lines as rain beat down on the windshield.

"Chantico's."

"Why there?" Bennett glanced over at the side mirror. A blurred image sparkled in the neon lights and turned their way, but fell back as she eased down on the gas.

"Allen had a thing for Chantico. Maybe it's something to do with the shooting. Christ Almighty, I don't know. Ever since you showed up at the *Rum Runner*, everything I know has turned crazy." Grant waved at the stop sign coming up. "Turn left at the highway. Maybe Chantico can help us contact that deputy, Wellington. We need somebody to back us. Your friends haven't been a lot of help so far. Let's try mine"

He had a point, so she drove. The sky and road both pitch black in the rain; shifting winds whipped at the truck trying to tear the steering wheel from her hands. Bennett concentrated her driving on staying between the white lines, but her mind raced, getting nowhere. She was stuck on the run with Grant. The only friend who had offered to help was dead. Everyone else she called had blown her off.

"Slow down."

Ahead their lights flashed over a sign marked with a heron, announcing they were coming to Chassahowitzka. Oh, Lord. Grant had led her back into the swamps. Behind them a pair of lights blinded her for a moment in the rear view mirror. Someone had come up quick behind them.

"Turn left. The Madero house is down this way, down toward the Gulf." He turned to look out the back window. "Have those lights been following us all the way?"

Bennett shook her head. "I don't know. I've been trying to keep this beast on the road."

Bennett let up on the accelerator as she rounded a tight curve. Ahead, flashing red and blue lights reflected through the rain drenched trees. She bent over the steering wheel, squinting to see through the pulsing multi-colored lights marking an ambulance that pulled out in a sweeping turn toward them.

"Oh, my God," Grant whispered.

A hauler followed the ambulance. As the hauler turned in front of them, their headlights swept across a burned out pickup chained down in the back.

"That's my damned truck."

Bennett let up on the gas. The trailing headlights came up close behind them, then braked and turned in the driveway. She rolled down her rain-streaked side window and glanced out the window.

"Keep going. Easy, just keep going," Grant whispered in her ear, face close as he leaned over and stared through the window. A sheriff's deputy stood in the middle of the driveway in a yellow rain slicker. His broad brimmed campaign hat protected his head from the driving rain, face lit by a flare burning between the ruts. His green and white car blocked the entrance to the driveway leading through the trees back to the old house. A highway patrol cruiser seemed poised to pull out after them.

Bennett took a deep breath and coughed, the heavy smell of smoke filling her sinuses. The steering wheel jerked in her hands as the right front tire dropped off the edge of the pavement and caught in the mud. She clutched the wheel tighter and eased the flatbed back onto the pavement.

"Pay attention, damn it," Grant hissed at her. "They'll think you're drunk and pull us over." He turned and stared out the back window, fingers drumming on the dash.

Bennett shook her head and focused on the white lines. "What happened?"

"I don't know. Patrol car pulled out, coming this way. Just keep it slow and straight."

Bennett took a deep breath when the highway patrol car raced around them and accelerated away into the thickening mix of fog and smoke, emergency lights still flashing.

When they eased around the next curve, Grant said, "There's a small bridge coming up. Just before we get to it a road leads to the left, no more than a pair of ruts. Fishermen use it to launch boats down the creek. Turn when you get there."

Bennett leaned even closer to the windshield and the squawking wiper blades, squinting into the blackness. She slowed as she picked out tiny reflectors glistening from the bridge abutments. On the left all she could see was a low screen of weeds. "Where is the road? Good Lord. I don't see any road. I'll drive into the river."

"Turn, now, damn it," Grant barked.

She twisted the wheel, and they bounced off the pavement and through a dark tunnel formed by a line of oaks. Spanish moss dragged across the windshield and tangled in the wipers, smearing the glass even more. Bennett snapped off the wipers.

"Turn off your lights. Don't touch the brakes. Foot off the gas. Just let it roll."

Bennett slammed the light switch off and let the truck coast, straining her ears for the sound of water. When the truck finally rolled to a stop she switched off the ignition and turned toward Grant, a dark blob by the window. The smell of crushed dog fennel filled the cab. "You give orders like you expect people to obey, Lieutenant."

Grant twisted in the seat and stared out the back window. "No use in giving orders if no one pays attention. You're doing better." He continued looking back toward the highway. "I don't think anyone saw us turn. You hear anything?"

Bennett cocked her head. "Nope. Just the river and frogs. And rain." Big drops drummed down on the unlined roof and splashed through the open window.

"Crank it back up. No lights," Grant muttered. "Just ease forward. Pay attention and I'll guide you."

Right, she thought. Look where he has taken me so far. To a bunch of killings, the middle of a shootout. No, make that two. This guy is full of lies, deceptions, with an aunt who is his mother who calls him Charlie. Wilson had said Grant was into heavy stuff. And now he is dragging me into it. She thought again about the kiss. *Rather it had been Flash*, she thought.

But then again, Silva had tried to kill her, twice in one day. She had wanted to deny her old boyfriend was behind the shootings, but the look on Silva's face when he pointed his pistol at her had been enough. Now, of all people, Grant was the closest person she had to a friend. Or he was playing her for an even bigger fool.

She yanked the wheel, jerking the truck across the ruts in frustration. *Damn him*! Was this all staged to suck her in? Some scheme Wilson and Grant had cooked up?

CHAPTER 23

Grant stared into the darkness, retracing the track in his mind, the good times when he and Juan and Eustis and Roberto wasted their summers fishing and wandering the rivers and swamps in search of excitement. Well, he finally had found it. Grant's head nearly slammed into the windshield as Bennett bounced across the slick ruts leading to the boat ramp. All that time in Iraq, boredom shattered by bullets cracking around his head, he had never really felt fear. Concern for the men and women he led; yes. Apprehension that he had not planned correctly, or that he had not asked the right question in an interrogation, or that he had misinterpreted an answer; yes. But never the gut wrenching dread that tore at him now. The back side of the Madero family's old clapboard house should be directly ahead, tin roof reflecting the dim star light that occasionally broke through the shifting clouds. But all Grant could see was rain, swaying long leaf pines and scattered cabbage palms. "Stop!" Grant barked, and braced himself against the dash as Bennett stomped down on the brakes.

After the truck had slithered to a stop she turned off the engine. "Where are we?" Bennett asked.

"Close to the boat ramp. Chantico's house should be just up the path." Grant kept his voice low and peered through the dark screen of trees.

Bennett squinted though the smeared glass. "Oh, I remember. This is where Juan brought us in the boat, up behind Chantico's house; I can see the big tree with the rope swing by the boat landing. But I don't see the house. Where's the house?"

Grant suddenly felt woozy, like he had taken a fistful of OxyContin all at one time. Where was the house? Where was Chantico? And Juan? And the child?

He sat in the musty cab, listening to the rain drumming on the roof, first loud, then soft as the wind shifted, imitating that familiar *Take Five* opening drum sequence. Trees twisted in the gusts like brushes on the cymbals. Distant lightning flicked out over the Gulf, thunder rumbling in moments later, bass drum accents. A spring in the worn seat poked his butt, a painful reminder he was wasting time. No questions to be answered sitting here listening to the music throbbing through his head.

GULF WINDS

Grant got out of the truck and walked though the dripping grass, ignoring the rain pelting his head and running down the back of his neck. A smoldering smell clogged his throat. He stopped and took a shallow breath, fighting back the tears that suddenly filled his eyes. A bolt of lightning crashed down into the swamp, outlining a row of— something—that led back to the trees. Behind him a door slammed. Across the clearing, emergency lights flickering through the trees marked the patrol car at the highway. Bennett called out from the truck. Her feet whispered across the wet grass as she hurried up the path to stop by his shoulder.

Was his hearing getting better, or his imagination?

"Uly. What happened here?" Bennett's voice took on a shrill tone, grating on his ears. "I told you I want some answers. Now tell me what is going on."

"I don't know, damn it." Without looking back he waved her away and took another step forward. He stopped as something crunched underfoot, something more than wet grass, something black as death. Another stroke of lightning flashed across the clouds. A soft glow illuminated the clearing, followed by a drawn out growl of thunder. He stumbled and wiped at his eyes, trying to make sense of the scene.

When he was a boy, his momma had taken him up to Midway, Georgia, to visit relatives. Sunday, after church, they had walked a graveyard littered with crumbled statues and tilted headstones. She had told him they had an ancestor buried there, her grandfather Marion Grant. They looked, but never found the headstone.

This looked all too much the same, a place of death. He squinted through the rain and walked into the middle of his confusion. What first appeared to be statues were crumbled brick piles, foundations that once held the cracker house's hundred-year-old heartwood pine frame off the sandy ground. Charred timbers lay in a tumble by the sooty bricks, surrounded by sodden piles of black and silvery ash. He stumbled over a twisted bed frame. Gradually he recognized the warped sheets of roofing tin, finally the remains of the concrete block steps. A toilet perched up on a burned section of flooring as if waiting for someone to use it.

"Chantico?" No answer, just the drum of the rain on the warped tin. "Juan?" He strode across the clearing, ignoring the twinge that shot up his leg as he quartered the ruins. The smell of smoldering wood rasped harsh in his throat. Drooping streamers of yellow crime scene tape marked where the house had sat for all the years he could remember, from when he and Vicente had chased snakes and hid from their mothers underneath the old cracker house. He randomly pulled at the charred timbers, some still warm where tin roofing protected the ashes from the rain. For an instant the flashing lights reflecting from the trees silhouetted a figure, then nothing. *Ghosts.* Ghosts that would haunt him the rest of his miserable life.

Grant searched the darkness for a sign of anything good.

Bennett had followed him and stood, hands on her hips. A flash of lightening revealed a defiant look on her face. Rain plastered the new blouse to her skin. Glistening goblets of water dripped from the hem of her skirt.

She yelled at him over a gust of rain that rocked her back on her heels. "Don't look at me for sympathy, you lying son of a bitch. You've been playing me. All these phony names, whining for sympathy, pretending to save me from the boogeyman. Did you stage this crap with Allen, just so you two can cut me out, get Bobby to think I took his weed?"

Pain took over his body; aches from his leg, throbbing from his arm, a pounding behind his eyes. He stepped toward her, stumbled over a partially burned timber and fell to his knees. He felt the crusty ash of the timbers under his hands and struggled back to his feet until they were nose to nose. He shook his head, flinging water into her face. "Whatever happened, Kat, I never lied to you. Never took anything from you. I'm not the cause of your problems." His voice rose. "But I did try to help you. And see what happened." His voice was almost a scream. "My friends are gone, maybe dead. Eustis, Chantico, Vicente's baby." He squeezed his eyes together, shutting out the pain. He spun away from Bennett's accusations. "Angelica," he screamed into the storm.

He staggered through the grass and knelt down by a rut where the rainwater had puddled. He scooped a double handful of cold rainwater, splashed it on his face and scrubbed at the soot on his hands, struggling with his rage. He finally stood and shook the water from his eyes, turned to Bennett and let go.

"God damn you to hell. I told you the truth, and now I want it from you. When I finally figure out what happened here, I'm going to start settling scores." He pointed a dripping finger at Bennett. "And if you caused any of this, I'll bury you in the swamp with your ranger."

Bennett stared at him for a moment, mouth open. Before she could answer she jumped back as a mottled form darted though the grass and disappeared. Grant twisted, trying to follow the movement. He yanked at his pistol, deep in a cargo pocket, until the seam ripped and the pistol came free. *Fool*! He jammed the empty pistol back in his pocket.

He slowly backed toward the path to the truck, scanning the edges of the clearing.

"Here, boy," he heard Bennett whisper behind his back.

Grant turned to see Bennett silhouetted in a sudden flash of distant lightning, kneeling in the wet grass. She held Flash's head against her. The greyhound's body shivered, tail curled up under his rear end.

Grant squatted and ran his hands over the dog's skinny frame.

Flash jerked, rolled his eyes back when Grant's hand slid down his side. He buried his muzzle under Bennett's arm.

"Easy, boy," Grant whispered. His fingers traced an ugly wound, hot and damp, across Flash's ribs. Grant gathered the dog in his arms and carried him back down the slick path to the truck. Without a word Bennett opened the truck door, and Grant laid Flash across the bench seat. Bennett slid in and cradled Flash's head in her lap, gently pulling his lanky body over her legs to give Grant room to ease behind the steering wheel. Bennett reached out for the door handle, but before she could pull it shut Flash struggled out of her lap, slithered down to the ground and limped out into the darkness.

Bennett hopped out of the truck and followed Flash through the rain. "Flash," she called softly. "Flash. Come back, boy."

Grant put his head down on the steering wheel, exhausted. Tired of killing, tired of running, just tired. He jerked his head up at a sharp whistle from the darkness.

"Come help," Bennett called out from the shadows in the edge of the tree line, a sharp edge to her voice. "Now."

The tone of her call broke Grant from his stupor. He followed Bennett's trail through the wet grass until the track gave out in a soggy bed of leaves under a cluster of old oaks. Grant shivered as cold rain drops ran down his neck. The rain coalesced, gathering up the fine drizzle until huge drops pattered from the trees to the ground, his shoulders, his head. Grant spun at the sound of palmetto fronds rustling under the trees behind him. He shook the water from his brow, staring into the dark. "Where are you?"

"Uly, don't be silly. We're over here where we are supposed to be." Bennett stepped out of the tangled undergrowth with a child in her arms. "Look, Angelica. Uncle Uly came to take us some place nice and warm, someplace to get something scrumptious to eat, and dry clothes and everything."

"Can Flash come, too?" a small voice asked, muffled against Bennett's neck. "He's got a boo-boo on his side that makes him cry."

"Of course, honey. I'll carry you, and Uly will take care of Flash." Bennett waited until Grant had gathered Flash up again and led the way to the truck. Smeared raindrops glistened on seats that smelled of charcoal and dog as Grant waited for Bennett to slide the little girl across the wide bench set. "How can we do this?" he asked.

"Lay Flash across my lap and we'll let Angelica put poor old Flash's head on her lap." She turned to Angelica. "That way we can all say warm, can't we, honey," Bennett whispered, settling the little girl in the middle of the bench seat.

Grant held Flash as gently as he could, feeling the dog's heart beat, an irregular throb against his fingers. "Chantico?" he asked Bennett as he settled Flash across Bennett's soaked skirt.

Bennett shook her head. "I didn't see her anywhere. You look around while we get warm." She reached across and turned on the ignition key and fumbled with the levers on the dash until the fan blew the damp air across them. Grant leaned across Bennett and the kid and the dog, this time twisting the key until the engine started.

"Go see if you can find her," Bennett told him. She hugged Angelica closer. "We'll wait right here, won't we, honey."

Grant tromped around the clearing, his cries of "Chantico. Juan," smothered by the rumbling thunder. He ignored the red and blue sparkles reflecting off the wet trees, at this point more interested in finding his friends than caring about the deputy out front. *Nothing.* The rain seemed to ease up a bit, but still no one answered. He crisscrossed the ruins one final time, stopped and turned full circle, his head filled with the smell of charcoal and something else he didn't want to put a tag to. The sparkle of lightning reached across the sky, followed by a sharp crack.

He trotted down the path to the river and stood by the truck door, shaking his head. "Can't find anybody else." He looked across at the little girl snugged up under Bennett's arm. "Angelica. Do you know where Chantico is?"

She brushed her hair back from her eyes, every bit a tiny Madero. "We played a game. Then a man came and started yelling, so Chantico let me climb out the window all by myself and go hide. I got under a big bush and then Flash found me, and he was all hurt. I stayed there with Flash. And then, the lightning came and everything boomed, and a big fire, so we stayed under the bush waiting for Momma Chantico. When all the trucks came I got 'fraid."

"What kind of trucks, honey?" asked Bennett. "A truck like this?"

"Noooo, a big red fire truck like I saw at the parade one time, and lots of cars with lots of lights, all different colors. Momma Chantico told me not to go with strangers. I waited for her to come back, but I never saw her."

Water dripped down through the trees, pattered on the truck roof, a soft tympani across the roof and counter point to the rumble of the muffler and the cymbal clangs of thunder. Grant shivered as the rain trickled down the back of his neck. He climbed behind the steering wheel and closed his eyes against the warm air from the heater.

He had lost everything.

Everyone.

"Uly?"

He jerked his eyes open and looked across at Bennett.

"Can you take us somewhere safe?"

"Me, too?" chimed in Angelica.

Foolish. He still had much more he could lose. "Sure." He turned the truck in a big circle, slowly followed the ruts, and turned left across the bridge, flicking on the lights when he hit the wet pavement. "I'll take my princesses to the fortress where no one can get them."

"Is your head straight?" Bennett asked. "Do I need to drive?"

"I'm straight." He understood her question. "No pills. I hurt. But I'm in control." He took a deep breath. "I'm finally in control," he repeated.

CHAPTER 24

Grant wound through Homosassa Springs and turned on to the highway headed toward Crystal River and home. He wanted to lower the window and hang his head out in the damp air to clear the cloying smell of death from his head, but Angelica's tiny frame shivering beside him reminded him of other priorities. He followed a twisting maze of slick roads toward the Gulf until his headlights flashed across the sign for the tiny community of Ozello, perched out on the edge of the Gulf of Mexico. His mind raced, wondering, worrying about Chantico and Juan. Grant drove through the relentless rain, staring down the headlight beams until he spotted the rural mailbox embedded in a coquina post. He slowed and turned, let the truck roll past the mailbox to a stop beside a gate post. He flicked off the truck lights and peered through the rain. Trees leaves fluttered, glittering, reflecting a pair of headlights far behind them, still on the far side of the last bridge.

They were home.

Not the boat yard and the *Rum Runner*—his real home, where Angelica and Bennett, even Flash, would be safe. Grant rolled down the window and stretched his aching arm out until his fingers found the rain slick cover and, below it, an access pad set in the side of the post. He punched in the code and a dim light came on at the side of the house as the garage door slowly opened. Grant drove inside and turned off the engine. "Home, kids. Sit tight for a minute until I can check things out." He slid out of the truck and scanned the thick line of undergrowth and trees between the house and the road. A single pair of headlights flickered through the trees, heading toward the causeway and the abandonded restaurant where the island ended and Crystal Bay began. Grant punched the button to close the garage door and walked to the back of the garage as the overhead door rattled shut. On the back wall, the alarm indicator LED glowed a steady green. No messages indicating anyone had disturbed the house since he had secured it, before he had met Bennett and her schemes, before the killings. He punched the security code in the keypad and opened the door leading into the utility room.

"Uly?"

He reached inside, flicked on the house lights and then turned back to the truck. The truck door flew open and Flash slowly clambered out.

"Uly. I can't get out of this damn truck carrying Angelica. Come help us."

Grant gathered Angelica in his arms, dripping wet and smelling of leaf rot and charred timbers, and led the way inside. At the doorway Flash eased inside, limped to his crate in the corner of the utility room and plopped down with a groan. Grant kept going through the kitchen and across the hall until he reached the guest bedroom. When he laid Angelica on the patterned quilt covering the guest bed her eyes slowly opened. Big, brown, Madero eyes blinked, stared up at him.

"Is Momma Chantico going to put me to bed? I gotta go to the bathroom first."

Bennett eased Grant aside. "I'll take care of you tonight, sweetie." She looked over at Grant. "Got a couple of clean tee shirts around? Dry panties?" She wrinkled her nose at him and giggled with Angelica. "Actually, if you do have any panties around, I don't want them. I brought my own, some extra stuff I bought, if you'll get them out of the truck. The bag behind the seat, girly stuff." She and Angelica both grinned at him. "Hurry up. I want to get out of this wet skirt."

Grant glanced down at the mud and grass speckled skirt, her scratched shins. How in the hell could she joke after today? Lord, he would never figure out women, big or little. Grant left them and went to his bedroom, pondering. As far as he knew, he didn't have anything in the house for a woman or girl to wear. He rummaged through his dresser until he came up with an oversized tee shirt with a big flower design—a joke gift—and one of his old soft, faded Army PT shirts. Next he retrieved Bennett's bag from the truck, still smelling all girly, powder and makeup like from his mom's stuff. Something new for this house. When he returned to the hall he heard a murmur of voices inside the bathroom. He left the tees and the bag outside the closed bathroom door.

Back in the kitchen, he opened the refrigerator and stared at the row of Ybor Gold bottles. Not the time. Instead he started the coffee maker, Army strong.

What to do now? Something right, for a change. Something positive, something that doesn't get anyone killed.

He walked back to his bedroom, stripped out of his damp clothes and slipped on a dry pair of pants and a black tee shirt. He slid aside a back panel in the closet and blinked when a bright incandescent fixture flickered, then came on full, along with the whir of a small exhaust fan. Too tired to do a decent cleaning job, he laid the empty Kimber on the workbench for later. In the wall rack the twelve gauge Maverick pump shotgun's short barrel glistened in the blue-green light alongside Grandpa's worn Garand rifle and Colt .45 automatic. Faint scents of Hoppes bore cleaner and Militec gun lubricant lingered in the air. He stared at the empty slot in the rack for a moment. The Tamer .410 was probably at the bottom of the river. And had likely saved his life when the pistol round smashed it against his forehead.

He shook his head. Focus on the here and now. As a start, he hadn't done a very good job of checking the perimeter. Morris had always taught him that too many distractions were just an excuse. Look past them to what was important.

So focus. Focus on securing the area, after that he could take the time to find out what the hell was really going on. He picked up a remote; put it back down. No cameras. He needed to get some air to clear his head, walk the battlefield.

Grant slipped the Maverick from the rack. He cycled the slide and a shell flipped out on to the bench, confirming the shotgun was loaded. After the Tamer fiasco on the island, he wasn't leaving details like that to chance. He fed the ejected round back in the magazine as he slipped through the front rooms. Except where the light spilled from the kitchen and bedroom into the hallway, the house was dark as a tomb. At the front door he stopped, still, and listened for a moment. Soft voices came from the bathroom. A light flashed into the hall as the door opened.

Bennett reached a bare arm and shoulder out and picked up the clothes, then closed the door.

Grant let the image of her freckled skin rest in his mind for a moment. Back to reality, he shivered, cool air wafting over his damp hair, and slipped on to the front porch. He dropped to a crouch behind a thorny bougainvillea vine entwined around the balustrade. He pushed aside a section of vine, a sharp thorn raking the scab from the inflamed cut on his hand. He scanned the matted screen of trees and undergrowth between the house and the road. The aroma of the blooming bougainvillea floated heavy in the sultry air, almost suffocating on the small porch, but welcomed after the stench of the burned house. He slid his throbbing hand along the shotgun, wiping away beads of moisture where the humidity condensed on the cold steel.

He stepped from the porch and across the grassy mound resulting from the many dump truck loads of fill Juan had brought in to raise the septic tank, topped by a layer of turf, up from sea level. The rain had finally stopped, but the breeze floating in from the nearby Gulf was tacky, heavy with moisture. A faint twinkle marked a star trying to shine through the cloud cover as his night vision returned. To the north, the Crystal River Nuclear Power Facility security lights reflected against the high clouds. He let his eyes float over the shadows, all too aware that his beat up ears wouldn't be much help.

Nothing seemed out of the ordinary. Bushes that were supposed to wave in the light breeze bowed and twisted in sync with the Australian pines screening the house from the road. He walked on around the house, a slow circuit past the rotten pilings leading down to the abandoned boat ramp. He stopped, stared at a ghostly shape in the water. He eased the shotgun to his shoulder, safety off, finger poised over the trigger until he recognized the outline of his flats boat with the crumpled poling platform. Closer, he saw the battered Yamaha had been replaced with an ancient Johnson two stroke. Juan must have brought it over. A dark line stretched from the boat back toward the house. Grant dropped to a knee. An extension cord led to a battery charger, LEDs winking as the boat rocked. Grant silently thanked Juan and stared into the darkness, wondering where Juan was now, what had happened at Chantico's house. Grant continued around to the front yard, searching for answers in the dark.

The crickets suddenly went silent. Or were his ears failing him again? Lightning flashed over the Gulf, followed by a roll of thunder. His ears worked, to a degree. Something, someone was out there. *Or in his imagination.*

Grant stepped up onto the front porch and settled into a rocking chair. He brushed away a section of bougainvillea and propped his tired feet on the top of the balustrade. Lightening crashed inland, the thunder exploding around him. Like the day Vicente died.

Sheet lightning out over the Gulf startled Grant back from Iraq to the present. He twitched in the rocker, sweat running down his face despite the cool breeze, his throbbing hand a reminder of the flames flickering up from the floor boards, singeing his arms as he fought to pull Madero free.

The image of Wilson crouched on the road below Snyder, rifle pointed directly at Grant, blood streaming down his face, had been permanently imprinted in his mind.

The scene replayed like an action video in Grant's mind. *Every night since.*

His next memories were of hospitals: Landstuhl and Walter Reed, tired orderlies, exhausted doctors and pain. Where he had discovered how to escape in a pill bottle. He shook his head, exchanging the memories for a blinding headache. Had something moved, there, in the trees? Only ghosts. If Vicente, Chantico and Juan would only come strolling out, laughing, another nightmare at his expense. Lord, if only.

CHAPTER 25

Allen Wilson walked along the shoulder of the road, searching for any sign of the flatbed he had followed from the retirement center. Where in the hell had the truck disappeared? He turned into the trees at the edge of an unkempt driveway, almost falling when his foot slipped on a rotten branch. He grabbed a vine draped across two trees. "Shit." A thorn stabbed his palm, drawing blood. He stopped when another limb crunched under his feet. Not to worry about sound. Grant was deaf as a post from the car bomb, enough that a snapping twig wasn't a problem.

The real problem was Uly Grant. Wilson had first thought sending Bennett to his cousin would put a little money in everybody's pocket, mostly his. This stupid attempt to double cross Bennett had more than backfired; it had gotten Silva on his ass and given Wilson another reason to even the score with Grant.

Sometimes it bothered Wilson that he was going against family. But Grant was only a second cousin. He'd never even acknowledged his Seminole heritage, a bastard disgrace to the family, closer to his Mexican neighbors than his Seminole cousins. He got that from his momma. Woman had no pride. She worked for a bunch of Mexicans, for Christ's sake, preferring to manage a bait store for the Maderos rather than taking Tribal money.

Wilson peered at a house set back behind the pines, out of sight from the road. No sign of the truck, Bennett or Grant. A light flickered inside, and then everything went dark again. Enough walking around with the spiders and snakes. When they were kids Eustis Rankin had kidded him that he was the Indian; he should lead them through the swamps. But Wilson had always preferred big trucks and fancy apartments to the swamp his ancestors roamed through, evading Andrew Jackson's soldiers until the soldiers finally gave up and let the Seminole tribes be. He eased back through the trees and trampled through the damp dog fennels to the road. The sooner he was back in Tampa, the happier he would be. All he had to do was cover his ass with Silva. Grant and Bennett had made their own bed. He climbed in, gunned the big truck around and headed toward civilization.

GULF WINDS

Why did the road, everything look so familiar? The light at the entrance to Madero Builders and then the bridges connecting the small island with the rest of Florida flashed by when it struck him. The dark house behind the trees perched on the edge of the water exactly where the old bait shop sat for years—where Grant had lived as a kid. *He had the son of a bitch!*

Wilson dialed his cell phone. Silva's voice answered, a recording the voice mail program beeped, and Wilson left his message.

"I came up to Homosassa after work, trying to straighten this deal out, man. Beetle called, said they got the stuff and fixed you up, so that should be squared away. But I wanted to let you know what Bennett was up to. I followed her up to a speck in the road called Ozello over on the Gulf outside of Crystal River. Looks like she's holed up in a house on one of the islands. Call me back and I'll give you the details." He added just before the dial tone buzzed in his ear, "—and I've got a tag number for you, at least a partial."

Wilson wondered if this was a mistake, letting Silva catch up with Bennett. When she met him for lunch, what he had thought was the prelude to a real date, the dumb bitch had confided in him, said she was planning to intercept Silva's weed and asked for his help with the computer records. He had played it cool, acted unconcerned, even uninterested, not wanting to get involved, and passed her off to Grant. From the beginning he had intended to let her and Grant do the dirty work, then grab the weed for himself.

And for Grant? The son of a bitch finally might get what he deserved. Grant had beat him out on the girls, school, even got the only officer slot available in their Guard unit, ended up as Wilson's commander in Iraq. Wilson hadn't felt the slightest twinge of guilt when the car bomb exploded; instead, relief that the car had targeted Vicente's Humvee, not his. He rubbed the scar across his forehead. He even received a Bronze Star and Purple Heart for the ensuing firefight; the only recognition he ever got while serving with Grant. His only regret was that he hadn't been quick enough to finish his bastard cousin when he had the opportunity.

Wilson had always envied Grant, all the way back to their schoolboy crushes on Chantico. Now, finally, he had found someone who Grant didn't even know. He dialed her number. No answer. On an impulse, he slowed, turned south onto the Suncoast Parkway. If he gave the information about Grant to her, maybe the FDLE would take care of him. Even better than Silva. Like they said in the casino, double down on this one, a sure winner. Once Wilson passed along what he knew to his friend in the FDLE Operations Center, Bennett and Grant would be put away for a long, long time, if Silva didn't get to them first. Maybe not long enough to make up for the times Bennett had turned him down or Grant passed him by, but a start.

An hour later he pulled up in front of her apartment. One of hundreds clustered around the University of South Florida, the complex was quiet, set back from the busy street. Midnight had long since gone, but lights glittered through slatted blinds, flickered with movement inside. Wilson wondered if she had company. She had whispered that there was no one else, but women lied, even more than men. Should he call up first? Christ, what a wimp. Grandpa Tiger would rise up out of his swampy grave if Wilson didn't act like a Seminole instead of a coward. Wilson pulled his black hair back and wrapped it with the braided leather tie with the silver ornament. Never mind the tie was Navaho and nothing a Seminole of the old days would wear. It had taken him half a year after his deployment to grow his hair back long enough to use the tie, but she had once admired it; so he would wear it. Maybe to his cousin's funeral. He might even leave a ceremonial pot by his grave—to piss in.

CHAPTER 26

Grant shook the drowsiness from his head, stood and sniffed at the humid air drifting across the island, heavy with the scent of skunk vine and dog fennel, salt marsh and mud flats. Over and over, he had gone through the last two days' events, but still couldn't connect what happened with any logic. Swaying pines laced with nightshade tendrils had lulled him close to sleep for a moment. Rejuvenated by the brisk breeze blowing in from Crystal Bay, he blinked away the drowsiness.

He needed to do something more than whine and mope. Grant slipped back in the house and reset the alarm. His mind raced as he cleaned the Kimber and sorted out what to do next. He dropped the reloaded pistol in his pocket and returned to the kitchen where he could hear the thump of the clothes dryer running in the utility room.

Who could help? His old Military Intelligence unit commander, Greg Talbot? Talbot had returned to the FDLE and was probably wrapped up investigating the terrorist attack. Who else did he know in law enforcement? Eustis was dead. Gunner, Patricia Snyder, his team machine gunner and female interrogator? Last he heard she had applied to the FBI or DEA or some law enforcement agency. Hell, she was probably out somewhere, gun in hand, searching for him.

Wellington. The deputy might still be on his side. Grant poured a cup of coffee and looked at his watch. After midnight. Too late to get a reasonable answer, but his wasn't a reasonable question. Then it struck him.

If anyone, Father Roberto Escobar would know how to get in touch with Wellington. Grant opened a kitchen drawer, pulled out one of several prepaid phones he kept on hand and turned it on. Battery was good, reception was better than he expected inside the concrete reinforced walls. He booted up the laptop on the kitchen counter and searched down through the contacts file.

Roberto's listing was under friends, a truth long before Roberto put on the collar, back from when Uly, Vicente, Eustis and Roberto had been the terror of Homosassa. Grant punched the number in the phone and sipped the coffee as he waited. A tired voice answered immediately, not the sleepy pause and cigarette cough that Grant expected this late at night.

"Roberto. Are you alone? Can we talk in confidence?" Grant swallowed the remaining slug of coffee from the bottom of the cup and glanced up as Bennett padded into the kitchen wearing the floral print tee shirt draped down over her bare legs and feet and, from the sway of her breasts, no bra. She poured herself a cup of coffee and rummaged through the refrigerator for milk. She looked around, eyebrows and coffee cup raised as Grant talked to the priest.

Grant pointed at the sugar dish on the counter.

Bennett poked around in the drawers until she found a spoon and added a mound of sugar to the mug. She grimaced at her first sip. The rhythmic clicking of the spoon against the mug was the only pleasant noise in the kitchen.

Roberto's harsh voice told him the authorities were pretty sure they had found human remains in the burned house, and they were looking for Grant and some woman.

The room swam as the blood drained from Grant's head. He cleared his throat, suddenly constricted by the news. "Roberto. I just went by the house. I swear to God I didn't have any part in whatever happened there. Juan and Chantico were fine when we left, just after breakfast." Grant raised his eyebrows and motioned with his head toward the bedroom as he listened to Father Escobar.

Bennett laid her head to one side on her hand, indicating Angelica was asleep.

"At least I have some good news, Roberto. We found Angelica in the woods. We're taking care of her for the moment. But until I can make things safe, I don't want to bring the little girl out in the open. Please don't worry about her; she's not alone with a heathen." He tried to smile at Bennett who had pulled out a dinette chair and sat with her knees tucked up under the tee shirt, aware he didn't have control of his face muscles. "I have a lady friend with us who is a great mom, taking care of her."

Bennett stared back at him, frown wrinkles across her brow.

"I'll call back when I can." Grant stared at the phone. Not the news he wanted to hear. He shook his head, powered the phone down and dropped the phone in a cardboard box along with several other once-and-never-again-to-be-used phones.

Bennett stirred the coffee until it sloshed over the edge onto the granite countertop. "Did that Roberto know anything?" Her soft tone told Grant she suspected the answer.

"Roberto Escobar is an old friend. Padre, Father, Priest, pretty much the leader of the Mexican community around here, active in the workers coalition." Grant kept talking, not wanting to answer the hard question, but finally deciding it had to come out. "He said the fire inspector found remains in the ruins."

Bennett's face paled. "Chantico?"

"Unidentified. But who else would it be? And maybe Juan." Knees weak, he leaned over the counter, palms flat, head down. If he had any tears left he would cry. "Apparently my truck, the one we left the weed in, was parked by their house, the pickup we saw hauled away. So now I'm the prime suspect in whatever happened."

Bennett's chair scraped and her feet padded over the tile floor to him. She put a hand on his shoulder, then both arms around his chest, her head against his back. "Thank God we found Angelica, got her away from there." After a minute she rubbed her face against his back, damp tears soaking through his shirt. "It's dark in here. Is the storm getting worse?"

"The sky's clearing. Stars are coming out. I just haven't gotten around to opening the hurricane shutters. I didn't want to give away that we were here."

"What will we do now?"

He turned to face her, took her shoulders in his hands and eased her away. "Is Angelica O.K.?"

Bennett nodded toward a syrup bottle and the remains of a toaster waffle on the counter by the sink. "You need to buy milk. And some more waffles if you like them; kid cleaned you out. But Angelica says you gotta buy some Scooby Doo Berry Bones; that she and Flash really, really like them." Bennett scrubbed a tear away from her cheek and smiled. "She's gone to bed, already asleep."

"Good for her. There's another box of waffles in the freezer, top of the fridge." Grant shook his head, frowned. "Flash. I can't believe I forgot to take care of him."

"Then what?"

"Then? Then I'll do what I should have been doing for the last couple of days. Find out who is doing this to us, and why. And stop them." He stared at Bennett, wondering what secrets the fluorescent lights reflected in her eyes hid. "We've got to be honest. Stop the games, sliding around the truth. I ran an interrogation team in Iraq, searching for the truth. Sometimes, if I thought I had to, I didn't go by the rules, but we got the job done, hopefully saved GI and Iraqi lives. Then I got a taste of real combat, maybe liked it too much. That's where Vicente and I had been when the car bomb got us. My fault. So I buried all that under a bunch of pills, forgot how to look people in the eye and tell if they were lying. Now I can't tell if what you have told me is half true, or all lie." He pulled away from Bennett and went into the utility room. "Come here, buddy." He dropped to his knees in front of Flash's crate and patted the top of his thighs, ignoring the spasms shooting up his hip. Flash wasn't whining. He wouldn't, either, not any more, not till this was over and done.

She followed him into the utility room. "You don't trust me."

He looked into her eyes. "Just as much as you trust me."

She shook her head, her wry grin on her face. "Yep. Just about as much. We really make a team, don't we?"

The greyhound slid forward, half a slink, half a crawl, and lay on his side on the old crocheted rag rug. An angry red tear marked his skin from his belly across his bony ribs, half scabby, half seeping. Grant leaned closer. Ugly powder burns marked the end of the tear toward Flash's belly.

Grant stroked the dog's head. "Look in the kitchen cabinet and bring me the first aid kit, and then some clean rags from under the sink, one soaking wet." Flash closed his eyes and lay back with a groan.

Slowly, gently, with Bennett's help, Grant cleaned and swabbed at the wound as Flash twitched, but didn't bolt. He gently rubbed in an antibiotic ointment and sat back on his heels. Flash's big eyes looked up at him.

"Yeah. I screwed up, boy."

"Do you want to try to bandage it?"

"Should, but he'll probably pull it off so he can lick it, dumb dog."

"I think he saved our butts yesterday in the boat going to get Juan. More important, he led us to Angelica tonight. Maybe he's smarter than both of us."

Grant looked at her. She was dead serious—and right. Grant tore open a sterile pad and smoothed it over the wound. "Hold up his rear haunches." He slid a length of gauze under the dog and repeated the process, finally cutting the wrap and securing it with a pair of butterfly clips. "Directly over the sink is a cabinet with a bunch of prescription bottles. One's Flash's painkillers. Label says Trimadol, and lists a Doctor Draper, his vet. Bring me one pill." Grant gently stroked Flash's muzzle, clearing the crusty matter from the corners of his eyes with the damp rag until Bennett returned. Flash gave Grant a wide eyed look, then let Bennett coax the pill down his throat.

She grinned at the two of them. "Just like a kid."

Grant pointed to the crate. "Can you get back in by yourself, boy?"

Flash got up, one leg at the time, and crooked his head around. He sniffed at the bandage, then walked to the crate, nails clicking on the tile floor. Inside, he took a couple of hesitant turns and lay down.

When Grant tried to stand, a wave of dizziness washed across his eyes. He steadied himself with a hand on Bennett's shoulder for a moment.

"Let's start. First, I'll tell you what I'm all about. Then you. Deal?"

"Deal. But more coffee first. Not quite so strong." She opened the cabinet below the coffee maker and pulled out a canister of coffee and a filter. Grant sank back in a chair by the old wooden table. Just hours in his home and she already knew where he kept the coffee. What else did she know?

"So talk," she said, filling the pot from the sink and pouring the water into the coffee maker. "Who are you? Really."

"The woman you met at the retirement center is my mother, Elizabeth Grant. She named me Ulysses Grant to keep my father from having anything to do with me." Grant couldn't help but grin at the absurd story. "My father had a Confederate flag tattooed on one cheek of his ass and a swastika on the other, a real cracker, probably kin, at least in spirit, to those yahoos we left out on the island. She figured my name would be enough to keep a dyed-in-the-wool 'South-will-rise-again' nut away."

Bennett's eyebrows rose. "Oh? You've seen this artwork, I suppose?"

Grant lost his grin. "I never knew my father when I was a kid. He left us and Homosassa when I was still a baby. Momma told me about the tats. She always got a big laugh out of it." He scratched at the adhesive pad on his arm.

"Come here, by the sink and let me take that off." Bennett pulled Grant over to the kitchen counter and started peeling the bandage away from the wound. "So how does your daddy fit into this masquerade?"

"When I first got out of Walter Reed I needed something to do. After laying around a couple of months, I did some research, talked to mom in one of her more lucid moments. Found out my dad was in Phoenix. Sorry bastard was living on the streets and had called mom asking for money. Nothing else to do, and I was feeling sorry for myself. Got myself together and went out west to find him."

"Did you?"

"Barely. I was sitting by his cot in the homeless shelter when he passed. Alcohol-soaked liver quit on him." *Enough of that. His heart still ached when he remembered that day.* "By the time I got back, Juan had finished the house."

"Juan? He looked like he was in construction. Is he a carpenter?"

"Carpenter?" Grant smiled at the thought. "He runs his own company, Madero Builders, currently has fifty-seven employees." Realizing what he had said, Grant clenched his right hand into a fist, but Bennett grabbed his arm before he could pound the counter. "At least he did. God knows, I hope he and Chantico are still alive out there somewhere. Juan runs the business and is part owner."

"You know a lot of details about Juan's business." Bennett threw the old bandage in the trash, tipped the alcohol bottle onto a sterile pad and swabbed the open wound.

"Yeow!

She grinned at him. "Be a man. Flash didn't whimper." She patted the wound one last time and then opened a sterile pad. "Keep talking."

"I installed a pretty good computer set up and went back to cracking into al Qaeda accounts.

Bennett pulled back, a funny look in her face.

Money. It always seemed to jack her up.

Suddenly he swayed as a rush of pain swept over him.

"Uly. What's wrong?"

"I keep talking big, but I hurt. When you are whole, before crappy things happen to you, you think you can get through anything. You know, the old tough-it-out bull shit. I came home intending to turn on the computer, start doing some searches, analyzing information, making plans, figuring out courses of action. But instead I keep going blank." He stared deep into her eyes, but couldn't figure out what to look for. "You got to help me."

"We're both tired." She opened the cabinet, took out the OxyContin bottle, shook out two capsules and filled a glass with water. "Here. Take these, then to bed. I'll get you up in the morning and we'll get to work."

He took the pills and the water, wishing for more. "Doing what?" *Work? His mind was addled.*

"Whatever it takes." She took a step back. "Goodnight, Uly." She smiled and walked out of the kitchen, her hips swaying under the thin tee shirt, enticing, but far distant.

Grant turned out the lights and the house went coalmine black. Could Juan and Chantico really be dead because of him? He flipped the switch that opened up all the motorized storm shutters. As the shutters rolled up, the row of windows looking out over Crystal Bay glittered with stars. The bay waters shimmered, reflecting the lights glowing over the nuclear facility.

He leaned his forehead against the cool glass. What could he have done? If he gave up now, that cracker Billy was right—he was just a crip. Grant turned off the alarm and eased his way out onto the back porch, down the steps and onto the damp grass. At the water's edge he flung the OxyContins out into the rising tide. He needed the pain to stay focused. He thought back to Iraq. He had always kept himself, his soldiers in check, sometimes on the edge of the rules, but never so far over that he worried about his soul. Now, if need be, even his soul was forfeit.

If only he had gone to church Sunday instead of fishing. *If only.*

CHAPTER 27

"Click, click, click, click." A faint noise tickled his ears.

Grant didn't move. As usual, he woke up on his right side, protecting his injured hip. A warm lump pressed against him, the distinct impression of a clenched fist pressed between his shoulder blades. Warm breath slowly pulsed against his neck. He forced his eyes open, blinked. His eyes were crusty after watching the stars circle the house from the back porch until the dawn mists began to rise over the water.

Angelica stood by his dresser in his faded Army tee shirt, galloping a miniature silver camel across the top. She turned and squatted beside Flash, sprawled on a prayer rug between the bed and the dresser, to guide the camel in a gentle trot between Flash's ears. She looked up to see Grant watching her and turned on a wide smile. "Morning, Uncle Uly," she said, matter-of-factly, like she always started her day in Grant's bedroom.

Grant winked at Angelica, willing her away from the nightstand where his pistol lay exposed, loaded and cocked. Going to bed in the wee hours of the dawn was no excuse. He should have remembered a small child might be wandering in his house. The bed shifted as the knot uncoiled and pressed flat up against his back and legs, a warm body, soft and moving sensuously against his bare skin. The fist unclenched, one hand slid under his arm and crawled up to his chest. The other arm worked its way under his neck until the two hands clasped across his chest, holding him tight.

"Uly," Bennett whispered in his ear. "Are you really going to bury me in the swamp?" She squeezed him tight.

"No, Kat." He twisted until her short hair tickled his lips. The smell of fresh soap floated from her neck, soft as he touched his lips to her skin. He felt every inch of her legs laying across his, even the sawgrass scabs, a heat building, a sensation almost forgotten. "Can't kill you now," he whispered back. "You have to look after the kid." He flinched when she pinched his chest.

Angelica stood up on her toes and stared over Grant's shoulder. "Oh, Aunt Katrina. What happened to your pretty hair?" Angelica made a face as she stretched out Bennett's name. "It used to be all sun-streaky like my finger painting. Now it's icky black." Angelica led the camel, a memento purchased from an Iraqi *souk*, in a canter up the sheet dunes, to slowly slide down the other side, stopping directly in front of Grant's nose. Angelica's gaze slid from the camel to Grant, to Bennett and back to the camel as the silver beast made its way over to the edge of the bed. "Aunt Katrina and Uncle Uly," she sang in a little sing song. "Did you get married?"

Bennett propped her chin on Grant's shoulder. "No, honey. I just lay down beside Uncle Uly to take a little nap." She smiled down at Grant, slowly eased her arms free and slid out from under the sheet. "All that late night coffee and I had to get up early and go to the bathroom. So, I came to see if Uncle Uly was all right. I think he was having a bad dream." She sat up on the bed and tucked the long tee shirt under her knees.

Angelica twirled over to the dresser and put the camel out to pasture, replacing it with a miniature crystal angel, a gift from Chantico the previous Christmas. She stared at it for a moment. "Momma Chantico has one like this at her house." The big eyes turned back to Grant and Bennett. "I saw the house get all burned up. I cried, and Flash came and found me." She leaned her elbows on the bed, her face inches from Grant's, and studied the details of the crystal angel. "Did Momma Chantico go to heaven?"

Grant's throat swelled. He couldn't answer.

"We don't know, honey; but she might have. What do you think?" Bennett asked

Angelica's head nodded. "I think she went to heaven." The crystal angel soared as high as Angelica's arm could reach.

The finality of her steady voice shamed Grant. Ashamed that he didn't have the guts to look Angelica in the face and be the grownup.

"There was a mean man in the house and a big boom, lots of booms." The angel swooped low over Grant's head with a little guidance from Angelica.

Bennett slid off the bed. "O.K. Everybody's rested." She leaned over and ran her hand over Grant's heavy stubble. "Time for Uly to shower and shave." Bennett herded Angelica out and shut the door behind them.

Mean man in the house? Who? Grant didn't have the will to try and pry it out of Angelica. Intending to take a quick shower, Grant found himself standing under the beating water, letting every bone in his body relax until his fingertips began to prune, letting his mind race across the possibilities as he scraped at his beard. With Angelica, everything had changed. Especially his perception of Bennett. He needed to start getting his perceptions right the first time, stop waiting until it was too late to change course. He retrieved the Kimber from the nightstand, made sure the hammer was cocked and the thumb safety engaged, and dropped the pistol in a pocket.

Dressed in clean cargo pants and the freshly washed blue shirt he discovered on his bedside chair, Grant began to feel like a real person as he walked down the hall, pistol balanced, to a degree, by the hefty Buck automatic knife, a modern switchblade conversion his momma had given him. Mom sincerely believed a man wasn't a man without a sturdy knife in his pocket.

In the kitchen Angelica, dressed in a pair of flower covered bib overalls and pink tee shirt, attacked a defenseless waffle. Bennett leaned on the kitchen counter nursing a cup of coffee, wearing tan slacks and a pale blue blouse that Grant didn't recognize, the blouse still sporting a tag dangling from the untucked tail.

Angelica carried on the conversation for all of them as Grant turned off the security alarm and opened the screened door onto the back porch. Flash gingerly sidestepped down the steps. To Grant's surprise, he still wore the improvised bandage.

Grant followed Flash and made a quick circuit around the house. At first he felt foolish, lugging a pistol around his own yard, but then as he watched Flash gimp around the yard and he remembered the burnt ruins at Chantico's, his anger built.

He stopped, held his face up to the brilliant blue sky. The sun had burned away the last hint of rain. Faint tracks from his walk around the night before were the only signs of people in the yard. Flash trotted over to commune with a small flock of immature ibis, feathers still a dull brown, pecking away in the weeds growing from the limestone make-shift seawall along the water's edge. Squawks and a flurry of feathers, and much to the greyhound's disappointment the ungrateful birds took wing before Flash reached them. Grant wondered if the birds were high on his OxyContin. He shouldn't have thrown the capsules in the water, but lately he had done a lot of things he didn't like.

Grant squinted against the glare off the water. Real Florida summer hovered around the corner; hot and humid, hit and miss for a flats fishing guide, good for an occasional big tarpon in close. The horizon hinted of the early tropical storm pushing a long line of thunderstorms through. Grant wished weather was all he had to worry about as he whistled Flash back and followed him across the porch and into domestic uncertainty. In the kitchen Bennett was scrambling up a mound of eggs. The smell from a plate of bacon on the table made Grant's mouth water.

"Can't find any bread for toast," Bennett announced.

Grant dug a carton of English muffins out of the back of the freezer and popped four into the microwave to thaw. He watched Bennett for a moment, then walked to the office and powered up the computer system. He left the system to boot while he went back to the kitchen. "Stop for a minute," he told Bennett. She held still, ladle in hand, as he snapped open his Buck knife and snipped the tag off her blouse, resisting the sudden urge to reach out and touch the back of her neck. Instead he turned back to the counter, split the muffins and dropped the first pair into a toaster. He motioned toward Angelica with his head. "Any suggestions where she can stay while we sort out things?"

Bennett nodded. "I've been thinking about that. I'll call my ex. He and his wife are good people. I trust them with Chris." She smiled at Grant's raised eyebrows. "My son." She placed the eggs on the table with the bacon and muffins, putting another pair of muffins in the toaster. "That is, if you'll let me use one of your phones. I lost mine somewhere."

"All for the better. I'm sure yours has a trace on it by now." He plowed into the eggs and was halfway through before he realized that the food was good. Amazing. Food hadn't tasted—at all, not good, not bad—since his return from the sandbox. Eating had been just a means of sustainment, nothing to do with pleasure.

Across the table Bennett slowly dribbled syrup onto Angelica's remaining waffle. Angelica squealed with delight as the outline of an angel appeared. As a finishing touch, Bennett carefully sprinkled a sparkling sugar halo over its head. "Sweetie, would you like to go out to a farm and meet Chris? He's a little older than you are, but he's a pretty good kid, for a boy."

Angelica nodded her head, her mouth full of syrup-soggy instant waffle.

"What do you say, Uly?"

Grant handed her an unused prepaid cell phone from the cache in the drawer. "Here. Call, but don't stay on very long. Never know who's listening." He wiped his mouth and motioned toward the hall. "Reception's spotty out here. Best if you stand by the widow, or better yet, the back porch. While you call, I'll be in the office, up the hall. I've let business slip during all our troubles."

Sitting in front of his main computer, Grant scrolled down the outstanding transactions list. He really had let his friends down over the last couple of days. He rectified the situation with a multi-hop transfer of funds from a newly discovered Indonesian account, controlled from Pakistan, to the Banc Ixcateopan. Actually, his bank, the majority owner if someone dug deep enough and waded through a maze of corporations, mostly Mexican. He also was the majority owner in Madero Builders, the titular owner of his house, along with Juan and Enrique, the oldest Madero brother. And a handful of other businesses in Florida, Arizona and the small town of Ixcateopan, Mexico, the Guerrero State ancestral home of the Maderos and many of the Mexican immigrants who had settled nearby. Al Qaeda accounts unwittingly provided financial security for many.

Bennett padded up behind Grant and rubbed his shoulders as she leaned down and stared at the transaction records. Behind her, Angelica and Flash sprawled on a braided rug where Angelica proceeded to wipe the greyhound's long muzzle with a soft cloth. Bennett chuckled, her breath warm on his neck, and pointed at the screen. In the reflection, Flash stretched his neck out so she could better work her way between his ears.

"What are all the numbers?" Bennett asked, bringing his attention back to his computer.

"This is how I move money." He slid the cursor over the latest transactions. "I tracked down a new al Qaeda account and appropriated about three-fourth of the total last week. I just transferred a little over fifty thousand dollars through a couple of cutouts to an account that is accessible by a business acquaintance in Mexico. He'll invest it in the Mexican markets, sell in a few days, maybe a week, or a month, depending on market conditions, and assign the proceeds to a list of individuals I provide him. He usually makes sufficient gains on the transactions to bring himself a substantial profit, and ends up passing along, in this case, about forty thousand. If I pick up any useful al Qaeda info, I forward the data to Central Command's Joint Intelligence outfit out at MacDill so they can follow up. That's why I cringed when I saw Lester Scanlon on the TV at the retirement center. Lester's the guy I send the raw data to in Central Command, although I don't think he knows the information comes from me." Grant turned the desk chair to watch Bennett, trim in her new khakis, as she knelt to the floor beside Angelica and Flash.

"That's a lot of money. A lot." She shook her head. "Why do you do it? And for whom?"

"Why? A debt that goes back to when my father left my mother. Carmencita and Alphonso Madero, Chantico's mother and father, opened up a bait and tackle shop about the time my father ran away. They made mom the manager. Job included a place to live, upstairs over the shop. That's where I grew up." He studied her face. "People are strange. The locals figured the only thing Mexicans could do was pick fruit and run Mexican cafes. So the Maderos let everyone think the shop was mom's. That was back before property records were accessible on the Internet, and the county courthouse was a world away. We all lived in peace, pretty much, except when us kids raised—" He cut his description short when Bennett cut her eyes over toward Angelica, now carefully cleaning a skinny dog leg, softly talking to Flash about very important things.

"What did the Maderos do for a living?"

"They came over as migrant workers, broke out of the debt cycle after years of working up and down the east coast and eventually bought their own farm. This was before I was born. I don't know the details, but I think mom used her name to front for the Maderos when they bought the place. She let everyone think the Maderos, and the other Mexicans they hired, all worked for her. Their oldest son, Enrique, still runs their farm."

"Mutual benefit society, huh?"

Grant shrugged. "Pretty much."

She pointed at the computer screen. "How did you figure out how to set up the front companies?"

"The companies aren't fronts; they're real. Just the principals' names are a little tricky. Juan got in an argument with a competing contractor and spent a couple of days in the Pasco Detention Center when I was in Iraq. Since they seemed to have a lot of spare time, a fellow inmate taught him the fine art of identity theft. Juan loves to play the dumb spic, but he's got a Masters in common sense." He swiveled around to face the computer, wondering if Juan was down at *El Sombrero Rojo* having a beer or in heaven with his brother. He blinked, looked to see Bennett's reflection in the flat display. He was spilling his guts to a woman he threatened to bury the night before. *You have to trust somebody in this world. She was who he had today.*

"I used what Juan taught me to hijack my father's identity and set up a network of credit and bank accounts, originally based on my father's Social Security number. I operate three small financial companies. They process small loans, mortgages, similar transactions, under several names. I channel financial transactions through them so anyone with an interest, like the IRS, will think the companies are legit, pay taxes and are reputable. The companies hire people who need a little help, mostly Mexicans, and help them in qualifying for a Permanent Residence Card, what everybody calls green cards." He continued typing as he explained. "Never thought I would like, much less hire them, but two of the companies are managed by lawyers. Their legal work is mostly on immigration issues and keeping the companies legit, especially in the eyes of the IRS. Plus they do a bit of work on the side that actually generates income. The one nonprofit helps pay the naturalization fees, if the applicants can meet Immigration qualifications, gives out school grants, that sort of thing."

Bennett stared at him wide-eyed. "Illegal immigrants? Aren't you afraid you're helping terrorists?"

"Look around. Lot of people are blind at what goes on around them, don't realize how the trades are dominated by Mexicans, all across America. Back before our time, African slaves, Irish and English indentured servants came across the Atlantic, then the Chinese to work the railroads, laundries, kitchens. America has always used immigrants looking for a better life, and treated them like crap when the bosses could get away with it. And, yeah, immigrants have brought their own problems. And maybe some bad eggs slip in. What's new? We try to run background checks, but sometimes the information isn't there. What I really do is help immigrants become legal. "

She waved her hand around her head, encompassing his world. "How do you keep the companies, everything a secret?" She walked over to a bookshelf and pulled out a creased and yellowed Matt Helm novel. "Randy was right. You really are a spy."

"Not me. But secrets aren't hard to keep around here. You would be surprised what goes on in Ozello. This is an old timey community. People live in campers, old shacks, even tents, without any government recognition. No Social Security registration, no drivers' license, never pay a penny in tax, never take a dime in welfare, totally anonymous. The Maderos were the only ones who knew I lived here. Juan was really proud of the house, and should be. It's unique. The shell is pre-stressed concrete, covered with cedar lapboards so it looks like a rundown Florida cracker house, complete with fake rust metal roof. The flooring is real wood, not that pretend stuff; salvaged pine boards from the bait shop, all refinished."

Grant pointed at the computer. "I get TV through a dish mounted under the skylight which gives me Internet access, all billed to a mailbox in Phoenix, supposedly for one of those big RV's you see with satellite dishes up on top. Electricity and water are run over from the cabinet shop next door, part of Madero Builders, so no utility bills show up in my name. I pay all the taxes through Madero Builders, so it's legal. My—Uly Grant—home of record, telephone, everything else for everyone else, is the boat yard and the *Rum Runner*."

Bennett made her way down the row of old classics to the dusty Robert Louis Stevenson adventures. "Looks like you read a lot. My daddy was never much for books in the house. I grew up on soap operas and talks shows." She turned to Grant, back to the point. "What happens to all the money? How have you gotten away with stealing it?"

"Appropriate, not steal," he corrected. "See the leather-bound book on the shelf, under the New Testament.'

Bennett picked up the Army-issue pocket Bible. "Never took you for the religious type."

"Did my time in Sunday School as a kid, even attended Mass with the Maderos. Now I'm not much of a church-going guy, but if you want to understand what's going on in the Middle East you got to be able to grasp the basic conflicts between Christianity and Islam."

She replaced the New Testament with the Koran.

Grant's heart skipped a beat when the tattered blue notebook fell from between the pages, enough he had to close his eyes to fight off the woozies. When he opened his eyes Bennett was scanning the notebook.

"I found that in Iraq the day Vicente died. When I got back home I figured out the numbers were al Qaeda accounts. I followed those transactions trails to other, mostly offshore, accounts and learned the electronic transaction signatures to locate new ones. I let the gap between fiddled records get wide enough so whoever manages a particular account can't easily discover what's happening to the funds. I figure the terrorists are so paranoid, and thieves themselves, they don't have any idea of who is doing what with the money. The radical Islamic charities and Arab oil bigwigs financing the terrorist operations start most transactions with cash deposits in places that don't keep easily accessible records, like Indonesia. Apparently they don't try to track the funds, so far as I can tell. They probably figure any audit might lead back to them."

"So, the money is all from terrorists' accounts?"

He laughed. "Mostly. Unsecured porno sites are dead meat when I run across them. When I can, I divert their charges to a charity site like the Red Cross, and then corrupt their servers with a virus." Grant chuckled. "I doubt the people who end up donating to the charities ever challenge the loss to their credit card company. I'm very careful with those, because most of them are eastern European or Russian mob operations. Sometimes the transaction trace leads to plain old criminals, mostly drug dealers, ironically often Mexican, or an illicit gambling operation. That's where your buddy, Allen Wilson fits in. Accounts that are associated with criminal activity, I drain what I think I can get away with, then pass the account specifics on to Allen and let the FDLF and FBI dig them out. That means Allen gets the credit and my name never gets associated with the case. Allen knows something's going on, but I don't tell him enough that he can figure out exactly what I'm doing, or if he did, enough to track the transfers back to me."

Bennett replaced the notebook, shaking her head as if she was having a hard time believing.

Grant swept his hand around the room to take in Angelica, twirling around on the polished wood floor in her stocking feet. "The only people who know the details about my financial operations are right here. Flash and Angelica I trust." He stared at her. "How about you?"

Bennett leaned closer to the four foot gator hide mounted on the wall and grinned her crooked smile. She ran her hand over the gator hide. "Did you trust this varmint?"

"Nope. When we were kids Eustis teased me about the gators in the canal behind the barbershop. 'Tiny things,' Eustis teased. 'Anybody can wrestle a baby gator. Your cousins do it all the time down at the reservation.' When I was about ten, I jumped a gator in that canal we floated down, Tarzan style, knife in hand. To everybody's surprise, I lived and the gator didn't. A friend of Mom's cured the hide and gave it to me. He told me the kill had made me a man. Mom was really pissed." *Now was time to prove Morris right.* "But I'm asking you."

"Trust? Sure."

After all her obsession with money, he had spelled out the details of his finances for her, and all she had to say was sure?

"Just sure?" he confirmed. "No more questions?"

She shrugged. "Why not. You've seen——." She grinned as she glanced at Angelica.

He smiled back. "Not much to see."

Another pinch, and she left, Flash's toenails clicked as he followed the girls down the hall. *Abandoned again.*

CHAPTER 28

Grant stared at the screen saver image dancing from edge to edge of computer display, thinking for a moment before he directed the computer to more important tasks than stealing others' money. Juan had called the house a fortress, but this morning Grant felt the walls were more of a prison, more of a restriction than protection. Somewhere outside were bad people, threats that should be stopped. He let his fingertips touch the keyboard. He needed processed intelligence, not more raw information—specific targeting information. Where, why, and, more importantly, as Bennett had asked and he had never really answered, who?

First he scanned the public Florida Department of Environmental Protection web sites, tracking down their servers' IP addresses. Then he accessed the federal Department of Environmental Protection files. They both focused on upcoming legislation on oil exploration and leasing options. Recent activity focused on the spill. He quickly scrolled through them, but nothing popped out. Damn! Grant closed his eyes. Patience. This was a search, not a chase.

He changed tasks for the moment; Allen Wilson's visit to his mother still a bothersome question. Was Wilson trying to warn him? Grant opened up the DMV data base and did a quick look up on Wilson. His cousin drove a black Ford truck, a F-250 with a Purple Heart tag. Grant had seen a truck like that last night at the assisted living facility, and then back at the Maderos' place. Had Wilson been following them? All this was making his head hurt. Maybe Wilson was concerned about Chantico. Certainly he had cared for her, even had a crush on her as a kid. Except for her brothers, all the boys did. So it made some kind of sense.

Down the hall he heard a screen door slam. Suddenly a sharp worrying thought pulsed through his concentration. Had he told Bennett to stay out of sight from the road or passing boaters? He set an automated search engine to work scanning every file in the DEP server for her name and walked down the hall.

Angelica lay on her tummy on the screened porch, feeding crackers to Flash, one tiny bite at the time, dog lips quivering in anticipation. Across the yard, shallow water and small islands stretched north, to where the steam rose from the Crystal River Energy Complex's signature cooling towers that most people associated with nuclear reactors, and curved out of sight toward Cedar Key. Several fishing boats crisscrossed on the far side of Shark Point, some heading toward Crystal Reefs, the scattering of low islands buffering the nuclear facility. Others headed out to the where they hoped monster tarpon were feeding. If he had a lick of sense, he'd be out with them. On the horizon a single white cumulous cloud grew from a puffy white cotton ball to a towering colossus as he watched. Lord, he loved this place. And now he had set himself up so he might have to leave, forever.

Bennett held up a cell phone. "I called my ex. If we need to, we can drop Angelica with them for a few days." She paused, stared across the water for a moment. "You and I have unfinished business to attend to, and I don't want to put Angelica in danger. I heard all your fortress talk, but I've figured out that nobody's ever as safe as you think you are, not when jerks like Bobby Silva are involved. Just wanted to let you know I had a plan, in case we have to leave Angelica somewhere for a bit."

Grant stared at her for a long minute. "How's your son?"

Bennett smiled, both corners of her mouth turned up, a new look for her. "You think you're beginning to figure me out? Chris is fine. For the moment. But that's not what we're talking about."

"What does that mean? I showed you mine. We agreed we would talk, but you haven't told me anything."

Bennett just smiled. "You go back to your magic computer while I fix us lunch, if I can find anything in the pantry other than dog food." She stood and opened the back door. "Come on in, kids. It's getting too hot out here." Angelica popped up, followed much more slowly by Flash, his bandage beginning to sag under his gaunt belly. Bennett held the door open for Flash to amble into the house. "Where'd all the neat pictures come from?" She motioned toward the row of paintings hanging in the hallway.

"Florida Highwaymen."

She looked at him with a quizzical frown.

"Mostly itinerant artists, all black men, and at least one woman, who painted local scenes and sold them along the roadside." He took her on a tour of the paintings as they walked to the kitchen. "Morris, the guy who cured the gator hide, gave Mom these. It took me until I was about twelve before I figured out he was more than a friend; that he and Mom had a thing going. He came around at lot, taught me most of what I know about fishing. I helped him build the old fishing shack out in the refuge." Morris had been a long time ago, before college and war and Bennett.

"Mom hung the paintings in our old home upstairs over the bait and tackle shop." He pointed at the framed piece in the center of the group, a trio of palms on a sun-dappled river bank, herons, brilliant blue sky and white clouds. "My favorite. Guess it's because it reminds me of life along the river. Slow, quiet, all the things my life have stopped being, lately."

"Since you met me?" Bennett asked. A sad look returned to her eyes. She spun on her heels to follow Angelica and Flash into the kitchen.

He shrugged and trailed along.

After a lunch of hot dogs, baked beans and canned peach slices, silent except for Angelica's chatter, Grant unwrapped Flash and inspected his wound. Flash rolled his eyes, but lay back and let Grant ease the bandage off and gently swab the dried crust from the wound. Grant had seen wounds like this before. An old cowboy movie would have called it a flesh wound, a grazing wound that tore and burned the skin but didn't penetrate. "We got to be more careful, buddy," he whispered to Flash, replaced the dressing and left him resting on his rug in the utility room.

Grant returned to a quiet kitchen. Giggling came from the guest bedroom where Bennett was trying, without much success, to get Angelica to take a nap. His smile generated by the giggles slowly drained away as he fished out a fresh phone. He really didn't want to call, to confirm what Flash's wound suggested. *Do it, damn it*, he said to himself, and punched out Father Escobar's number. A half ring and a hacking cough, and Roberto answered.

"Roberto, this is your old friend. *Que pasa?*" Grant bit his lower lip and pressed his free hand against the counter to stop the trembling as he listened to Father Escobar's report. He answered after clearing a catch in his throat. "Confirmed? Juan? Oh, Lord." After a moment he replied to Father Roberto's next question, "I don't know if we'll make the Mass, Father, but we'll pray, just as good, a genuine old-timey Baptist prayer for their souls." His voice thickened. "But you're on your own to pray for the ones responsible for the murders. You want to save their souls; you better get with it. The sons of bitches will need more than prayer." He listened another minute, and in response said, "Don't worry. We'll take especially good care of Angelica. Goodbye, Father," disconnected and tossed the used phone in the box with the others.

As he walked by the guest room Angelica's giggle seeped through a crack in the door, but not enough to lighten his heart. Someone had killed his friends. And was trying to kill him—and Bennett.

He returned to the kitchen and retrieved the used cell phones, walked outside and pitched them, one by one, far out into the shallow water. He had never really worried about the phones before, but with Homeland

Security involved, some smart tech could milk volumes out of the old phone records. No use making life easy for whoever was after them.

By the time he returned to the office, the computer had completed the search and listed all the files with "Bennett" that were accessible on the State computer servers. Grant scanned the long listing, and then started sorting by likely categories.

An hour later, he had nothing.

Two hours later, he still had nothing. Bennett, Angelica and Flash rejoined him in the office. While Grant pounded the keys, the three relaxed in the cool of the air conditioning, sprawled on the floor. Flash took up most of the thick braided oval rug in the center of the room, while Angelica galloped the camel around him on the braided ovals like a multi-colored racetrack.

The screen flashed.

"Ah, ha. Finally."

"Ah, ha?" Bennett looked up at him from a paperback like he was crazy. "People only say that in old movies. What in the world have you found?"

"Looks like email account files on your Department of Environmental Protection server. Come over and see for yourself." Grant pointed at an alphabetical list of names on the screen with Bennett and Silva in the appropriate order. "You know any of these other people?"

Bennett scuttled across the braided racetrack on her knees and leaned on his forearm, mouthing the names as she read down the list. "I recognize everybody, people in our office. Except one." She pointed at a name on the screen. "This 'Rusty' doesn't ring a bell. Nobody in our office with that name. Not even a nickname, no redhead in the bunch I can think of."

Grant downloaded the mail file and disconnected from the distant servers. He opened the file and scanned the messages. Most of the sent messages were signed "Bob" and addressed to an anonymous email address, several more to a Florida legislative address. A couple of messages at the bottom of the list caught Grant's attention, sent to a FDLE addressee Grant recognized: Allen Wilson. Why did Allen's name keep popping up? Grant shook his head. *Because he got me involved with Bennett in the beginning, likely got himself mired in the drug business*, Grant decided.

Bennett tapped his shoulder and pointed at the first message on the list. "What does it say?"

Grant opened up the message. The text mentioned a delivery of flowers, giving a date and time, all surrounded by a meaningless garble of too innocent minutia, all butterflies and magnolias.

"Bastard'" Bennett whispered. "I recognize this email address. It's the same person who set up the marijuana shipment."

Grant opened up several other messages, including the ones to Allen, and scanned the message texts. "Nothing that clearly reads drug trafficking here."

She nodded her head. "But look the contents. Each one includes dates, scattered over several months, and times, all late at night. I saw a printout of a message like this on Bobby's desk. Magnolias be damned These are more marijuana air drops, I'd bet my ass."

Grant dead-panned and rolled his eyes at her at her language. "But nothing that incriminates you, so far. Let me check the fax files." He worked back through the computer connections to the DEP server.

He pointed at a line on the screen. "Here they are. Image files, all in a fax console folder."

Grant opened up the first file, scanned it and then hit the print key. A printer whirred in the alcove to the left. He looked over at Angelica. "Hey, sweetie. Take Flash and give him three—" He held up three fingers, "—just three of his special treats. They're in the kitchen, the drawer closest to the utility room."

Angelica hopped up and screwed her mouth around as she bent down her little finger and held up three fingers and a thumb. "Just three." She looked down at Flash, who was watching her with one eye. "Want a treat? Come on Flash." Flash groaned, slowly got up and followed her into the hall.

Grant selected the remaining fax files, added them to the print queue and swiveled his desk chair around to face Bennett. "Now you want to talk?" He could tell from her eyes that she had read enough of the first fax to understand his question.

She took a deep breath and nodded her head. "Silva's in the middle of an influence peddling scheme. Soon as they sort out the leak business, a vote is coming up, soon, on off-shore exploration and drilling. He set up a deal to buy votes." She pointed at the legislative email address. "Some legislator—maybe whoever this is—will guarantee the vote goes in favor of a particular oil exploration company. Which legislator or company, I don't know. I found out about the arrangement when I saw the email." Her face reddened. "I went along with Bobby and stayed out of the whole affair at first. Then I told him I knew what he was doing and wanted a cut."

The mass of oil related files now made sense, but didn't help. He focused back on Bennett's words. "Blackmail?"

She stepped back and looked at the floor, nodding her head. "Look, Uly. I really need the money for something very important," she said, so low Uly had to lean forward to catch her words. "I didn't tell you everything—." She shook her head."I knew I was in over my head. I didn't want to make it any worse."

Grant reached out and took her by the shoulders. "I've seen your butt, remember. Tell me what the hell's going on."

When she raised her head, her lips had a determined set. "Bobby started treating me like I was his property or something. We had dated before, but he got physical, abusive physical. He scared me, bad. I tried to get out. I told him I would pay the money back; whatever he wanted. Then he got real ugly. Said he would turn me in, blame the whole scam all on me if it went sour. That's what the faxes are all about." She twisted away from Grant and walked to the hallway, looked out back toward the water like she wanted to bolt and run. "Now the son of a bitch is trying to kill me."

Grant held up the first sheet off the printer. "This fax reads as if it's from you and sent to Allen. Says the southerners will deliver ten packages at the arranged drop point. Read Mexicans and marijuana bales." He studied the sheet for a moment. "Unless they make an awful lot of drops, I'd guess this was the stuff we picked up. It's dated three days before Sunday, so looks very incriminating for you two, not an after-the-fact memo that could be easily disproved. He's setting both you and Allen up." He scanned the second sheet. "Silva isn't mentioned anywhere in the fax. Reads as if you guys are the ones bringing in the dope. Is this oil business big enough for Silva to be a real threat? Players have a lot of juice behind them?"

"The marijuana money was just to prime the pump. I'd guess millions, maybe billions are at stake over the oil exploration and drilling rights. Once the public gets past the cleanup mess, they figure it will be more oil, as usual." She picked up the first sheet, jaw muscles clenched as she slowly read the incriminating words.

Grant leaned back and stared at her. "And you wanted a cut? Always the money, huh?"

"Not for me, Uly. Not for me." She paced across the room. She stopped, looking out the window. "Damn it. I made a mistake. A big mistake. Haven't you ever made a mistake?"

He nodded. "Sure I have. And I damn well regret each and every one. Was this one worth what has happened?"

She turned to face him, wadded up the fax and threw it to the floor, hands on hips and a defiant look on her face that slowly crumpled as her hands slid down to her sides, shoulders slumped. One tear trickled down a cheek, followed by a flood.

She wiped at her cheeks. "No." She came over to Grant, knelt on the braided rug at his feet. "It's Chris, Uly. My son. We're trying to get him in a special treatment program, but the cancer keeps spreading. Logan, his dad, got laid off, company went into bankruptcy, and he lost his medical insurance. Liz, Logan's wife, her insurance won't cover the program we want to get him into." By this time she was snuffling so hard Grant had a hard time understanding her. He tried to pull her close, but she pushed back. "You can think what you want. Whore, drug dealer, whatever. But I'll damn well do what it takes, as long as I can help Chris."

"What kind of money you talking about?"

"I don't really know the total, probably chump change to you and all your al Qaeda loot. I think Chris, or rather the clinic, needs about fifty thousand bucks above what the insurance will pay, just to commit to the treatment."

Jaw clinched, Grant swiveled his chair back to face to the computer. "Which clinic?"

"Why. What are you doing?"

Grant logged on to an account in the name of Charles Howell, a fictitious director on the board of The Sun State Society, a real, if misleading, nonprofit corporation chartered in Arizona.

Bennett's warm breath wafted across his ear as he typed. She scrubbed her wet cheek across the back of his neck, sharing her tears. Bennett's fingers clutched his shoulders. "I take him to the Florida Kids Clinic, the one on the USF campus where you saved my ass yesterday."

"Ow. Easy on the shoulders. One of my corporations, the nonprofit that solicits donations for various farm worker aid societies, can handle this." Grant bent his head over, squeezed her hand between his cheek and his shoulder. "Arabs are always giving to charities. They've given buckets to this one, even if they don't know it." He rattled the keyboard with a series of quick strokes, bringing up the web site for the cancer clinic. He copied the clinic address, then clicked over and logged into a bank site. "What are Chris's legal name and social security number, and his legal parent's?"

"Christopher Lee Stevens." She thought for a moment, pointed at the space for Social Security and rattled off a string of numbers. "His dad is Logan R. Stevens." She snuffled back what Grant hoped was the last of her tears, and then recited another nine digits.

Grant punctuated the last keyboard entry with a thump of this forefinger. "There. The Sun State Society just initiated a payment of fifty thousand dollars to the clinic against the account of Christopher Lee Logan."

Bennett slid both arms around his neck and practically strangled him. "Dear God. I need to go out and tell Logan that he and Liz can bring Chris down and start the treatment. Can we go tonight? We can take Angelica with us." She trembled with excitement.

"Sure. But first, we need to talk about how to deal with the faxes I printed. And we need to warn Allen." Grant brought up his contact file and printed out a map showing Allen's apartment. "When we get all that taken care of, we need to figure out how to stop Silva and clear ourselves—and Allen—before somebody kills us." Grant picked up one of the faxes. "You still don't think Silva had paper copies?"

She shook her head. "I don't think so. He swore he had it all on computer."

"This guy can't lie?"

She picked the fax she had crumpled and smoothed it out. "Like a rug."

"All right. I can wipe the data files clean from here, at least from the one network computer I found. Your boyfriend—"

Bennett pinched his neck, a painful habit.

"—ouch—tried to hide the files in a fake mail account and in fax files, which isn't super smart. Hopefully, he isn't computer savvy enough to have the files backed up on a remote server that we don't know about. Grant scrolled back to the emails addressed to the legislator and read through them. "These are so bland they don't make sense. Unless they are just codes." He pointed to the first one. "This one mentions a tourist trip to Houston that could potentially result, it says, in significantly increased tourist revenue. Think this is a cover for a message relating to the bribery scheme?"

Bennett shrugged her shoulder. "I don't recognize the address."

"We need to figure out who the emails are addressed to, so we can close down the bribery deal, or at least pass the information to Allen and the FDLE Computer Crime Center folks. I'll start by sending Allen copies of the messages sent to the legislator. See if he can track them. Then I'll destroy the incriminating files so they won't be proliferated into the wrong hands." Grant forwarded the email files to Allen's email. He then deleted the original files, one by one from the DEP server, and then deleted the fax folder.

"A good computer analyst could find the file records, but it would take a forensic specialist to reconstruct the actual files or find the backups. At least you're safe from Silva simply retrieving or printing out the files, or faxing them to someone else." Finished, Grant powered down the computer and spun around in the chair. "I'll take Flash out, check his food and water. You get Angelica ready."

Bennett frowned at him. "We're going now?"

"Right now." Grant started to tell her about Roberto's report on the human remains, the likelihood of Juan's death, his own optimistic hope that Chantico might still be alive. He decided to let it pass. They had to move on. "I'll see to Flash. You get Angelica ready to go meet Chris."

Grant followed her out into the hall and watched her veer into the kitchen, a spring back to her step. Grant thought about the weight pulling at his pants. He was a believer in the stopping power of the .45 caliber Kimber loaded and cocked in his hip pocket, but he had no concept what he was getting into when they got to Tampa. This might be another day he had to kill somebody.

CHAPTER 29

Silva ignored the red glow of the sun burning through the early morning mists. He hadn't been able to sleep, wondering if the lingering smell of dog piss was real or in his mind, how he was going to find Bennett and, more important, how she was going to die! The building was silent as he shoved the door open and walked back to the Department of Environmental Protection office he shared with Bennett before the other staff arrived.

He threw the beach bag, fat with bundles of bills wrapped in dirty clothes, behind the desk and pulled out a couple of Fed Ex boxes from behind a credenza. He'd use these to ship the payoff to the Senator and his payment to his pals up north. He counted out the bills, addressed, stuffed and sealed the boxes. Finished, he dropped into his desk chair, grunting when the holstered Glock bit into his side.

"Bitch," he muttered, and slipped the Glock and its holster from his belt and into a desk drawer. He rubbed the teeth marks on his sore wrist and pondered for a moment, wondering if he needed to lose the pistol. He didn't think it could be traced by bullet analysis. He had loaded the 9mm Glock with MagSafe frangible bullets, powerful shotgun-like loads with lead pellets, not a single slug that could be put under a microscope and compared. Plus, all the shooting at the clinic and Suitcase City he could lay off to a righteous chase of dangerous perps, backed by his Vice and Narcotics buddies in the Tampa PD.

His only regret was that he hadn't been able to nail Bennett when she stood by his Corvette with the throwdown in her hand. Now he had other plans for the tiny Kel-Tec. He shook his head at the fiasco in Suitcase City. He should have taken her alone, not asked for help. A missed opportunity, but too late to whine now. Only thing to do now was make sure anything she said or did was discredited.

He turned on the desktop computer and pulled up the fax program. Somehow he had known he would need some protection against Bennett. She was too damn smart, sneaking around and digging into his personal deals. He'd send copies of the faxes anonymously to the FDLE; let them assume they were from an outraged clerk who had stumbled on a terrible drug scheme, or something as stupid. He'd make sure nothing in the faxes linked to him or Russell, only to Bennett and that pothead Wilson. Silva paused, fingers poised over the computer keys. Where could he send them? FBI? Don't need that bucket of worms spilled. The fax console program already had the FDLE Tampa Operations Center in the speed dial, why not them? Silva dropped the cursor down to the miscellaneous file and opened the folder.

He stared at the folder for a moment, his anger building. He clicked open each folder in the fax console. He slammed his fist down on the desk. Damn files were missing! The planted messages were gone, the folder empty. He clicked on the properties for the folder, and looked up at the calendar on the wall. The folder's creation date was today, obviously overwritten, all the messages erased. Now he knew. That son of a bitch Wilson had conspired with Bennett to hijack the dope and clear all the incriminating files from the computer.

Silva spun his chair around, unlocked the cabinet drawer, pulled a laptop computer out of the cabinet behind the desk and fired it up. When the laptop finished booting, he quickly found the backup copies of the fax documents he had stored in the laptop files and pulled them up on the screen to confirm they were the correct ones. He connected to the Department's wireless network, this time logging on as Katrina Bennett. Then, one by one, he faxed them to the Tampa Operations Center. Whatever she said now, the faxes would pin it all on her and Wilson.

Had he missed anything? Bennett was on the run with a fugitive on drugs and a suspect in the death of at least two law enforcement officers. Silva didn't have a clue how Bennett had gotten involved in the other shootings, but figured she, or her partner, had killed the two Brotherhood bozos when she hijacked the weed. As he thought about it, he decided he really didn't give a shit about how she was involved, she was dead meat anyway it worked.

With luck, she and the joker she had teamed up with would be killed when either he or the law caught up to them. But Allen Wilson was a loose cannon. As far as Wilson was concerned, the faxes were flimsy evidence. He needed to silence that pot head, personally.

Silva leaned out the office door to make sure no one else had come in yet. Hallway clear, he unlocked the bottom drawer, took out two blister packs of MagSafe 9mm rounds and reloaded the Glock's empty magazine. He slipped his driving gloves on and speared the Kel-Tec out of the beach bag with a pencil up the barrel, thinking back as he laid it on the desk. Bennett had held the pistol by its grip for just a moment before she flung it back at him. Must be at least a smudged print somewhere on the pistol. He popped the magazine release with the rubber eraser tip. Two .380 rounds left in the Kel-Tec's magazine. Should be one more left in the chamber. He clicked the magazine back into the pistol with a gloved fingertip. *A present for Kat*, he thought, *a special present.*

He opened a credenza behind Bennett's desk. He flipped open the top of a box of chocolates sitting on the top shelf, took out the remaining piece and popped it in his mouth. He let the pistol slide off the pencil and into the box, then closed the lid. Silva looked around the silent office, chewing on the caramel center, searching for any evidence that could connect him with the shootings or the drug deal. When he spotted the laptop still on his desk he thought of one more perfect touch. He retrieved the laptop, wiped it clean with his gloves and slid it in the credenza beside the chocolate box. He spun around, startled, when he heard steps in the hall.

"Morning, Mr. Silva. Got anything to go in addition to these?" The mail clerk dropped a stack of papers and envelopes on Silva's desk and picked up the Fed Ex boxes stuffed with money.

Silva took a deep breath. "That's it. Thanks." When the kid was gone Silva picked up a bulletin from the top of the stack. It named Bennett with a man identified as Ulysses Grant as suspects in a felony. Silva smiled. It had started.

He had figured he had plenty of time, but the word was out. He needed to get his hands on Bennett, Grant and Wilson, before they could implicate him. The sooner dead, the better. Like the spics and that damn dog.

CHAPTER 30

Delina Karkoff eyed the nameplate on her FDLE desk identifying her as Delina Sanchez, administrative assistant. One day she would have her own assistant, in a new Havana, perhaps, or maybe even London. Yes, London would be better, if her father's associate and newly promoted Special Agent in Charge Ernesto Raphael followed her instructions. She closed her eyes. Agents' voices echoed through the Tampa FDLE Operations Center, now eerily quiet after the frantic activity caused by her brother's rocket attack. The investigation had ground down to a snail's pace as agents traced the owner's registry of the boat found in the bay and argued with various agencies over jurisdiction. Identification of the partially burned body of Zakariya al Bandri had intensified the investigation, everyone speculating that America was under some massive new terrorist attack, especially when the boat was eventually traced to the Bahamas. She had to stifle a laugh when Special Agent Talbot had commended her on remaining calm in the midst of the threats. Threats? Ludicrous. If anything, she posed a greater threat to America than al Bandri.

She scanned Raphael's latest report. Following her suggestions, he had ordered wire taps on Bennett's family and requested a federal background check on Grant. She had planted the idea that perhaps Grant made some contact with al Qaeda when he was in Iraq. Raphael's manipulations had everyone running in circles, none even approaching her or her family. Amazing what the promise of riches produced. She had been wise to become more than a friend to Raphael. Together, they could do much.

Her eyes popped wide, startled when the phone connected to the fax machine behind her desk rang. Seconds later the first page slowly emerged. Startled by the content, she plucked off the sheet and read it as the following pages fed out of the tray. When she got to the last fax she looked around to make sure no one else had noticed the machine's activity. She read through them again. The faxes clearly incriminated the Bennett woman. Delina took a sharp breath when she read the final page, identifying Allen Wilson as one of the conspirators. Hands trembling, she quickly scanned them again. No mention of her, Ivan, or anything about the rocket attack. The messages all had to do with drugs. Delina looked at the fax header and confirmed her first impression that they came from Bennett's DEP office. Had Bennett sent them to the FDLE Tampa Operations Center by mistake? Was the woman that stupid? Delina carefully folded the final sheet, the only one mentioning Allen, and slipped it into her purse. She sat back and stared at the fax terminal, unsure of what to do next. Across the room, Talbot had returned to his desk, munching on corn chips from the vending machine as he listened to his phone. Delina picked up the faxes implicating Bennett and stood in Talbot's doorway until he slammed the handset down, a frown on his face. She must be careful. With her help, Raphael had manipulated the system to replace Talbot while the senior agent was deployed to Iraq. Talbot was smart and, now, especially, angry—not a man to be trifled with.

"What do you have?"

Startled, she handed the remaining faxes to Talbot. The man saw everything—almost. "These just came in. I'm not sure what to make of them. Perhaps they came to us by mistake." She glanced up at the wall clock. Her extended shift was almost over. "Anything else for me." She needed to make sure her father and Ivan had not made another hasty move that would upset her plans.

Talbot's cheek twitched as he read the first page. He waved at her as he continued reading. "Go, go. It's late. Raphael won't be back until tomorrow. I'll check these out." He picked up his phone and scrunched it between his ear and shoulder as he read the next fax.

Back at her desk Delina took out her cell phone and dialed. "Hello, father, it's Delina." She frowned and repeated her name, louder this time. "Delina." She covered her mouth and the phone with her hand so she could speak loudly without Talbot overhearing her. "Yes, yes, your daughter Delina. I wanted to make sure you were home. I need to speak with you. And Ivan."

Within the hour she had pulled into the inner courtyard that hid the back entrance to a faded red brick building, once a cigar factory on the edge of Ybor City when Ybor was the center of the world's cigar industry. She parked beside a vehicle she didn't recognize, a white pickup truck with a metal frame attached to the back. The signage on the truck advertised a highway surveying company.

She wrinkled her nose at the smells, roasting coffee, curing tobacco and something else too sour to describe, that met her at the door and followed her up the staircase. On the second floor she found Ivan and their father, Colonel General Roman Karkoff, sitting behind a desk, looking over a large map.

Ivan nodded without looking up. Her father offered her a pale cheek which she pecked. "Are your treatments going well, Papa?"

The retired Soviet general raised an unlit cigar and waved it with a trembling hand. "The American hospitals, with all their fancy technology, do not have the skilled doctors, not so good as the Russians who treated me in Havana. Sometimes I wish I were back where I could at least visit your mothers' graves. But time for travel, for me, has passed." He leaned over the map and pointed with the cigar at a promontory jutting out into Tampa Bay marked with crossing runways, MacDill Air Force Base. "Ivan still has one more mission to fulfill."

Delina stepped across the room to the window and stared down at the tourists beginning to fill the Ybor City streets. *More foolishness.* She turned back to Ivan. "Please convince Father that we can stop with these ineffectual attacks. The Ministry believes it is time to escalate the nuclear issue."

The general shook his head. "No, no. The attack on the port was only the first phase of our operation. Already the media are filled with warnings of environmental disaster resulting from the oil spill. Soon, they will connect our attack to the potential threats from offshore oil drilling and pipelines. Even though the attack did not cause much damage, the *Norte Americano* media made it a bigger disaster than it was. Are your office and the FBI following the Islamic terrorist leads?" her father asked. "What help can you provide?"

"I saw a FBI report today that identified al Bandri's body. They have also confirmed the boat was stolen in the Bahamas. FDLE, FBI, they are all convinced that the cigarette lighter Ivan left in Homosassa implicates Arab terrorists." Delina started to pull the fax from her purse, but stopped, wondering if now was the time to tell Ivan what she knew. "I hope you left no other evidence. If so, there is a danger that they will link you to the two events. We should not underestimate their investigation."

"Ivan only used weapons al Bandri brought in from the islands. I made sure the rockets can be traced back to Africa, even more proof to the Americans that the Arabs were behind the attack. It may even suggest to the Americans that more Saudis are involved and further influence the price of oil products in our favor."

Delina frowned. "I think this is all getting too complex, for little value. FDLE is in constant contact with Homeland Security and other security agencies through them, including the CIA. Be careful that you do not leave traces for them to follow. Ernesto will alert me to any danger, but I cannot be sure."

The general looked up from the map and stared at Delina. "Your Ernesto should realize you hold his career, his life in your hands." He shuddered with a deep cough. "We must continue. Any disruption to the American oil industry and future exploration legislation will support our cause."

Delina turned to Ivan. "I asked you to interrupt the drug transaction in hopes of slowing the process that I discovered through my Indian. You went too far. The attack of a police station was very risky, too risky. Now you have lost both your lover and a comrade."

Ivan sat back, anger flashing in his eyes. "I didn't realize the woman had gone to a police station. I believed she had stopped to deliver the drugs to the Mexicans in the cantina." His voice rose as he continued. "Just as I had no suspicion the woman would be with an armed bodyguard. The man's appearance was of a crippled fisherman." Ivan turned to Delina, a scowl on his face. "Your Indian left out important information." His look implied that for some reason she was at fault for Petite and Agustín's death, not his own impetuousness.

Delina swallowed her rage as Ivan accused her. Her mother had been a beautiful woman, an official in the Cuban government, a friend of *el Comandante* himself. Ivan's mother was only a street whore, someone for father to bed on cold nights. But Ivan had been the perfect son, serving with the Cuban Army in Angola, even traveling to Afghanistan for their father while perfecting his hatred for America. She knew better than to stand between them, or even more dangerous, to argue with Ivan. Sometimes she even wondered if he had been the cause of her mother's death. Ivan found killing too easy. The fools, both of them, should realize that she was the one controlling the information flow, and, more importantly, the flow of funds to support their actions. Father still thought of her as his little girl. Not for long. She had found others who could kill for her. Let Ivan rant, as long as he did as he was told.

"What do you want me to do next, father?" Ivan held a match to the end of the general's dark Veguero, then snipped the end of a second with his teeth and lit it for himself. A cloud of smoke enveloped their heads.

Enough. "Ivan. Father. I decide. We cannot wait for the Canadians to form a new exploration consortium. My contacts with the Russians insist we must move now while the Americans agonize over the consequences of the oil spill." Delina hated the smoke as much as the bickering. The cigars were killing father, almost as surely as the cancer from his radiation exposure. She waved away the cloud and tapped the map between Havana and Key West. "The recent Russian exploration contract has made our efforts even more important to Cuba. I am in constant contact, and the Russians have promised continued financial support."

Delina paused as the General interrupted her with a bout of coughing.

"The new consortium expects to find more oil in Cuban controlled waters very soon, and the Russians simply want world oil demand to outstrip supply, especially American demand. There are further plans to sabotage more oil rigs in the Gulf which will increase demand even further. In both cases, domination of the American oil market is the goal, with the side benefit of the long term degradation of the American economy and the destruction of the fragile American-Arab business arrangements."

"Very good," The General smiled at Delina, as if he were teaching her lessons of which she knew nothing.

"Father—" Delina began, about to explain how she had put the authorities on the trail of the drug dealers, thwarting their attempt to obtain bribery money.

"Yes, girl. I know you are in charge." The general waved his infernal cigar at her and pounded the map with his other fist. "But we must watch closely, pounce upon each opportunity to influence the outcome of the legislative process."

Delina leaned over and placed her hand on his fist. "That is why I called. Allen Wilson came to my apartment last night, told me the drug transaction was completed, despite Ivan's attempt to intervene." She thought of the faxes and the action that Talbot was sure to take. "Others are now aware of the bribery plot. We need not interfere further and possibly expose ourselves. The Americans may delay the oil exploration program themselves when the scheme is uncovered."

Ivan jumped to his feet. "*Que pasa*? I thought that woman and the pig who shot Petite were killed or in hiding from the authorities. How did they get the drugs? Who else have they brought into their schemes?"

Delina frowned at him. "Apparently the woman recovered the drugs and is handling the transaction now, with the help of her friend. Allen thinks he is gaining my favor by exposing her to the authorities, through me." She lifted her chin, stared through the smoke at her brother. "I have passed this information to a senior agent in the FDLE. You need to take no further actions to undo your mistake." She stood and turned to the general. "Father. Do not concern yourself. I have taken adequate precautions to stop the woman and her friend."

"Ha." Ivan barked out a puff of smoke. "Who are you working for? This Indian, or for our father and his patrons? This is work for soldiers, not women."

Delina waved the cloud of cigar smoke away. "I do what I do for Cuba, Ivan; not you. You let your hatred of Americans cloud your judgment. But I—"

"Stop, stop, you two," barked the general. "Do not bicker. Let us remain focused. Delina, you must find out more information on the bribery scheme, and let Ivan take any needed corrective action to be certain it stops."

Delina's face froze. Her father hadn't heard a word she had spoken. If he only knew what she had accomplished. The Cuban minister had promised her a senior position in the Economic Ministry as a result of her efforts to secure the Russian contract.

Let the two of them live in their clouds of cigar smoke.

Ivan turned to Delina. "How many of your friends have died at the hands of the Americans?" He drew a cloud of smoke from his cigar and blew a stream toward the ceiling. "You, you have lived in America too long. You are one of them. Just tell me where they are hiding, and I will kill the bastards."

Delina bit back a rebuke. "I understand your frustration, losing Petite, but we must stop toying with drugs and ports. We must address the long term issue of nuclear power. Let the Americans continue their internal squabble over off-shore exploration. Soon the Russians will suck the oil out from under through the Straits of Florida wells." She pulled a copy of a report from her purse. "We need to direct opinions in opposition to any new facilities or expansion of the existing nuclear power plants. There is talk of a new reactor in the center of the state. I intend to make it my personal goal to make sure no new nuclear plants are built. They have been an abomination to the entire world. Just look at you, father. You would be a well man if ..." She stopped, aware the two men had resumed talking, ignoring her completely.

As the general scattered ashes, ideas and Leninist philosophy across the table, Delina wondered which of his words had meaning and which were the ramblings of a man embittered and sickened by his exposure to radiation. The skin on his once handsome face was drawn, ravaged by the battle inside his body brought on by his work at Chernobyl. If only he had stayed in Cuba with her mother, so much would have been different. She started to interrupt, then stopped, decided to leave them to their wild schemes of revenge, her half-brother's focus on becoming wealthy with his drug trade. "Here." She handed her father the map Allen had given her. "This is where Allen Wilson believes the man, Grant, lives."

The general handed the map over to Ivan.

Ivan's eyes lit up. "This is perfect," he said, tracing a line from the marked location, across the water, to the nuclear power facility at Crystal River. "*Muy perfecto.*" He stood. "I must go and find Stephan. We have some work to finish." He smiled at Delina. "Americans to kill."

CHAPTER 31

Ivan shook the heavy framework extending from the rear end of the truck bed all the way across the top of the pickup's cab, satisfied the assembly felt sturdy and stable. He stepped back and squinted along the frame. One of the four PVC tubes was slightly misaligned. He tightened the strap securing the tube to the frame, moving the tube a centimeter or so to the left, visually gauging the tube's movement. Satisfied, he sighted across the tubes and toggled the switch operating the jury-rigged boat winch cable. The motor whined as it took up the slack in the cable.

Stephan jumped back in alarm when the frame creaked and groaned.

Ivan chuckled."I see your wound has not seriously impeded your movements."

Stephan blushed. "I thought it was falling."

"Not with the heavy bolts we used to attach the frame. Unless you failed to tighten them."

"They are tight."

The ball inclinometer attached to the frame slowly rotated to designate a forty-five degree angle as the back ends of the four tubes dropped. Ivan cycled the switch and the tubes rose back to a horizontal position.

"Will these missiles do any better than the ones on the boat?" Stephan asked.

Ivan shrugged. "If we do our job correctly, and the rockets perform as they are designed."

Stephan cocked his head and looked at Ivan, questions apparent in his eyes.

"Don't be afraid to ask questions, Stephan. If you have something to say, speak."

"The other missiles missed the tanker. Why do you think these will do better?"

"You're thinking, Stephan. Good." Ivan slapped his hand against the side of the truck. "This time the launch platform will be much more stable." He grabbed the frame and rocked the truck. "Once we get in place and have the tubes correctly oriented, we will deflate the tires so the truck sits directly on the ground. The shocks are old, so they will allow only minimal movement." He pulled a portable GPS device from his pocket and held it so Stephan could see the miniature screen. "I have programmed the nuclear facility location in the GPS. Once we arrive at the launch site we should be able to visually sight the cooling towers, but if not, the device will also display the exact azimuth and range to the target."

Ivan hopped up onto the loading dock and peered at the large door screening them from the alley, checking to make sure they had no unwanted observers. "Come and help me load the launch tubes." He opened a wooden crate labeled "Fragile - Survey Equipment - Do Not Drop" and lifted one end of an olive drab tube with yellow Arabic markings clear of the crate. "Are you ready? Careful. Each rocket weighs about seventy kilograms."

Stephan picked up the other end, sweat dripping from his nose.

They raised the first rocket up to the level of the PVC tubes attached to the framework. "Gently, guide it into the tube. The missiles damage easily. We have four spares, but I don't want to use them unless we must. I have other plans, even more important. I have located Central Command headquarters on the GPS. I could hit it from right here, from our rooftop, when the time is right. One day soon, I will kill all the bastards."

"Will Delina approve?"

Ivan ignored his question and held the rocket steady as Stephan slid it into the tube. "Now secure the front end with a cap." He pointed to PVC caps on the loading dock.

Ivan stood back as Stephan hammered an end cap firmly on the tube with his fist.

"Gently. The rockets are fused to explode on contact."

He laughed as Stephan noticeably paled.

"Good. Now for the others."

The other three rockets loaded quickly.

Ivan stepped back and surveyed their work. "Now strap the two ladders across the sides."

He thumped one of the four PVC tubes strapped to the framework. "When the rockets inside these tubes hit their targets, Delina's Russian and Cuban associates will pay us well. We can expand our other business interests, buy more grow houses with the real estate market so cheap. Diversify, as the capitalist bastards say."

Stephan still looked doubtful. "But can we actually strike the reactor?"

"The range should be about eleven kilometers from the launch location to the nuclear plant cooling towers." Ivan pulled a creased sheet from his pocket and again checked the trajectory table. "These are the Iranian *Arash* model of the Soviet *Katyusha*, not those old Egyptian pieces of trash we fired from the boat." He held up a hand and showed Stephan the missing fingers. "My experience with the Egyptian rockets is not so good. That is one reason I let our Arab friend fire the ones on the boat, in case they exploded on ignition." Ivan squinted down the length of the PVC tubes. "These are accurate within one hundred meters of the aim point at the range I have plotted. If we aim correctly, the rockets will land very close to the reactor containment facility." Again his broad shouldered shrug. "As Father said, even if no radiation is released, the wailing over the facility's vulnerability will be sufficient to halt any further talk of building new nuclear reactors." Ivan slammed his hand against the truck. "And the *Norte Americanos* will blame the bastard who killed Petite and Agustín, whether or not we can find him ourselves."

Stephan frowned. "How will the police make a connection between him and the rockets?"

Ivan pulled a second creased sheet of paper from a shirt pocket, a map with a penciled circle around a cross mark. "Delina discovered the location of the man's home." Ivan tapped a mark on the sheet. "We will launch the missiles to strike the nuclear reactor from there."

Stephan suddenly turned to Ivan, a worried look on his face. "If you deflate the tires, how will we escape after we fire the missiles?"

"Stephan, comrade, this is not a suicide mission. I do not believe in any god, but if there is one as our Arab friends proclaim so loudly, I doubt he is waiting for me to kill myself. He will have to take me when I fail myself, not before." Ivan pointed to the airboat on a trailer parked beside the wall. "We will tow the boat behind the truck and place it in the water close to the launch point. After the rockets fire, we will then escape by boat. We will leave what is left of the truck to further implicate this American. Perhaps the authorities will even kill him for us." He looked at Stephan for a moment, his smile gone. "You had your opportunity to kill him at the dock, and did not."

Stephan averted his eyes. "I was concerned about Agustín."

"Look at me! I understand. And you were wounded. The first time, it always frightens. In combat there is a time to help and a time to fight. I remind you only so you will learn." Ivan sat on the steps, rolled one of his Vegueros cigars between his fingers, bit off the end and lit the cigar with a wooden match. "Do you remember what I have taught you about the firing circuits when you fabricated the control box?"

Stephan nodded, rubbing his bandaged shoulder.

"Then you wire the missiles, while I watch." Ivan tossed a screwdriver and a pair of wire cutters to Stephan. "First, pass the wires through the end caps, and wire the rockets. Don't forget, we capped the front end of the launch tubes, so do not trigger the rocket motor by mistake. The warhead could detonate here in the courtyard, and you will not have the opportunity to purchase your fancy new car."

After ensuring the battery leads were disconnected from the black metal box bristling with toggle switches and connectors, Ivan watched closely as Stephan began connecting the firing wires to each *Arash*.

"And you are very certain no radiation will escape from the reactor." Stephan's inflection implied his words were more question than statement.

Once again Ivan shrugged. "Come, boy. You have stopped being a thinker and started being a worrier. Finish here first. Then go check all of our plant rooms. Remember, regardless of the outcome of this rocket business, we are rich men. The drug dealers hunger for more product, so do not let the room conditions get out of control. We will leave soon, before dawn, so we can set up in the early morning." Ivan blew a dark cloud of smoke up into the sky, watched it twist and float in the hot air. "In the morning you will see a grand spectacle. And perhaps an opportunity to avenge Agustín and impress Delina."

CHAPTER 32

Grant tried to focus on driving the flatbed, but the girls' chatter was beginning to make him wish he had indulged in a handful of OxyContin instead of only two Tylenols. He should have taken at least four, but the docs had warned him he was killing his liver if he didn't ease up. And the OxyContin put him in a funk. How long had it been? One, two days since he took a blue bomb?

Grant glanced over when the girls laughed. He pulled the ragged straw hat down to his ears and made a face at Angelica. She giggled even louder.

"You look ridiculous." Bennett pressed a big straw hat to her head to keep it from blowing out the open window. "Doesn't he?" she asked Angelica.

Angelica smiled up at Grant, then Bennett. "I think you look like Miss Miranda in the book about Rebecca that Mrs. Sanchez reads to us at school. Rebecca wore a straw hat in the picture, with a flower on it. Can I go back to school soon? Can I get a little straw hat like Rebecca in the book? With a flower?"

"Yes, sweetie. You can go back to school real soon. Let's just take a couple of days of vacation." Bennett took off her straw hat and plopped it down on Angelica's head. "Here. You can wear my hat till we find you one like Rebecca's. With a flower." She held up a top for Grant to see. "See what we bought Angelica." Bennett had insisted they stop on the way so she could get Angelica some clothes. "Just boy's stuff at the farm," she had explained, as if that was enough reason to risk being recognized.

"It's very pretty." Angelica pushed the hat back so she could see from under the brim. "Are we going to a farm like Sunnybrook? When we get there will we set up a fruit stand like Uncle Enrique?"

Grant glanced in the rearview mirror and chuckled at the row of empty produce boxes. "Yes, we just might. But first let's go find Chris." He followed Bennett's directions and turned down a secondary road leading away from the highway. About fifty miles southeast of Homosassa and Ozello and less than twenty from Tampa, the landscape around San Antonio changed dramatically from the familiar flat swamps and cabbage palm thickets. This land rolled, real hills so different from the coastal landscape where he grew up. Scattered dogwoods and camellias, blooms long since come and gone, lined the road. Cypress stands marked the low wetlands between the grasslands and the scattered lakes. Herds of cattle grazed among the low cabbage palms, some standing knee-deep in the cool water. Real Cracker country.

Blowing in the breeze, Bennett's dyed hair had developed several weird orange streaks, almost a match to the wild flowers blooming along the roadside.

Grant turned onto a one lane gravel road and crossed a rickety bridge over a creek that probably burbled if he could hear over the truck's exhaust. He bumped down the road under a canopy of ancient oaks. Past the oaks he skirted around a hill thick with mixed hardwoods and a tangle of wild grape vines. When they cleared the trees, Grant spotted a small frame house halfway up the low hill, flanked by a pair of tall magnolias just beginning to bloom out. Planted garden rows circled the foot of the slope, and a plot of tall corn extended along the bottom land between the slope and the creek. The road, now little more than a lane, bumped over the exposed roots of a giant live oak then followed a line of pecan trees to a weathered barn and fenced pens.

Bennett pointed at a figure emerging from the corn rows. "There's Logan," she said, with a lilt to her voice Grant hadn't heard before.

Grant glanced over at the wide grin spreading across her face. Did he actually feel emotion, jealousy, at her tone? He let the truck roll to a stop in the shade of a pecan tree.

Bennett opened the door, slid down from the high truck seat and lifted Angelica out, holding the little girl on her hip. "Look, Angelica. That's Chris over there."

A boy skipped along behind the man, then broke into an awkward run toward Bennett, arms waving over his head. "Mommy, mommy. I didn't know who you were till daddy said it was you. He said you might come see us, but I didn't think it was you, your hair all funny." The boy wrapped his arms around her legs as the man, a curly headed, large scale replica of the boy, walked up, sat a basket of green corn on the ground and gave Bennett a peck on the cheek. The man stepped back and looked at her hair, a question in his eyes.

Grant got out and walked around the truck, feeling very much the odd man out.

"Logan and Chris, this is Angelica. She came to stay with you for a little visit, if it's all right. And Logan, this is Uly, the fellow I told you about." Bennett tousled Chris's curly hair. "Uly's a really good friend who's helped me, us, a lot."

Logan stuck out his hand. "Glad to meet you, Uly."

When he gripped Logan's calloused hand and smelled the fresh corn and bottom land dirt, Grant instantly liked the man. He hoped all his judgment wasn't leaving him simply because Logan reminded him of old Alphonso Madero with his bib overalls and giant tomatoes.

Logan turned to include Bennett and the children. "Come on up to the house. Liz is still at work. Chris and I put a treat in the smoker for you. Katrina, can I carry Angelica?"

Angelica answered the question by slithering down Bennett's leg and walking over to Chris.

Chris took her hand. "Come on, Jelly. I'll show you the pigs, and the pretty rocks in the creek. Maybe we'll see a frog." The kids ran around the side of the barn, already friends.

"Don't stay long, and don't get wet in the creek," Logan called after them. "Supper will be ready pretty soon. And don't let Angelica get all nasty around the pig pen." Logan led the way up the hill, Bennett close by his side.

Grant lagged behind carrying Angelica's new clothes, sniffing at the air. Wood smoke drifted down the slope from the house. Surrounded by the old oaks draped with Spanish moss, they could have been a thousand miles from anywhere. He hurried up the hill after Logan and Bennett, a twinge shooting up his leg as he climbed the grass covered slope.

Logan dropped the basket of corn on the porch. "Let me get cleaned up. Liz won't be home for a bit, but I can fix you some good fresh corn for supper, along with some pork shoulder cooking in the smoker." He turned toward the barn and whistled. An answering yell came back and moments later Chris and Angelica's heads bobbed into sight. They darted up the hill to arrive sweaty and grinning.

Grant watched Bennett's face, saw the concern when Chris arrived, outrun by Angelica.

"Momma, I helped Daddy butcher the pig. It was really yucky." Chris made an appropriate face that Angelica carefully mimicked.

"And I found a pretty rock in the creek. Chris said it looks like a frog face." Angelica held up a polished pebble that did actually look like a frog.

Logan smiled. "You kids go wash your hands in the sink before you touch anything."

The kids ran into the house, screen door slamming behind them. Logan caught the door on the bounce and motioned Bennett and Grant inside.

A black cat with brilliant green eyes stared at Grant from the corner. Logan cracked the screen. "Out, Rocky." The cat darted out the door followed by a squeal from a startled Angelica. Logan laughed. "Our guard cat. He keeps the mice at bay. Uly, would you help Chris feed in some wood while I shower?"

Chris hopped down from the sink. "We'll cook it good. Come on, Uly." He led Grant to the back of the house where Chris explained in grand detail how to add two hickory billets into the smoker without burning his fingers. The boy exuded happiness, belying his frail exterior and measured movements as if he were conserving energy.

When they came back inside, the smell of fragrant hickory smoke laced with a hint of spices followed them through the screen door. Grant stood in the middle of the kitchen, feet throbbing as he recognized the muted vibrations of an attic fan pulling the warm summer air through the old frame house, a memory Grant savored from his mother's bait shop. Air conditioning didn't seem to be in Logan's budget, either. By the sink, Bennett finished shucking a stack of sweet corn ears. Angelica stood beside her on a chair picking tiny bits of silk from the shucked ears.

Bennett wiped Angelica's hands with a dishrag. "Chris. Why don't you show Angelica your things? Just don't make a big mess for Liz to clean up. And take things easy. You've been outside with your dad working hard. I don't want you getting too tired."

"'Kay, mom. Come on, Jelly. I got a real neat dump truck." Chris took Angelica by the hand and led the way to a corner filled with toys.

"You got any crayons? I like to color." Angelica and Chris sprawled on the worn linoleum. "Auntie Katrina." Angelica held up a yellow crayon. "When are you going to make your hair sunshiny again?"

Bennett ran her finders through her chopped up hair, the orange streaks even more pronounced under the incandescent fixture. "Soon as I can, honey. It's just a rinse. It'll come back out the next time I give it a good shampoo. I'll be just like before."

Bennett slid the pot on to the stove and turned the burner on high. "Chris is playing big brother already. Notice he's given Angelica a new nickname?"

"Good kid, you got there, Kat." Grant packed the corn shucks in a brown grocery bag. "And Logan seems like a nice guy." Grant used the edge of his palm to sweep stray bits of corn silk and shuck off the counter and into the bag.

"He is. Logan had a pretty good job managing a grocery store, but got laid off when the chain went under. He still hasn't found anything steady, so he spends most of his time working the farm. He puts food on the table, and adds a few dollars from selling at the farmers' market." She bit the end from a homemade pickle she plucked from a jar on the counter, made a face, and ate the rest. "We got married in college; after I found out I was pregnant with Chris. One of those marriages that never should have happened, except both of us felt like we owed it to the baby to have a home. We ended up separating. It just seemed sensible for Logan and Liz to keep Chris."

"Are they married?"

"Yeah. Finally. Just last year. Gun shy after me, I guess. It took Logan a while to pop the question. Liz is as good a person as Logan, and Chris dearly loves her. We looked into my assuming guardianship, but my insurance includes a preexisting clause that screws him, the same reason Logan hasn't taken some other crap job. He and Liz decided that she'd take a job at Wal-Mart to pay the bills, and Logan would look out after Chris. I help as much as I can from my salary. Medicaid has kept his treatments going, so far, but now Chris needs more, a lot more than the government is willing to give." She picked the corn silk from her fingers and looked up at Grant. "You may have saved Chris's life."

Grant shrugged. "Usually what I do is for people I don't even know. Which is all right by me. I spent enough time in Walter Reed to appreciate what you're going through. When you're really hurt, it's like you are a kid again, needing somebody else to look after you. Exasperating. Like when you have to let a nurse put a bed pan under your butt so you can go to the bathroom, then wipe your ass after. When you're hospitalized for something bad, you're helpless, frustrated. I think a lot of the wounded men and women I knew in Walter Reed will heal physically, but some will never quite get their mind straight." He folded the top of the bag down. "I'm probably one of them."

After supper Grant cleaned up the dishes while Bennett and Logan talked out on the porch. They looked to Grant like they should still be married, the way they walked together. His ability to judge people had left him, but at least hand washing and drying with a faded dishtowel had come back to him. He had grown up broke as dirt, but happy as a kid can be without a dad. Chris was lucky, despite the cancer, to have a mom and dad who loved him. Suddenly a plate slipped from Grant's fingers and clattered to the floor, rattling around on the worn linoleum.

He had almost forgotten that Angelica didn't have a father. Because of him, because he hadn't paid attention, let himself get drawn into a mixed up drug deal gone wrong. Eyes squeezed shut, he let the pain in his arm and hip wash over him, a reminder of what he had done, what he had not done.

A hand touched his arm.

"Uly. You all right?" Bennett asked.

"Yeah." Grant bent down and picked up the plate, a scratched and stained Melmac piece. He rinsed and dried the plate again, this time carefully handing it to Bennett who slid it back on the shelf on top of a stack. "Kat. You and I got to get going." He turned to Logan. "Mind if we leave you with the kids for a bit. If she hasn't told you already, Kat and I need to take care of some business."

"I saw the TV news this morning. Somebody thinks one of you, or you two together, have killed several people. I got to confess, when Katrina told me you had put some money in the clinic for Chris, I wondered there—" He threw up his hands and shook his head. "—I wondered if maybe you were up to your ears in drugs or something worse." Then he laughed. "I know that's stupid. Go. But be careful, both of you.

Bennett smiled and glanced back at Grant, guilt apparent in her eyes.

Was he getting back his old interrogator skills, or was her guilt just too heavy to hide? More important, was it guilt about lying to Logan or was there still more to come?

Logan apparently didn't notice. "At least you look different from the TV pictures. I think they actually used an old yearbook photo for Katrina. I've always trusted her." It showed on his face "I guess now I've got to trust you, trust that you guys are not who the TV says you are."

Trust. The word burned Grant's ears.

Grant wondered what Logan would say if he knew how many men he had killed since he met Bennett; how many of his friends had died. He turned and walked over to the front screen. He cracked the door so he could get a clear view of the lane at the bottom of the hill, his attention suddenly focused. "What kind of car does Liz drive?" he asked Logan.

"She's got an old red Ford Escort hatchback, but she won't be home until after nine."

Grant turned to Bennett. "Somebody nosing along the pecan trees. Looks like a big SUV, probably some kind of law enforcement. We got to go." He grabbed Logan as he started toward the door. "You and the kids can't come, not the way the cops view this. Got anyplace you can hide with the kids? If it's cops, you come out and tell them we were here, but left." Grant shoved Bennett toward the door as Logan nodded, speechless. "It could be Silva and his goons. If it is, he won't stick around long. Just stay out of sight till you figure out who it is."

Bennett stopped in the doorway. "Wait a minute, Uly. If it is the police, and they find Angelica here, what'll happen to her?"

"Don't worry. Chris and I will take care of that." Logan turned to Chris. "Hey, buddy. Before it gets dark, let's take Jelly and show her your secret tree."

Chris looked at Logan, head cocked to the side and the corner of his mouth twisted with a question. "But then it won't be a secret."

Logan waved all of them out, shooing them like they were a herd of his pigs. "Well, it'll still be a secret between you and Jelly. Just don't tell me. I'll be down in a minute and do our special whistle for you before it gets real dark. O.K.?"

Chris grinned, loving the mystery. He took Angelica's hand and they skipped across the porch and toward the tree line behind the house.

Logan held the screen door open. "You two go now. I'll make sure Chris and Angelica are fine. Follow the road from the barn back across the creek. It comes out the other side of the oaks. Turn right when you get to the road. It will take you back toward Tampa."

"Uly?" Bennett's anguish was apparent as she stared after the children.

"Logan will do what's right. If we stand here much longer, we'll probably be in jail by dark, or worse." Grant pulled Bennett out the side door. "Do you know the road Logan was talking about?"

Words coming between pants, she replied as they ran down the hill. "I've seen a pair of ruts leading away from the barn, but never been down them. I don't think Logan goes that way, except to get over the creek and to his back fields. You want me to drive?"

His hip was cramping, His head hurt worse. Grant felt his pistol banging against his buttock as he lugged his way down the slope and toward the truck. "You drive." The physical pain he could deal with, plus he had Bennett.

He could trust her. He hoped.

CHAPTER 33

 F lorida Department of Law Enforcement Special Agent Talbot stood back as Special Agent in Charge Raphael deployed the response team along the overgrown lane. Their vehicles disappeared behind a screen of intertwined wild grape and air potato vines bordering a track that led to the farmhouse. Talbot could barely make out the agents in their dark jumpsuits flitting through the lengthening shadows. Only a spectator on this operation, Talbot held his face up to the faint breeze that stirred the leaves with an illusion of coolness and a hint of hickory smoke.

Idyllic came to mind. Along with retirement and a smooth sip of single malt. But not tonight.

Talbot peered at the briefing sheets. The photos of Grant and Bennett were barely visible in the fleeting twilight. The DMV report noted Grant was the registered owner of the 1985 half-ton Chevy pickup found at the burned house. Bennett shared ownership of a 1989 red Mustang with her credit union. Raphael's rationale for the assault team was the report filed by a missing and presumed dead Citrus County Deputy. In the report Grant admitted killing two reputed drug traffickers on an island out in the Gulf, the remains of one identified as a member of the Aryan Brotherhood. Raphael's decision to go in with his team "locked and cocked," as he had said, was clinched by the last page sent over from the FBI. Grant's war record confirmed what Talbot knew first hand: Grant had seen extensive combat in Iraq. Back then Talbot had pegged Grant as a bit of a hot shot, but he got the job done. In addition to running an interrogation team, he had been the unit computer forensics expert until a car bomb blew him off the Baghdad highway. More damning was a footnote handwritten across the bottom of the sheet alerting officers that Grant was known to be on medications, to include OxyContin, a widely prescribed addictive pain medication and a favorite recreational drug well known to the law enforcement community. Local searches in the Tampa area hadn't given Talbot a lead, but the faxes from Bennett's office had led him to Bennett's DEP personnel record and a short conversation with her HR administrator in nearby Temple Terrace. The administrator had put Talbot on to Logan Stevens, her ex, and this farm on the backside of Pasco County where cattle ranches and citrus groves were being replaced with strip malls and sprawling developments.

Talbot's heart pounded as the evening drew darker. *Too old for this shit*, he thought. Ought to be back in the office, filling out the retirement forms he had stashed in his desk drawer. But once he had brought the intelligence report to Raphael, along with the local report that the shot up Jeep used in the substation attack had been stolen from a location close to where the rocket attack on Port Tampa originated, the jerk took the entire case out of his hands. The possibility of resolving the drug killings and the terrorist attack all in one fell swoop had pumped everyone up. So here Talbot stood, a useless appendage to Raphael's operation.

Raphael suddenly paused, hand to ear, listening to his radio.

"Someone's turned in, coming this way," Raphael barked out to the agents along the road. "Old red Ford. Woman driving. Sounds like Bennett. Stop her before she can alert whoever's in the house."

Talbot watched from beside a thick oak as the car drove up the road. He frowned. He could be mistaken in the dark shadows. Something wasn't right. The vehicle appeared to be an old Ford hatchback, not a Mustang. And hadn't Bennett's car been impounded as part of the investigation? Before he could speak, one of the team members stepped into the lane, dim headlight beams sweeping across the agent's legs. The car swerved; brake lights flashed. The agent held up one hand palm up, shouting for the driver to stop. The other held a pistol pointed at the vehicle. From both sides of the road, powerful flashlights pinioned the driver, clearly a woman, eyes big behind the windshield as her head pivoted around, one hand up to shield her eyes from the lights. The car skidded sideways across the ruts. It lurched as the driver ground the transmission into reverse before it had come to a full stop.

Raphael yelled at his agents, words smothered by the roar of the engine and squeal of the spinning tire on the damp earth and weeds.

Back up lights lit up a team member diving from behind the car. Talbot shielded his face as gravel and dirt flew up from a spinning tire, ricocheted off the trees.

The agent in front of the car had shifted to a wide stance, both hands cradling her pistol. A shot rang out from the side, twanging off the roof and into the trees. An instant after the first report a shotgun blast smashed out the windshield.

Talbot, already in a half-crouch after the first shot, flinched when a ricochet thwacked into his vest. The car bounced over the ruts and careened toward him. Talbot jumped back as the back bumper crumpled against the oak, engine screaming, right side wheel still spinning. Pistol drawn, Talbot threw down the papers, stepped to the car door and jerked it open. The smell of burnt oil and blood washed over him.

The woman didn't move, hands still locked on the wheel. Her face was gone. The interior was smeared with gore.

"Cease fire, cease fire!" Talbot screamed at the agents surrounding the car, waving his pistol over his head. He reached in and turned off the ignition.

The lane was suddenly silent except for the ticking of the overheated engine.

"We got one of them," yelled Raphael. "Get out of the way, Talbot." He shoved Talbot aside and squatted, scanning the back seat with his pistol extended, smoke curling from the end of the barrel.

"You fucking idiots," Talbot muttered. This was worse than the panic he had witnessed in Iraq when an IED exploded, triggering an uncontrolled volley of random gunfire into a civilian neighborhood.

"Take down the house," Raphael yelled into his radio. "Go, go, go." His eyes shimmering with excitement, Raphael turned to Talbot. "I told you my hunch would pay." He waved the agent still standing in the road toward the car. "Check out the vehicle," he yelled, still oblivious it was a hatchback, not a Mustang.

Talbot holstered his pistol, closed his eyes and leaned against the cool tree trunk to steady himself. *Dear Lord, take me away from this mess.*

"Take down anybody in the house who resists," Raphael screamed.

CHAPTER 34

Bennett wished she had let Grant drive as she wrestled the truck over the creek bed, but he had barely been able to climb up and into the passenger seat after their sprint down the hill. She flinched when an indistinct boom rattled through the trees. She looked back through the side mirror. Lights flashed behind them. "Was that thunder?"

Grant twisted around and looked out the back window. "I can't hear anything but this damn truck. Probably another storm front. Go ahead and turn the lights on. We're far enough away that whoever came up to the house can't see us."

"Will they be all right?"

Grant shrugged. "They might give Logan a hard time if he goes back to the house, but he hasn't done anything to get him in real trouble."

She shook her head. "I'm not worried about Logan. He's certainly not like you, but he'll survive. I was thinking about the children. I hope they're safe, now that it's turned dark." She jerked upright when she pulled the light switch and realized she had the right wheel off the track and the left was following. She steered back into the weed filled ruts alongside the creek bed.

"Just focus on the road. He'll look out after them. Liz will be home soon. Don't worry about the kids."

Cold son of a bitch. But he was right. Bennett slowed as the ruts disappeared in a tangle of heavy kudzu leaves. She gunned the engine and they bounced onto the shoulder of a road, unpaved with shallow ditches scraped along the sides. When she got them going straight between the ditches she glanced over at Grant, scrunched against the door frame, staring out the windshield. He didn't have a kid, didn't know what being a parent was about. Didn't have a clue what she was going through.

"Know where Allen Wilson lives?"

She shook her head, eyes flicking back and forth from the road ahead to the mirror where dust from the dry laterite surface boiled up behind them, orange in the light of the setting sun.

"First stop, I want to see what Allen knows about Silva, how we can get him off our backs. Then, maybe Allen can get word to the cops that we want to come in. This running will only get us killed."

Bennett followed Grant's directions into New Tampa and through a winding series of streets into a residential area. She reached out the window to adjust the big mirror at the corner, thinking for a moment that she had spotted Silva's battered Corvette trailing them. She decided her imagination was getting the better of her. No one had shot at them all day, for crying out loud. A new record for traveling with Grant.

"Slow down." Grant held the map up under the windshield so the streetlight illuminated it. "Next block of apartments. Second floor." He pointed across the intersection to a row of two story buildings.

Bennett pulled to the side of the street a block past the address and parked the truck in the shadows. "What now?"

"I'll go in. Find Allen. See what he has to say. You sit tight until I get back."

Bennett watched him walk away, his gimp noticeable as he crossed the street. She knew why she had gotten in this mess. She just didn't know if what they were doing was the right way to get out of it. She closed her eyes and leaned her head back against the seat, wondering, hoping Chris and Angelica were safe in bed. She rolled her head back and forth over the worn seat and pushed that thought out of her mind. They had to be safe. She should be thinking about how to get away from Silva, how to get her life back. Grant—

She jerked her head up when the truck door flew open with a screech.

Bobby Silva stood by the open door, pistol in hand, face ghoulish in the mercury vapor light.

"What you dreaming about, baby? Come on. Let's take a ride back to the office while your boyfriend jerks off with Wilson. You and I got to have a serious conversation." He grabbed her arm and yanked her out of the truck, pistol pressed against her back, arm twisted behind her. "Don't give me an excuse to blow your guts all over the sidewalk. You'll be dead, and I'll probably get a medal."

The pain was excruciating as he half dragged her through a gap in a row of shrubbery and down the sidewalk to a car. She tried to struggle, but he bulled her to a car and into the passenger seat where he looped a plastic tie around both wrists and yanked the tie until it cut into her skin.

He leaned close and pressed the pistol's cold muzzle against her cheek. "Damn, you're ugly with your hair all screwed up. Don't give me an excuse to pull the trigger. I'll be pissed if I have to clean your shit out of the car, but I'll get over it." He returned his pistol to its holster, slammed the door and got in the driver's side.

Bennett squeezed her eyes shut as she listened to Silva make a call on his cell phone, the pain in her shoulder vying with the pain in her heart. How in God's name had she let him slip up on her.

"Darrell. Just wanted you to know that I have solved my problem. Payment's made. Got the shit bird in hand, right here with me." He glanced over at Bennett. "Don't you worry. I'll take care of everything." He finished the call and eased away from the curb.

"Where are we going, Bobby?" Bennett asked. She tried to flex her wrists under the tie. Too tight to escape. Felt as if they were cutting her hands off. Dear God, and to think she had slept with this monster. She searched the car with her eyes. He had exchanged his Corvette for an Agency fleet car, bare, nothing in it to help.

"Let's go back to the office, hon. We got some unfinished business." He made a second cell call. "Hey, Beetle," Silva said into the phone. "'Nother job for you. Should be easy with your connections. Guy's name is Uly Grant. He lives in Homosassa; the one who popped the Brotherhood guys, so you should give me a discount on this one." Silva grunted. "O. K., regular rate, just do it, soon as you find him. Your EME buddies probably know him, from what Wilson tells me. He's in Tampa right now, but I expect he'll finish his business here tonight and head back home." Silva shook his head. "Yeah, you're right, dude, I want you to clean up my mess. I'll pay, dammit. Never have welshed on you, have I? Just find him and get him out of the picture. For good."

Bennett strained at the tie. It only bit deeper into her wrists. She had never felt so helpless. *Uly, where are you*? Please, God. Please find me.

Silva dropped the phone in a pocket. "Your buddy go up to see Wilson? That's where I was going when I spotted you two pretending be farmers. This truck belong to some of your Mex friends? You're such an unreliable bitch he'll figure you ran out on him. I sure as hell didn't miss you. Doubt he will. Probably won't live long enough to worry about you." He shook his head, brow furrowed. "Got to make sure you and Wilson are connected when the cops sort it all out. Pot head and his babe, all turned bad over drugs." He leered at her. "Maybe I'll leave a pair of your panties at Wilson's place when I pop him. That ought to do it."

"You shit!" She swung her clasped hands at his face, grazing his ear as he jerked back.

Silva slapped her, a stinging blow with the back of his gloved hand. "You sit still, bitch."

Bennett blinked back a tear from the stinging slap. Where were they? She recognized the bridge over the Hillsborough River, the turn onto the lush grounds of Telcom Park and the Department of Environmental

Protection Offices. Silva pulled her out of the car and shoved her toward a side entrance.

Frantically she searched the streets for anyone to help. Not a soul in sight. Security lights cast dark shadows along the DEP building and empty parking lot. Somewhere close a sprinkler stuttered rhythmically, but no chatter of late workers, no sign of a security patrol. Grant wasn't coming to rescue her this time. She had to get away from this bastard on her own.

Silva swiped his security card through a reader, muttered, swiped again until the lock clicked. He jerked one side of the double glass doors open and shoved Bennett through the doorway, down the hall toward her office.

"Sit down, Kat." He waved toward her desk with the pistol. The DEP building was silent except for his voice. "You tried to play me, bitch, but you picked the wrong guy; you must have figured that out by now."

Bennett looked around the office with a sinking feeling. Surveillance cameras all around the front entrance, but nothing back here where the peons labored. She spotted a red fire alarm station across the hall by the door to Silva's office. Time was running out. Silva wouldn't let her live the night. She lunged out of the chair and reached toward the alarm.

Silva caught her by the shirttail and spun her back into the office. His hand closed on her throat.

Bennett gasped for air as the pastel walls swirled around her. His fingers dug deep in her throat.

"Easy, baby. You'll get all bruised up. Bet the cops will think your new squeeze got mad and banged you around." He slammed her back against the wall.

Bennett's head rang and stars floated around inside her eyes as she slid to the floor.

He opened a box of candy on the credenza. He laughed at her and fished a small pistol from the box, one like the gun he had held out to her in the car. Silva grabbed a fistful of blouse and pulled her back up to her feet, laughing. He pointed the pistol at her face. "Went to a lot of trouble to keep your prints on this peashooter. Waste of time, now that I think about it. You know what, I'll make sure the cops find Wilson's prints all over it, another pot head Indian all dead from remorse. You guys are so stupid." He waved the pistol toward the laptop on the credenza. "Smart asses. Thought Wilson deleted all my files, didn't you? I'm smarter than you or that jerk ever dreamed of being. There's enough evidence in there to fry you all."

Bennett took a deep breath when Silva stopped, head cocked to the side as if he were listening to someone, something. Maybe a guard had heard them. She took an awkward step toward Silva, following him as he backed to the doorway and looked to the left, then right. Then she heard the noise, a screech from the back of the building.

Silva swung his pistol away from her.

Bennett raised her left knee to her chest and kicked out with her heel, harder than she had ever kicked before.

CHAPTER 35

G rant gasped for breath after his run down the curving entrance-way from the truck. He itched to get Silva in the Kimber's sights after seeing Silva drag Bennett out of the car. Every step he thanked the Lord that Wilson wasn't home; he hadn't waited around for his cousin to return; got back to the truck in time to see Bennett led away. Grant snatched up a piece of discarded galvanized steel pipe from beside a trash bin, poked it under an overhead cargo dock door and pried. A screech, but the door held.

He squatted, got his shoulder under the pipe, and lifted with his legs, hip screaming at him. The pipe groaned and began to bend. Flecks of old paint popped off, bits sticking to the sweat running down Grant's face. He leaned in toward the door to get a better angle, straightened his knees; up, up until he was on his toes, trembling with the effort. With a screech of shearing metal the door moved. Grant paused, worked the pipe further under the door for more leverage. He lifted again until he thought either the pipe or his collar bone would snap.

An aluminum strut smacked him across the shin as the door exploded, spilling him to the concrete floor. The door flew up with a clatter, rattled along its rails and slowed to a stop, uncovering a dark hallway.

A thud reverberated down the hall.

Grant dried his sweaty hand on his pants, scrambled to the connecting hallway and dove to the thin carpet, pistol in hand. As he wormed around the corner on his belly, a man dressed in a blue blazer, button down shirt and tie stepped out of the office and peered his way. Grant hesitated. The car outside wasn't a Corvette. His hesitated. Was it Silva, or some bureaucrat with shitty timing?

Before the man gave any indication he had spotted Grant, Bennett stumbled out into the corridor behind the man. She lashed out and sank her heel into the middle of the man's back. He crashed, face-first, against the wall. He spun back toward Bennett with a scream, pistol in hand.

"I'll kill you, you bitch. Just like the Mex whore."

Grant finally saw his face. The same face he had seen in the Corvette. Silva!

Silva screamed and lunged back into the office. The sound of ricocheting bullets filled the hallway.

Grant sprang from the floor and charged down the hall, skidded across the office doorway.

Silva swung toward Grant, surprise in his eyes. Flame spurted from the pistol.

The photo on the wall behind Grant exploded, flinging bits of glass into the back of Grant's neck.

Grant's Kimber bucked in his hand. The roar of his .45 drowned out the crack of the small pistol in Silva's hand.

Silva fell back against a desk; strained to raise the pistol.

Grant's next shot spun Silva back against the wall, now spattered with blood. Grant scrambled to his feet as Silva slid to the floor.

"Kat." Grant yelled, his voice a tinny reverberation in his head. A pair of dirty canvas shoes stuck out from behind a desk, the wooden top gouged by several shallow furrows. Grant shoved the desk aside with his hip. Bennett lay curled in a ball on the floor, hands lashed together with a plastic tie. Grant shoved his pistol in his pocket and grabbed her shoulders.

Bennett jerked away and her eyes flew open, wide with fear, bound hands clutched to her chest.

"Easy, Kat. Silva's down." He dug the Buck from his pocket and sawed with the serrated blade until the tie popped free.

Bennett rubbed her wrists and looked over his shoulder. "Bobby. Where is he? Outright told me he was going to kill me, that son of a bitch!" With Grant's help she struggled to her feet.

Bennett's fingers dug into his arm. He grimaced at the sharp pain. "Dammit, turn loose." She fell against him, chest heaving as she struggled for her breath.

"Silva won't hurt you, or anybody else."

She pushed Grant back and stepped over to Silva's body. For a moment he thought she was going to spit on the dead man.

A pounding noise reverberated down the hall, from the side door.

Grant grabbed her arm. "Come on. I don't want to be here when the cops arrive." He pulled her past Silva's body and toward the loading dock. Hand still gripping a wad of Bennett's shirt tail, Grant paused at the entrance. Flashing lights reflected from the nearby buildings and a siren growled down from a wail on the front entrance. At least one more, maybe two, sirens pierced the heavy night air, coming closer as he urged Bennett through the shadows. Grant pulled Bennett through a dew-damp hedge. Crouched low, they ran through a gap in a hedge, away from the building. When they got to the truck he shoved Bennett toward the passenger door and ran around to the driver's side. As he wrenched open the door he saw Bennett standing on the sidewalk, staring back at the building. "Get in, Kat."

She stared back at him.

"Dammit, move!"

She blinked and slowly climbed in.

Two police cruisers with flashing lights pulled up in front of the DEP main entrance, followed by a dark sedan with alternating red and blue lights flashing through its grill. Guided by the street lights, Grant twisted in the seat and slowly backed the truck down the street. An emergency vehicle emerged from the nearby fire station, horn sounding as it careened around the corner.

Grant let it pass, switched on the headlights and drove, oblivious to where he was going for the moment.

"Uly. I got to go back."

"Look. I heard the son of a bitch. He tried to kill you. Take a deep breath. We took care of him. He's not going to hurt you, or Chris."

"No, not back to the office. To hell with Silva. Take me back to the farm. Chris, Angelica, Logan and Liz. I'm worried about them."

He shook his head. "Are you crazy? You saw all the cops. With Silva dead, they've got one more reason to shoot us in our tracks."

"But we should be able to go back to the farm."

Dumb move, Grant thought, but probably what he would do if some kid was ever so unfortunate to have him for a parent. "O.K., you win. But I'm all turned around. Can you find the road back to the farm again?" The steering wheel was slick from his sweaty palms. He wiped his hands on his shirt, concentrated on driving.

About a half-hour and several wrong turns later, Bennett said, "slow down," and pointed ahead and to the edge of the road and tracks churned through the kudzu vines, glistening in the moonlight. "There. See where we pulled out, the tracks."

Grant turned on to the shoulder, rolled down the slight slope. He let the truck slow to a stop, dust settling behind them, and turned off the lights.

"You want me to walk the rest of the way?" she asked.

"No. Just let me get my night vision back." Grant closed his eyes for a minute. When he opened them, light from a quarter moon glistened down through the live oaks. Ahead of them he could see where they had driven out, faint wheel tracks meandering back and forth across the old ruts. He slowly eased down the track until they lurched back over the gravel filled creek bed and up the low bank. Grant stopped with the truck half hidden by a fragrant hedge of Confederate jasmine, careful to keep his foot clear of the brake pedal. Ahead, lights flickered through the trees. Figures in what appeared to be dark uniforms strode around, long shadows following along.

"Oh, Lord, Uly. What do you think happened?"

"I don't know, but I don't think we need to get tangled with that bunch. Pretty obviously law enforcement. Do you see Liz or Logan?" As he leaned forward for a better look, an ambulance stopped at the barn, reversed and drove back down the lane. Flashing lights strobed through the trees.

Bennett kicked opened her door.

"Wait, Kat!" Grant lunged after her. He snagged her by the waistband and jerked her, flopping like a bait fish on a hook, back into the truck. He tightened his grip, gathered her up close and focused on driving as she pounded on his chest, sobbing incoherently. He turned the truck in a wide sweeping arc and lurched across the pasture.

"Kat, Kat. Stop struggling. Listen for a minute. What would running in there get you, except pitched in jail?" His time as an interrogator had put him around law enforcement types enough to understand their thought process. Two sheriff's deputies, a wildlife ranger, Silva, whatever the hell he was, all dead. If Bennett ran up that slope, some trigger-happy cop would likely shoot on sight. Grant glanced back through the mirrors at the house. Vehicle lights bloomed back at the road, jammed in a cluster, all vying with the ambulance for the lane leading out of the farm.

The wheel jerked in his left hand and Bennett squirmed in his right as they ripped through the Confederate jasmine. Grant tore his eyes away from the mirror and concentrated on driving. Cold spray, gritty with a hint of pasture muck, splashed across his face as the truck's big tires dropped into the creek bed. The engine sputtered, and Grant punched the accelerator. Bennett clutched his arm and bit off a scream when the engine backfired with a loud bang.

The rear tires whined and spit water and globs of clay onto the side mirror, distorting the red and blue flashers that strobed across the corn rows heading their way. The truck began to crab sideways as the rear wheels lost traction on the muddy bank.

Grant winced as a bullet cracked past the open window. Son of a bitches were shooting! He glanced at the mirror, but the lights behind him were indistinct through the muddy smears. He eased up, forced his foot to feather the accelerator, straightened the steering wheel and let the truck find a purchase. The tires finally caught and they lumbered up out of the creek bed, heading toward a dark mass of trees, engine staggering. Grant pumped the gas and the truck accelerated under the low limbs. He steered back toward the ruts, hoping he didn't drop into a gully or slam into one of the massive live oaks as they roared through the shadows under the trees. Bouncing back out of the trees, he followed the crushed grass back toward the paved road as the engine finally smoothed out. Grant ignored Bennett's protests and concentrated on driving, dancing the truck across the ruts, guided by the streaks of moonlight that penetrated the trees.

He twisted in the seat and stared back toward the house, now half hidden behind a mantel of trees. Vehicle lights flickered through the big oaks, coming toward them. Ahead, the laterite roadway glistened in the moonlight. Grant gunned the truck.

"Uly, you got to let me go back. I need to see about Chris, Angelica." She pounded both hands on his chest, sobbing. "Please."

Grant shook his head and pulled her close. "You walk up that hill and you'll never see the kids. If the kids do see you, it'll be with the cops dragging you down, cuffing you and tossing you in the back seat of a cruiser, if we should live so long. Let Logan take care of them. I know you trust him. Right now he and the kids are better off without us." Grant bounced across the kudzu, onto the road and accelerated until he reached the paved road. He whipped the truck toward Ozello and drove blind, winding through the dark back roads. When he was sure no one was behind them, he finally switched on the truck's headlights.

"Oh, God." She buried her face against his chest. "Did you see the ambulance?"

"Yes. Probably brought in as a precaution for the kids. Listen. You did everything for Chris, right? It's done. Silva's dead. Let's get back to my house and figure out what happened here, what to do next. Listen to me. We'll be safe back at the house. Let Logan and Liz worry about the kids for now."

"When we get to your house, what will we do?" she whispered into his chest.

Grant took a deep breath and loosened his grip on Bennett. She stayed close beside him, her head still resting on his chest. "I don't know, Kat. If you want to give yourself up, you can, maybe under Roberto's protection. Maybe Allen, if I can find him, maybe he could see we get taken into custody without anymore shooting. We could be charged, probably put in jail. But I don't think a jury will ever convict either of us of killing anybody. But the legal system is crazy, sometimes. So let's don't rush into anything." He pulled her chin up and looked into her eyes. "All right?"

She wormed one arm under his back and held him tight. "I don't care about us. Chris, Angelica. Logan. What if something did happen to them?"

Grant didn't have the answer. Should they just turn themselves in? Silva was dead. Whoever else was on the other end of the drug deal, the crooked lawmaker, would any of them come after them now? Grant didn't have a clue.

He shoved the straw hat down over his eyes as he twisted through a maze of back roads and back toward his Gulf retreat. Pushing the groaning truck up to the speed limit, Grant's mind whirred as he barreled toward home. With Silva out of the picture, maybe he could convince the cops that—what—that he hadn't killed the two crackers and Silva? Crap, and the guy on the dock; he had forgotten about him. Who would believe their story, when it all started with hijacking a load of dope.

CHAPTER 36

Talbot hit the button and the car window slid down, exchanging cigar smoke for steamy humidity. He cleared his throat and spat. Even that didn't seem to clear the bile from his system. The raid, the entire day had gone wrong. The deputy at the driveway entrance stopped a line of oncoming cars already slowed by the plethora of flashing lights and waved Talbot out on to the paved road. Talbot pulled away from the disaster scene, still shaking his head. God damn that trigger happy Raphael and his crew. Raphael claimed he had eliminated a terrorist, but Talbot figured in the end they would discover the Department had killed an innocent woman while Talbot had stood right there, not in control of a damn thing!

Talbot shook his head as he headed toward the FDLE Tampa Bay Regional Operations Center, a stone's throw from the Buccaneers' football stadium. After Raphael had announced he had the suspects in custody, a man and a couple of kids, for Christ's sake, Talbot decided it was past time to leave Raphael at it. The imbecile had used some half-ass random logic to replace Grant with this Logan guy as the prime suspect. What a jug fuck! Enough had gone wrong that Talbot now questioned Raphael's judgment, his entire logic for the direction he was taking the investigation. But Talbot had been around long enough to figure the bosses would probably discount his concerns, finger him for a disgruntled employee pissed that he had been bumped from the supervisory position. Whine enough, and they would accuse him of an imagined anti-Latino bias.

Up till now Talbot had been convinced the terrorist attack against the bulk petroleum terminal at Port Tampa and the shootings in Homosassa were connected, based solely on the engraved lighter the deputies had found at the scene of the substation shooting. But he was getting absolutely no help from Homeland Security either way. He had known Grant well enough in Iraq to put him at the bottom of the suspect list. More and more, it seemed the connection was barely circumstantial, more of a coincidence that the drug incident and the rocket attack all happened the same night, not that the same people were responsible. Wilson was an unknown quantity. But where and who had the incriminating faxes really come from? How had the engraved lighter gotten to Homosassa, fifty, sixty miles north of Old Tampa Bay? Maybe the Florida Computer Crime Center analysts upstairs could help. They could access both Wilson's files and the Department of Environmental Protection's computers. Maybe tell him what was really going on. As he walked in from the Operations Center parking lot he saw the lot was at least half full. Good. Meant Beth and her folks were putting in a little overtime, along with the rest of FDLE.

"Dammit, what the devil's going on here?"

Talbot spun around at the harsh voice. "Hey, Beth. I was about to come up to see you." Talbot followed the chief analyst down a polished hall and upstairs past the faded prints on the walls. "You guys need a few ficus plants to break up the sterility, maybe add a mural like down in the main lobby. You know, keep the hostility level in check."

The fuming C3 supervisor opened the door to her office and motioned him inside. He had barely cleared the door when she slammed it behind him. "Is Raphael on a power trip, setting me up for something?" she asked, a not-so-quiet fury in her voice. "This better be real, accusing one of my people."

Talbot swallowed his reflexive response to bark back. Instead, he took a deep breath. "I don't have the vaguest idea what you're talking about, Beth."

"Temple Terrace PD just reported a shooting at the Department of Environmental Protection office in Telcom Park. They recovered the victim's cell phone at the scene. The tech support folks jumped on this one, determined the last call on the cell went to a pay phone down in Riverview, known to be used by a drug trafficker, a member of EME, the Mexican Mafia." She looked at him, eyebrows raised as if she had asked a question to which he was supposed to know the answer. "Please tell me you know what I'm talking about."

Talbot didn't. "I didn't think there were any pay phones left in Florida, at least any that worked. Phone must be under the protection of the EME boys." He sat down in the armless chair in front of her desk, slid it back and propped his feet on the corner of the desk. "I don't know anything about the shooting." He held up his hand, interrupting her. "And I'm tired. Saw the king of stupid reign today. Don't rail at me about something I know nothing about. I didn't piss in one of your pots; Raphael thinks he's in charge of this operation; not my piece of dirt."

"Screw territory." The supervisor sat down behind her desk. "You know Allen Wilson?"

Talbot froze to keep from leaping from the chair; instead he shrugged his shoulders and nodded his head. "I know an Allen Wilson. Why?"

Beth stared at him, a hint of a smile at his reaction. "This one works for me, and I think it's the same one you know. Some hotshot agent downstairs ran down the call history of that pay phone and linked it to Wilson, apparently multiple calls. Raphael connected your suspect, this Grant guy, to Wilson. Discovered they are cousins, for Christ's sake, and put out a BOLO on Wilson. The highway patrol spotted a vehicle with Wilson's tag number heading up toward Crystal River, close to where the drug incident, the shootout with the drug guys, or terrorists, or—" She shook her head. "This damn case is so screwed up I got no idea what I'm talking about. Bottom line, one of my guys is a suspect. I haven't had a chance to talk to him. I can't even get my hands on him. I need this Grant in custody so I can figure out if Allen was burning me." She tapped on her desk with a lipstick tube, apparently empty from her pale appearance. "I trusted Allen enough to authorize him an informant account. He's been paying a confidential source a lot of money for some very good leads, or at least we thought they were good. Son of a bitch! He better not be playing me."

Talbot grinned at Beth. "All that cop talk. You been watching too much TV." He dropped his feet down to the floor and looked around. "You guys got any coffee?"

She leaned toward him, jaw clenched. "If I had a cup, I'd dump it over your head. You been listening?"

He put his elbows on her desk, his face inches from hers. "Yep. But let's go over the facts, which, by the way, most of which are new to me. Listen to what you just said. If all the connections ring true, Wilson is at least a person of interest I'd like to sit down and have a chat with." He tapped the desktop. "And you're more than welcome to lead that conversation."

Beth closed her eyes and shook her head. "What a screwy day."

"Well, let's unscrew it. Here's what I do know, and what you can do to help me sort it out." When Talbot finished describing the faxes Delina had dropped on his desk, Beth called in two of her analysts and had Talbot repeat the few facts to them.

"You two find out where the faxes came from, and if you can find any other electronic transactions in the system that might have come from DEP." She held up her hand to hold the analysts, thought for a moment, then added, "Find Mister Special Agent in Charge Rafael's office assistant, that floozy fake blond Cuban gal, have her check his fax logs. See what else is going on I don't know about." The analysts scurried out.

"Gee, Beth. What you got against Delina? She might be blond and Cuban, but she works hard, not like some of the lowlifes that came with her on the boat lift. Christ, she was just a kid, a baby, back then." Talbot twisted around to retrieve his BlackBerry vibrating on his hip.

"Talbot," he answered. He listened for a moment, thanked the caller and turned back to Beth. "The missing deputy has been found. He crawled through the swamp to some priest's house. He's alive, but critical and in a coma, so he's won't be any help for the moment. Attending physician isn't sure of the prognosis. We may never find out what happened to him. Poor guy had been shot and burned. The down side is traces of dope were found in the trunk of his cruiser. For all we know at this point, he was part of the deal."

"The same deputy wounded in the initial incident in Homosassa?"

Talbot nodded,

"Damn. I hope this Grant resists arrest and somebody jams a shotgun up his ass."

Talbot frowned and shook his head. "I got a little different take. Grant and Wilson both served with me when our Military Intelligence unit deployed to Iraq."

She looked at him in disbelief. "What?"

"Yeah. We served together in the Guard. Grant ran one of our interrogation teams, a lieutenant. Wilson was enlisted, on Grant's team. Snyder, the new agent downstairs, was on his team, too. She and Wilson saved Grant's life in an ambush. Grant isn't the kind of person I expect would drop into the drug world, or help terrorists. Wilson had a few bumps along the way, so you would know better than I how he turned out."

Now it was Beth's turn to frown at him. "Greg, don't let your friendship get in the way—"

Talbot held up his hand, stopping her. "Uly Grant was one of my boys, Beth, and got hurt bad. People got killed with him. Wilson was wounded. But if the evidence hangs anything on either of them, I'll do my due diligence." He pointed his finger at her. "But I don't want to hear anymore shotgun shit out of you, or anyone." He looked at his finger and grimaced. "Sorry. You carry a lot of baggage when you've been to war. Mine weighs kind of heavy when I'm tired."

Beth's face softened and she nodded. "You're right. Maybe I spoke too soon. But be careful out there. When a cop goes down, lots of law enforcement types jump to conclusions, just the way I did before you brought me back to the world. I'll let you know what we come up with ASAP." She stood. "Now get out of here. I got a meeting with Internal Affairs. You know how that goes. If I had any, they'd cut them off."

"I'll keep you informed, too." He smiled at her. "Didn't mean to sound harsh."

"Yes, you did. You're a cop."

CHAPTER 37

Grant flexed his fingers, took a deep breath and relaxed his grip on the steering wheel as the flatbed rumbled past an unmarked Mercury Grand Marquis at the next intersection. The extra antennas, glint of lights hidden in the grill and a faint sign of exhaust mingling with the morning mists gave away the Highway Patrol cruiser. Grant glanced back in the mirror. The cruiser didn't move. No lights, no siren, no interest in his produce farmer routine. Either the cops were doing a great job of clandestine surveillance or they were ignoring him. He wound through the back roads, staying just below the speed limit, taking a round-about route to Ozello and home. He blinked with exhaustion. It must be far past midnight. Thankfully the air had cooled with the fresh breeze blowing in from the Gulf. He slowed for a stoplight in Weeki Wachee, his eyes on a Hernando Sheriff's cruiser parked in the shadow of an antique shop.

He was tired, senses gone stupid. Was the deputy sitting there, watching, waiting for him to pass? The truck engine stumbled and Grant glanced at the fuel gauge. It sat firmly at the bottom of the scale. Well, he'd find out about the watching part right now or run out of gas. He turned into the convenience store across the highway from the parked deputy.

Bennett lay curled up on the beach seat, apparently asleep. He gently shook her shoulder, held her down when she started to sit up. "I stopped for gas. A deputy's parked across the highway, so stay out of sight. We're almost home."

Grant pulled down the straw hat's brim to avoid any cameras and swiped the Louis Anderson credit card through the pump. "Dumb," he muttered as he realized what he had done. When he had set up the accounts, he made a rule that he would never use a card with an assumed identity twice while under duress. He could have paid cash, but this late any jerk waltzing into a convenience store with a hat pulled down over his face and a pistol in his pocket was likely to be greeted by a shotgun and the deputy across the way. Nope, let the fictitious Mister Anderson sweat this one out. He'd shred the card tomorrow.

Tank filled, Grant climbed back in the truck. He wondered if the cruiser was empty, a speeder's decoy, and all his bravado had been for naught.

He started the truck, let it cough for a moment before the fuel pump caught up and the engine smoothed out. He waited for a pair of headlights coming down the highway to pass. A black Ford pickup flashed by. Grant watched the truck's lights fade into the midnight mist rising up from the Weeki Wachee Swamp, wondering if the truck was Wilson's. He had left a note on Wilson's door telling him they had to meet, to call Roberto to set it up.

Before he could pull out, a second vehicle passed, a Mercury Grand Marquis; too fast, too dark to tell if it was the unmarked cruiser. Seconds later, the deputy across the highway flicked on his headlights and pulled out to follow.

Jesus, they were gathering an army. Grant felt a smidgen of guilt flicker through his mind. He never expected Allen to come warn him, if that was him in the pickup. Cousins, yes, but never good friends. In fact a great deal less, most of the time. Grant wished he had caught up with Allen back at his apartment. But then he wouldn't have seen Silva take Bennett. Life was just too damn complicated. Grant stared back up the road and let a big SUV cruise past. Nothing else coming, at least with lights, so he followed the pack.

The lump under his leg, deep in his cargo pants pocket, reminded him that he was tired, not thinking with any logic. He shifted his butt so he could wiggle the pistol out of his pocket. If he got caught up in a roadblock, a gun in his pocket might well get him and Bennett killed. And if some trigger happy cop didn't shoot him, ballistics would surely tie him to Silva. As he approached a bridge he held the pistol by the barrel. He hesitated, shoved the pistol back in his pocket. He might need the damn thing again before the night was out.

Grant glanced across at Bennett, back asleep. Had her touch, her kiss, brought him out of his lethargy? He pushed the thought away for later. Too much at stake to worry about his psyche. He had to think about the ones he was responsible for. Figure out a good home for Flash, pack what was essential, then goodbye Kat Bennett, if need be. In fact, goodbye Uly Grant.

Mom would be all right. He had a trust set up for her. She'd never know he was gone. The only tangible things he would really miss were the Highwaymen paintings. And Flash's groan. Even as he had the thought, he knew he was lying to himself. He didn't want to let go of any of those things. But what else could he do?

GULF WINDS

Bennett? He tried to push her out of his mind, but the touch of her head against his leg made him wish, for a long moment, they had met in a different life.

Ahead of him, tail lights flashed as the train of vehicles twisted over the narrow bridges crossing the tidal marshes and connecting the small islands. Too much traffic heading toward Ozello for this time of morning. He scrubbed at the dirty mirror, wondering what he would do if a deputy pulled out, lights flashing. *Dumb thought*. He'd stop. Then they would arrest him for murder. All his grand schemes would have been for naught and his Mexican friends would have to fend for themselves as the law dismantled his shadow world. Ozello Trail dead ended at the Gulf of Mexico, the wrong road to be on tonight. He should be headed for Utah, anyplace with no connections back to Florida.

Grant slowed when the convoy ahead of him broke into a circus of blue and red and white flashing lights. With relief, he realized the lights had passed his house and were stopped at the end of the island by the abandoned restaurant, too far away to make out the individual cars. Grant let up on the gas, coasting, wondering if he and Bennett should just abandon the flatbed and head out into the tangle on foot, when an Argon security light flickered through the trees ahead. He whipped into an overgrown driveway, punched the flatbed's headlights off and let the truck sputter to a stop beside an abandoned singlewide trailer, half-hidden under a tangle of shadowy vines and overgrown shrubbery. He was home. Almost. Only the Madero Builders shop and a screen of cabbage palms draped with wild vines separated him from his house.

Bennett sat up, her face hidden in the dark shadows. "What—"

"Hush." He put his finger over her lips. "I think the cops followed Allen down here. Let me slip into Madero Builders. I can check the house's alarm status from the shop."

She leaned across him, staring at the flashing lights, her warm breath a mixture of barbeque sauce and homemade pickle juice.

"Stay here," he whispered.

His hands were clammy when he stepped to the ground, not so much from sweat but from the thick mist drifting in from the tidal flats just feet away. He froze. Loose siding rattled in the breeze, held together by rust and dried vines. The trailer had belonged to old man Morris. Like a lot of Grant's life, Morris was dead, passed away while Grant was in Iraq. The pungent mix of rotten vegetation and exposed oyster bars wafted in with the breeze. He stood for a moment, peering through the tangled growth, listening to the familiar sounds of the tidal marsh. He thought he could hear an engine running. A car door slammed, the sound blown across the water by the wind. He was half deaf, but not that deaf. A powerful beam shot out from one of the patrol cars, spotlighting a black pickup parked at the far end of the island. He didn't think his cousin knew about his house, but Allen apparently knew more than Grant had suspected. At least neither of them needed to worry about Silva any more.

Grant slipped through a tangle of skunk vine and dog fennel, past Morris's rusting mackerel smoker and to the edge of the chain link fence surrounding Madero Builders. Grant stood in the shadows, on the opposite side of the building from the security light, wondering if the cops were lying in wait at the house. He could go back to the flatbed, try to slip out of the area. *With nothing.* Or he could try to get to his house where files and accounts awaited him. *And don't forget Flash,* he reminded himself.

Grant worked his way along the fence line until he found a gopher tortoise burrow that had collapsed under the edge of the fence. On his knees, he dug away at the sand, hoping any snakes that had taken up residence with the tortoise were asleep deep in the burrow. *Do snakes sleep?* He sure as hell hoped so. Grant flung sand to each side until he had enlarged the opening enough he could wiggle under the fence, rolling over on his back to work his way under, ignoring the grinding pain radiating from his hip.

He flopped back to his stomach and was on his knees brushing away the sand when he saw the glow of a cigarette. He dropped back to his belly, worked the Velcro flaps open and slipped the Kimber from his cargo pocket. How many rounds had he fired? One in the chamber and seven in the magazine to start. He had fired, what, three shots at Silva?

He disengaged the thumb safety and crept toward the glow. It came from inside a big SUV beside the loading dock. The driver's elbow leaned out the open window, occasionally flicking ashes from a glowing cigarette. Grant stopped when he caught the acrid scent of marijuana. Christ. All he needed was a run-in with a pot head sneaking a smoke. But why here? He glanced over at the gate. It appeared to be closed, a funeral wreath strung from the posts. Whoever was in the SUV must have a key, access to Madero Builders. Maybe one of the employees.

He worked his way slowly behind the vehicle. The driver had parked facing the flashing lights, but far enough back in the shadows that no one else would notice, especially with the SUV sitting at the loading dock entrance. This was dumb. Smart thing was to get the hell out of here. Then he spotted the specialty plate with "EME" and a soccer ball followed by "13." Grant paused, brought his pistol up to train it on the windows. Wellington had mentioned the EME gang. This might be the bald man, the one who killed Eustis. Grant felt the blood rush though his temples. He didn't care the cops were swarming down the road. If the bald man were here, he'd kill him on the spot, consequences be damned.

Grant crept up to the side of the vehicle. The driver's profile in the mirror implied he was focused on the activity around the black pickup. One disappointment, he had a heavy shock of hair. Not the bald man. Who the hell was this? One way to find out. He held his breath, eased under the window and slowly stood. Grant punched the Kimber into the side of the driver's neck.

The driver dropped the glowing joint to the ground. The flashing lights glinted from the interior surfaces of the windows; enough to confirm a second man in the passenger seat. The back seat looked empty.

Grant leaned closer to the driver, ground the muzzle into his neck. "This fucking .45 is an instant away from taking off your head. What the hell are you doing here?" Grant jammed the pistol harder when he heard a metallic click from inside the SUV. "Freeze, stupid! I can put a bullet though your neck before I die, most likely take out your buddy with the same bullet. Guns on the seat, hands on the steering wheel."

"Easy, Boo. We here to talk." The driver raised a single finger from the steering wheel and pointed toward the flashing lights. "Now, ain't you glad it's us over here and not them cops?"

Grant ground the muzzle harder into the man's neck. "Tell your friend to put his hands on the dash where I can see them."

"Uly?" Bennett's voice whispered from over his shoulder.

Grant glanced over his shoulder.

Bennett stumbled into view, a man beside her. A long blade glimmered in the glow of the security light.

The driver chuckled. "Now, why don't you put your hands where I can see them, 'migo."

"Crap." Grant cursed his deafness and his ineptness.

The driver turned his face toward Grant. "Don't get jumpy, man. I just got a question for you. 'Sides, my boys got you outgunned. You ain't got no chance. I die for them; they die for me. We don't really give a shit. Now take that fucking gun out of my neck." The driver's right hand came into sight, showing Grant a plastic lighter. The left hand slid toward the dash and came back with a new joint. The lighter snapped and a flame illuminated the driver's broad, pocked face. The man waved the glowing end of new joint at Grant. "Want a smoke while we talk, Uly Grant?"

How the hell did this guy know his name? "No thanks. What are we going to talk about?" He lowered his pistol to his side.

"All them cops over there, they following that big black truck, Wilson's ride. We was, too, but too much heat, so we peeled off in here.

We watched. Wilson, he done took off into the swamp. Yo here thinks he heard a boat, so Boo, I don't think the cops ever going to find Wilson's ass." He nonchalantly turned to the passenger. "Now ain't this great, Yolander. We didn't even go fishing and still caught what we was looking for, without ever having to ask old Wilson."

The driver drew on the joint and the momentary glow illuminated a tattoo on the driver's cheek. The glow subsided before Grant could be sure, but thought the tattoos extended down the side of the man's neck. Grant was starting to get dizzy, so close to the smoke. This was all out of his control. "Why are you looking for me? What have we got to talk about?"

"Surprised, huh?" The man chuckled again. "I got a call, from a man I done some business with before. You are Grant, right? He say you need to go away, am I the man for it?" Another long draw on the joint. "Am I the man, I tell him. Shit!"

The passenger chuckled at the very thought.

Grant had a problem with the humor, but hadn't yet figured out why these men had been told to kill him.

"You kinda hard to find, then I asked Yolander, here, my other friends 'round Homosassa 'bout you, even go to the Padre. Got a big surprise."

"Yeah, Beetle, big surprise." The passenger echoed.

"So tell me, Boo. You really the *patron* helping all our *hermanos*, like the Padre say? The glowing joint waved at the building. "You Juan's *amigo*, you help the little girl? Padre say so in the confessional, but sometime I lie in there. Maybe he do, too."

The joint glowed.

Grant's mind raced. He should be asking, not answering the questions. This Beetle might have the answers he needed. As if he had a choice. So see where this goes.

"Sure, I've heard Father Roberto lie before. He and I grew up together. But he didn't lie about the Maderos. Them, my momma and me, Allen Wilson; we all grew up together." Grant glanced around. Bennett and the shadow behind her stood a couple of steps back. Grant wondered if he had missed anyone else in the parking lot. The angle was wrong. He didn't dare take a shot toward Bennett with the Kimber. Snap shot, with his nerves all fried, he wasn't sure he could hit the side of the shop. Back to what he used to be good at, asking questions. "Where did you know Juan?"

The joint waved toward the passenger. "Yolander was Juan's roomy in the detention center. Juan was a good guy. Not a brother, but a good *Mexicano*, give Yolander a job when they get out, right here. Juan told him, said he had a friend who helped out with immigration, legal shit. If you really Grant, Juan's guy, you got Yolander here his papers." Beetle chuckled. "I got more friends, too, back in Ixcateopan, same place the Maderos from. My *tio* works at the bank, says a *Norte Americano* is running money through accounts, lots of it for good things, help poor people like my pop when he come to America." The man twisted in his seat, leaned both elbows on the door frame. "Tonight, man, it's simple. You that man who help people, we O.K. You not that man, I honor my contract and you're floating out in the river, gator bait. So you 'splane to me, Boo. Pretty soon, now, or I tell Rafe to cut your girlfriend's throat, real quiet like. Then Yo shoot you dead, like the man want."

Despite a cool breeze, Grant felt the sweat running down his face. How the hell did he explain his setup to a gangster, prove he did the deeds? "You got a phone that can call Mexico?"

"Yo," Beetle commanded. "Hand me a phone." The passenger opened up the glove compartment, pulled out a cell phone and passed it to Grant. "Take it, man, make your call. We gotta finish up here. Too many cops around."

A yellow light flashed over Beetle's face. Grant looked up to see a wrecker blow past the entrance, heading toward the gaggle of lights across the island.

Grant took the phone and powered it up. He dialed the international access code, 011, the code for Mexico, 52, the Ixcateopan exchange, 736, followed by the bank's number. He held the phone to his ear, listened to it ring. Chill sweat ran down his spine.

A deep voice finally answered in Spanish; thank God one he recognized.

"*Señor* Nochtli. This is Charles Howell," Grant replied, using the name the man on the other end would expect from him. Grant prayed his contact in the bank understood the urgency calling this odd time, and that Beetle would take the word of a bank manager in Mexico for the truth. "I need to ask a favor of you. A gentleman here wants to confirm my identity as a member of the bank board of directors, and perhaps he may want to ask some other personal questions. It is very important he understand my position in these matters. You have my permission to answer all his questions." In response to Señor Nochtli's query, Grant squinted his eyes, visualized the numbers from his master account and repeated it into the phone for confirmation and then handed the phone to Beetle.

A rapid exchange of Spanish followed, so fast Grant caught only the rudimentary phrases. Beetle clicked the call off and nodded. "So. You are also Mister Howell, too?"

"Yeah. I think I might have used some of Yolander's information on how to be a lot of people, all at one time."

"That's good for you, not so good for me. Now I got to tell Silva his contract no good. Tough shit, hey?" Beetle laughed, joined by Yolander.

Silva. Somehow Grant wasn't surprised at the name.

Beetle took back the phone. "I know you know this, but I say it. I got to get rid of the man who say for me to kill you, or I got problems everywhere. So don't speak about our deal. *Muy importante.* I don't break a contract unless I find out family gonna get hurt. Juan say you a friend of family, so you kinda family now." Beetle leaned over and spoke to the shadowy figure behind Bennett. "Rafe, open the gate. We ain't got no more business here."

"Wait a minute," Grant said. "I can save you some trouble. Don't call Silva. He's dead. I already took care of that." He couldn't help but let a wry grin slip over his face.

Beetle cocked his head and smiled back at Grant. "Hey, Boo. You get around. Maybe we need to work on some jobs together, you keep you nose clean."

"Sure. Give me a call anytime. But I got a question for you. Know a big bald guy, dark? Speaks Spanish, but I don't think he's Mexican. He's the one who shot the deputies in Homosassa."

Beetle flipped the glowing butt to the ground. "I saw all about that on TV. That was a dumb shooting. Everybody know you pop a cop, you going to die, like that dude who whacked the cop and his dog over in Polk County. Son bitch never had a chance after that. Cops put a bunch of bullets in him." Beetle shook his head. "I keep my ear to the ground; know a lot. Ain't no big bald guy speak Spanish hang with the brothers I know."

Rafe waved from the gate, now standing wide open.

"Listen, Boo. The cops all think you done the deed, man. You take care, or they going to do you, too." Without another word, Beetle started the SUV, drove out to the road, picked up Rafe and turned back toward Crystal River.

Barbeque and pickle breath drew his attention away from the road. When he turned Bennett put her arms around him in a bear hug. "Kat?" Her whole body trembled as if she had a fever.

" I knew; I knew. I should have said something; that they were after you. I wasn't thinking straight. I was worried about the kids. I'm sorry, Uly," she whispered.

He held her at arm's length. "What do you mean you knew?"

"When Bobby took me, I heard him call, tell somebody to kill you. And I didn't warn you."

He pulled her back tight, her gritty cheek against his. "Don't worry about it. We got ambushed. Not your fault. We lived through it. If Silva sent them here to kill me, he's too damn late. One of the gang bangers worked for Juan; says I set up his immigration papers. They even knew about my connections in Mexico. God, this is tangled." He pushed her back, this time to see if she could muster one of her grins. No luck. "Too many people know too much. We got to get going, or those cops will be on our asses." He pulled Bennett over to the building where he checked the LEDs in the security system panel on the loading dock. The house indicators glowed green.

Grant tugged Bennett deeper into the shadows as a string of police vehicles left the island heading toward Crystal River. A tow truck followed with a pickup lashed down to its rollback bed. Grant waited until all the lights had disappeared across the bridge. When the traffic cleared he led Bennett out to the gate where he looked up and down the road. No sign of lights or life down the road toward the tip of the island.

"Thank you, Lord," Grant said to the sky. He closed the gate behind them. "I don't think the law has connected us with the house. Come on. We can get cleaned up, see about Flash and figure out what to do next."

Files to delete, tracks to cover. Corporations to transfer, trusts to be established, accounts to be closed. Uly Grant had to vanish. But first, take care of a couple of important things, like Flash. Then he was out of here; to Mexico, someplace, anyplace he could just rest. Maybe even Utah, wherever that was.

CHAPTER 38

T albot grimaced at the tepid coffee and re-read the faxes, ignoring the BlackBerry and its annoying vibration. Two minutes later it vibrated again. Things were beginning to unravel around the office. The lab report had confirmed the dead woman was an Elizabeth Stevens, a resident on the farm, not Bennett. Now Raphael was in a panic mode trying to cover his ass, announcing Stevens probably was a conspirator in the attack on Port Tampa. He had scurried off to a late night interagency task force meeting spouting his shit. At least he was out of Talbot's thinning hair.

Talbot's Blackberry vibrated again. He scrolled through the menu and turned off the vibration mode, hoping for a little peace. *Damn phone.* It lay on his desk, screen blinking with a new call. Not the damn phone's fault. He gave up and answered the call. "Talbot."

"About time you answered. Where the hell you been?" Beth rattled on, not waiting for a reply. "Not sleeping, I hope. My boys got some info for you. They think you should have received four faxes from Bennett. You only mentioned three. One more fax should show up, in addition to the three you have. Go over to your machine and find this batch of log numbers." She read him a series of fax log numbers. "I'm also sending down some of Wilson's files you might find interesting. Apparently he recently received a bunch of messages that appear to be related to illegal financial accounts. Maybe from his informant. But my guys will sort that out later. Let me know if you need anything else. We'll keep looking on this end. By the way, turns out the shooting victim in Temple Terrace was Bennett's boss. Plot thickens, huh?" She disconnected before he could response.

Talbot stood up holding the scrap of paper with the log numbers. Now wasn't the time to learn how to operate the new combination fax/printer/toaster. Delina wasn't at her desk. He looked across the room at the high windows. Dark as pitch. The LED clock on his phone flicked past 05:17 to 05:18. Delina was probably home, asleep, like regular people. Talbot scrubbed at his eyes. Sleep could come after this mess got sorted. He walked over to the fax, fiddled with the menu until he found the log files. As Beth had said, apparently he was missing one of the messages. Talbot compared the log numbers with the sheets on his desk. Satisfied he had found the missing fax, he printed it out. He read the fax on his way back to his desk, then sat down and read it again. This one he could believe, in a strange way. It implicated Allen Wilson. Wilson always seemed a little devious, but never had gotten into any real trouble that made its way up to battalion headquarters where Talbot would hear of it. This message, if true, linked Wilson and the Bennett woman to the drug drop. That, with the phone logs, put Bennett and Wilson in deep shit and, by association, Grant. No wonder Beth was so abrupt. Wilson was one of her boys now.

Talbot logged on to his computer and downloaded the email files dredged from Wilson's office computer. Most were routine office business, a couple of personal messages that obviously shouldn't be on State computers, but not incriminating. Then, the surprise. Two messages, highlighted by Beth's guys, originated from a free email service, the kind you can set up anonymously. Each of these messages had provided Wilson the details of offshore financial accounts, and linked each account with criminal activity that had subsequently been turned into active investigations. Must be Wilson's confidential informant Beth had mentioned.

A penciled comment from Beth noted these cases eventually resulted in criminal prosecutions, indicating solid information; but she would have to get her hands on Wilson to identify the source. A trace back through the Internet service provider to the informant had led to a dead end. Possibly traceable over time and with additional research and subpoenaed files, but tedious and time consuming. If all that was going on was domestic crime or drug trafficking, so what. Beth would track it down and somebody else, likely FBI, would take it from there. But, if this had anything to with the attack on Port Tampa and terrorists, he didn't have time to wait.

He needed to find Grant, take him into custody before Raphael shot him down where he stood. In Iraq Talbot had learned to dance down the fine line dividing protection and prosecution. Sometimes you had to kick the door down, worry about legalities later when lives were at stake.

Talbot need to find a door to kick.

CHAPTER 39

Grant grabbed Bennett's hand and pulled her through the dew-damp weeds along the fence. On the other side of the fence, his house appeared and vanished again in the cottony haze rising off the water, just enough pink in the mists to hint at the coming sunrise. Somewhere close an airboat engine whined, coughed, then revved up to full speed like it was clearing a trailer, idled for a moment. Almost as quickly it went silent. The air felt heavy, full of rain. As the mist floated past, details resolved from the haze: the attached garage, the empty boat storage area. The road stretching to the end of the island appeared deserted; the cops, Beetle and his cutthroats, all gone.

Grant crouched and ran down the fence line to the water's edge, Bennett close on his heels, splashed through the shallows and around the fence. He picked his way through the dripping pines and cabbage palms separating the Madero Building from his home. He stopped, looked for a moment, then trotted across the yard to the back porch. He paused, pistol in his hand. *No more fucking ambushes.* A light rain began to patter down. Grant opened the back door and stepped back as Flash burst past, sprinted out to his favorite clump of bushes and squatted. Somewhere along the way he slipped his bandages. Grant secured the alarm as Bennett climbed up the steps, looking weary and worn.

"Go in," Grant told Bennett. "Get cleaned up, whatever you want to do. Maybe make us something to eat if there's anything left."

"Can I call Logan?"

"Sure. Use one of the phones in the kitchen. Just not too long. Somebody probably listening."

"Have I got time to shower and change clothes?" Bennett brushed past him. "Between Bobby and those creeps in the parking lot, I feel nasty."

Grant scrubbed at his stubble, suddenly aware of the sand grinding against his skin under his waistband. "Yeah. I don't think we have to rush. With Silva out of the picture and his contract with Beetle null and void, the only thing we have to worry about now is figuring out where to go from here and, eventually, clearing the police charges. I figure we're safe for a day or two."

GULF WINDS

Grant waited for Flash to come back in and shut the door behind them. "We'll miss this place, won't we, Flash?" He followed Flash down the hall past the Highwaymen paintings. Grant had lived in Homosassa all of his life, right on this very same piece of land except for time in Tampa attending college and at various Army schools. Not to forget almost twelve months in Iraq. He would miss the people. He paused. Not so. Most of his close friends were gone, dead. Flash paused in the hallway to shake, splattering rainwater on the floor. "You got no respect, boy. Momma would give me a good whipping if she saw this mess." The polished pine boards were tracked with damp sand. No time for house-keeping, not till more important things were taken care of.

He logged on his computer and, one last time, opened his email program. A new message popped up addressed to one of his fake accounts. His shook his head. From Scanlon's Central Command email address. In the text Scanlon addressed him—Grant—by name. Ah, crap. Scanlon, or someone using Scanlon's email account, had figured out he was the intelligence source.

He quickly scanned the message, surprised anyone could have tracked him through all of the cutouts, wondering what telltale he had left. Scanlon wrote that he thought Grant had been caught up in some-body else's bad deal. He suggested he turn himself in. That might be good psychology on his part, the "come on in and talk" routine, but Grant would have to think on that one a bit. From someplace far away. While he was reading Scanlon's message, another popped up on his screen, again from Scanlon. An even bigger surprise.

Scanlon had tentatively identified the bald man from the shooting, an Ivan Karkoff. He was Cuban, ex-military, somehow linked with al Qaeda. Scanlon suspected Karkoff had participated in the terrorist rocket attack, and wanted to know if Grant could add any information. Most important, Scanlon emphasized, was that he was concerned about Grant's safety, warned him to get help. And probably would keep feeding him emails until someone knocked on the door.

With a battering ram. *If al Qaeda didn't find him first.*

Grant reached down to rub Flash's bony head. "I'm concerned about our safety, too, boy." Grant worked his way through the DIA data base and ran a quick search on the name "Karkoff." The only hit popped up an ex-Soviet general now living across Tampa in Ybor City with connec-tions to Cape Canaveral and the space program. Grant pasted the Ybor address in his contact files, hurrying so he could log back out before anyone could put a sniffer on him. Next he copied his banking account information and contact files to a IronKey secure flash drive, along with the incriminating faxes and files from Silva. He dropped the flash drive into his pocket, set the computer to clean all data from the hard drive and started the wipe that would make the files irretrievable. How in the hell had he let this all come down on him? Too drugged up to notice? He had been in the Army long enough to know—excuses don't cut it.

"About time to disappear," he told Flash, who seemed to sense something strange was going down. Rather than retreat to his crate, he stayed snugged up to Grant's leg. Grant reached down and scratched between the dog's ears as he waited for the drive to finish chattering. "Those girls spoiled you rotten."

Bennett padded into the office, barefoot and in a pair of his nylon gym shorts and tee shirt, cell phone in hand.

"Talk to Logan?"

She shook her head, those frown lines back again. "Voicemail. I'll try again later. What are you and Flash doing now?" She dropped the phone back in the drawer.

"An email from Scanlon said he thought the bald man was a Cuban, with al Qaeda connections."

She looked at him, her eyes narrowed in an expression becoming all too familiar. "So they *are* after you, not me. Anything about Chantico and Juan?"

He shook his head. "Not from Scanlon."

Her eyes went from hard to sad. "Did we cause all this?"

"Maybe. But we didn't kill them, or even try to put them in danger. Don't take this on your shoulders or put it on mine." Even as he spoke, he knew both he and Bennett would carry this guilt the rest of their lives.

"Poor Angelina." Bennett closed her eyes for a moment. "If the deputy is alive, he can testify for us. Shouldn't we just turn ourselves in?"

"Everybody else seems to think so. Let me think about it, get all the loose ends tied up." He looked up from the computer. "You can always do what you want."

She squeezed his shoulder "What *we* want. We're a team now, buddy. You said so." Bennett scrubbed her head with a towel. She had returned her chopped hair to a soft brown, streaked with natural looking highlights.

Angelica would approve. Wherever she was.

"What are you doing now?"

Data wipe complete, Grant shut the computer down. "Cleaning up some files, the ones that have to do with my businesses. Which reminds me." He pulled the used Louis Anderson identification and credit cards from his pocket and fed them into the crosscut shredder. "Hand me those mosquito cigars." He pointed at an ornate wood humidor on the bookcase.

She handed him the box. "What are mosquito cigars?"

"Ones that smell so bad the only thing they are good for are to chase away mosquitoes." He opened the humidor and dumped two layers of cigars on the desk along with a thick envelope. He pulled a wad of hundred dollar bills, a Florida drivers license and a credit card from the envelope and returned the cigars to the humidor. "I'm running out of identities."

Bennett stared at the money for a moment, then nodded her head, her face lined with exhaustion. "I'll wash some clothes and fix us something to eat while you finish."

Grant nodded, and then flipped off the master uninterruptible power supply switch, blanking out an array of red and green LEDs. When he returned to the kitchen Bennett had pulled eggs and bacon out of the refrigerator. He grabbed a small backpack from a hook in the utility room.

"Do you think they are really all right?" She placed strips of bacon in a frying pan.

Grant immediately understood the question, even if he really didn't know the answer. "Logan will see they're fine, Kat." He added the cash, a cell phone and the small laptop from the counter top to the backpack, and draped it over the back of a chair. "Let's catch our breath, then you try Logan again. I'm sure the kids, everything's all right." What had he forgot? He fished the IronKey flash drive out of his pocket and held it up. "Important files, to include all my contacts. Password to access the secure files is 'Flashdog.'" Lord. He was giving his life's secrets away.

"What are our alternatives?" She broke two more eggs, as if she was keeping her hands busy to keep her mind channeled away from the kids.

"Get ready to run. I got to quit letting people surprise me." Like his interrogation team, he and Bennett had been through the fire, shared secrets. Surely they were now a team. "Surprise us."

Grant put plates and flatware on the table, then dropped into a chair, Flash stretched out on the floor by his side. Flash looked as he was healing pretty quickly for an old dog, quicker that he was.

He glanced at the wildlife calendar on the wall. A red circle on the calendar marked the appointment to take Bennett on her Sunday fishing trip. Today was—he had to count the days, blurred in his mind—Thursday. He let his eyes run from Bennett's chopped hair to her red painted toes. The fluorescent light accentuated the bruises on her taunt thighs and neck, some yellowing from the Sunday night on the island with Billy and Hoop, scabs starting to peel away, some fresh purple marks from Silva. At least she wouldn't get any more bruises, from Silva or the Aryan brothers. They were home free. Then Scanlon's comment about al Qaeda and the Cuban wormed its way in to his mind. A different question. Puzzling, but he didn't know how it figured in with them.

The smell of frying bacon filled the kitchen. Bennett stood at the stove, her body lines apparent in the nylon shorts and tee shirt.

Suddenly Grant was starving. For a lot of things. He buried the sudden thoughts of her warm body and soft breath. Bennett wasn't his, to have or protect. He pushed himself up out of the chair. *Just a team member.* "I'll take a quick shower and throw some clothes in the washer."

"I've already put mine in. I was waiting for you to turn it on."

He showered, letting the hot water wash away the blood, play over the wound on his arm, run like a soothing touch down his back and across his hips as he lathered and shaved under the running water. Grit and beard cleared away with some of the aches and in a clean set of clothes, he walked past Bennett piling their plates with food, and threw the sand-caked clothes in the washer. He was too tired to sort. What got washed, got washed.

They ate in silence, Bennett with her elbows on the table, head propped on one hand.

She stopped eating for a moment and looked around the room. "No TV, no radio. Doesn't the quiet drive you batty? I'm a TV nut, living by myself. Especially the sitcoms. And music. When the TV's not on I keep some good country music going, you know, everything from Garth Brooks to Reba McEntire. I even like the Dixie Chicks. Just none of that pickup truck and dead dog stuff." She laughed at Grant's look.

"We got class around here, lady." Grant slid his chair back and opened the drawer with the cell phones, dug around until he found a remote. He pointed it toward the wall, and a panel slid open displaying a flat screen TV. A soft piano riff filled the room from hidden speakers, the bass set heavy. "Whole house is wired for satellite TV, including music channels. My ears are so bad I forget to turn the music on. When I do all I can really hear is the bass beat. Getting better, though. I think my ear drums are healing. Lots of Miles Davis, Amad Jamal, Theolonius Monk, Bird, good stuff with a rhythm I can feel, even if I can't hear worth a crap." He stopped talking to finish the last bite of grits and eggs. "I saw so many stupid soap operas and talk shows while I was in Walter Reed, I swore I would never look at another daytime TV show. Seems my evenings have been busy lately, not a lot of extra time. I—"

Bennett's fork clinked against her plate. Her head slid down onto her arm, eyes closed.

Grant glanced at a wall clock. Just after seven o'clock. He was so tired he had to stop and think. The hurricane shutters were still closed tight, no view of the outside to give him a hint, but he was pretty sure it was morning. They had been on the run all night. No wonder they were exhausted. He put one of her arms around his neck and slid his arms under her. The side of her neck looked as if she had been scratched by a mean cat. Beetle's lookout, Rafe, had been a little heavy with the knife.

"What?" she whispered, snuggling her face into his neck.

"Go back to sleep, Kat." Grant gathered her up and carried her to the guest bedroom. He laid her on the bed and pulled up the sheet, folding it so it didn't touch the fresh scab. He walked back to his bedroom, arranged his knife and pistol on the night stand and clicked off the overhead light. Grant supposed he was as tired as Bennett. He wasn't sure he could sleep, but he stretched out on his bed and closed his eyes, anyway. Maybe a little rest would make his mind work better. Just a few hours. With Silva no longer a threat, he and Bennett—and Wilson— should be safe from whoever was behind the bribery scheme. Ivan? That one he just couldn't figure out.

Eyes closed, his mind raced. Beetle and the rest of his EME boys were another quandary. Grant would have to work on breaking all connections with his Mexican interests. Then he would have to make the hard decision. Turn himself in, or vanish. The more he thought about disappearing, the more he realized that Bennett, Allen, and now Scanlon all knew too much about him. Even Angelica could probably provide clues that would lead a savvy investigator to him. The more he though, the tougher it got. Technically—crap—not technically, really, he was still in the Army on convalescent leave. DoD had his fingerprints on file under his real name and Social Security number. Eventually someone would catch up to him. If he ran, he would be AWOL. That wouldn't do, not to sully Vicente's memory that way. And there was Flash.

Too much to think about now. He listened for the music coming from the kitchen. All he could hear was a faint beat, Jim Cammack's throbbing string bass counter point to Ahmad Jamal's flowing piano, now largely lost in the buzz of James Johnson, heavy on the drums. Grant let his eyes close, imagined music floating through his head with all the other unknowns, and drifted into a dream.

"Uly. Wake up. Uly." Bennett's voice whispered in his head. For real. He rolled onto his back and reached up for her, pulled her down and kissed her. Her lips were soft and her body was warm from head to foot as she sprawled across him. A weight he was more than willing to bear. For the first time since the car bomb exploded he felt like a man, a real man. He held her tight and laughed.

"Stop."

"You taste like bacon and grape jelly." He kissed her again and ran his hands down her back, over the nylon gym shorts to her thighs and back up.

She kissed him, a short peck, then pulled away.

He opened his eyes, and reluctantly let her go.

Her eyes were wide. "Someone's outside."

Grant rolled over and off the side of the bed. He slid the Kimber in one hip pocket and the Buck in the other, blinking the crust from his eyes.

"I woke up with Flash poking me with his nose and whining to go out. I had opened the back door before I heard somebody driving up the driveway. I didn't know anyone was there. I'm sorry." She shook her head, lips pursed. "I shut the door before anyone saw me, I think. Flash had already scooted outside before I could stop him."

"Not your fault. You didn't see them." Grant stuck his feet into the scuffed deck shoes that had been new just the day before. He clicked the remote button that displayed the bedroom monitor. A wide screen TV divided into a sequence of views, each from a security camera mounted at each corner of the house and over the front, back and garage entrances. The view from the garage showed a truck parked in the driveway.

Bennett stared at the screens. "Why didn't you tell me about this yesterday? Can you make the pictures any clearer?"

"I didn't think anyone was watching us yesterday. And we still had secrets, remember." He pointed at the screen "Blur's from the rain."

"It looks bad outside, rainy and dark. Poor Flash."

"Don't worry about Flash. You did the right thing. He can take care of himself. Remember, you told me yourself, he saved both our butts." Grant took Bennett's shoulders in his hands and looked in her eyes, almost black in the dim light. He shoved her off the bed and toward the door. "Go get some clothes on."

He grabbed a handful of tee shirt and pulled her back as she started out. "Wait." He pulled the Kimber from his pocket. "This is loaded and cocked. Take off the safety, pull the trigger and it shoots. Know how the safety works?"

She shook her head. "No."

He held the pistol so she could see the safety, and motioned with his own thumb how the lever worked. "Push this down and it's ready to shoot. It's loud and kicks, so if you have to shoot, be ready. After it fires the first time you'll know what to expect."

She shook her head "I—"

"No, I don't expect you to shoot anybody," he interrupted, glancing up at the monitor to see a shadow flash by the front door. "But I want you to be ready to help if Flash and I need it. The pistol's perfectly safe until you push the safety down. You can use the damn thing for a hammer, drop it and it won't go off, so don't be afraid of it."

She took a deep breath and took it. "Right." She nodded her head and looked down at the pistol cradled in both hands.

GULF WINDS

Grant took her trembling hands in his and pressed her thumb over the safety, clicking it down and back up. "See how the safety feels? Click down, it's ready to shoot. Up, and it's safe. But don't put your finger on the trigger until you're ready to shoot. And don't point it at me or Flash," he added. "Remember, we don't know what's going on. If it's law enforcement out there, they should identify themselves. If it is a cop, lay the pistol down immediately and get away from it. But if it's somebody threatening us, be ready to point it at them and pull the trigger. O. K.?" He gently shook her shoulder. "Dammit, Kat, you gotta help me out here." He shoved her toward the hall, watching the curve of her butt as she walked out. *My, how he had missed the small joys of life this past year.*

Grant stepped into his closet, racked back the slide on the old Colt .45, a grown up ancestor of the smaller Kimber. Grandpa George Grant died when Grant was twelve, but he had already taught Grant how to safely handle and shoot the WWII relic, lessons Grant had carried with him as he followed his grandfather's legacy into the National Guard. Grant let the slide slam forward, round in the chamber, hammer cocked and safety on, remembering the wild stories Grandpa told of the Dixie Division's participation in the invasions of New Guinea and the Philippines. Oh, how exciting Grandpa had made combat seem to a young boy, teaching Grant how to handle the pistol with the prancing pony on the slide. Grant shook his head at the memories and jammed the worn pistol into a pocket. His own combat time had seemed exciting. Until Vicente died. Then war had stopped being so glorious.

Grant dropped a handful of shotgun shells into his left side cargo pocket and felt his pants sag under the combined weight of the pistol, knife and the shells, exacerbated by his skinny waistline. *Lord, I hope I get a chance to eat more of Kat's cooking.* He pulled back the shotgun bolt to confirm a brass case in the chamber, and let the action snap closed.

When he met Bennett in the hall she had slipped on her khaki slacks and deck shoes. With the black Kimber in her hand, she would have been macho if her lack of a bra hadn't been so apparent. All of a sudden he seemed to be sensitive to such details. He shook the image from his mind. "Come on." He led Bennett to the kitchen, shotgun in hand. "Let's see what's going on." He clicked the remote and brought up the outdoor monitors.

Grant stepped closer to the screen and pointed at the view from the garage door. A white pickup truck sat next to the house, an unrecognizable face behind the windshield wiper. "Looks like a plumber or a gutter installer with ladders, PVC pipes and tools in the back of his truck." Grant glanced over at the wall. Damn. He had left the security alarm system unsecured when they came in, turned off along with the rest of his mind.

Bennett pointed at the display that showed the back yard and Crystal Bay. "I see Flash. I think he just hopped into a—" She leaned forward and stared at the screen. "Is that your boat by the water?"

"Yeah. Juan must have brought it back after we left the Maderos' house." Grant pushed off the shotgun safety with his forefinger. "Stay in here where you can see what's happening. I'll find out if this is something to worry about, or just some guy looking for work."

She suddenly clutched his arm, pointing with the pistol at the screen. For a moment a bald head glistened in the rain behind the truck.

Grant pried her fingers from his arm.

"Look. The man that shot the deputy."

Grant nodded. "Scanlon thinks his name is Ivan Karkoff, a Cuban, warned me about him."

The man disappeared. A moment later he came around the truck, stopping at the front tire. He bent, stabbed the tire with a long knife. The truck settled on the flat as the man walked back out of sight behind the truck. The back ends of the PVC tubes jerked, then slowly dropped toward the truck bed, leaving the front ends pointing up into the sky.

"Son of a bitch."

"What is he doing?" Bennett whispered, as if the man could hear her.

He pulled her away from the screen, into the hallway. "I think he's set up a jury-rig rocket launcher."

"What in the world is he aiming at?"

Grant looked back at the screen, paused. "The Crystal River Nuclear Facility across the bay."

Bennett suddenly seemed frozen to the floor.

"Don't worry about radiation or any of that crap. The nuclear reactor containment chamber is designed to withstand the impact of a crashing airliner. Piss-ant *Katyusha* rockets will scare the bejeasus out of everybody, maybe put the coal fired generators offline. But we're all right."

Her eyes were wide.

"You hear me? The plant is safe."

"You promise."

"I promise." He shoved her toward the office, hoping he was right.

Bennett paused at the door and looked over her shoulder at Grant, the pistol clutched to her chest. "What are you going to do?"

He ran his finger over the safety button on the shotgun. "Stop him."

CHAPTER 40

When Grant slipped out the back door, a sudden gust of wind whipped a fine spray into his eyes with enough salt to sting, despite the ball cap pulled down to his ears. Heavy raindrops pelted down against the cap brim. The pink glow had faded to a swirl of dirty grey. The dark squall line and distant streaks of lightning out over the Gulf warned of more to come.

Grant started when a damp nose prodded his thigh. Flash leaned against his leg, shivering in the chilling rain. Grant grabbed Flash's collar. "With me, boy. We got to check this out." Grant led the greyhound to the corner of the house. Quivering, Flash curled his lean body against his leg. "Easy, Flash." He stroked the greyhound's neck, fur slick with rain. Grant squatted and slowly poked his head around the corner, squeezing the shotgun's wet pistol grip, finger hovering by the trigger.

The white pickup truck sat at the near end of the driveway. The logo on the door said something about Ybor City and surveying, too blurred by the rain to be sure. The bald man, presumably Karkoff, had disappeared.

"Flash, I got to move where I can see better." Grant led Flash back to the back porch and shoved his rump through the screen door. "Stay, boy," Grant whispered, and got that sad smile in return. Keeping the house between him and the truck, shotgun at the ready, Grant trotted out toward the water. He worked his way around and through the trees until the truck sat between him and the house. Behind the house the sun struggled up over the trees, firing shards of yellow through a thick bank of clouds.

Grant froze behind a screen of wild passion vine trailing down from a pine when the man walked around the side of the truck. Big, bald; Grant could see him in his mind's eye at the plate glass window, face set in a snarl as he fired through the glass.

Karkoff leaned closer to the framework and flicked a switch. The back ends of the PVC pipes jerked, then dropped.

Plenty close for ought buckshot. Grant ran his finger over the safety. Maybe twenty feet away, the twelve .32 caliber pellets would pattern out to a ragged twenty inch circle. *One way to stop this, right now.* Grant stepped from behind the tree and raised the collapsible stock to his cheek.

Karkoff's head bobbed down behind the PVC pipes before Grant could pull the trigger. *For crying out loud!* Had he forgotten everything he had learned in Iraq? Vicente always carried a shotgun because he preached that the perfect shot never sat still for you, and the first hit always won a shootout. Grant shook his head, flinging raindrops off the brim of his hat and squatted, searching for Karkoff's legs behind the truck. Whatever his excuse: OxyContin, exhaustion or stupidity, he had just let the man who killed Eustis out of his sights, the man who controlled four rockets aimed toward the nuclear facility across Crystal Bay.

He flinched when a sudden flurry of heavy drops plopped onto the cap brim. He glanced up and blinked into rain drops splattering down from the trees. A fat squirrel bounded along the limb overhead, scampered to the next moss draped tree, stopping to flick its tail up and down, followed by a second, urging the first along and around the tree trunk in a scurry of little feet. Grant shook the water from his eyes and searched for Karkoff. Distracted by a bunch of squirrels, he had let the son of a bitch vanish into the driving rain. When he looked back toward the truck a movement at the front of the house caught his attention. Grant swung the shotgun, stopped. Bennett, crouched by the corner of the house, stared out at him. Damn. Why hadn't she stayed inside?

Grant duck walked to the edge of the waist high dog fennel until he was only yards from the truck and the inclined pipes. Out of the corner of his eye he finally spotted Karkoff, now far to Grant's left, back in the edge of the trees. He held a black box connected to the truck with a bundle of wires. A remote firing switch. Grant had seen one before—on the road to Baghdad.

Grant was in mid-step, shifting back into the trees to circle behind Karkoff when the first rocket fired with an explosive crack and a spout of fiery rocket exhaust from the end of the closest pipe.

A flaming tail following the missile as it streaked up and over Crystal Bay.

Grant coughed as superheated steam from the scorched ground behind the truck enveloped him, filled his lungs, then dissipated just as quickly as a wind gust whipped around the corner of the house. He cringed, expecting all four tubes to fire in a ripple, one big salvo of destruction. But instead of the roar of the other three rockets firing, all he could hear was a rushing hum in his ears.

As if he launched rockets every day, Karkoff calmly stepped out into the open. He raised a pair of binoculars to his eyes and looked out over the bay toward the nuclear facility.

GULF WINDS

Grant glanced over his shoulder in time to see a dirty column of smoke climbing into the low clouds scuttling around the cooling towers. The grinding yowl of an emergency warning siren shattered the heavy morning air, followed by a chorus of wails from the multiple warning sites scattered around Crystal Bay and the nuclear facility. His heart began to pound; the bruise on his head seemed to swell. He sucked in a deep breath, so deep hyperventilation stars spun in his head, mixed with the blood his heart insisted on surging through his body. *Get a damn grip!*

A motor whirred on the back of the truck. The four pipes of the launcher dipped and then moved upward another few inches. Karkoff let the glasses drop and toggled a switch on the box.

With the distant impact Grant lost any confidence in the capability of the nuclear facility to absorb more rockets. Not enough to stand by and let Karkoff launch them.

Wisps of steam still rose from behind the truck, enveloping Karkoff. Not a clear shot. Too far. Was Bennett clear?

Stop thinking. Grant snatched the shotgun to his shoulder and snapped off a booming shot.

Karkoff twisted away, maybe hit, but not down. He dove out of sight behind the thick trunk of a longleaf pine.

Grant racked the shotgun, spun and fired a wad of buckshot at the makeshift launcher. The frame and PVC tubes jerked with the impact. He jacked a new shell into the chamber. He ignored Karkoff, focused on the launcher. He fired again, this time toward where he imagined the rocket motors would be in the tubes.

Flames roared out of the rear of one of the tubes. Smaller plumes spewed in all directions through holes in the PVC. Shotgun butt still at his shoulder, he racked another shell into the chamber and fired again, this time toward where the warheads would be.

A blinding explosion slapped the shotgun back across his nose, slammed him on to his back into the wet dog fennel. Dazed for a moment, he rolled to his stomach and crawled on his hands and knees toward the trees, dragging the gun behind him by its sling. Another explosion flattened Grant to his stomach and sent bits and pieces whistling over his head, rattling through the leaves. The next explosion slammed his face down into a matt of wet weeds.

Grant clawed his way to his knees and scrabbled around behind a slender pin oak. Cheek pressed against the wet bark, he peeked around at the truck, now an unrecognizable tangle of wreckage, and searched for Karkoff. Not to be seen. Grant shuffled back into the trees as the gas tank exploded with a whomp, shooting a tongue of fire into the sky and rolling a wall of intense heat across his face and hands, sucking the air from his lungs.

A gunshot rang out, cracked through the trees.

Grant dropped flat and searched through the weeds. There. By the side of the house. Karkoff ran toward the water. He disappeared into the rain and wind-driven smoke plume that billowed up from the truck, rolling the smell of burning cedar and plastics over Grant. The next gust blew away the screen of smoke. Cedar boards curled away from the pre-stressed concrete sides of the house and burst into flame.

Steam and smoke and bits of ash swirled up into the sky.

Grant reloaded the shotgun, slowly circling around the tree line toward the front of the house. Shivering in his wet clothes, gritty shotgun to his cheek, Grant walked through the trees toward the water. He fired when Karkoff burst into an opening. He pumped the slide, fired again as Karkoff dove behind a cabbage palm.

A rifle report cracked past his ear from behind, smacking into the pine in front of Grant, splattering shards of bark into his face. Grant dropped to a crouch, spun to see a man running toward the front porch. To his right a gunshot from the water's edge hummed through the air. He had let himself get trapped between at least two shooters. *Dammit. Where was Kat?* He prayed she had barricaded herself inside and wasn't a part of this melee. Grant ran toward the front of the house where he had last seen her. The shooter scrambled behind the balustrade and its tangled screen of bougainvillea vines.

Behind him the sound of an airboat engine rumbled through the rain and built to a high whine. When Grant turned toward the water a bullet snapped by his head. He dropped to the ground and rolled toward the cover of the trees. Confused, looking for Bennett, he had lost all track of where the shooters were. He crawled into a skunk weed thicket and looked back toward the house. The crushed vine's heavy scent, mixed with the acrid smell of burnt rubber and plastics bubbling from the wrecked truck, clawed at his throat. When he rose to his knees a gunshot cracked from the front porch, the bullet snapping through the weeds to his left, another over his head as he buried his face in the skunk vines.

"Bull shit," he muttered, spitting out damp leaves. This was his house, his home.

He scrambled to his feet and charged the porch, shattering the railing and bougainvillea with buckshot as he ran. He fired and jacked the pump shotgun as fast as he could move his arms. He dove to a stop on the slick grass and searched for the shooter.

The shooter obliged. He rose from the far corner of the porch, blood streaming down his face, and swung a rifle toward Grant.

Grant pulled the trigger on the shotgun. *"Click."* He dropped the empty shotgun and dove to his right behind the tiny bit of cover offered by the septic tank mound.

A full automatic burst stitched the yard, splattering oyster shells, turf and sand into the air.

Grant flopped to his side and reached in his cargo pocket for Grandpa's pistol. He looked up to see the man from the porch slam a magazine in his AK, pull at the charging handle. Grant dug at the big pistol, hung deep in his soaking wet pants pocket. He rolled across the thin grass and glanced toward the porch where the shooter stood, half-hidden behind the bougainvillea, reloaded rifle now tracking Grant. A single bullet splattered sand in his face. Grant finally jerked the .45 automatic clear, fumbling to get a grip on the wet grips. A second bullet plowed into the ground by his head, bits of oyster shell stinging his ear. Son of a bitch was learning.

CHAPTER 41

A heavy report reverberated across the yard from inside the porch. The shooter dropped the AK and clutched at his shoulder. He bolted off the porch and disappeared into the rolling mists.

Bennett walked out on the porch. Smoke curled from the Kimber dangling from her fingertips. She squatted, carefully placed the pistol on the top step.

Grant climbed to his knees and looked around. Grandpa's Colt was nowhere to be seen. Where were the shooters? He picked up the AK, forearm shattered and slick with blood, and ran around the side of the house.

An airboat accelerated away from the shore, bouncing over the light chop kicked up by the squall.

Grant dropped to a sitting position, wiggled his butt into the sandy ground, propped his elbows on his knees and fired the AK. The first shot kicked up water far short of the boat, the second just short. He lifted slightly and triggered off the remaining rounds in rapid fire, tracking the airboat. It lurched, as if it had lost power, then slid around Bear Island and out of sight. Grant cocked his head, listening. Had the airboat engine quit? Shit, he had started the day half deaf, and now the only thing he could hear was his heart pounding and the nuclear warning sirens wailing. He looked up to see Bennett staring out over the water. "Can you hear the airboat? Can you tell if I hit him?" he yelled, not sure if his throat still worked, his voice a thin echo in his head.

She shook her head. "I'm not sure," she shouted back. "Shooting—" She waved one hand at the sky and pushed her hair back from her eyes with the other. "—sirens. Exploding rockets. Lord, I don't know anything, anymore." Her hands were shaking, but she had the most determined look he'd seen in her eyes since she had told him about Chris.

Grant stood, took her in his arms and hugged her close, wet sand and all. "You're safe, Kat." He wiped his hand on his gritty shirt tail and pushed her chin back. "You and Flash. Just keep saving my butt." He looked over her shoulder at his house. The damp cedar siding smoldered over precast concrete panels in spots, but his home was intact.

"I was so damn scared when the rocket fired I ran back inside." She buried her face in his neck. "Then I saw the other man on the monitor, shooting at you. I didn't know what to do. Good Lord, I was scared."

Her hand in his, Grant pulled Bennett back to the front porch, picked up the Kimber and held it out to her. "I'll be back in a minute."

He ran in the open door to the bedroom and grabbed grandpa's old M1 rifle. On his way out he stopped in the kitchen, retrieved the backpack and a second phone for himself. Dashing back out, he handed the backpack to Bennett.

"Go see what's happened to Chris and Angelina. Try Logan again after you get away from here. If you really need me, press 'speed dial one' on the phone in the backpack. It's set to call a voice mail account. Leave a message if you want me to know where you are or where you're going."

"Whoa," she interrupted him. "If?" she asked, eyes wide. "After all we've gone through, you ask if?"

"Christ, Kat. I don't know what you want, other than Chris being safe." He dropped the second phone in his shirt pocket. "But I want you safe." He pointed through the trees toward the fence where they had met Beetle. "Go find the flatbed truck back up in the brush. Key's still in the ignition. Take it to the boat yard and the *Rum Runner*."

She shook her head, a confused look in her eyes. "Where?"

"The boat yard, in Homosassa. Where we first met."

Bennett threw the backpack over her shoulder and squeezed his fingers, her eyes pleading. "Uly. Please go with me."

Grant shook his head. "The guy in the airboat. He murdered Eustis. Don't know about you, but I got enough Indian blood and Scotch-Irish pigheadedness in me to enjoy true justice." He pointed with the rifle at the body bleeding out on his septic tank. "You got yours for Olsen. I'm not stopping until I've got mine for Eustis. I'll call you on the cell if I can't get back to you by dark. If you don't hear from me, send Lester Scanlon, the guy you saw on TV, an email. Tell him everything. Email account information is on the flash drive, laptop in the backpack." He kissed her, a short smack on the lips, spun her around and shoved her toward the road.

He shook his head, wishing the sirens would stop. Things he wanted to hear, he couldn't. Things he didn't want to hear drove him nuts. The incessant din reminded Grant that pretty soon Homeland Security, local cops, the world, would come down on their heads, searching for the source of the *Katyushas*. "Go," he yelled back at Bennett as he ran toward his boat. "Get out of here before the roads get blocked."

Grant snatched the extension cord loose and untied the flats boat, hoping the water puddled in the bottom was only rain. He primed the bulb on the fuel line and searched for the choke, finally finding the lever on the side of the old Johnson. Three pulls on a frayed starter rope and the motor barked, sputtered a cloud of grimy smoke. The engine died when he jammed the gear shift into reverse. "Damn you," he muttered.

This time he let the motor run for precious seconds while he loaded the one clip of eight .30-06 rounds into the M1 and brought the unfamiliar weapon up to his cheek. Even if he had missed Karkoff with the AK, maybe he had hit the airboat's engine, slowed him. Grant squinted through the tiny peephole in the battle sights and picked out a distant tree on Shark Point, along the imaginary boundary between Crystal Bay and Homosassa Bay to the south. If he could get Karkoff in his sights, the old rifle would take care of business. He propped the rifle against the wrecked center console and eased the motor in gear, this time nursing the throttle until he had the boat headed toward the islands.

Grant felt he was moving in slow motion as he guided the flats boat across Crystal Bay with its replacement motor sputtering under his hand, backfiring every minute or so until it finally smoothed out a hundred meters or so away from the boat ramp. Grant twisted the throttle, willing the wounded boat to cut through the water faster. Rather than stepping up to a plane, the old Johnson shoved the boat through the water in more of a wallow. Grant crouched and searched the islands. A pair of Great Blue Herons flushed out from a slender gap in the trees to his left, rising majestically into the air. Grant throttled back, scanning the edge of the water. No airboat, Karkoff to be seen.

Far out in the Gulf a big sportfisher slowed as an even bigger boat pulled alongside. Grant squinted across the glittering water. The chaser had the boxy profile of the *Guardian*, the Coast Guard's big jet drive catamaran, probably herding everything away from the nuclear facility.

He powered back up, barely making headway against the outgoing tide as he entered a skinny channel between an exposed mud flat and Bear Island. Grant shaded his eyes and searched the water. No Karkoff. He turned south toward Shark Point, marked by a pair of islands separated by a shallow bit of water. In the shallows and out of the tidal flow, he killed the motor and pulled the lower drive up. Another bird, too fast to identify, burst from the trees on the far island, squawking at something. A movement on the other side of the trees caught Grant's attention

He stood and began poling the boat along the shore, sweat soaking his sand-caked clothes. The water was slick as glass in the lee of the island, the mud bottom littered with limestone, oyster shells and patches of sea grass lined with tracks where boaters had run their motors too shallow and chopped into the bottom. Grant let the boat drift and searched the overgrown waterline. It could be a scene from one of the

Highwaymen paintings—herons wading the tidal flat, an anhinga on a stump drying its wings, the ripple of a cruising snook, the sudden splash of a jumping mullet. But no airboat.

The sun broke though the overcast, hot on his arms. A flicker caught his eye, the sun reflecting off a pair of helicopters swooping around the power plant. As the sun burned away the clouds, thin contrails circled and intertwined high above. In Iraq, this usually meant high altitude loitering air support, awaiting a call. Here, today, the big circles most likely indicated fighters scrambled as a result of the rocket attack on the nuclear power plant. The helicopters were of more concern to Grant. Especially if Homeland Security had brought in an AWACS or a Joint STARS with its side looking radar. Either of the big birds could track him and have a helicopter run him to ground in minutes. He didn't have time to evade a searcher. He wanted to do the searching. And the killing.

A closer glitter in the shadows, on the far side of the next island, the rising sun reflecting off the vertical rudders of an airboat partially screened by the trees. Grant shoved the nose of the flats boat toward the bank and with a grunt drove it as far as he could get it up a tiny slough, pinioned on both sides by mangroves. He reached back, grabbed the M1 rifle and started forward.

A mottled shape crawled out from under a tarp and grinned at him.

"Flash," Grant whispered. "I thought I left you on the porch."

Flash stretched out one long leg, then the other, hopped out of the boat and on to the bank where he waited for Grant.

"Think you can stay behind me, boy?" Flash's answer was to trot ahead toward a stunted oak poking above the tangled mangroves and sawgrass scattered across the tiny oval of high ground. His lean body disappeared in the grass. Grant followed, bent low on the game trail. Game trail was too kind of a description. Probably a marsh rabbit or raccoon trail, at best a tiny tunnel through the underbrush.

Without warning, Flash stopped.

Ahead, a stretch of water, ten or so meters wide, separated the two islands. Dark ruts in the mud spoiled the smooth surface of the flats barring the channel entrance. Along the far side the mangrove roots showed fresh scrapes and roots, marking where the airboat had skidded through the channel. Across the island the rudders hadn't moved.

A school of mullets rushed single file between the islands, searching for either an escape route or food. After all these years on the water, Grant never had been able to figure out why mullet did anything. Made about as much sense as his chasing the Cuban. A low line of oyster shells marked a limestone ridge under the water's surface, obscured by cascading ripples as the tide drew down the water level. Crouched behind a low stand of mangroves along the water's edge, Grant crept between the trees, trying not to flush a trio of white bellied sandpipers scurrying along the edge of the water. He picked out the metal framework of the airboat through the mangroves, still on the far side of the next island. Something moved.

"Stay, Flash."

Flash looked at Grant like he was a fool, walked out to the water and sniffed at a tiny crab that scurried under a rock, then turned his head to watch a pair of pelicans gliding inches above the water.

Grant crouched and followed until his feet squished down into the mud., listening for the roar of the airboat engine. All he could hear was the water swirling along the channel with the ebbing tide.

Grant knelt to his knees in the mud and engaged the rifle's trigger guard safety. He slid down, prone in the mud, and pulled himself into the water. About a foot deep, the water gave him just enough buoyancy to dig his fingers into the bottom and drag his way across the channel. The tide pulled at him as he worked his way through the warm water to the far side and crawled over the mangrove roots.

Grant stopped. Inches away, his old buddy, a wrist-thick rusty orange salt marsh snake stared at him from a branch, round pupils unblinking. The snake wasn't venomous, but this was the snake's island, not his. Grant wondered if this was his friend from Sunday night.

The snake hissed, arched its neck.

Grant slowly lifted the M1, reaching the muzzle out toward the snake. He eased the rifle higher, until the snake seemed to leap from the branch and vanish in the mangrove roots. Grant looked back. Flash had decided enough was enough. He sat on his haunches in the mangrove shade, head held forward as he intently watched Grant worm through the mud, nose lifted as if he had caught the snake's scent. He twisted and began licking at the scab along his side. Flash must have decided everything was all right.

Grant slithered through the gritty mud until he reached a padding of leaves. He snapped off the safety and tilted the rifle until the water ran out of the barrel. If he could pull the trigger and had a bullet in the chamber, the M1 would fire, and probably feed the next round out of the clip. A movement caught his eye. Old Flash on the move. The greyhound had trotted down the bank, looking back at Grant like he had missed something.

An engine started with a roar.

Grant stood, swung toward the sound and slammed the dripping rifle to his shoulder, cheek against the muddy stock.

CHAPTER 42

The airboat burst from behind a screen of mangroves, engine screaming. Karkoff looked back from the driver's seat, high up in front of the big engine and propeller.

Grant jerked the M1's trigger, startled by the sudden appearance of the boat, even more with the jackhammer recoil of the old rifle. He swung the rifle and fired again, the recoil rattling his teeth and spraying grit into his face. The boat cleared the mangroves and slid across the mud flat at the end of the island, skidding sideways as Karkoff momentarily lost control. The boat bucked into the air when the boat bottom scrapped over a limestone shelf, spoiling Grant's aim. He settled the rifle, fired again as the boat pulled away, kept firing. Steam crackled from the wet forestock, heated by the barrel, stinging his eyes. Grant blinked, wondered if he had hit anything. He swiped at his eyes in time to see the airboat slow. About forty meters out the airboat engine began to screech like it was going to seize up.

The airboat's back end began to oscillate up and down on the water in a wild dance. An explosion of steam and smoke burst from the airboat engine followed by shattered propeller chunks and engine parts crashing through the cage on the back of the boat and splattering into the water.

Grant slammed the stock to his cheek and fired again at Karkoff, clinging to the front seat. The clang of the ejecting empty clip announced he had fired all eight rounds. Grant threw down the M1 and ran to the edge of the island as Karkoff hopped down from the boat seat. The Cuban stood on the airboat's bow and brandished a big knife toward Grant, blade glittering, then jumped into the water.

Karkoff swam with an uneven stroke, laboring in the water, almost fifty meters away in the shallow water and passing a channel marker. He headed away from Grant and toward shore.

A big pelican, spooked by the commotion, squawked and dove down from the marker, swooping low, wingtips leaving streaks in the darker green water of the channel.

Karkoff angled toward an opening in the mangroves that led back to a house perched up on stilts, another two hundred meters or so away, each choppy stroke marked by a huge spray of water.

For an instant Grant considered going back to the flats boat, crank it up and swing around to intercept the Cuban? *Take too long.* He dove, scraping his elbows on the shallow bottom. Warm and salty, the buoyant water seemed to carry him toward Karkoff as the bottom quickly fell away. Grant's arms, shoulders, hips, thighs worked together better than they had for months. Glide, stroke, ignore the jolt to his toes when he kicked the bottom. Two strokes out he lost his shoes, and thought about losing his cargo pants as the tidal flow edged him out into the deeper channel and down the coast. He broke the surface and saw he was gaining.

Karkoff's bald head glistened in the sun rising above the trees. Grant pulled harder, straining his shoulders, long, even kicks. What would he do when he caught him? The Cuban was bigger and taller. Grant slowed, shook the water from his eyes.

Karkoff turned to face Grant, neck deep. Motionless, he waited. Eddies rippled around his thick neck as the tide ebbed, knife held high.

Grant veered to his left so he could let the current sweep him down to Karkoff. On his next stroke, face in the water, Grant glanced at the bottom. A shimmer of white sand, but deeper than he could stand in. When Grant looked up and blinked the salt water from his eyes, Karkoff was gone. Grant switched to a breast stroke, pushing his head higher up out of the water, searching, tingling at the thought that Karkoff might be a better swimmer than he, that the Cuban was somewhere out there, about to pull him under.

Karkoff's head and shoulders emerged from the water at the mouth of the inlet leading to the house, ten meters away. The big man's shoulders swayed back and forth as he struggled against the tidal outflow.

Grant power stroked through the water toward Karkoff, head high so he wouldn't lose him again.

Karkoff lunged toward the bank and chopped at the thick roots with his knife, carving an escape through the mangroves.

Grant took a deep breath and angled down until he was gliding along the bottom, kicked hard into the current, tendrils of sea grass reaching out toward his face. He swam under the shadows of the low mangroves leaning out over the cut. Tiny fish flashed past, weaving in and out of the roots and washes in the sand, around shadowy movement—Karkoff's legs, moving across the channel.

Grant wondered if Grandpa's pistol was as reliable as the M1 when it was water logged. Then remembered. The Colt still lay somewhere in his yard. He reached down and ran his fingers ran over the heavy Buck in his pocket. This was stupid. He wasn't a knife fighter. Grant worked the knife from his pocket and kicked his way toward the far bank. He found the button and snapped the knife open as he surfaced an arm's length from Karkoff.

Karkoff spun and, with a shriek, lunged at Grant. Karkoff's long knife glinted as it swept in a high arc through the dappled shadows.

Fighting against the tidal flow that pushed him back toward the open bay, Grant sidestepped to his left, chest deep in the water. His movements felt like slow motion.

The knife sliced through the air, missed. The blade swept a spray of water in Grant's face as Karkoff fell back in the channel. Karkoff broached the surface and thrust the knife toward Grant, dark eyes focused on Grant like lasers, lips pulled back from his teeth in a grimace.

If Grant had a chance, this was it. Just pretend Karkoff was the gator in the canal, big teeth ands all. Grant dropped under the surface, bent his knees and drove up from the bottom. He slammed his shoulder into Karkoff's gut and grabbed at Karkoff's knife arm. Karkoff jerked his arm back, out of Grant's grip. Grant clutched a handful of cloth and slashed out with the Buck.

A blade sliced his ear, painless, but drawing a sheen of red into the water. Grant stabbed at Karkoff; sliced, chopped, stabbed again, not sure he made any contact.

They rolled through the shallow water, stirring a scrambled mass of bubbles, silt and bits of sea grass.

Grant finally clenched his fingers around Karkoff's knife arm. Together they swirled, twisted, danced around the two blades until Grant's toes grazed the channel floor, scoured to hard sand by the tidal flow. He blew out the last of his air and drew Karkoff with him to the packed sand, bent his knees and drove up, toward the sun. He snatched a breath as he broke the surface and rolled over Karkoff, forcing him on his back. He kicked, long, wide scissors kicks, pulling Karkoff down with him back to the sandy bottom before Karkoff could get a full breath.

Karkoff struggled in Grant's grip, kicked.

Grant locked his elbow, holding Karkoff's knife hand an arm length away. Karkoff twisted his wrist, trying to get the long knife's blade to slice. The current caught them, forced them down the fast-running channel toward open water, deeper, further under the surface as the blade sliced, this time deep, into Grant's arm. Blood swirled into the warm water.

Karkoff's free arm clubbed him across the head so hard Grant felt his neck crack. Karkoff twisted and struggled, fingers clutching at Grant's face, fingernails gouging his throat.

Grant's toes touched the bottom, brushed across a log, then a tangle of thick branches. He poked his left foot under a limb and stared through the shimmering water at Karkoff's dark face. Grant wriggled his toes in the sand, embedding his foot under the rough wood.

Karkoff clutched Grant's knife arm in a steel grip. His twists and jerks becoming more desperate.

Grant held on to Karkoff's arm, his fingers beginning to cramp.

Karkoff kicked his legs, lunged with his massive upper body.

Grant held fast, foot embedded under the limb. He felt his foothold begin to loosen as the tide washed at the sand.

Pink eddies swirled around them. Grant didn't know if any of his cuts, given or received, were deep, but he would hang on, right here, until the decision was made. This was the way Eustis and Vicente would expect him to end it, right in their back yard, in their water with the gators and the manatees and the snakes.

Karkoff's movements became more frantic, uncoordinated. A sudden burst of bubbles streamed from Karkoff's nostrils. He kicked away, almost escaped Grant's grip.

Grant jammed his other foot into the tangled limbs, firmly pinning them to the bottom as he held on to the struggling Karkoff.

This would be easy. He had once held his breath for four minutes hanging on to the manatee statue deep in the cavern where the spring fed Kings Bay.

Karkoff's movements slowed, seemed less frantic.

Time dawdled as Grant stared into Karkoff's eyes. Grant focused his thoughts on his fingers and his toes, the pelicans soaring above the water, the mullets flashing past. He held on to Karkoff and the old tree buried in the bottom, thinking about what Eustis would say.

The water became very peaceful. Grant enjoyed studying the bronze manatee, now still as the statue it was supposed to be. It was serene, resting deep in the cavern sluiced from the sand and limestone by the incessant spring, quiet. He wondered where Vicente and Eustis were. His lungs ached. They were supposed to time him, tell him when he had broken the old record. He looked up. The surface shimmered, so close, but out of reach.

The manatee wavered, indistinct, as if Grant were sighting down a dark funnel, pink tendrils streaming from its nostrils. He turned the statue loose. Grant watched it float away, slowly twisting in the clear water. Grant pulled his feet free of the limbs and kicked toward the light. At the surface he gasped, lay back and breathed deeply, again and again, letting reason return to his mind. Where was Karkoff? He dropped back under the surface. No statue. No Karkoff.

He kicked back up and let himself drift, head laid back and face in the sun, wondering how long it would take him to float down to Tampa Bay. No. That wouldn't do. He had left Flash on the island.

By the time he had slowly stroked back to the island, Grant realized he had almost drowned himself. Fool. He had probably damaged what he had left of a brain. Visions of manatee statues and alligators floated through his head as he pulled himself back onto the island and lay with his cheek on the warm mud, letting the sun warm his exhausted body. Grant started, an image of a big iguana's tongue flashing through his mind. Grant jerked his head up and Flash gave him a big lick across the lips.

"Hey, boy. You all right?" Grant pulled himself to his knees and realized Flash was in much better shape than he was. Slices across Grant's arms and shoulders oozed blood. His left ear stung and his hand came away bloody when he touched it. Felt like a notch had been added. At least it was still there. His head throbbed. He looked down at his right hand. His fingers clutched his knife in a death grip. He wiggled his fingers loose, released the blade lock and dropped the Buck in a pocket, patting it to make sure it was secure. Mom would never forgive him if he lost it.

His shirt was wet, muddy, a gritty mess. The bottom half was sliced into ribbons, some trailing almost to the ground. He pulled the fabric up to find a shallow slice across his taunt belly weeping blood. His feet were raw from where he had lodged them under the tree limbs. Grant stood, wavered for a moment, and took a deep breath. The M1 rifle lay a few feet down the beach, brass shell casings scattered in and around his footprints. Grant knelt and carefully selected the shiny cases from among the bits of shell and twigs. He dropped each one in a shirt pocket along with the empty clip, shoulders still heaving as he tried to sort reality from the fantasy of asphyxia. He picked up the rifle and painstakingly brushed bits of sand and leaves from the polished wood and worn steel. Had to get home, oil it before the old metal rusted away, or Grandpa would have his butt.

Grant stared at the rifle, shook his head. Get it together. He had won. Karkoff was dead. Silva was dead. Find Bennett. He almost fell over when a cold nose poked his kidney. He reached back and pulled Flash close, running his hand over the smooth fur, slicking back the dog's long ears, gently running his fingertips over the scab along Flash's ribs. Propping on the rifle, Grant pushed himself up and hobbled barefoot through the low mangroves and followed the trail to the back side of the island, across the shallow water and on toward the battered flats boat. He stopped for a moment to lean against the solitary oak and let the tears wash the salt and grit from his eyes.

"We won, Eustis. Me and you and Flash, we won this one for Vicente."

He pushed the bow down with his bare foot and let Flash clamber past him to the console where the greyhound parked his haunches on a boat cushion. Before Grant could pull the Johnson's starter rope, he sensed a rumble as a shadow flashed over. Grant raised up just high enough to see over the mangrove screen. A red and white Coast Guard MH-68A helicopter banked over the shoreline, angled back toward him. Grant dropped to the bottom of the boat, nose to nose with Flash.

CHAPTER 43

Bennett blinked, eyes watering with the acrid smell of gunpowder and incinerated truck still heavy in her head. She wrestled the flatbed from the tangle beside the remains of the old singlewide and headed up the road toward the mainland where she met every emergency vehicle in the county screaming across the island bridges. Fire rescue, sheriff's deputies, black Crown Vics all passed her on the narrow road. With the damp straw hat jammed down on her head, no one seemed to pay her any attention. She wondered what they would think of the carnage she had left behind on the island.

And Grant? Where was he? When she first met him, his eyes seemed to have a drug-induced dullness, his body lethargic. When he had kissed her at the house and shoved her toward the flatbed, a fire raged in his eyes; his body taunt.

When she came to the state highway she let the truck roll to a halt. Which way? What had Grant told her? *Wait for him at the boat yard.* After winding her way across a series of back roads Bennett finally found herself at the dock by the river. She parked the flatbed and grabbed the back pack. Inside a pistol clunked against a laptop and a cell phone. She wanted nothing more to do with guns. She tossed the pistol back in the truck. Backpack in her hands, she walked toward the old boat, her solitary footsteps a low crunch across the soft sand. Mid-morning sunlight flickered down through the thick oaks as she walked up the ramp. Back on the *Rum Runner* the air was still, but hot enough that the sweat began to run down her sides. A dove cooed from its perch on the electrical wire. *All so peaceful, safe.* Thank the Lord.

Below in the cabin she picked up the old rotary phone's battered handset and dialed Logan's number. Had she ever used one of these before, or had she just seen them in black and white movies on TV? It seemed to work. A distant voice told her the line had been disconnected. When she closed her eyes, the images of lights and people rushing around the farmhouse intruded on her mind. When she opened her eyes her hands were trembling. Where was Logan, the kids?

"Dammit!" she muttered. She peered out the porthole at the empty road. Was she safe? What if that man had killed Grant and was coming for her?

She pulled out the cell phone and tried the preset. A computer voice prompted her to leave a message. "Uly. I'm worried. Call me." Who else could she call? Maybe Wilson? Grant obviously didn't trust him, but who else? Surely he would help. She opened the computer and inserted the flash drive. She smiled at the password prompt and entered 'Flashdog." She would never thought she would ever miss an old dog. And his person. She scrolled down, found Scanlon on the contact list and composed an email, telling him about the attack by the Cuban. She paused, wondering if she should send it. Maybe Grant would come. He would make everything right. But, just in case, she hit the "send" key.

Then she called Wilson.

CHAPTER 44

"Get down, Flash," Grant urged. A second smaller helicopter abruptly reversed direction and veered low over the channel. He twisted his head to the each side, trying to drain the water from his ears. He still couldn't hear crap. He parted a gap in the mangroves and watched the smaller helicopter come to a hover, drop a swimmer. The helicopter shifted position and a basket descended toward the water. Moments later the twirling basket left a trail of sparkling droplets as the helicopter winched the basket up, then dropped it back down for the swimmer. Maybe they had found Karkoff. Grant hoped it was only a recovery, not a rescue.

He eased a little higher to watch the helicopter winch up the basket, turn back and arrow straight toward the nuclear facility. Grant guessed they had set up some sort of command center to investigate the rocket attack. He dropped back down when the big Coast Guard MH-68A swooped back along the shoreline, turned back and followed the marsh back toward his house. He took a deep breath as the helicopter circled, about where his house should lie, where he last saw Kat.

"You reckon Kat got away?" Grant asked Flash, who ignored him and plopped back down on the old tarp.

Should he stand and wave, distract them? No. Bennett should be long gone by now. Grant decided he didn't want to mess with the Coast Guard bird. Armed with a .50 caliber sniper rifle and a machinegun supported by sophisticated surveillance devices, that bird could put him in a world of hurt. "O. K., boy. Let's just rest another minute. Wait till the law gets tired, goes for a cup of coffee. Then we'll leave, find Kat."

Where? Did Bennett even need him? First he'd find her, make sure she was safe. After that he'd figure out where his own path lay. A helicopter whirred overhead and slowed over the shore. Grant dropped back down beside Flash and waited until it had circled back toward the nuclear facility. By the sun it was around noon, heavy Florida hot on the small island.

Every muscle in his body ached. The cuts stung and snagged on the salt caked shirt hanging around him like a shroud. Now if this were only a deserted island, Grant figured he would rig a pole and they would feast on some kind of seafood. Blue crabs, sea trout, maybe even snook fillets grilled over an open fire. His mouth watered at the thought. No fire, no fish today, not unless it was served in handcuffs. He pulled the old tarp over him and Flash, closed his eyes and took a deep breath. Kat got away, he told himself. Now Flash and I will, too, in just a few minutes, after everything calmed down a bit.

The hot breath of a huge grey manatee stirred him from a fitful dream. He opened his eyes and rubbed his neck, cricked from where he had napped curled up on the fiberglass bottom. A furry face stared back at him.

He rolled on his back and peered around the island, the bay, scanned the sky for helicopters. Tiny birds wheeled around over the big cooling towers, so far away he could barely make out they were the helicopter kind and not big buzzards. Not even a fisherman in sight, unusual for Crystal Bay, anytime. Feds must have made it a restricted area, one he and Flash should leave.

Grant poled island to island across the shallows until he reached the channel, every shove pouring a little more fire on the cuts on his arms. He tried to keep trees between him and the helicopters and any possible scopes on board.

At last the tide gently pushed the boat south along the edge of the marsh away from Crystal Bay toward the open Gulf. Grant sat and stowed the pole. Resting a moment, he stroked Flash's head until they drifted past Mangrove Point, leaving the helicopters distant flyspecks on the horizon.

"Ready to go, boy?"

Flash climbed to his feet, stretched, and walked to the bow.

Grant shook the gas can at his feet. At least a couple of gallons. He squeezed the fuel bulb, and then pulled the starter rope. A loud pop and a cloud of smoke rose around his head. He worked the choke back and forth and tried again. This time the outboard sputtered. It caught as he twisted the throttle to give it a little more gas. Underway, Grant guided the crippled boat south around the point and close ashore in Homosassa Bay waters. He puttered close by the marsh, risking discovery by the mosquito squadrons rather than being caught on the open water by one of the helicopters.

He would have to face the big boys eventually. But first, he wanted to get to the *Rum Runner* and make sure Bennett had made it to safety. He estimated about ten miles to the boatyard, if he remembered his charts correctly. In easier times he would make this run in about two hours, taking into account the Manatee go-slow zones in the river channels. Grant puttered down the coast and turned into one of the meandering channels leading to the Homosassa River, mind churning. *What next?* Would Bennett be long gone when he got there, a mystical dream?

Afternoon shadows stretched from the trees along the bank when the last bit of gas gurgled up through the fuel line and the outboard began backfiring. He killed the Johnson and dropped the electric motor into the water. As he crept along the last stretch of river, willing the boat to go faster, a single bark sounded though the trees. Flash stirred, stood to lean out over the gunwale. Another bark and Flash made some sort of noise in reply. Grant wondered if greyhounds used a low frequency woof, like giraffes and elephants to communicate at frequencies so low humans couldn't hear. Another sharp bark echoed between the trees. Betsy knew they were home.

The *Rum Runner* sat silent up on the chocks as he tied the battered flats boat up to the dock. The flatbed truck sat equally silent. Bennett had made it to the boatyard. He glanced in the truck, surprised to see his Kimber on the seat. She must be O. K. To have left the pistol. But no sign of her up on the old cruiser's deck. *You'd think she'd be watching for me,* Grant thought.

Flash trotted by, hellos already said to Betsy. His toenails clicked on the plywood ramp. Grant followed, the hair on the back of his neck tingling, anticipating the men in black windbreakers jumping out from behind the trees, guns and handcuffs waving.

Grant paused at the top of the incline. Flash already lay curled on his pile of towels. Grant slowly opened the hatch. The cabin was empty. "Kat," he whispered, and crept forward to the berths. No answer, no Kat.

Had she left, or had someone beat him to her? Was she in jail? Could he get one of his Arizona lawyers in touch with her if she was in custody? *Getting ahead of himself,* he thought. Or wishing. He stopped searching, struck with the thought. If Homeland Security linked her to the rocket attack, Lord only knows where they would take her. Or if they would ever let her see a lawyer. Was she on her way to some off-shore detention center? His own vaguely formed plans for changing identities and escape evaporated as he stood in the middle of the sweltering cabin. How could he help Bennett? First he had to figure where she was and if she needed, even wanted his help.

He sniffed. Coffee. The coffee maker switch glowed, the carafe half full. The pot had an automatic cutoff at what one, two hours? Bennett had been here, not too long ago. The laptop sat on the table, with his IronKey flash drive plugged into the USB port. What had she been doing? When he swiped the touchpad the email program flashed on the screen. She had sent a message to Scanlon. Good.

He stared at the old Bakelite phone. He had told her to leave a message on the cell phone. He patted his pocket. The last time he remembered having the phone was when he put it in his pocket, just before he got in the boat. He vaulted over the side rail, stumbled down the ramp and trotted to the boat, willing away all the aches. He poked through the wrecked poling platform, the smell of gasoline heavy around the old Johnson, trying to remember his movements. *Damn.* He had cranked the engine, shook the gas tank trying to keep it going. Had he dropped the phone overboard? He patted around the gas tank, feeling with the tips of his fingers through the bilge water, then worked his arm under the console until he touched a piece of pipe. Must be part of the poling platform. To his surprise the pipe turned out to be the Tamer's barrel. He held the gun up in the light. The receiver was dented where a bullet had smacked it, shattering the stock in the process of beating a purple bruise on his forehead. He tossed the busted gun into the bait well and continued his search for the phone. Back under the console he nudged something with his finger tips. Ignoring the weeping cuts, he forced his hand deep into the corner, bent his wrist until he could feel—the phone.

He worried the phone free and out of the bilge water. He gimped up the ramp and slid over the rail into the cockpit, sweat mingling with the bilge water stinging the cuts to his arms, almost falling in his haste to call Bennett. He waved the phone in the air to dry it, telling himself he shouldn't be worrying. Bennett was probably having a big dinner, somewhere far away and safe, trying to forget he ever existed. Had she called someone else for help—again? All he really knew was that she was safe from the Cuban and Silva. Those were verifiable facts. But what did he not know?

Flash opened one eye, and then curled his nose back under his long legs as Grant dropped down into the cabin. Grant found a rag, patted the phone dry and hit the power button. He waited impatiently until a green screen glowed back at him. He punched in the voicemail preset. His smiled with relief when he heard Bennett's voice. A short message, *worried*, she said, asking for him to call. The time stamp was just after noon. He tried the next message.

"Uly," crackled through the phone.

He could barely understand her. "Damn!" He shifted the phone to the right side of his head, his best side, so the doctors said, and pressed the speaker tight against his bloody ear.

A tinny voice. Bennett? "Allen's here, at the boat yard." A short pause; a loud voice in the background. "I don't know what's going on,

Uly. Hurry. Something's not right." Bennett sounded muffled, as if she were whispering into the phone.

A loud clank, static, and the call ended, followed by the automated service asking him what he wanted to do next. *Good question.* Grant's face turned somber. Bennett knew Wilson. From what she had said, Grant thought she and Wilson were friends, of a sort. What could be wrong? He reran the message. The recording time stamp said the call came in at three o'clock.

He hadn't missed anything. He'd heard it all.

The brass clock on the bulkhead chimed eight bells, four o'clock. Grant stared at the phone, wondering what else he could do when the old phone on the table rang, a startling jangle. This line was in his real name. On the Internet his fishing guide service and this number was listed on several of the community links. Might be a fisherman calling for a trip. Or the cops. Or Bennett.

He slipped the cell phone back in his pocket and picked up the Bakelite handset. Grant closed his eyes with the handset pressed to his face. Could he smell her shampoo on the handset, or was he just losing the rest of his mind? A brusque voice said, "Hello?" snapping Grant back to the stifling hot cabin.

Roberto's gruff voice barked out of the phone. "Uly. Is that you? Are you all right? The police have been looking for you, questioning every-one."

"I'm fine, Roberto. But I'm looking for the woman who was with me. Her name is Katrina Bennett."

"Yes, yes. They are looking for her, also; but I have not seen her."

Grant shook his head in frustration. "Have you see Angelica? We left her with a friend of Bennett's, but the police came to their house"

"Yes. I have spoken with Child Services. Angelica is with Enrique and his wife. She is safe. But now I call about you. Uly, your soul is past my ability to do more than counsel," Roberto continued. "But I still worry for your body. Several men, gangsters, came around asking about you. I'm concerned they might do you harm. I told them—well I told them more than I should, but it seemed necessary, with everything else happen-ing."

"You mean a guy named Beetle? Don't be distressed, Roberto. We talked, and I thank you for what you told him. We settled our concerns. And my soul? If I don't go to jail I might even sit in the back of your church during Mass if you don't do the Latin thing anymore."

Roberto's laugh degenerated to a hacking cough. "More Spanish than Latin, Uly. Come—"

Grant interrupted Roberto. "Roberto, I'm really worried about Bennett. I told her to meet me here at the *Rum Runner*. The truck she was driving is here, but she's not."

"Have you talked to Allen? He was here yesterday, asking for you."

Grant's fingers suddenly felt cold. "No. Is he around?"

"He came to my door last night and told me his truck was broken. He seemed very agitated; asked to borrow a car. I thought it was just because he is so proud of that fancy truck he drives. He borrowed the church's old panel van, and I haven't seen him since."

"Did he say where he was going?"

"No. He was just his usual arrogant self. You know how Allen gets when his toys break."

Grant paused, but couldn't think of anything useful to ask. "Thanks, friend. And stop smoking those mosquito cigars. They're killing you. *Adios, amigo.*"

Roberto laughed. "*Y tu*, Uly. *Vaya con dios.*"

What information did he have? He was supposed to be an intelligence officer. Were all the clichés true? Was military intelligence really an oxymoron?

Her message bugged him. Where would Wilson take her? Why? Grant didn't have a clue, other than they might be in a rusted-out ministry van. The last time Grant remembered seeing the van, the Mexican kids had painted it to resemble a '60s hippy rig, all psychedelic flowers and rainbows. Startled, Grant flinched when the cell phone in his pocket rang. He snatched it out and punched the answer button.

"Kat. Where the hell are you?"

"Uly. Help me. Allen took me to Ybor City, some cigar place." Her voice was muffled.

"Are you all right?"

"Yes, but I don't understand what's going on. I'm calling from a bathroom so Allen doesn't hear me. He's arguing with some Cuban woman. Come get me, please."

Grant's heart seemed to skip a beat. "Where, exactly?"

Before she could answer, the phone hummed in his ear, disconnected. *Dammit*! One last hope. He called the cell number for the one person he knew in law enforcement, his old commanding officer, Major Talbot. He grit his teeth in frustration when the system buzzed him over to voice mail. What could he say that made sense?

"Boss. This is Uly. I expect you are looking for me, and we'll talk first chance we get. First though, I'm trying to find a woman named Bennett. I think she may be in danger, maybe in Ybor City. I, I—" He paused. What did he really know? *Nothing Talbot could act on.* He didn't know what else to say, so he hung up the phone. He'd face his old boss soon enough.

Grant stripped out of his ragged shirt and salt-soaked pants, stood under the cold hose just long enough to sluice away the salt, sweat and blood. He pulled on a shirt and pants from the cabinet in the forward berth, ignoring the blood seeping from the cuts across his body and arms. *What could he do*? The obvious. Go to Ybor and look for Bennett.

"Hey, boy. Stick around here. Hang out with Betsy if you get hungry," he called out to Flash, dumping a handful of dog food into Flash's bowl. He jammed his feet into a pair of paint-splattered work boots he pulled from a corner of the open cockpit and tied the laces in a big bow, too impatient to lace them up correctly. He hopped over the rail and clomped down the incline. He had to find Bennett, make sure she was safe. With Wilson?

The flatbed threatened to skid into the ditch as Grant attacked the winding road and drove like a banshee toward Ybor City, taking every short cut he could dredge out of his memory.

"What am I doing?" Grant muttered to himself. Well, he had a handful of answers to that question, but the most important seemed to be to make sure Bennett was safe. He glanced down at the fuel gauge. Only a quarter of a tank. He had filled it last night. Should be full. When he looked in the mirror he could see a dark stream trailing the flatbed down the dirt road. Hell of a time to take a short cut, running out of gas!

The engine chugged, hiccupped. When he looked at the gauge again it had dropped even further. He called the voice mail number again. The mechanical voice announced he had no more messages. The next time he looked the gauge had dropped almost to the bottom, fast on its way to empty, and he was only on the edge of Tampa.

CHAPTER 45

Talbot ignored his vibrating BlackBerry, too impatient to be returning BS calls. He snatched up the desk phone and hit the extension for Beth's office. It was almost five in the afternoon, a hell of a long day. Her boffins must have tracked down the message source by now. Surely she had an idea of the informant's identity. He drew circles on the scratch pad, waiting for her to answer, wondering if there was any coffee left this late in the day. He didn't think he could stand another cup of the ersatz mess from the machine in the hall. He forgot his coffee craving when Beth answered.

"My techs analyzed the message traffic from the anonymous account. They also traced traffic from the account to a military address assigned to a retired Chief Petty Officer Lester Scanlon, currently employed as an intelligence analyst with Central Command out at MacDill. Anyone you know? Are we in over our heads? With the rocket attack on Crystal River Nuclear facility this morning, the heat is really on."

"Scanlon?" That was a surprise. "Yeah, I worked with him in Iraq, and we're so far over our heads I can hardly breathe. Somebody must have a handle on things, though. So far as I can tell, the Department isn't involved in the Crystal River investigation. Seems we're out of the loop, probably because of your boy Wilson being with FDLE. Everything's in Homeland Security hands, like they didn't trust us or something. No surprise, after Rafael's fiasco." His pencil point broke. "Thanks for the info on Scanlon. I'll call him right now. You know I love you."

Talbot flipped though his phone listings while he tapped the cradle button. When a fresh dial tone buzzed in his ear, he punched in Scanlon's number at MacDill.

"Major Talbot for Chief Scanlon," Talbot growled at the clerk who answered the phone. He didn't feel like trying to explain to an Air Force clerk why a FDLE agent wanted to talk to a Department of Defense intelligence staffer, and anyway, he really was an Army major. "When will he be back at his desk?" Talbot ground his teeth at the answer. "Tell Chief Scanlon to call me back immediately."

He looked up at the clock. Close to closing time. "No, tell Lester to sit tight. I'm coming out to sit down with him. Important. I know it's late, but tell him to please wait. And ask him to clear me in, O. K.? I'll be there in thirty minutes."

By the time Talbot fought his way through the afternoon rush traffic and the MacDill Air Force Base front gate security, his growling stomach protested missing lunch and the threat of missing supper.

At the Central Command security check point, Talbot waited impatiently for Scanlon to sign him in as the familiar flow of men and women in camouflaged fatigues surged around him. The security policewoman traded Talbot's Glock 22, BlackBerry and credentials for a CENTCOM visitors pass and waved him in. Finally seated in a conference room, Talbot inhaled the rich aroma from the cup of honest-to-God military coffee Scanlon handed him.

"You look tired, Greg. Wondered when you would come out. Did you get the stuff I set you through Homeland Security? The lawyers would choke if I passed it directly."

Talbot looked up, surprised. "No. I haven't gotten anything. I thought this visit was on my dime." Talbot motioned with his cup toward Scanlon's arm dangling in a sling. "Saw you on TV the other night. You put in a good word for Uly Grant."

Scanlon shook his head. "Uly is a good guy. He was easy to work with, knew a hell of a lot about computers, financial transactions and al Qaeda. And fishing," he added with a grin. The grin turned sour. "Sorry he got beat up pretty bad by that car bomb, and you guys lost a soldier." Scanlon thumped the cast on his arm. "For me, wrong place, wrong time. I was lucky I didn't get my ass blown off. Crap, we're lucky Port Tampa didn't turn into an inferno."

"Yeah." Talbot took copies of the emails from his inside pocket. He looked around. No apparent cameras, microphones. "How secure are we in here?"

"Good as it'll get, outside of a SCIF." Scanlon pulled out a chair and sat, waiting for Talbot to start.

"We got to talk about some emails you received."

Scanlon looked at him with a frown. "You reading my mail?"

Talbot shrugged. "Not exactly." He took a sip of the coffee. "My new boss at FDLE is trying to make Grant the principal suspect in a bunch of shootings and the rocket attacks, and he's tangled somehow in a murder."

"Yeah. The TV folks tried to get a rise out of me on that." Scanlon's face took on a blank look, as if he were hiding something very important. "How does Grant connect with me?"

Talbot wondered what had spooked Scanlon. "His emails. Our Computer Crime Center identified two messages sent to you by the same person who emailed some tips to an Allen Wilson. Wilson was also a member of my MI Guard unit in Iraq, along with Grant. Wilson works for FDLE and is up to his ass in this." Talbot slid the faxes across the table. "I don't have copies of the messages sent to you yet, just records of transmittal, so help me out. Recognize the sender address? Were your messages and these sent to FDLE from Grant?"

Scanlon scanned the messages and nodded. "The emails are from an anonymous account, but I had the account traced when the messages started to make sure I wasn't being scammed. Took the cyber folks over a month to finally trace them back to Grant. I didn't want to get tangled up in domestic shit and the lawyers, so I routinely pass information from the messages to our cyber security people and let them run with it. I understand at least one has tracked back to an al Qaeda shell account in Great Britain. I never alerted Grant that I suspected I was on to him, just let the information keep coming. It was good stuff, mostly." He looked up at Talbot. "You sure you didn't read the ones sent to me?"

Talbot grinned. "Not yet, Lester, we're not that good. But, Grant, or whoever sent the messages, is certainly connected to Wilson, and possibly to the shootings up in Homosassa, plus another murder last night in Temple Terrace, and maybe the rocket attacks." He waggled his hand at Scanlon. "Fingers all point to Grant. He's certainly involved, but as a friendly or a bad guy, we can't figure out. He's the common link tying all the players together." He shifted in the uncomfortable conference room chair. "I know I'm biased, but I can't see Grant going bad. I just can't put it all together. Thought maybe you could help."

Scanlon shrugged. "If Grant wants to disappear, you're in better shape to track him down than I."

Talbot scrubbed his eyes. "Grant's still on active duty, on convalescent leave. Technically still under Army jurisdiction, subject to the Uniform Code of Military Justice. Can you access his hospital records?"

"Not me." Scanlon shook his head. "And man, I sure don't want to go there. To get Department of Defense involved, somebody's got to start an investigation. Army Criminal Investigation could, with federal interest. You really want to go that route? Even then, you'd probably never get any medical records because of the Privacy Act. Lawyers are still skittish they'll pinch somebody's civil liberties."

"Lester, the State of Florida has a warrant out on him as a murder suspect involved with drug trafficking, killing a law enforcement officer and possible links to a terrorist attack. If I don't find him pretty soon, some cop will. If that happens, chances are our boy will come home in a body bag. We got to do something before Grant gets himself in even more shit."

Scanlon opened his mouth, stopped. "I really don't want to get into anymore details, Greg."

Talbot scrubbed his knuckles across his tired head. Why was Scanlon being so obtuse? He flipped a business card toward Scanlon. "My email's on the card." Talbot pointed to a console on the corner of the table. "Can I call out on that phone?"

Scanlon nodded. "Sure, non-secure, though."

Talbot dialed his office.

"Snyder. Pull Raphael's file on Ulysses Grant. Yeah. Our Uly. Forward the specifics to Homeland Security, with a copy to the Army CID liaison office at Fort Gordon, requesting any information on his whereabouts and connections with our Allen Wilson. Call me if you get any feedback, any time. This is very important. And remember; do not let your personal feelings about Uly or Allen mess with your objectivity, newbie." Talbot put the handset back in its cradle and nodded with satisfaction. "Got that started."

Scanlon leaned back in his chair. "Wait a minute before you go too far." Scanlon slid an unmarked folder across the table. "God dammit, this better not come back to bite me."

Talbot picked up the unopened folder. "Is this what you wanted to tell me, the stuff you sent through Homeland Security?"

Scanlon scratched under his cast with a ball point pen. "Part classified shit, Greg, part CYA. I'm not telling you any of this, understand, the classified part. Not until Homeland sends it to you, if ever. Since it has to go through the Bureau and your Department is implicated, Lord knows when you will ever see it, or how much will be redacted. Let me get you another cup of coffee." Scanlon picked up Talbot's empty coffee cup and left the room, leaving Talbot with the folder in his hand.

Talbot quickly scanned the report inside the folder, red with all the classification markings. Talbot had the clearances as a result of his National Guard position, but everyone got hung up on need to know, usually to cover their ass or protect their turf, so he understood Scanlon's hesitancy to share.

The first page was historical background detailing the activities of an Ivan Karkoff, a Cuban national and an officer of the Cuban Army with suspected intelligence ties. Talbot flipped to the next sheet, a yellowed newspaper clipping and English translation that described Karkoff as a soldier in the Cuban Army of Liberation, and included an award citation. The article said Karkoff's T-72 tank was disabled by South African anti-tank fire along the bank of the Cuito River in Angola back in 1975. Karkoff, according to the translation, bailed out of his burning tank and scrambled over to a battered Soviet truck with a "Stalin Organ" in the bed, abandoned by its Angolan crew. Apparently Karkoff, in all the chaos, figured out how to salvo twenty *Katyusha* rockets across the river and into the South African Defense Force and UNITA rebels, then run like hell after being severely wounded when one of the rockets exploded in the launcher. When he returned to Cuba, Castro personally decorated him for his heroics. A grainy photo topped the original article, Ivan posed beside a heavyset soldier all decked out with medals. A note penned on the back of the photo identified a Colonel General Roman Karkoff of the Soviet Strategic Rocket Force stationed at the time with a missile site at Guanajay, Cuba. Talbot looked up as Scanlon returned with a fresh cup of coffee.

"Sit down, Les, damn it. Don't just dump this shit on me with no explanation." Goose bumps actually ran up his arm when he recognized the name in the next paragraph. Ivan Karkoff was linked to the al Qaeda terrorist, Zakariya al Bandri. "Who else knows about this?"

"The part about Ivan?" Scanlon shrugged. "That's when we come to the cover my ass part. I sent a message to Grant, warning him after I heard he was involved. Figured he needed the heads up. From the descriptions of the attack in Homosassa, sounded a lot like Karkoff to me."

Talbot all but flew out of his chair. "How about telling me, for Christ's sake?"

"Uly was the one being shot at." Scanlon shrugged. "And now you know. We don't get kept up to speed on domestic issues. I didn't have a clue what was happening with you guys."

"Lord help me." Talbot threw the folder back to the conference table. "Bandri. Is he the same one we identified on the boat that launched the rockets against Port Tampa?"

"Samo, samo. Over in Special Ops one of the old time operators reported getting in a brawl with the two of them at the Havana Café in Luanda, a nightclub themed to honor Cuba for its combat sacrifices in Angola while fighting US-backed rebels in the 1970's and '80's. Our guy said the Americans used to go there just to piss off the Cubans. One of Karkoff's friends was killed in a bar brawl by some DIA cowboy. After Angola, Ivan reputedly helped train Taliban militants at the *al Farooq* guerrilla training camp in Afghanistan, has a real hard on for Americans. I expect he's one of several thousand Cuban soldiers that still hate us."

"Just thousands?" Talbot asked, eyebrows raised.

"Whatever." Scanlon pointed to the remaining sheet in the folder. "This last page hits closer to home. Ivan's pop, the general, came to Cape Canaveral as part of the US-Soviet space cooperation program in the 1990's. The general lives in Ybor City in one of the old converted cigar factories, dying of cancer linked to his exposure from the Chernobyl clean up. Nobody thinks he's a threat, so no surveillance, wiretaps, nothing. He's domestic, a US citizen now, so DoD can't touch him, that's why I'm so skittish with all this. Nobody has any real proof that this dude Ivan is the general's son, even though DIA points to the picture and the last name as sufficient evidence."

Talbot squinted at the photo. "Ivan is dark skinned, the general isn't."

"A Cuban convention. The Cubans are proud of their mixed racial heritage. The Soviet soldiers stationed in Cuba jumped right in, so I wouldn't bet against Ivan being his son."

"Too many connections to be coincidences."

"Damn right. That's why I wanted to get it to you ASAP, but didn't think it was worth the risk to bypass channels. Can you get the FDLE to start something on the general without burning my ass?"

Talbot stood up. "Be tough without any leads I can show my boss. They put in a new SAIC while I was deployed. I think he's in over his head, and he's a real cover-your-butt type. Let me mull over that one, figure out how I can show probable cause for the State Attorney." He tapped the file folder. "We both know I can't acknowledge what's in your files, but I've got another source. Our admin gal, Delina Sanchez, came over on the Mariel boat lift as a baby. I bet she's got a lot of Cuban contacts I don't know about. I'll see if she can help."

"Whoa!" Scanlon snatched the file off the table.

Talbot stared at Scanlon, trying to decipher the look that came over the old Coasty's weather beaten face when Talbot had mentioned Delina. "What the hell's wrong now?"

"This has gone too far. Sit back down. I got to go get another file I can't show you."

Scanlon returned with a single sheet of paper and slapped it on the desk.

"What's this?" Talbot picked up the paper and read it once, then again, making sure he had the names correct. "My own Department? Raphael and Delina—and Ivan, all linked back to Cuba and the Russians through poppa Karkoff? Where did this crap come from?"

"I'm sure as hell not going to tell you." Scanlon snatched the sheet from Talbot's hand and stuck it back in the folder. "Ongoing investigations and all that homeland security shit. That's why I hadn't already given you a heads up."

A tap at the door and an airman poked his head in. "What?" Scanlon barked.

The airman took a step back. "Sorry, Chief. I know you said not to disturb you, but I got a weird one here. Has to do with the rocket attack. I thought you needed to see it ASAP." He closed the door.

Scanlon bolted over to the door and snatched it open. "Jerold, come back. Thanks. You were right. I did need it. Sorry I yapped at you." He returned to the table with a message in his hand. "From Gulf Winds Guiding Service," he read. "That's Grant's business up in Homosassa. But I've never got an email from that address before." He read down the page. "Holy Mother of God. This Bennett; is she the woman connected with Grant in the shootings?" He handed the message to Talbot.

"Son of a bitch!" Talbot stood and handed Bennett's message back to Scanlon. "Got to go." When he got back to his car he pulled out his BlackBerry and turned the nuisance back on. A voice mail message from Grant waited. He listened to Grant's message, shaking his head at the mention of Ybor City. "Dammit," he muttered and dialed the Operations Center. Only one person he knew without a doubt he could trust. "This is Special Agent Talbot. Get me Agent Snyder." He drummed his fingers on the steering wheel until she came on the line. "Gunner, is Delina at her desk?" Talbot listened. "When did she leave?" Snyder's voice murmured in his ear. "Get a car and meet me in Ybor City." He flipped open the folder on the table, pulled out the report and read off an address. "And make sure Raphael doesn't know what you are doing, or where you are going."

"Get me out of here," he told Scanlon. "Raphael's got every cop in the State looking for Grant, with an armed and dangerous tag. Plus it all ties with what you just told me. How, I'll have to figure out as I go."

CHAPTER 46

The flatbed's engine sputtered as Grant coasted into the fenced compound.

Sherman stepped out of the door. "Hey, man. Where's my sweetheart?"

Grant slammed his shoulder against the balky truck door, popped it open and slid to the ground, rubbing his arm. "Don't know, Randy. I was trying to find her when I figured out the truck had a leak."

Sherman walked over, squatted by a puddle of gas dripping from the flatbed and looked up under the side frame. "You ain't got a leak, pard. You got a cut fuel line." He looked over at Grant's arms. "Bunch of other stuff cut up, too. You want me to take you to a walk-in clinic?"

"No time. I got to find Kat. I think she's in trouble, but I don't know exactly where the hell she is."

He really needed help. Grant dialed Greg Talbot's desk phone at the FDLE Tampa Operations Center. A woman answered. "Agent Talbot, please" Grant asked. He paused for a moment, then added. "Tell him Lieutenant Grant's calling."

"L. T.?"

Grant started at the familiar voice. "Gunner?"

"L. T. You're in a pile of shit, but I can't help you right now. I got a call from Talbot. Thought you were him calling back or I would have ignored the phone. Got to meet him in Ybor. Some kind of tip on a terrorist involved in the rocket attacks, and your name's all mixed in. There's a BOLO out; every cop in town's looking for you. Wherever you are, hunker down and call me back in the morning. Stay alert and hang tight, buddy. Gotta go."

She clicked off the phone, leaving Grant with dial tone buzzing in his ear.

Ybor? Grant turned to Sherman. "Randy. I got to get to Ybor City, right now. Can I get a ride?"

"Sure." Sherman pulled the door closed behind him. "Jump in the wrecker. Only thing on the lot I trust."

Grant grabbed the Kimber off the seat and followed Randy to the wrecker.

Using the Randy Sherman school of driving to bull his way through traffic, Sherman had them across Tampa and cruising on Seventh Avenue, Ybor City's main drag, in less than fifteen minutes. Most of the clubs hadn't opened yet, just a couple of cafes. The smell of dried beer had largely burned off the sidewalks in the day's heat, waiting for dark to start all over. As they cruised down Seventh the smell of roasting coffee beans filled the air.

"Just cruise, slow. I'm looking for an old van, hippy paint job." Grant pulled his cap down lower as Sherman drove by a sedan parked at the end of the next cross street—a Crown Vic with stubby antennas and dark tinted windows. Grant resisted the urge to look back. If he wasn't dreaming, the driver was Gunner Snyder. She had beat him here.

Sherman tilted his head toward the Crown Vic. "Spot the cop? They still after you?"

"Yeah. Kat and I were out at Ozello, took care of some problems. I sent Kat to Homosassa, but when I got there, she was gone, left me a couple of messages. She's with a cousin of mine, but I'm still worried about her. I think he brought her to Ybor, but the message didn't make sense."

"Ozello. That's down from the Crystal River nuke place! That terrorist stuff on the TV? That you?" Sherman's voice rose in pitch. He rolled his eyes at Grant, whispered, "More spy shit, huh?"

Sherman gunned the wrecker through a gap in the traffic, turned left and eased past an alley cutting through the middle of the block. A flash of color caught Grant's eye. Rainbows and flowers.

"Stop. Let me out here. You go back to the Crown Vic. I think the woman behind the wheel is a friend, a cop now. Name's Snyder. Old Army buddy. Call her Gunner, give her a hooah and you should hit it off. If it is her, tell her I need help."

"What if it's not?"

Grant shrugged. "Beat's the hell out of me."

Sherman circled the block then stopped at the opposite end of the alley. The van hadn't moved.

Grant checked the magazine in the pistol butt, racked back the slide and let it slam home with authority, more than he felt. He dropped the pistol in his side pocket and slid out of the wrecker, wondering what he would find down the alley.

CHAPTER 47

Grant scanned the surrounding buildings as he gimped down the alley, focusing on the windows and rooftops. Was he the one being fooled? No obvious watchers or shooters out back. He shook his head. Too much thinking. Maybe Snyder had stopped for *Cakes de Cangrejo*, crab cakes, from the Columbia Restaurant over on Seventh. Maybe he was seeing things and the driver wasn't Snyder.

Grant walked down the side of the alley, old boots clacking on the bricks. He hugged the wall, feeling naked without his M4, grenades and tactical vest. He searched the roofs ahead. For just a moment Grant thought he saw a head bob over the low parapet, but his attention was drawn to the ministry's pink and purple van sitting in the late afternoon shadows. The van blocked the main entrance to one of the restored cigar factories, faded brick with a fire escape leading from an end window up to the roof and down to ground level. Grant opened the van and rummaged through the litter until he came up with a tire iron. No need. A small doorway leading into the factory's rear courtyard stood open. He shoved the door with his hip and edged around the doorway, pistol in hand.

The small courtyard was empty—at least of people. He climbed up the loading dock steps. Several pieces of large PVC tubing, random lengths of angle iron and a stack of wooden cases littered the dock. "Survey Equipment," Grant read aloud from one of the cases. A massive air conditioning unit rumbled from the corner. The air exchange unit blasted out hot air, the smell peculiar, a mixture of rich tobacco, burnt coffee and something Grant couldn't quite place.

Bloody hand prints splotched the top crate, but the surveying equipment was long gone. Grant dropped his pistol in a pocket and used the tire iron to pry up a cover from the next crate. Inside a dark cylinder nestled in a pair of wooden supports. Arabic markings ran down the outside of the cylinder. About five inches in diameter. Not survey equipment—a variant of the Soviet *Katyusha*.

A loud voice bellowed from inside the building, followed by a higher pitched response, a woman? Bennett?

He peered through the glass panes of an entrance door still embossed with an old cigar company logo. No one in sight. Grant used the tire iron to force the entrance door and edged inside. The odd smells were overpowering and the voices louder. He slipped out of the clunky boots and continued in his bare feet along a corridor. A dark trail of spilled beans led to a partially open door. A blast of hot air, infused with the smell of roasted coffee, washed out into the hallway. Inside, the room glowed as a machine fed beans from a hopper into a roasting oven.

Down the hallway, each door was labeled with Plexiglas placards marked with a series of dates and what appeared to be varieties of cigar tobacco. He pried open the next door. Inside, bright lights glared down on rows of hydroponic fixtures and plants. Rows and rows of plants, for smoking, but not cigars. He had stumbled into a massive marijuana grow house, complete with carbon dioxide generators, temperature and humidity controls. At least fifty plants in this room alone. No wonder the place smelled strange.

He slipped back out into the corridor. He damned his ears as voices seemed to come from upstairs, but with the roar of the air conditioners he wasn't sure. He crept up a flight of worn wooden stairs.

This was the part he hated. Clearing two story buildings never had good parts, unless you had enough guys to frag each landing and room before you entered. Even then, you had to be aware of closets, roof openings, even holes carved out of masonry walls for firing ports, watch out for civilians. A cleared room could turn into a trap, easy as not. But no frags today.

He eased his head up to the landing, high enough on the stairs he could see the hallway. Was Bennett here with Wilson, or had she high-tailed it with her crazy stories? Surely there weren't two psychedelic vans running around Tampa. A polished wooden floor gleamed, reflecting the light from a window at the top of the stairs to his right. A row of closed doors marked each side of the hallway, apparently rooms that overlooked the street on one side and the alley on the other. A large door at the end of the hall. One big mouse trap.

CHAPTER 48

Stephan stumbled up the iron fire escape, tears filling his eyes as the pain coursed through his body. He damned all *Norte Americanos*; Indians and Anglos; that Wilson who courted Delina; the others who killed Ivan. He especially hated the woman who shot him in the back and almost killed him at the house on the water. Thank God he had found a car at the end of the island that he could steal. He had given up waiting for Ivan and made his way back to Ybor City, holding his breath as each police car passed him on the narrow island roads.

With his one good arm Stephan dragged the heavy rocket to the far edge of the roof and propped it on the parapet. In the distance a military cargo plane lifted up over the skyline. He knew from watching Ivan study the aerial maps on the Internet that MacDill Air Force Base and Central Command headquarters lay close beside the runway. Stephan angled the rocket nose to point over the city to where he imagined all Ivan's enemies sat, comfortable behind their concrete walls. He wished he had Ivan' GPS to aid in aiming the rockets. He squinted across the rocket's nose at the rising aircraft. This would have to do.

The black box. He had left it by the edge of the roof.

Stephen scuttled across the roof to retrieved the black box and coil of wire. At the edge overlooking the alley he spotted a big black man staring back up at him.

Ivan?

No. A woman ran up to the man, a gun in her hand. They both stared up at him.

He would have to do it alone.

Stephan stumbled back to the rocket and began attaching the wires to the connecting posts.

He wiped his eyes with his sleeve. He felt faint, from the loss of blood, he supposed. He could not make the fingers of his left hand work. Shivering, he focused on connecting the wires.

Fire the rocket.

Ivan would be avenged.

Delina would know who was true.

He, Stephan would be the hero of Cuba.

CHAPTER 49

Grant crouched low at the top of the stairs. The voices boomed from the other side of the door at the end of the hall, louder.

He strained his ears trying to distinguish words from the constant roar of the air handler. He couldn't make out what was being said or identify the speakers. He sidestepped along the wall, back flat against polished cedar planks, edging closer to the voices, tire iron gripped in his hands, polished planks cool on his bare feet. He looked down. Blood had begun to flow from the scabs leaving a trail behind him.

When he got to the door he nudged it with his foot. Shut tight. He tried the knob. Locked. A heavy thump came from inside, followed by a yell. Was his damn ears playing tricks? Sounded like his name. Grant jammed the chisel end of the tire iron into the door frame, shoved until it hit metal. He wrenched it back and slammed his shoulder against the door. Wood splintered, but the door held.

He kicked the door with his bare heel, ignoring the jolt to his hip. The door swung open. Something moved to his left, half-hidden behind the open door. A gunshot exploded from the right. The bullet crashed into the door over his head, getting all his attention.

He spun toward the shooter. A frail looking old man sat at a desk covered with loose papers. Smoke curled up from a dark cigar. A woman stood behind him, one hand on his shoulder and a pistol in the other.

A door slammed behind him. *Where was Bennett?*

The man had a startled look in his eyes, the woman a calculating stare as she pointed the pistol toward Grant. A faint wisp of smoke trickled from the muzzle

"Who are you? What are you doing in my home?" The man ran his stare down Grant's arms, taking in the cuts and scabs and bruises, down to his bleeding feet.

"Karkoff, right?" Grant took a step toward the pair. "My name is Grant." He glanced back over his shoulder. No Bennett. "I'm looking for a friend of mine, Kat, Katrina Bennett. Where is she?"

The old man barked a sudden laugh. "Kat. How quaint. You wouldn't be referring to our *Katyusha*, would you?"

Grant stared at him.

"*Katyusha* is the Russian diminutive for Katrina." Karkoff shook his head. "You Americans are ignorant in many things, languages especially. Now, I have a question for you. Where is my son?"

Not much of a resemblance—but? Grant met the man's cold eyes. "If the big Cuban firing the *Katyushas* is your son, he's dead."

Grant glanced from Karkoff to the woman. Family? Neither showed any signs of grief. Karkoff answered Grant's unspoken question. "I suspected Ivan had encountered some difficulty when he didn't return. Why are you here?"

"I came here for Bennett. Where is she?"

"You, the Indian and the woman have become an irritation that must be eliminated. Since you are here, you may be the first." He turned to the woman. "Kill him. Now!" he ordered.

She raised the pistol to eye level. "Quiet, father. I will do what I must." She waved the pistol at Grant. " You. On the floor." She came out from behind the desk. "Father. I must deal with Stephan before he does something foolish." The pistol wavered in her hand.

Grant had seen pistols like this one in Iraq. An old Soviet Makarov. A piece of shit low-powered 9mm pistol. But this close she could—would—likely hit him.

"Kill him, Delina," Karkoff repeated. "Now." The old man pulled another pistol from the desk. "Ivan was a fool, but had his strengths. You were always too weak, girl."

Grant flung the tire iron toward the woman and dove. Not over the desk, but toward the front of the desk, out of the old man's line of fire. A pistol shot rang out, a scream. He slammed into the desk, feeling muscles tear as the heavy desk barely moved. He dug his toes into the carpet and shoved until the desk lifted, heavy legs rising up from the thick pile, shoved again.

The desk suddenly tipped, went light as it balanced on two legs. Another shove and it flopped onto its side with a reverberating crash. The sharp crack of a pistol punctured a drawn out scream. Chunks of ceiling plaster splattered down on the carpet as Grant rolled away from the toppled desk and to his knees, wobbly from crashing into the desk. He looked up to see Karkoff pinned under the desk, face slack. The woman, Delina, held her Makarov in both hands, inches from his eyes, so close he could smell that peculiar metallic-sulfur odor of fired gunpowder, feel the heat from the tip of the muzzle.

She screamed, poking her pistol toward him. Grant flinched as she fired. The bullet tore into his shoulder, sharp pain searing its way to his core. Her hands held the pistol steady, pointed directly at his face. The look in her eyes said the next bullet would be a kill shot. He watched her lips as waterfalls rushed through his ears, but couldn't understand her words. She waved the gun at him and shoved at the desk with her hips. She backed away as he climbed to his feet.

"Move the desk." Delina's shouts finally registered in his scarred ears.

Grant tilted the massive desk away from Karkoff.

"Get it off Papa," she screamed, cracked the barrel of the pistol across his head.

Another shove and the desk fell back to the floor, the thump more felt than heard as the wooden floor boards rebounded against the heavy weight. She knelt by the old man. The gun in her hand lay exposed, on top of the desk. Grant shook the floating stars out of his head, reached across and grabbed at the pistol. Too slow. She jerked back as he lunged forward. The pistol flew out of her fingers and plopped onto the carpet.

Delina dived across the floor after the gun. Grant grabbed her leg and dragged her back. She kicked, scraping her shoe down his arm, scraping off a fresh scab. Blood smudged the rug.

Grant looked up, fingers clamped around the struggling woman's ankle as the door to the hall flew open. Allen Wilson burst into the room, holding Bennett by the arm.

Grant pulled Delina back away from the pistol, her skirt riding up as she struggled to free her leg from his grip. *Damn*. First time he had ever felt happy to see Wilson come into a room.

"Darling," Delina cried out when she saw Wilson. "Help me." She kicked again at Grant.

Wilson swung a big revolver toward Grant. Lead bullet noses gleamed in the cylinder, at least .44 caliber, big enough to down a bear.

"Allen. Don't shoot me, you son of a bitch, at least not with your daddy's pistol, for Christ's sake." Grant dropped the woman's leg, presuming Wilson had her under control, and rose to his knees, his shoulder numb. He glanced down. Blood ran down his arm and dripped from his fingers. "Kat. You all right?"

Wilson shook Bennett when she started to speak. He stared at Grant, a strange range of expressions flitting across his face, finally settling on a sneer. More important, he didn't lower the pistol. "Thought maybe you'd run out of gas out in the swamp. Since you're here I've got a present for you." Wilson said. He laughed and shoved Bennett toward Grant.

"What the hell's going on?" Grant pointed at the pistol. "Point that thing somewhere else before it goes off." Suddenly he recognized the look that had taken over Wilson's face. The same look he had seen on the road to Baghdad.

Wilson thumbed the hammer back on the massive revolver.

Grant had seen Wilson's expression—the hard set of the cheeks, the unblinking eyes—on the faces of prisoners who were not going to talk, who only wanted to get their hands around your throat.

Bennett stumbled to her knees on the carpet.

Grant caught her with his one working hand and stood, pulling her up with him. Her face was bruised, jaw clinched. He pulled Bennett behind him. Her arm went around his chest and she pulled close to him, face buried against his back.

"You've screwed up everything I care about, ever since we were kids," Wilson snarled. "For once I had a chance to make some money when Kat decided to cross Silva. You screwed me out of that. Then when I tried to help Delina with leads on the oil deal, you had to interfere." He shifted the revolver toward Delina, rocking her father in her arms. "And finally I've figured out this bitch was playing me with that fucking Raphael." He looked back and forth between Delina and Grant. "Let's see, how will this work? The old man kills you two. Then I come in and he tries to shoot me. I have to stop him and his lying daughter. Save the world."

"No, please." Delina pleaded with Wilson. "I was about to tell you everything, help you arrest the Senator. You will be a hero."

Through the numbness and pain Grant felt Bennett fumbling with the Kimber in his hip pocket.

Wilson shook his head. "No more bullshit. I'm the computer whiz, not my doofus cousin. I ran a check on your records, Delina, deeper than you thought I could. You didn't come on the Muriel boatlift. Your adoption papers are dated before the boatlift. That was stupid. Did your father establish a new identity for you?" He pointed the revolver at Delina. "I found your emails to the old man, and from him to the Russians. Now I'll get all the credit for stopping an international terrorist ring and disrupting an oil exploration bribery scheme." Wilson snarled at Grant, face twisted with anger. "Not you, the Lieutenant, the one who always got what you wanted, using me. Now I get to use you. I made a mistake, not killing you before. The damn raghead got you before I could. But this makes the wait worthwhile."

Grant didn't care about oil exploration or terrorists, or Wilson's insanity. Right now he only wanted Bennett out, alive, before he bled out. He felt a tug at his hip, Bennett's fingers working their way in his pocket. The damn Kimber must be hung. *Time.* He needed just a little time before his nutty cousin killed them all.

"Think about what you're doing," Grant stalled. "Tiger Wilson must be rolling in his grave. One of his great-grand kids about to kill another." Grant waved the one arm he could move, trying to disguise Bennett's actions. "You and I always argued about honor among the Seminoles.

Some of us got it, some ain't. You finally showing your true colors? Tiger would call you a muddy frog, make up a good story about you to tell around the fire."

Wilson shook the revolver at Grant. "Damn you, Uly. Your mom barely got a trickle of Indian blood in her; even less in you after that cracker gave her a bastard child. Don't preach to me about Seminole honor and all that shit."

Grant felt the Kimber slip free. Bennett's breath was warm on his neck as she pressed against his back, sliding the pistol down his side away from Wilson. He could feel her heart, pounding away, her breathing erratic, the movement of the pistol stopping, then starting again, moving toward his hand by his side. He wrapped his fingers around the grip, letting Bennett ease her hand out from under his until he could slide his thumb up, confirming the safety was off and the hammer cocked. "Allen. It doesn't have to end like this—"

Wilson interrupted him. "Just shut up. Stop talking. You always talk too much, you and your interrogation crap. I know more cops will be here soon. But first, I get to finish this the way I want to."

Grant snapped up the Kimber. *Shoot, Vicente would have said, don't think*. But Wilson was kin. He stared down the sights at his cousin, felt Bennett gasp behind him. But he couldn't pull the trigger.

Delina screamed, "Stephan. Come and kill them all!" She lunged for the Makarov, snatched it off the floor and pointed it toward Wilson.

Wilson's pistol roared, flame shooting from the barrel. Delina slammed against the wall like she had been hit by a truck.

A glazed look in his eyes, Wilson swung the revolver toward Grant. *His damn cousin.*

"No, Allen," Bennett screamed.

Grant's pistol wavered in his hand. He took a deep breath and steadied the sight on his cousin.

A snarl on his face, Wilson fired, the massive explosion blasting Grant's ears, merging with Bennett's scream, the pressure wave from the huge bullet pulsing past Grant's cheek.

Bennett entire body shuddered; her fingers dug into his arm.

Enough, family or no. The Kimber bucked in Grant's hand.

Wilson, the lights finally out in his eyes, crumpled to the floor.

Dear god, what he had done? Grant lowered the pistol. *Jesus.* He had shot his own cousin. Great grandpa Tiger would haunt them both. He closed his eyes. His momma would never forgive him.

CHAPTER 50

Pounding steps reverberated from the hallway. Sherman burst through the door. He crouched, looked back over his shoulder when more shots echoed down the hall.

Grant pulled away from Bennett, the pain in the entire left side of his body screaming at him. "What the hell's going on?" He looked around at the bodies surrounding him, numb, partially from the shock from the bullet wound, but as much from the thought of killing kin.

"Uly. That cop, Snyder, she's gone up on the roof after some guy." Sherman pointed out in the hall. "Snyder said he's carried a rocket up top. She went after him."

He shoved Bennett toward a wide-eyed Sherman and ran down the hall to the open window. "Randy. Take care of Kat," he yelled back over his shoulder.

Large enough to step through, the window opened up to the old iron fire escape he had spotted from the ground. Grant stumbled on to the landing, pausing to lean against the railing. Looking for Gunner Snyder, he realized he was breathing hard; everything out of focus. "Next I'll have a manatee swimming up here with me," he muttered to himself. Blood dripped from his hand as he staggered up the metal fire escape, steps. The sun-soaked metal steps burned at his bare feet.

At the top of the steps, he peeked over the worn brick parapet to be greeted with a quick glimpse of a man with an AK in one hand and one of those damn black boxes at his feet. Wires ran from the box to a makeshift launcher, a PVC pipe propped against the parapet. The pointy nose of a *Katyusha* poked out of the upper end.

The man fired the AK across the roof one handed, spraying rounds across the flat roof and into the sky. To Grant's right a figure dove behind an air vent as rounds riddled the thin metal.

The shooter was the same one from the front porch, the one Bennett had shot. Dumb son of a bitch still hadn't figured out how to shoot that damn AK. When Grant eased back up, the man had dropped the rifle and picked up the black box.

Grant fired the same time as the person behind the vent.

Hit, the man with the box stumbled back against the low line of bricks. He fell with a prolonged scream, taking the black box with him.

Grant watched, transfixed as the rocket slithered out of the PVC pipe. Dragged by the wires, it snaked across the roof, caught on the parapet and spun around until the nose pointed directly at Grant. He ducked down behind the parapet, held his breath and waited for the rocket to blow him all the way back to Iraq.

A shadow fell over his head.

He looked up.

Gunner smiled down at him. "Damn, L. T. You took long enough getting up here. As usual, you look like shit." She held out a hand.

He took her hand and stood, every bit of him hurting. Finally, he could get some rest.

CHAPTER 51

G rant felt good. His arms and legs had a healthy tan, the scabs had peeled off and the scars were less obtrusive than many of the tattoos he saw down at the Riverside Resort's Monkey Bar. The extra notch in his ear didn't make much difference since he still couldn't hear all that well. He had a new flats boat on order, this time with a made-in-the-USA Evinrude E-TEC 175 horsepower engine. Sherman, some of the guys from the Guard unit and a crew from Maderos Builders had helped him replace and repair the burned cedar clapboards covering the scarred concrete. He'd have it all stained in a couple more days.

A shiny SUV turned into the driveway and crunched its way up the driveway. Flash came trotting from the front porch as Bennett got out of the SUV and Chris spilled from the other side.

Grant forced himself to not favor his healing shoulder as he climbed down the ladder.

"Uly, Uly, look what I got," cried Chris, waving a toy boat with one hand and petting Flash with the other. "Can I see if it floats?"

Grant wiped the stain from his hands and looked over at Bennett, who nodded her approval.

"Sure. Come on." Grant led them to the shallow water at the old boat ramp. "Watch for gators, now."

"Aw, Uly, no gators out here." Chris took off his shoes, waded out ankle deep and launched the toy boat, laughing and guiding it with a reed. Flash walked up to the water and sat, not quite willing to have that much fun.

"So, how you doing, buddy?" Bennett stood beside him watching Chris. "The lawyer told me to stay away from you until the hearings were over. Been kind of a long eight weeks."

"I'm still out of jail, although it was a close thing there for a while. That email you sent Scanlon from the Rum Runner apparently was my 'get out of jail card.' The way you spelled it all out, telling Scanlon we had stopped the rocket attack and I had gone after Ivan; somebody bought it." Grant shook his head with a wry grin. "When that came out in the hearing, I thought they were going to give me a medal instead of prosecuting all the bank fraud charges the DA had threatened me with."

He turned to look at her, blond hair glistening in the morning sun. "I agree with Jelly. I like your hair this way much better than black. You look good. No hard time for you since I saw you last?"

"Nope. I'm doing fine, thanks. I did have to trim the facts a little, probably helped me stay out of jail."

"How's that?"

She shrugged. "I told them I came down to find out if the drug drop was for real before I reported it. Since you and I tried to stop the weed from reaching to the dealers, and Wellington testified that we voluntarily told him about the drugs, no one was left but you who knew my real intentions. Apparently you didn't say different."

He shrugged, wincing when the scar tissue in his shoulder caught. "Didn't seem important. Anyway, since Wellington told the investigators Silva killed Juan and implicated him in Chantico's death and stealing the marijuana, almost anything you said had credibility."

She nodded, then looked up at Grant, a sad look around the corners of her eyes. "We ran around together for less than a week, but I felt like I knew what you would say. I guess our testimony didn't deviate too much, or we'd both be in jail." She turned to watch Chris and his boat.

Grant glanced over at the porch. Was he uncomfortable with this conversation, or was Bennett? Or the both of them? "Chris looks good. Filled out since I saw him last."

She nodded. "Got his new treatment schedule all set up. He started last month." Flash walked over to Bennett and nuzzled her hand.

"Looks like you're doing O.K." He motioned toward the SUV.

Bennett face turned somber. "Logan's filed a wrongful death suit. His attorney said the Attorney General's Office told FDLE that they had to pay restitution, so they started with a confiscated vehicle. Money won't fix everything, but better with than without."

"Yeah." He shook his head. "Listen, I didn't say anything when you first got here; I didn't want to upset Chris. I really am sorry about Liz. I just never saw that coming."

Bennett blinked back a sudden tear. "That bogus FDLE agent is under a bunch of charges. The lawyers say he was involved in some kind of conspiracy with the Karkoffs."

He took her hands in his. "Logan holding up all right?"

She nodded. "Logan and I have made some decisions, Uly. That's why I came over." She paused, looked over at Chris. "Felt I owed you an explanation."

Grant turned her face back so he could look in her eyes, gently running his finger along a faint scar on her chin. "You know you don't owe me anything."

"Yes I do. I owe you money. I owe you—" She stopped, her eyes red. "I really like you, Uly. You saved my ass, after I did a bunch of stupid things. But—"

"No buts between you and me, not any more. You said you and Logan had made some decisions. And I know Chris comes first with you."

She nodded. "I'm moving out on the farm. Back with Chris and Logan." She started to say more, but stopped.

Grant pulled her close and hugged her, then held her back at arm's length. "I think you're at the right place, you and Chris, and Logan. I'm happy for you." He grinned at her. "Really."

"I kind of felt I had made an implied promise to you."

"You did. That you and I would be friends. Maybe a little more, but that was under duress. What you did give me was more than I got from anyone else since I got home. You brought me back to the world, and I appreciate it."

She wiped at her face with the back of her hand. "Thanks, Uly." She pecked him on the cheek. "Chris and I got to go."

"Bring Logan and Chris by anytime they want to go fishing. And Kat. You know to let me know if money is an issue—for Chris—won't you?"

Bennett laughed "Sure." She cocked her head to the side. "You still have access to the accounts? I thought the government would shut you down."

Grant grinned. "I didn't tell you this, O, K.?"

She pulled back, a puzzled look on her face. "O.K. I'm not listening."

"I'm now an official government consultant now that the Guard has medically retired me. No one's going to audit my accounts or try to track down all of my dad's accounts."

"Your dad's?"

"Dammit, you know what I mean."

"Sooo. This means I can hit you up for a big loan if things get tight? You said I was all about the money."

He shook his head. "I did think that, but I was wrong. You were always about Chris."

She smiled, both corners up. "Thank you."

"My pleasure."

She hugged him, touching her cheek to his, skin soft, smells nice. After a long moment she pulled back.

"Come on Chris. We got to go." She turned back to Grant. "Listen to some good country music for me." She walked away, hips a little broad, chopped hair wild in the salt breeze, and waved as she backed past the yellowed spot where the rocket exhaust had singed the thick turf.

As Grant watched the SUV roll down the driveway, Flash trotted back from terrorizing a cow bird along the water's edge, stopped at the top of the porch steps and turned, waiting for Grant. Grant stopped, listening to Brubeck's piano solo from inside the house. He could actually hear the melody.

The screen door opened. The closing beats of *Take Five* floated out on the breeze

"Oh, shit, Flash. Are we in trouble?" he muttered. He swiped at his cheek.

"Maybe. Old girl friend, huh?" Snyder leaned out as Flash brushed past her. "Come on in L. T. and get cleaned up. Lunch is ready."

Grant stopped at the foot of the steps and looked up at Snyder. "You got to stop calling me L. T."

Her broad shoulders filled the doorway and her long brown hair brushed his face when she leaned down toward him. "Nope. You and me are L. T. and Gunner. That's the way we started, and that's still good enough for me, *Mashalla*." She kissed him softly, on the lips, and stepped back from the door.

"What will our grandchildren think?"

She wrinkled her nose and shoved him toward the door. "We'll never know if you don't go get in the shower. Now come on in."

"A Tropical Painting"
Reproduced with Permission from the Artist, B. L. (Bonnie) Butler

This original oils on canvas is very reminiscent of the original Highway men style art featured in GULF WINDS. First sold along the roadside for around twenty-five dollars each, pieces created by the small group of Highwaymen are now valued in the thousands. A few of the surviving artists continue to paint and sell their work, now recognized for their striking beauty. Bonnie Butler's contemporary art matches the beauty of the original Highwaymen and represents wild Florida at its best.

J. M. TAYLOR AND LUCY, FLASH'S STUNT DOUBLE

Taylor is the author of the award-winning south Florida thriller, FLASH OF EMERALD, the international thriller, BEHIND THE GREEN WATER and MISSING STICKS, his WWII D-Day novel set with the 101st Airborne Division Screaming Eagles.

Combining his experiences as a paratrooper, nuclear weapons specialist and operations research analyst with travels in the Far and Middle East, Europe and the States, he packs a ton of adventure into action-filled page-turners. First Place winner in the Mystery/Thriller (Unpublished) category of the Florida Writers Association 2007 Royal Palm Literary Awards Contest, GULF WINDS introduces Homosassa fishing guide and Iraq combat veteran Uly Grant to bribery, terrorism and romance along Florida's Gulf coast.

Read more about Taylor, Lucy and her friends and Taylor's books at http://johnmtaylor.com.

Lucy is a retired racer, now living comfortably in Ozello, FL with her buddy Molly, taking care of Pete and Pat Price. Learn more about adopting and caring for greyhounds in need of a loving home at http://www.bayareagreyhounds.org.